PRAISE FOR THE GUMSHOE GHOST MYSTERY SERIES

Dying to Know

"[A] great start to a new series.   —*Mystery Scene*

"O'Connor's debut ... provides plenty of suspects and an eclectic mix of motives among the living."   —*Kirkus Reviews*

"TJ O'Connor has a smash hit with his debut novel *Dying to Know* ... I couldn't stop reading."

—Stephen Frey, *New York Times*
bestselling author

Dying for the Past

"Murder and intrigue stirred with a little history and subterfuge ... TJ O'Connor has served up another fast, fun read."

—Wallace K. Fetterolf, Retired CIA Senior Executive and
Former World War II Office of Strategic Services Operative

Dying
for the
Past

Dying
for the
Past

A Gumshoe Ghost Mystery

TJ O'Connor

MIDNIGHT INK
WOODBURY, MINNESOTA

FIRST EDITION
First Printing, 2015

Book design and format by Donna Burch-Brown
Cover design by Lisa Novak
Cover illustration: Jesse Reisch/Deborah Wolfe LTD
Editing by Connie Hill

Midnight Ink, an imprint of Llewellyn Worldwide Ltd.

Library of Congress Cataloging-in-Publication Data (pending)

ISBN 978-0-7387-4206-0

Midnight Ink
Llewellyn Worldwide Ltd.
2143 Wooddale Drive
Woodbury, MN 55125-2989
www.midnightinkbooks.com

Printed in the United States of America

For Jean and Lindsay
Always sisters, always daughters, always my girls
I love you both.

ACKNOWLEDGMENTS

Many thanks go to those who helped me start writing over the years. Irene and Oscar, my grandparents, who gave endless support and encouragement; Ms. Sergio, my English teacher from Germantown High School, who told me I could write; and countless friends and colleagues who always nudged me forward when real life got in the way. Mostly, there are the steadfast few who have both helped out in many more ways than they know: my readers and editors—Jean, Nic, Natalia, and Gina; Toby, Maggie, and Mosby, who are constant companions in this lonely world inside my den; and, of course, Wally, who has been motivated by my first book to sharpen his whip to help make my stories better.

It goes without saying that none of this would be happening without Kimberley Cameron, my patient and always supportive agent, and my new friends at Midnight Ink for giving Tuck and his pals a place to tell their stories.

Yet, no acknowledgment would be finished without thanking my family for their encouragement and support in twisting arms, passing along posts, and rallying coworkers and friends to the pages of my world. Tuck and Angel thank you. Bear grumbles and waves. And Hercule wags, moans, and tosses you his ball.

Thank you to all.

ONE

Dying is not for the faint of heart.

Unfortunately, dying is also not reserved for the very old, the very ill, or the very deserving either. Sometimes, dying is unfair and ill timed. It is stressful and confusing. Almost always, it's irritating. Just when things are great—you're a hotshot homicide detective married to a brilliant, beautiful professor—then, wham, someone shoots you in the heart. I'm not being figurative here, I mean right in the heart. One minute you're alive and on this earth, and the next minute you're dead, and, well, still on this earth.

And to be clear, being among the living and being one of them are two separate things.

I'm Tuck. Formally, Detective Oliver Tucker. And I know about death and dying. Not only am I a damn fine homicide cop, but I'm also dead. Yes, *dead*. I'm just not gone. Or, to be more politically correct, I'm "living-challenged."

Sometimes, being dead is not so bad. Like poofing in and out of places on a whim without bothering with doors and stairs. And you never have to pee or get the flu again—big pluses. Then there are times, though, when dead is depressing and sad. It's the things you miss—the taste of good wine, the adrenaline rush of chasing a suspect, or the feeling when you're in the middle of the dance floor with the most beautiful woman in the room. Those moments hurt.

A woman with shoulder-length auburn hair and sparkling green eyes stood in the middle of the mansion's ballroom. Her long, silky gown was icing poured hot over sultry curves. All eyes fixed on her when she embraced a tall, distinguished-looking older man before a dance. He wore a tux—okay, yeah, he was striking, with gray hair and a strong, muscular build, brilliant, rich, blah, blah, blah. Big deal. The two could have been on a wedding cake but instead were the center of attention at Angel's big band-themed charity gala, leading a turn around the floor to Glenn Miller's *Moonlight Serenade*.

When they took their first step, I turned away.

She was my Angel. My wife. And while André Cartier was a father figure, uncle, and one of her closest companions—not a lover or suitor—an icy, sharp knife stabbed me.

Even the dead get jealous—and more often.

Angel was the queen of the evening. Around her, most of them watching, were two hundred of the area's most notable residents; read that "wealthy and powerful." Everyone was here to drink expensive champagne, eat, dance, and drop big checks into Angel's charity.

Drink. Dance. Eat. Write checks. Tough life, huh?

The dance floor was alive with starlight and magic cast by the glitter ball overhead as I watched her. I considered sauntering over and whispering some cute tidbit in her ear—just to make her laugh and her eyes roll—but a big, two-hundred-and-sixty pound dinner jacket slumped against the bar and ordered a double-bourbon. Detective Bear Braddock was over six feet tall and filled his jacket like too many potatoes in a sack—except this sack was hard and strong and packed a Glock 40-caliber and a gold detective shield.

Bear took a long sip of his drink and watched the crowd. He peered over at two deputies costumed as 1930s coppers standing nearby. One was a short, wiry, bald white guy in his early thirties, and the other was a tall, lean, strong black man just a little older. These would be Detectives Mike Spence and Calvin Clemens—my nemeses on the sheriff's department in my breathing days. Tonight, they were babysitting the guests and the swell of donations filling the crystal donation bowl.

With money come problems.

Bear gave Spence an exaggerated nod and took a long pull on his bourbon. Spence refused to acknowledge him and turned away. "Jerk."

They are pals—really.

I leaned close to Bear and whispered, "Tie's crooked, pal."

He spilled his drink trying to straighten it. "Dammit."

"Slob."

Bear wiped his hand on his tux pants and flashed a frown around the room. Yeah, sometimes the big oaf heard me and sometimes he didn't. He knew I was here—back, I mean—but wouldn't admit it. He's stubborn and tough, and, like Hercule, my big black Lab, loyal and trustworthy. He's also afraid of what he can't see. That includes me.

The band lowered their instruments as the bandleader switched on an old phonograph. Cab Calloway scatted away as guests tried to find the sassy rhythm to *Minnie the Moocher*. Most failed miserably.

I caught Angel's eye and she looked straight at me. Bear fumbled with his drink and she caught me laughing. She shook her finger at me and headed for him.

Passing me, she whispered, "You're underdressed."

She was right. This was a black-tie affair and I was in blue jeans and sneakers, blue oxford without a tie, and my favorite old blue blazer. But, for a forty-year-old, hundred-ninety-pound dead guy, I still looked good. It's not that I don't have a tux back home, it just fits someone more, well, alive.

As you can imagine, the dead need not worry about evening wear. I could be in dirty underwear and holey socks—every mother's worry when you leave the house—and no one would care. So I had that going for me.

Angel never reached Bear before the room went fuzzy. The music slowed like the phonograph was dropping Quaaludes. Cab Calloway droned in pitchy, lethargic groans. The crystal dance ball erupted with lightning strikes around the room. The air shimmered and the room shook, and for a time, I wasn't in Kansas anymore.

Then, as easy as it began, it was over. *Minnie the Moocher* played on again. No one seemed to notice, but I knew things weren't right. Something more than champagne was being uncorked.

Across the room, standing alongside the dance floor, was an uninvited guest. He was a stout, striking man in a black pinstripe double-breasted suit. He wore shiny, buffed wingtips and a gray felt fedora. The only thing missing was a big cigar hanging out of his mouth and a violin case. Then, he swept his hand across his jacket and revealed a heavy semi-automatic in a shoulder holster. Did someone invite Al Capone?

He looked at me and winked. Winked?

The mobster started across the dance floor, angling toward the table where Angel sat with several guests I didn't recognize.

A few more bars of *Minnie* played.

A plump, middle-aged man sitting across from Angel was having an animated conversation with a young—very young—platinum blond to his right. They could have been father and daughter, but his chopping hands and her accusing finger suggested more. The man wore round, wire-rimmed glasses and a carnation. Even with the big white tie against his all-black tux he was frumpy and out of place compared to the dinner jackets and suave tuxedos around the room. While she stabbed the air at him, he looked away at the dance floor and fumed.

The girl spun around in her chair and whispered something to the handsome young man sitting at her other side. A second later, she was floating across the floor, her partner leading in a too-cozy clutch. Neither looked at Mr. Carnation when he grabbed his champagne glass, jumped to his feet, and swooped Angel up for the light fantastic.

That's my girl—the belle of the ball and an eyeful of oh-my-God.

An assault of fire spread through me.

Did I mention spirits get jealous?

The song playing—something Benny Goodman, I think—carried Angel and Mr. Carnation to the center of the floor.

They made it halfway before things got weird.

Mr. Carnation slowed to a stop and spun Angel around, trying to catch the eye of his wayward blond laughing on the young man's arm. The blond pulled away from her partner and approached Mr. Carnation. He glided toward her with Angel still attached—the three met in the center of the dance floor as the room fixed on them in an awkward *voir dire*.

Mr. Carnation hailed a passing waiter for a refill of champagne. After downing the glass in a single gulp he lifted Angel's hand for a melodramatic kiss.

His glass shattered and spasms jerked his body all the way to the floor. His right arm thrust out and pointed at the crowd; his left still held the broken glass stem. His body twitched a few more times and stilled.

The blond stood staring down at him. Her hands flew to her face as she gasped for breath—a slow, wailing cry erupted.

For a long moment, the couples dancing slowed but didn't stop. The young man knelt down at the body and waved for the lights. The crystal dance ball's glitter hid the details, but I didn't need to see.

I'd seen death before—and murder too often. Not just my own, but dozens.

This one was unmistakable. It wasn't the way Mr. Carnation collapsed in a jerky, melodramatic spiral to the hardwood. It also wasn't the way his dull, lifeless face caught the dance ball light. It was much simpler.

It was the blood pooling around his body and the bullet hole through his torso.

Someone murdered Mr. Carnation—shot him in front of two hundred witnesses. A killer jitterbugged in and gunned him down to Benny Goodman.

The guests erupted.

Bear rushed in and pulled Angel away. Spence and Clemens tried to push the crowd back. The lights snapped off—just for a second— flickered off-on-off—and flashed on. Voices hushed as eyes fell on the dead man.

Not me, though; I watched the crowd, looking for the killer and any telltale sign of the smoking gun. But what I saw, or didn't see, unnerved me more.

The gangster in the black pinstripes was gone … vanished— *poof*. He arrived just in time for a killing and left before the body hit the floor. No sign of his spats and black tie remained. He didn't leave his fedora or heater behind either. He was as dead and gone as Mr. Carnation.

The question was, however, would he stay that way?

TWO

THE STOUT, MUSCULAR LATINO waiter—Jorge, according to his name tag—set his tray of hors d'oeuvres—escargot and oysters—atop the piano in the corner of the room. The sheriff's men were still kneeling beside the dead man in the middle of the ballroom dance floor where they'd been since he'd fallen there, dead. The crowd was crushing in on the deputies and the room vibrated with angst and shock. Jorge glanced around, poured three oysters from their shells into his mouth, and slipped away into the outer hall. There, he made his way to the kitchen in the rear of the house and up the servant's stairwell.

So far so good. No one noticed him. He reached the second floor and started down the hall. Someone ran down the second floor hall and he ducked into a bathroom. When the footsteps passed, he emerged and crept to the end of the hall, down to the last room on the left.

The door was locked, but he used an old skeleton key—relocking the door once inside. More footsteps in the hall made him press his hip against the door should anyone try to enter. When he was sure the danger had passed, he moved across the room without turning on the lights and disappeared into the walk-in closet.

A few moments later, two floors above, Jorge emerged behind piles of old furniture and three steamer trunks stacked in the darkness. He slipped a penlight from his waiter's jacket and used it to maneuver around a labyrinth of boxes and decades of piled-up attic clutter. Three dress mannequins nearly stopped his heart. His reflection in a cobwebbed, dusty mirror made him cry out.

God, what next?

In the far corner of the attic was a narrow doorway leading to the southwest attic wing and on to the mansion's southern tower. At what seemed to be the attic's end, he searched with his light and found the correct wall beam—he released the hidden latch.

A narrow section of the attic wall popped open.

Jorge was inside only a moment and returned tucking a short-barreled revolver into his waistband. He checked a small package with his light and slipped it into a pocket. After relocking the panel, he retraced his steps past the junk, mirrors, and mannequins. His breath eased with his hand resting on the curved butt of the .38 special.

On his climb back down, he stopped at the second floor and listened to the sound of the crowd rumbling through the walls as sheriff's deputies barked orders and herded guests out of the ballroom.

When the sounds faded, he continued down a dark, too-tight passage until he smelled the rich scent of coffee. From there, he used the rickety stairs to the wine cellar long ago concealed in the basement. He sat against the stone wall and waited.

It was going to be a long night.

THREE

SOMEWHERE BETWEEN YOUR LAST breath and death is a strange, awkward place that defies definition. For me, it was an elevator stuck between floors. The trouble is, I don't know whether I was heading up or down when the doors closed behind me. But when the doors reopened, I was still here—ladies' lingerie, sporting goods…dead guys. Perhaps my life's work will decide what floor I'll end up on.

Perhaps not.

For now, though, I'm content to be back home in Winchester— the wonderful historic Virginia town ninety minutes west of DC. The alternatives to being here, both of them, aren't for me.

My life was stolen a few months ago by a madman: Professor Ernie Stuart. Ernie was Angel's surrogate father. Angel, of course, is Doctor Angela Hill-Tucker, Professor of History and my widow. Ernie was her mentor and university boss, and a member of our family. But Ernie had a secret. Ernie was insane. He had killed when he was a young man. He had killed when he was old. He had tried to kill Angel.

And then he made a very big mistake.

He killed me. And it cost him his life, too. Murder keeps me in the here-and-now—catching killers and fixing old wrongs. It started with old Ernie and I knew not where it would take me.

And now Mr. Carnation was dead—I watched him die. Coincidence?

No. Coincidences are like politicians—they say they're one thing but they're always something else. The "something else" is often very, very bad.

"Stephanos Grecco," Bear said, standing up from Mr. Carnation's body sprawled on the dance floor. Bear was talking to no one, unless to me, which he never did. He made some notes on the back of a cocktail napkin—his tuxedo didn't come with his detective ensemble. "Poor bastard. All this money and for what?"

"Bear?" It was Spence. "You better come outside. We got something weird."

Saying "weird" around me was an oxymoron. Even if Spence didn't know I was standing there.

"Weird how?" Bear asked. "Weird like Sasquatch or flying saucers, or—"

"Ghosts?" Spence still gets the jitters when he thinks of me. When Ernie died, everyone, including Spence, saw things they never talked about—me, two dead girls, and more. "Not that weird. Looks like someone broke into the basement after we did our sweep this evening. And I'm thinking they might still be here, too."

Before Bear answered, Angel walked up and stood opposite Grecco's body. She was pale—murder can do that. "Bear, the guests want to leave."

"Not until we've taken their statements. It'll be a few hours."

After Grecco's shooting, Bear's men secured the ballroom, closed all the mansion's doors, and refused to allow the guests to leave. Deputies guarded the outside of the house while Bear, Spence, and Clemens searched the guests, trying to find the killer among them. No one saw the killer and none of the guests seemed suspicious. Bear called for reinforcements. That was thirty minutes ago.

"A few hours?"

Bear nodded. "Sorry, Angela. But we have to get statements first. And I have to check something Spence found. Can you help our deputies corral everyone into a couple rooms so we can interview? This mansion is big enough that we should be able to handle them all elsewhere without disrupting the crime scene."

"Yes, of course." She stole a glance at the corpse who used to be Stephanos Grecco. "He just donated a hundred thousand to my foundation."

A hundred thousand? "Holy crap, Angel. I hope it was cash."

"No, it wasn't." The words slipped out before she realized Spence was still there. "I mean, how awful. I'll see to the guests."

"Yeah, okay. Let me know if you have problems with them." Bear leaned close and whispered, "And take *him* with you."

I whispered back. "Fat chance, Bear." Even ghosts have feelings. "It's a homicide. You and me. Just like the old days. I'll do the thinking and you do the doing."

My voice was often just a buzz in his ear—he told Angel it was, anyway. But, buzz or not, the words got through. He wasn't fooling me at all.

Outside, the May evening thunderstorm was no more than a fine mist. The sky was overcast but a few stars poked through, giving Bear and Spence a little natural light to see by.

Spence led us around the side of the house. We were west of Old Town Winchester where money and antebellum history were guarded by giant oak trees and antique iron fences. The Vincent House was named—I just recalled—for an old gangland hood who hid out here when the atmosphere in New York and Washington DC got too warm. The Vincent House was a three-story brick and stone mansion consuming a half-block. The Vincent House reminded me of a castle, with two four-story towers on each side and a brooding, stalwart façade suggesting an impregnable fortress to any passersby. Two other homes on the estate—mansions in their own right—consumed the other half-block. Together, the compound sat far back from the surrounding streets and was protected by a tall stone wall and wrought-iron gates.

Stephanos Grecco wouldn't think it was so impregnable. Obviously, the way to penetrate the Vincent House's armor was to be on the guest list of a highbrow party. No stealth required—just your checkbook.

Spence stopped at the rear corner of the Vincent House where the grand oaks and walnut trees blocked the moonlight. He flipped on a flashlight and shined the beam at a secluded basement door made of tin and wood.

"Someone forced the lock. The one down on the inner door, too." He toed the hasp. It was bent back and open; its metal frame was gouged and scraped. "We checked this place two hours before Angela's bash. Everything was okay."

"Then we missed something." Bear yanked open the bulkhead doors and took Spence's light. Then he pulled his handgun from beneath his dinner jacket and stared down the timber stairs into the darkness. "Wait here."

"Bear," Spence said. "Wait. I wanna ask you something."

"What? You afraid of the dark, Spence?"

"Listen, this is the first murder we've worked since, well, since—"

"Yeah, I know. Since Tuck's. What of it?"

Spence looked around, uneasy. "I gotta ask. The day, you know, when we got Ernie Stuart at the farm. After he killed Tuck and all those folks. Ah, you know what I mean."

I did. Spence wanted the answer to the question plaguing Bear. Was I back?

Yep. Ernie thought he got rid of me. But like gum on his shoe, I wouldn't let go. I came back and stopped him. Oh, I had help, of course—Angel and Bear. They did the tough stuff; the breathing stuff like running and chasing and shooting and fighting. And there were a couple spirits of murders past and an old coot named Doc. They all helped, too. Even Spence and Clemens played a role.

But without me, Ernie would still be killing.

I couldn't let him, so I called his elevator, and it dropped him off in hell.

"Get to the point, Spence, or you can search the basement alone."

"Come on, Bear, you know what I want to know. Did you see him? I mean, did you see them all? When Clemens and I caught up to Ernie, he was going nuts. Shooting at nothing and screaming he'd already killed *them*. After, and I hate saying this, but after, didn't you see them all—the two girls and ... the others?"

"Them all" haunted Spence these past few months. Old Ernie had been on a rampage for decades. He'd killed five people we knew of, and we guessed there were more. When we caught up to him— we being me, Amy, and Caroline, who were two of Ernie's earlier victims—he died. No bullet took Ernie; guilt and terror did. He had a heart attack right in front of Spence and Clemens. In the moments afterward—how, I don't pretend to understand—Angel, Bear, Spence, and Clemens saw us—me, Amy, and Caroline. There were others there, too, but I don't know if anyone noticed. Since then, it was the one fact of my case that no one—not even Bear Braddock—ever talked about.

If you don't admit it, it ain't real. Right?

"Okay." Bear shined his light into Spence's face. "What do you want to know?"

"Bear, none of us talk about it, ever—" Spence turned away. "Did you see him? Tuck, I mean. And those two girls? You did, right? You saw them standing over Stuart's body. Didn't you?"

"I don't have time for this, Spence." Bear started down the basement stairs, and a second before he disappeared into the dark, he said, "Did you see them, Spence?"

"Ah, heck, I don't know. But if you didn't, I didn't. I just figured after Ernie died, Tuck would go. But sometimes—a lot of times—I think he's still here. Not that I see anything, you know."

"Spence, you sure remember pretty well what you never saw. Just keep your eyes open and don't miss what you should be seeing." Bear disappeared into the basement darkness.

Spence is right. After Ernie died, no light came for me. I don't even know if there is a light, or maybe I haven't paid the bill yet. I didn't leave and there was one reason—one much bigger than my own unfinished business, if you believe in that sort of thing. I do. You see, while trying to solve my murder, other spirits sought me to solve theirs. Because I can do what the other victims can't—I can work with the living and be their detective.

I'm back to work for the dead and stop the living from creating more unfinished business.

I waited with Spence in the pitch black. Just for fun, I whispered in his ear a couple times. Nothing important, just a few silly *hi theres* and *boos*. Each time he swatted at the buzzing. Each time he cursed and asked me to stop—*me*.

Deep down, Spence knew I was here. He just refused to admit it. Ignorance is bliss.

Three loud, heavy bangs on the lower basement door startled both of us. Spence stumbled down the stairs and opened the door. Bear stood inside. "It locked behind me."

"I should have warned you," Spence said, "It locks automatically. You need a key to open it from the inside."

"You think the killer wasn't a guest?" Bear found a switch on the wall and flipped on the basement light. "Maybe he came in this way and got locked inside?"

"Yeah, maybe—that means he's still here." Spence was thoughtful. "When Grecco was shot, I radioed the deputies outside to lock the house down—it took a few seconds at best. They were posted all around the perimeter. No one came out—some of the guests tried. So, if—"

"If the killer did get in this way," Bear said, "he's still locked inside."

Spence nodded. "I got four deputies on the outside. And a patrol cruising the area."

"Bear," I said as a hot, sharp fingernail etched my spine. "You gotta move fast—the killer's upstairs."

His eyes darted around, listening.

"Angel and the guests, Bear." I touched his arm. "You gotta get back upstairs."

He grabbed Spence's shoulder. "Yeah, okay. Spence, brief Clemens. Put two deputies in each room of guests. No one leaves. The four of us will search the house again from the top down."

"We did that already, but—" Spence started for the inside cellar stairs but stopped and turned around. "Which four of us?"

"You, me, and Clemens. Three—I meant three."

"Sure you did, Bear."

"Just go," Bear snapped. "Clemens takes the second floor. You take the first. I'll take the third. Move."

Spence relayed the orders on his radio and led Bear to the inside cellar stairs and up into the mansion. The hall between the kitchen and the mansion's smaller rear dining room led to a narrow servant's stairwell to the upper floors. At the first landing, Spence nodded to Bear and headed down the hall. We continued up to the third floor.

Three steps from the top landing, Bear jolted to a stop.

"Shush. Did you hear something?"

Shush? Did he shush me?

Overhead, attic floorboards creaked under unseen weight. Bear wasn't carrying a radio, and he cursed about it as we headed farther down the hall searching for the attic entrance. We'd passed three closed doors—he checked each and found bedrooms—before we found the right one.

He reached for the knob.

I said, "Be careful, Bear. You don't know—"

A shot cracked from behind us. Wood splintered the doorframe just beside Bear's head. He dove for the floor and rolled up behind an antique grandfather clock. I followed him down, but for the death of me I didn't know why.

Bullets can't hurt the dead.

Two more cracks split the air—one whistled past and the other smacked the grandfather clock and started *Westminster Quarters* chiming. Footsteps ran from one of the rooms we'd passed and down the servant stairs behind us. Bear jumped up and started back, adrenaline pushing him faster—experience slowing his progress.

One floor down—stomping feet.

Clemens shouted, "Freeze!"

Another shot followed by a louder, deeper retort. Another.

Someone cried out. A heavy thump.

Man down.

FOUR

"The perp shot me!" Clemens lay on his back halfway down the second-floor hall. Blood oozed from his shoulder as he tried getting up. "Hurry. He went down the stairs."

"Stay down, Cal. Who shot you?" Bear jammed a handkerchief under Clemens' shirt and pressed Clemens' hand over the wound. "Any description?"

"No. I heard movement and then wham, I'm down. I got one shot off but I don't know if I hit anything."

"Stay put. I'll send help."

We were off.

Taking the stairs three at a time, we reached the first floor and ran into two uniformed deputies on their way up. Bear ordered an ambulance and more backup. One of the deputies radioed the instructions as he dashed up the stairs to Clemens. The other followed. Bear started for the front of the house but hesitated, looking down the hall to the many rooms ahead. Each had a deputy guarding the doors so he turned back and headed for the kitchen.

The rear kitchen door to the back yard was open. Standing just beyond the door light, a deputy—Hoskins—called out to Bear.

"No one has come out this way, Detective. We've got deputies around the front, back, and other side, too. No one came through. The shooter must still be inside."

"Dammit." Bear jammed a finger toward Hoskins. "Stay here. No one goes in or out. Get a canine unit here to search the grounds. I want them here in five."

"Yes, sir."

Something finger-walked up my spine—the kind of something normal breathing folk would call *paranoia*. Me, I call it a signal.

"Bear, I don't think the perp is here. We should—"

Too late.

Bear ran back inside.

"Okay, good idea," I said, following. "Let's go back inside."

On the way to the ballroom, he checked with the deputies in each of the rooms. Everyone had the same story—after the shots, no one was in the halls and all the guests stayed put in the rooms. The house was locked down.

"Dammit." Bear stood in the ballroom entrance. His face was tight with frustration; his eyes darted everywhere, searching for an answer evading us both. "There's nowhere left to hide."

"Ah, Bear," I said as the strange, cold tingling started up my spine again. "Come with me. I think I know where the shooter is. Back to the basement."

He blinked a few times and looked around. Then, without a word to the deputies standing in the hall watching him, he returned to the basement door. He probably thought it was his idea, but I was three steps ahead of him.

I led him around the cavernous basement into the far corner room where there were old wine shelves and storage racks cluttered with junk. The junk was cobwebbed and gritty and the few bottles of wine were long ago forgotten. The small room was sectioned off from the rest of the basement and lit by only two overhead lights.

"He's here, Bear. Somewhere." Something pulled me to the wine rack closest to the corner of the room. It took hold of me—what, I don't know—and pulled me into the rack. I knew not to resist and stepped through the wine racks, passing into darkness…

———

The darkness consumed me. No, it didn't scare me or leave me feeling alone. I mean it *consumed* me. The stone floor fell away beneath my feet. The brick walls and wine racks withered into nothing, leaving a dull, black void. Darkness enveloped me and I was lost—nowhere—gone from the basement and standing helpless and abandoned in empty, inky nothing.

Except for the 1932 Packard barreling toward me down the street.

I dodged the old four-door—old was wrong, this one looked brand-new—and jumped onto the sidewalk. I stood in front of a soda shop where a mother and two children emerged. They were eating ice cream. The children—two chattering girls in bright, frilly sundresses—were giggling over their sweets as the mom shooed them to a nearby bench. The mother wore a dark, below-the-knee skirt, long-sleeved blouse, and a wide-brimmed hat perched on her head.

A hat? A Packard? Ice cream shop?

1930-something was everywhere. Round-fender Chevys and Fords drove past. Businessmen in their pinstriped, double-breasted suits and fedoras stood smoking on the street corners and reading newspapers. A paperboy hawked his news across the street. Somewhere a radio blared swing music.

Everywhere was an era long gone in some Dashiell Hammett novel. And I was its newest character.

Across the street at a storefront—my eyes were pulled there like steel to a magnet—was a strange building lost between a clothing store and stationery shop. The front windows were papered over with posters and billboards chiding some politician and calling for interested people to join a meeting inside on American patriotism. The glass-paned front door opened, and a short man with dark features and thick, slicked-back black hair emerged. He was in a business suit of the day—double-breasted, wide lapels, wingtips, and a hat in one hand. He stopped at the sidewalk and looked around as though expecting someone. No passersby greeted him.

He tightened his hat on his head and walked with brisk determination down the street and around the corner out of sight.

Before I knew why, my feet were carrying me in his wake.

I followed him four blocks and after just two realized we were in Washington DC heading east toward the Mall. Three times, the man stopped and double-backed, crossed streets only to cross back a block farther down. He purchased a Washington Star from a young paperboy hustling folded papers to anyone with a nickel. When he reached the mall, he went to a row of park benches. He sat, unfolded his paper, and pretended to read.

I say pretended because his attention was above the paper— not the fold, mind you, the paper.

I tried to approach him but something kept me at bay. Each time I tried to move closer, my feet became mired and my legs refused to obey. An unseen force kept hold and refused to let me get closer than fifty yards. What, I have no idea, but it walled me to a patch of sidewalk opposite the Washington Monument where I stared across the grass at the dark-skinned man and his newspaper.

There were perhaps twenty other people on the mall nearby. A mother with a carriage and child. Two lovers holding hands and strolling nowhere. Businessmen striding here and there on their way to important meetings. Even a uniformed beat cop ambled down the sidewalk, taking little notice of cars and pedestrians. And each of these people caused a ruffle in the man's newspaper and a peek over its edge. Twice, when someone neared him, he turned on the bench, re-crossed his legs, and continued "reading."

Just as I tired from boredom, he did a curious thing.

After the cop passed him and headed north along 15th Street and the Ellipse, the man slipped something from his inside suit coat pocket and tucked it into his newspaper. Then he stood, folded the paper with care, and walked back to Independence Avenue. At the corner of 15th, he jammed the newspaper down into a trash can and hastened across the street. He continued farther down

Independence, hailed a passing cab, and disappeared before I could make chase.

And it was a good thing I did not.

Whatever restrained me before held tight—a force telling me my visit to 1935 was not over. The fun was just beginning.

A tall, thin woman beneath a floppy hat and wearing a matronly, long-hemmed dress appeared down Independence. She ambled toward me and crossed the street at 15th, stopping at the corner. She went to the trash can, dug around inside, and retrieved the folded newspaper. Then she recrossed Independence and waited.

A city bus approached.

My legs were free and movement restored. I ran across Independence and made the bus just as the door closed. The thin woman was aboard, sitting one seat behind the rear side door. I made it three seats down the aisle before the invisible hand seized me and trapped me in the aisle—I could get no closer to her.

Several blocks later, somewhere in Northwest DC, the woman left the bus and walked a circuitous route several blocks north to a small family restaurant—Quixote's Windmill. At the front door, I peered inside the window to see what became of the mysterious woman and her newspaper.

She was gone—nowhere inside. In fact, the restaurant was empty and closed.

A tornado of darkness whirled around me, scooped me up, and returned me, not to Kansas, but to the here and now of Winchester in 2014. The sidewalk vanished and the basement floor returned beneath me again. The dark, empty basement surrounded me.

When the swirling stopped, I looked around. The dark-skinned man, his newspaper, and the curious thin woman were gone. And with them, 1935 was back in history.

———

Bear stood at the foot of the basement steps, looking up.

I said, "Bear, this isn't gonna make sense, but Grecco's killing is connected to 1935."

"Hmmph."

"No, really."

Bear called up the stairs to a deputy in the kitchen. "Ski, recheck the house and search the other houses on the property—everything. Something's going on here; I can feel it. And it's not going to make sense."

Didn't I just say that?

FIVE

"Partners?" Bear said to the petite, dark-haired woman giving orders at the crime scene team scurrying around. "You want me to partner with Spence? No way."

"Save it, Bear." Captain Helen Sutter's laser eyes made her order clear. "Clemens will be out for a few weeks. You haven't had a partner since Tuck was killed, and Spence needs one, too. Enough. What did the ME give us?"

Bear leered at Spence standing opposite Grecco's body from him. He snorted and gave his report. "Clemens and Grecco were hit with a .22 caliber slug—more after the autopsy. Grecco's shot came from a down angle based on the entry and exit wounds. We think the shooter was on the second floor in one of the rooms at the top of the stairs. He shot over the balcony railing and through the open ballroom doors."

Captain Sutter cocked her head. "Is it possible?"

"I went upstairs and checked it out," Bear said. "The ballroom entrance is two stories tall and wide enough. There's enough visual from the second floor above the main hall to see into the ballroom where the dancing was. I stood just inside the doorway of both bedrooms—out of sight of anyone below—and I could take a shot into the ballroom. A little patience and skill and boom."

"What a mess." Captain Sutter stood below the grand archway between the ballroom and hall and peered up to the second floor railing. "Find anything in the rooms?"

"Not yet. Now, Cap, about Spence—"

"No." Captain Sutter held up her hand. "Spence, finish in here and double-check the neighborhood canvass. Bear, make sure the guests are interviewed before they go. And play nice, boys, or else."

"I always play nice, Cap," Spence said. "Bear has the attitude."

"You tried to frame me for Tuck's murder."

"No I didn't." Spence held up his hands. "I was trying to—"

"Enough!" Captain Sutter yelled. "Will you two get over it already? Tuck's was a rough case—for all of us. Let him go."

Both men fell silent.

Looking around the ballroom, the donation table was still on the far wall with the crystal punchbowl on it. "Bear, what about all the charity donations? Whose got those?"

He looked over at the punchbowl. "Cap, whose got the foundation's money?"

"I'm sure Angela Tucker does. Check with her."

"Okay, soon as—"

"Holy crap, Cap." Spence stood up. "This guy's loaded. He has ten g's in cash in his wallet."

Bear forced a laugh. "Bull, Spence. Ten grand won't fit in a wallet. What are you talking about?"

Spence pulled several bills from Grecco's black leather wallet and fanned them out.

"Holy twenty-second president," I said.

Spence held ten bills—each a U.S. Treasury, Uncle-Sam approved, Gold Certificate, one-thousand-dollar bill. The bills were in immaculate condition and except for a little fading on Grover Cleveland's mug, they looked like they'd just rolled off the Treasury press.

"Are they real?" Bear slipped on a plastic crime-scene glove and took one of the bills. "Can't be."

"I don't know," Spence said. "I've never seen one before. I didn't know they were still around."

"Neither did I." Captain Sutter already had gloves on and took the bills from Spence. "They look and feel real. We'll have to get the Secret Service to examine them. They're evidence one way or the other."

"Cap," Bear said, looking at the guests in the lounge across the hall. "Who carries this much old currency? Or this kind of currency? Angel told me Grecco stroked her foundation a check for one hundred thousand. Why all the cash? And why—"

"Thousand-dollar notes?" Captain Sutter pointed her chin toward the hall. "Spence, seize the donations right away. We don't want anyone undonating. And I want a list of all donations tonight."

"Sure, Cap."

"Bear," she said, "make sure we check everyone's personal effects for any more dead presidents when we interview them. I want to know if anyone has any more Clevelands."

"Right." He started for the lounge but stopped and turned around. "Cap, about Spence and me partnering—"

"Zip it, Braddock." Captain Sutter walked over to him and drove a .50-caliber finger into his chest. She did, of course, have to get on her tiptoes to aim. "The friggin' sheriff and county supervisor are sitting in one of these rooms—right now, right here—waiting for answers. I gotta tell them Winchester's newest resident and biggest philanthropist got capped and we got diddly shit. I don't have time for this with you two. Got it?"

He nodded and walked off.

While I was alive, Captain Sutter and I got along just great—as long as I jumped when she yelled and didn't confuse her femininity with her rank. She was a fire-breathing dragon at work. None of us knew her off-duty. Rumor had it she had a calm, soft side hidden somewhere.

Rumors can be wrong.

"Go easy on Bear, Cap," I said as he walked away. "He's still in mourning for me."

She laughed and turned to Spence behind her. "Clever, Spence."

"Huh, Cap? I didn't say anything."

I started after Bear when the lights flickered off and on a few times—just as they had seconds before Stephanos Grecco's murder. When I looked up at the crystal chandelier, the raspy sound of Louie Armstrong croaked out *Ain't Misbehavin.'* In the hall, Louie's gravelly baritone introduced his old friend to me.

"Oh, no. Here we go again."

Standing in the hall was the stout, striking mobster in his shiny wingtips and fedora. He beckoned me to follow him into the lounge with a big smile and a wave.

I did.

My host had a drink in one hand and a big Cuban in the other. Bear, Spence, and Captain Sutter were gone. Instead, the bar was set up with bottles of expensive booze and the room smelled of good tobacco and dank night air. Even Angel's party and all her guests were gone—vanished to somewhere else—somewhere not here and not now.

Now wasn't 2014.

The mob boss lifted his drink in salute as I walked in. His broad smile consumed his puffy, dark face as he downed his drink. "Come in, Oliver. I've been waiting for you."

Oliver? The only two people who ever called me Oliver were dead. One of them turned out to be my guardian angel, Doc, and the other was Ernie Stuart. This gangster was neither.

He walked around behind the bar and took down a dark bottle from the top shelf. He put a second glass beside his on the bar and filled them both—one he slid over to me when I stepped closer.

"Hope you like bourbon, Oliver." He lifted his glass with a wink. "You look like a bourbon fella to me. Bottoms up."

I lifted the glass. "You know me but I don't know you."

"Ah, let me introduce myself." The mobster waved a hand in the air and started making sense of things. "I'm Vincent Calaprese of the New Jersey Calaprese families. You can call me Vincent—and this is my home."

SIX

THE BOURBON BURNED ALL the way down but it tasted like heaven. Among the many downsides of being dead were food and drink. They were not only unnecessary, they were disappointing. You see, the dead cannot enjoy a double-bacon cheeseburger with extra fries and a beer. If I'd known that before my death, I would have asked for a mistrial. But then again, nobody can punch me in the nose or stick a sharp stick in my eye either. Still, I miss rare, sizzling steak, cold Saturday morning pizza, and Angel's cherry pie. There was a lot I missed. Not just her cherry pie.

I sipped the oaky bourbon again and let the fire soothe my aroused taste buds. I could get used to this again. But how was this possible? If the dead run the still, do the rules change?

"Damn, that was good." I set my glass on the bar and Vincent Calaprese refilled it. "Now, Mr.—"

"Vincent, please."

"Okay, Vincent. I guess you know what I am going to ask you next."

He refilled his glass and raised it. "To your health."

Not wanting to be rude, I followed suit. Both glasses were emptied and set up for another round.

When you're dead and meeting new friends, manners are important.

"Vincent?" A silky, low voice said from behind me. "Who's the new fella? He's a cutie."

I turned as a sultry, red-headed siren slinked into the room. She was curvy and voluptuous and belonged pinned to someone's wall for nighttime ogling. Her face was soft and young and her eyes were lit with the fire of youth—fire dancing right at me.

Being dead might have some perks.

Vincent waved at her. "Sassy, go back upstairs. We got business." When she didn't retreat, he added, "You heard me—scram. This ain't no place for a dame right now."

Sassy sauntered over in time to Wayne King's *Dream a Little Dream*. She eyed me and smiled a faint, almost invisible smile more intoxicating than the bourbon in my glass. Her hair was short—the style of the more vivacious ladies of the thirties—and her saucy, floor-length red satin dress sizzled with each step. Regret at having missed my great-grandfather's era began tickling my ... spine. The satin struggled to conceal her bosom and lost all control over her curves gliding through the room. She stopped at the bar. Then she reached out, took my drink, and emptied it in one long swallow, watching me above the glass as the bourbon warmed her lips and dried mine at the same time.

She licked her lips and giggled, handing me the empty glass. "Hi ya, Tuckie. Thanks for the sauce."

I swallowed a bowling ball.

"Sassy!" Vincent snapped. "Out, damn you. We got business."

She winked and giggled again, then left as she arrived—slow and swishy—knowing I was watching her taillights leave the room. As she went, the tantalizing, unmistakable scent of Chanel No. 5 lingered longer than the mist into which she evaporated.

I turned to Vincent. "I'm beginning to like it here."

"Don't like it too much, Oliver." He tapped a finger on the bar. "You'll be welcome so long as you mind your manners. Got it? And so you know, Sassy ain't one for no dick."

"Excuse me?"

He smiled. "You know, dicks—coppers, detectives, gumshoes. You, right? I mean, you're a dick?"

Oh, yeah. I'm a dick. "Vincent, how about telling me what this is about?"

"I been watching you, Oliver." The gangster leaned on the bar. "Ever since the old guy drilled you."

I assume the old guy was Ernie Stuart. "Yeah? If you see him, tell him I said—"

"No, no." Vincent held up both hands in surrender. "Champ, trust me, he's one bruno you don't want to run into. He gives me the heebie-jeebies. Too bad you couldn't have repaid the favor on him."

I felt the same way. "What do you want, Vincent? This is twice you came to see me tonight."

"It's real simple." Vincent's face faded and the bottle of bourbon on the bar faded with him. "You bring me Benjamin. If you do, then you and me are square."

"Who's Benjamin? I don't know anyone named Benjamin. But I'll trade you. You tell me what you know about a restaurant named Quixote's Windmill and I'll find you Benjamin. Deal?"

Vincent was just a shadow but his voice was unmistakable. "Don't play with me, Oliver. This is a game you cannot win. Just bring Benjamin."

"So you heard of the place? Catchy name, don't you think?"

The music was gone and so were the bottles of booze and Vincent Calaprese. The sounds of Angel's guests rumbled in the next room and feet paraded up and down the stairs. There was no sign of my host or his sexy companion. The smoky taste of bourbon was gone from my lips and no Chanel No. 5 lingered.

As I turned to leave the lounge, Vincent's voice reached me again.

"Don't hustle me, Oliver. Bring me Benjamin. Bring him soon. Tell him I want my book. No double-crosses, Oliver. If you can taste my bourbon, you can taste my anger, too."

SEVEN

"WHO IS BENJAMIN? SASSY, come back—do you know Benjamin?" No one answered. "Oh, come on. A little help?"

"Tuck?" Angel asked from the doorway. "Is that you?" She walked into the lounge, glanced over her shoulder to see if anyone followed, and closed the doors. "Who are you talking to?"

"Angel, everything okay?" What a stupid question. One of her biggest philanthropists was dead in the ballroom. "I mean, other than—"

"I know what you mean. What are you doing in here? Who's Benjamin?"

Angel and I have a very unusual relationship—yeah, a lot of marriages do. But no one could top ours. Ever since we bridged the chasm of life and death after my murder, she can hear and see me. In rare moments, she can feel my touch. Other times, when emotions are intense—fear mostly—others can see me, too. Moving things takes a little more out of me. Often, I need a jolt of electricity for a jump start. Electricity to the dead is like speed—the drug, not a car. And, as interesting as it is, it doesn't last long.

"Tuck? Who were you talking to?"

I explained about Vincent. Common sense caused amnesia about Sassy. "This is Vincent's house. I don't know if he's haunting it or me, or if he's here for something more important."

"Like Benjamin? Do you know who he means?"

"No."

"A guest maybe? I don't remember anyone named Benjamin." Angel sat at the bar. "Could it be like last time, Tuck—like Carolyn and Amy? Could he need your help?"

Yes, it might be that simple. Carolyn and Amy were two young wraiths who came to me after my murder. They popped in and out for days, begging for my help—though what they needed wasn't clear until it was over. When I realized my killer was their killer, it all made sense. His demise was the key to it all.

I was the conduit—the link between the living and the dead— able to shake things up, work with the living, and help Bear and Angel unravel a serial killer. In the process, it unraveled Amy and Caroline and freed them, too. So, I'm sort of a private detective—or private dick, as Vincent called me—for the dead. A dead detective, spirit sleuth, a ghostly … you get it. I just don't charge for my services. What would they pay me in, dead presidents?

I said, "With gangsters, there's no telling what happened back in their day or what they want now."

"Gangsters? Like violin cases and fedoras?"

"Exactly. Hey, we got any fedoras in the attic at home? I'd look great in one. And you used to play the violin, right?"

"I played the piano."

"Too hard to carry. How about a fedora?"

"No." Angel turned on her stool to keep an eye on the door, making sure no one walked in on our conversation and branded her crazy. She got serious. "Tuck, do you sense anything? Anything at all on Stephanos Grecco? Bear thinks the killer escaped."

"Maybe." I moved onto a bar stool beside her. "Just before Grecco was shot, Vincent popped in for some champagne and caviar. He left a second before Grecco was killed. I have no idea who killed Grecco or how they got away—if they did. This place was locked up tight."

"There's more." Angel lowered her voice. "The lights went out when Stephanos was shot and someone stole the donations. They're gone."

"Spence and Clemens were guarding them. Cap said you had the money."

"No, Bear asked me, too. When Stephanos went down, everyone ran to him. Spence and Clemens, too. Someone took advantage of the chaos and grabbed the money from the punchbowl."

Terrific. "How much was taken?"

"I'm not sure. Most of it—about a quarter million dollars—was in checks. A few patrons put some cash in for show. The cash can't be more than a few thousand."

I thought about that. "Okay, so either someone took advantage of the murder or we have one really stupid crook."

"What do you mean?"

"Checks, Angel. They can be cancelled and reissued. Only the cash is gone, and there wasn't much."

She brightened. "You're right. I'll contact everyone about their donations. Everyone signed the donation book so I'll know the details. I can speak with each of them tomorrow." She looked down. "Tuck, the money isn't important. This is so horrible."

Murder is horrible.

"Yes, it is, but look at it this way—I got a couple good bourbons out, of it." She didn't laugh so I touched her hand. She smiled and I said, "Check with Bear, Angel. There is some benefit to keeping this quiet for a few days. Let's see who gets curious about the money."

She agreed before her faced darkened. "Poor Bonnie—she's Stephanos's wife. They were only married a little while ago. I met them last week, but they seemed like wonderful people. You have to find his killer."

Of course I did.

She went to the doors and hesitated, turned around, and looked at me. "Oh, one more thing, Tuck."

"Yeah?" The look on her face reminded me that women, like private dicks and coppers, have a sixth sense about all things dangerous.

"Later, you will explain about Sassy," she said, and smiled the smile I knew meant trouble.

EIGHT

JORGE THE WAITER PULLED his motorcycle into a parking space two lots west of the John S. Mosby Center for American Studies and turned off the engine. It was well after midnight and the security patrols were all at the campus security office having coffee. He'd have about forty-five minutes to get in and get out before the patrols made their next rounds through the University of the Shenandoah Valley campus. While he might fit in on campus during the day—he was twenty-seven, average height and build, shaggy dark hair, with three days worth of straggly, untrimmed growth on his face—explaining why he was roaming campus at this hour might be tricky. They might ask for a campus ID. In particular, if things went bad, he didn't want to explain the short-barreled semi-automatic on his ankle or the package inside his leather motorcycle jacket.

Forty-five minutes had to be enough.

The campus was empty and dark. He dodged the ornate street-lamps winding along the roads and courtyards, staying in the shadows. The campus was empty—not even a late-night jogger or strolling couple broke the cones of light. There were no sounds but an occasional night bird. No car engines. No town noises. Nothing but silence.

Jorge made his way across campus to the three-story brick history center where he stood beneath a tall oak watching the building's windows. Satisfied there were no faculty lingering and no teaching assistants cramming extra-credit, he took the long way around to the rear of the building where no streetlamp shined and both of the building's corner floodlights were off.

The double-security lock on the rear door was no hazard—Jorge had a master key—and he was inside and slipping onto the third floor five minutes ahead of schedule. Using only a small, red-beamed flashlight, he maneuvered down the main hall, past the conference room and reception desk, to the senior staff hall. There, he found the corner office door and master-keyed his way inside.

Once the door was relocked, he took out his cell phone and sent a simple one-word message: "Inside."

Jorge moved faster. First, he slipped a small, vinyl case from inside his black leather motorcycle jacket and opened it on the large oak desk. There were three electronic devices, none larger than a bottle cap, which he secreted around the room in strategic places he'd planned out earlier from diagrams. He placed one inside the desk phone and one in the extension on the small conference table across the room. He slipped the larger one behind a framed photograph of a handsome, fortyish man roughhousing with a large black Labrador retriever—the dog was getting the best of his master. The photograph was selected, not by random, but because it had more dust accumulated on its frame than the others sitting on the credenza behind the desk.

Next, Jorge sat in the plush leather chair behind the antique desk and began a systematic and careful search of its drawers. Then came the files atop the desk. The outbox. Credenza, bookshelf, and filing cabinet. No space was left untouched.

There was no frustration when his search failed to yield trophies. He hadn't expected any and yet he'd hoped for something to justify a late night report and perhaps a few more days on the job. Six-hundred a day went a long way.

Often, small failures meant bigger retainers.

Before he slipped out of the professor's office, he sent one more simple message. This time, it was two words. "Complete. Nothing."

Then, Jorge—who was neither a college student nor named Jorge—checked the outer office area, slipped into the hall, and re-locked Professor Angela Hill-Tucker's office door.

NINE

KATALINA—KAT TO HER FRIENDS at the county property office—
made the turn off I-81 onto County Route 37 and headed south
around Winchester. She was sleepy and knew she'd drank too much
at the club. But it was Friday night and it had been months since
she'd done more than work and sleep and work some more. Her
second job took too much out of her and paid her little more than
nothing—the cost of the right papers and a chance at a new life in
Virginia.

Her new girlfriends—two older divorcees and one loud party
girl who were as obnoxious as they were fun and friendly—
wouldn't take no for an answer and swept her to a night out. They
ended up at a nearby bar whose promise was cheap beer, loud
music, and country boys for any rodeo she wished to ride.

Kat wasn't looking for any bronco riding, but a few drinks and
some dancing made her reminisce about happier days. Days before

a man named Anatoly came into her life. She took fifty dollars from her rent money, donned a tight, bright-red dress cut too low for the meek at heart, and drove her dilapidated Escort ten miles across the West Virginia border.

Did she know what she was doing?

Hours later, and too many sweet drinks down, she wasn't sure.

She had to concentrate to keep the car steady and under the speed limit. She couldn't afford to attract the police. The alcohol coursing through her veins would mean jail. Jail would mean an unexplained absence. Both would mean Anatoly.

Fifteen minutes later, she navigated two backstreets, nearly collided with a bicycle left along the road, and turned into the entrance to her condo.

It was then she saw him. He was the cliché he portrayed—a tall, wide, muscular man with short black hair and dark sunglasses even at night. He wore a heavy black leather jacket and dark pants. He smoked a cigarette, leaning on the side of his dark four-door in the far corner of the center lot. Even in the faint moonlight, he was unmistakable.

Anatoly.

Her breath caught. Adrenaline washed the fuzziness of alcohol from her eyes. Her fingers screamed from her grip on the steering wheel. She was already committed to the entrance but she veered hard left and made a tight circle, accelerating out of the turn and speeding back to the main street before Anatoly could get a good look at her car.

His car headlights came on.

She crushed down on the gas and headed across town. She fumbled in her clutch bag and found her cell phone. Three times she dialed the wrong number. She was supposed to commit it to memory—stored numbers or speed dials were dangerous. But at the moment, fear was hiding it. On the fourth attempt, she connected with a voicemail.

"Dmitry, please answer—"

The voice on the mailbox was not familiar.

She swerved down a side street trying to remain undetected. "Think, Katalina." Finally, she reached a voicemail only answered with a number. "Dmitry! You say no call you unless important. Please. It is Anatoly. He come to house. He chase me. Help me. Anatoly, he coming."

She ended the call and turned right, heading south toward the highway.

The headlights behind her were gone, replaced by a higher, wider set she was hoping was a pickup truck like the local boys drove. She wheeled into an all-night convenience store and parked around the side where no one from the street could see her car.

She redialed the number again but got the same voicemail. Once. Twice. Three times.

Tears drained her makeup into black tracks down her cheeks. She could not face Anatoly—not tonight. Not again. Not ever.

Kat wiped her eyes and dug into her clutch bag again. This time, she slipped out a plain white business card secreted in her makeup kit. The card was simple—one name printed in the center and a handwritten phone number below it.

If she called the number, there would be no going back. Not to Anatoly. Not even to Dmitry. But if Dmitry did not reach her in time—if Anatoly found her first—there would be no going back *anywhere*.

She dialed the number, whispering a prayer, and cursed at the same time.

A grandfatherly voice answered, "Good evening."

"Yes. I ... I am sorry—" For a moment she considered hanging up but realized she had forgotten to mask her number with *67. She closed her eyes. "You say to call if ever I needing help. I am afraid. Dmitry, he will not answer. I am in very terrible fear."

"I understand, Katalina. Please, do not be afraid. Tell me where you are. I can have someone accompany you to my home. You will be safe there."

She sighed. "No. It must be you. I will not go with anyone. Just you. You must know this, yes? A man like you must understand, yes? Anatoly and you, you are not so different, no?"

The old voice laughed over the sounds of many mumbling voices. "Forgive me, I am unable to leave just now. And, Katalina, Anatoly and I are very much different people. Please, do not confuse us. Tell me where you are."

"Please, you must tell me, what will it cost—what must I repay you to help me?" Kat's hands trembled and she peered around the car as though someone might be just outside. "What must I do for you?"

The smooth, grandfatherly voice sounded sincere—comforting. "My dear, Katalina. You owe me nothing. If an old man cannot protect a young woman in trouble, then why grow old at all?"

She closed her eyes as rivers of black streamed down her face. "Thank you. I will meet your men. Please, hurry them. I am so afraid, Nicholai. I am so afraid."

TEN

AFTER WANDERING THE HOUSE for clues and snooping on all the hush-hush conversations the rich-folk were having—that's what private eyes do—I got bored and looked for Angel. A few of the conversations were, to say the least, *interesting*. Oh, one or two voiced genuine concern for Stephanos Grecco's murder, but most of the guests never heard of him. I listened to catty sniping about who wore what dress and the way Mr. Him undressed someone else's Mrs. Her with their eyes. Then there were never-ending complaints about the police taking too long, "Dear God, I want to go home—can't it wait until morning? He'll still be dead then, won't he?"

Someone even sniped the caterer should have been murdered.

Did anyone understand one of their own was lying in a pool of blood face down in the middle of the ballroom? Didn't they notice Stephanos Grecco bought it during a champagne dance in front of their eyes?

No. They didn't. "Oh, look, a murder. Waiter, the champagne isn't chilled right."

Still, I didn't think the caterer deserved to be murdered—no matter how slow the service.

I found Angel in the rear garden patio under the watchful eye of a uniformed deputy. She sat at a small wrought-iron table with Stephanos Grecco's wife, Bonnie. She was an elegant lady in her late twenties—*maybe* in her thirties. Her slim, sleek figure and platinum hair should have come with a removable sign reading "trophy wife" for whenever she was with the round, frumpy, and much older Stephanos Grecco.

But, based on what I'd heard in the crowd, perhaps the sign was unnecessary.

Bonnie wiped tears from her face—at least appeared to—and with each dab, she glanced into a compact mirror in her hand to check her appearance.

"I don't believe this happened," Bonnie sniffed. "I just can't."

"It's going to be all right, Bonnie," Angel said, touching her arm. "It's very difficult, I know. I recently lost my husband. Whatever I can do, just ask."

"Well, not too lost." I slipped into an empty chair beside Angel. "You two shouldn't be out here, Angel. The cops—"

"It's all right. Captain Sutter said we could sit here. Away from the crowd, I mean."

Bonnie looked at her and then around the garden. "I know."

Angel just smiled. Sometimes, without thinking, she forgets others cannot hear or see me. "I'm sorry, of course you know. I just didn't want you to feel rushed. Take all the time you need."

"Thank you." Bonnie dabbed a tear and straightened her gown. "I wish I had gone to the police sooner."

Excuse me? What?

"Bonnie?" Angel squeezed Bonnie's hand. "What do you mean?"

"Steph's murder is my fault. I could have stopped it."

Angel blinked several times and shot a glance at me as she leaned forward in her chair. "What do you mean?"

"It's my fault." Bonnie dropped her face into her handkerchief and sobbed for a long time. Then, she turned away from Angel and set me back on my seat.

"Steph's bullet was meant for me."

"You?" Angel stared. "Why?"

"Steph and I were arguing."

Angel nodded. "Yes, I know—it was hard not to see you two fighting. But how does—"

"I got real mad." Bonnie looked down. "He was drinking too much again. So I grabbed the nice man at our table—the very handsome *young* man—and Steph got madder."

"But why do you think the shooting was meant for you?"

"I know it was." Bonnie cleared her throat and looked around the garden as though there were spies behind the forsythias. "The letters."

"The letters?"

Bonnie took Angel's hand in hers and whispered, "I got two letters this past month. They said they were going to get even. I'd destroyed them and they were going to get even. One said that I'd betrayed him and I had to pay. They said I'd taken everything from him and he wouldn't let me go on hurting people."

Angel's mouth went agape waiting for more details. None came.

I said, "We gotta get those letters, Angel. And—"

"Do you still have them?" She was way ahead of me. "Do you know who sent them, Bonnie? Do you know what they mean?"

I had trained her well.

"No, I don't. The letters were like a computer printed them, not handwritten, and they weren't signed. I showed them to Steph and he laughed. He said he got letters, too, and it was old news. He said forget about it and he'd take care of it."

"Angel," I said, "you better get Bear. He needs to hear this."

Angel stood up but Bonnie held tight to her hand, pulling her back into her chair. "Please, don't go. I'm so afraid. He could be anywhere. If he can try to kill me here—if he can kill Steph in front of all of you—I'm not safe anywhere."

"It'll be all right, Bonnie. I promise."

"No, I'm not safe. He's going to kill me next."

ELEVEN

"REVENGE?" CAPTAIN SUTTER STOOD with Bear beside the wrought iron table watching Angel console Bonnie Grecco. "Revenge for what?"

"I am not sure, Captain," Bonnie said. "If I knew, I would tell you."

"Committing murder in public shows a lot of anger," Captain Sutter said, "or arrogance. And it takes a lot of planning."

"And no one saw him and there's no evidence yet." Bear's crossed arms and set jaw showed frustration. "We need a break."

For the past twenty minutes, Captain Sutter and Bear had listened to Bonnie's story over and over—pulling details and fishing for lost memories. None were caught. So far, all we had were a couple threatening letters and a dead Stephanos Grecco.

"Bonnie, where are the letters?" Bear asked.

She shrugged. "I'm not sure. Steph had them. I don't know what he did with them, but they must be at home in his office."

"Okay. As soon as we're through here, I'll have two of my detectives escort you home to search for the letters and anything else helpful."

Bonnie nodded.

Angel asked, "Would you like me to come with you, Bonnie?"

"No." Bonnie feigned a smile. "I'll be all right. I'm afraid I'm a little wobbly right now, and, to be honest, I don't want to stay at home tonight. I can't."

I understood. "She's terrified, Angel. And distraught."

"Take your time," Angel said, patting her hand. "It'll all sort out—we'll help you. Bear will find the killer."

"Thank you." Bonnie looked away. "I'm afraid I know very little about Steph. I don't even know about a will or his finances—not about burial stuff. I cannot believe I was so stupid."

Bear leaned in. "You're not stupid. It's normal—well, as normal as these things can be. Angel knows what to do. You're in good hands."

"Bonnie," Captain Sutter said, "You said you have no idea who sent the letters or what they meant. Do you think Stephanos knew? I mean, he seemed unconcerned about them, right?"

"No, he didn't take them seriously at all, so I never thought twice about the threats afterward. I asked and he dismissed it. Like always. If I asked about his past, he changed the subject. He never liked talking about it."

"Oh?" Bear's eyebrows went up. "Why?"

"He didn't like talking about his money. You know, about business. He didn't with me, anyway."

I said, "Bear, I've been snooping around. You know, listening to the guests. Nobody knew anything about him. Nothing. Zip. Crapola. Odd, don't you think?"

"Really?" Bear looked down and frowned. "What did your husband do for a living, Bonnie?"

She thought a moment; a moment too long for me. "He was a, what do you call it, a day trader? Yes, a day trader. He worked the stock markets and made private business deals. You know, like financing deals for people. He seemed to be very good at it."

"What company did he work for?" Bear glanced over at Captain Sutter and she didn't look convinced either. "I'd like to contact them."

"None I that I know of. He worked alone."

"But, you said he did business deals." Captain Sutter's eyes narrowed in the way I'd seen her when a suspect was weaving a tale. "We'd like some names, Bonnie. Did any of those deals go bad? Anyone whose money Stephanos lost?"

Bonnie raised her chin. "I wouldn't know, Captain. As I said, he didn't discuss his business. I knew better than to ask."

Disbelief telegraphed between Captain Sutter and Bear—telltale looks, raised eyebrows. Cop-intuition. Even my bullshit-meter was pinging.

Angel picked up on it, too, and broke a long silence. "Bonnie, how long have you been married to Stephanos?"

"He seems much older," Captain Sutter added.

"Yes, he is much older," Bonnie snapped, flipping her hair off her shoulders with more resentment than grief. "I know what you're thinking. We married three months ago, after we met six months ago on a cruise. Anything else? Am I your suspect?"

"No, Bonnie, no." Angel patted her hand. "They have to ask personal questions. They have to know everything about Stephanos. And—"

"And they have to see if I killed him for his money." Bonnie's voice was flat and cold. "I know what they're getting at."

"Yes, Bonnie." Bear sat down across from her. "It's unfortunate, but that's how this works. Look, we can do this later if you like. I understand—"

"No, Detective. Now is fine. I'll be honest—I don't know the details of Steph's will. But I'm sure he left everything to me. Why not, I'm his wife, right?"

"But you don't know, correct?" Captain Sutter asked. "For sure, I mean."

Bonnie shook her head.

"Does he have any other family?" Bear asked in a softer voice. "Children by another marriage?"

"None he told me about. But we've not discussed much of his past. What would it look like if I started asking him about his money and wills and business stuff? He would have been angry and suspicious. Just like you."

Bear and Angel exchanged glances. Angel said, "You're right, Bonnie. But they have to ask. Let's go find some tea. Okay, Bear?"

"Sure," Bear grunted. "We'll take this up later."

Captain Sutter agreed. "We'll get you out of here soon, Bonnie. I'm sorry about the questions. I am. If you don't want to go home, we can make arrangements for a hotel. But I'd like my men to be able to search your home tonight. It's important."

Bonnie nodded and followed Angel into the house.

Bear watched them leave and said, "She's different, isn't she?"

"Yeah—half his age and no clue about him." Captain Sutter shook her head. "I bet she inherits a fortune. She claims not to know for sure. I don't know what to believe from her, so just in case, we better put protection on her for a while, Bear. Starting now."

"Sounds like a job for Spence, Cap."

She forced a laugh. "Yeah, okay—Spence. He'll love you for volunteering him." Then she turned and looked at the house. "This case is bizarre."

Me, I think the entire evening was bizarre. Like this mansion of Vincent Calaprese's—of the New Jersey Calapreses—was one interesting, weird, bizarre place. What bothered me the most was that despite all my neat spirit-tricks and snappy detective skills, I had no idea what was going on. Neither did Bear. But, one thing was certain—either Bonnie or Stephanos Grecco had made someone very mad. And that someone was skilled and brazen; a very bad combination.

Then there was sweet Sassy and the Big Band mobster demanding I deliver Benjamin—whoever he was—or I swim with the fishes.

I better find Benjamin. After all, I'm not so sure ghosts can swim.

TWELVE

BEAR AND I WERE standing in the main hall when I spotted Angel arguing with a balding man in a tuxedo. I recognized the blowhard without introduction.

Professor W. Simon Hahn—"W" for weird, whiner, and worrywart.

Professor Hahn was a Senior Fellow—and senior pain-in-the-ass—at the University of the Shenandoah Valley, a muckety-muck in the University's College of History. Unfortunately, he was also a colleague of Angel's at the Mosby Center for American Studies. W. Simon Hahn was a historian by training and a bureaucrat and politician mixed with snake and earthworm on the evolutionary scale. When Angel's old boss, Ernie Stuart—the prior history department chair—took the heart attack train to hell, W. Simon Hahn was measuring his office before the crime scene was finished. Much to his irritation, the job was filled, albeit on a temporary basis, by Angel. The Board of Regents felt she was the most qualified and deserving, despite W. Simon Hahn's pending orders for new paint and furniture.

Since then, W. Simon Hahn was an ever-present lump on our backsides—no explanation of what I mean is necessary here.

He was having an animated conversation with Angel near a table just inside the ballroom and it didn't sit well with me. Arms flailed, chins jutted, and steam rose from his ears. Bear saw it too and made a beeline for their table.

Professor Hahn whirled around when Bear walked up. "I am speaking with Tucker—"

"Professor Tucker," Bear said in a stiff tone. "And you are?"

"Professor and Senior Fellow W. Simon Hahn. And who is addressing me?"

"'W' for whacko, Bear." I couldn't resist.

Bear stepped closer and let his shadow push Professor Hahn back from Angel. "Braddock. I'm a senior detective and senior deputy of the Frederick County Sheriff's Department and Major Crimes Task Force. I'm in charge here."

"How wonderful for you." Professor Hahn turned away and glared at Angel. "My business is with *Professor* Tucker. Not you, officer."

"Detective," Bear repeated.

I said, "Punt this little twerp, Bear. Angel's got enough troubles right now."

"Professor," Bear said, "this is a homicide investigation. If there's another issue, it'll have to wait."

"It cannot wait."

Angel shook her head. "Just tell me what you need, Simon. So far, all you've done is complain about the gala. And while I'm truly sorry about the way it ended, it is not my fault."

"Oh?" Professor Hahn straightened with an audible humph and took out a small, leather notepad from his tuxedo pocket. "I'm surprised to hear you say that. I would like the donations turned over to me for safe keeping at once. You have too many other duties at present to concern yourself with those. I think it appropriate as I am—"

"Sorry, Professor." Bear held up a hand. "Sometime during the murder, the donations were stolen. We're looking into it, but the murder has priority."

When Professor Hahn smiled, Dr. Jekyll turned into Mr. Hyde. "Uh-oh, Angel, Simon's happy. Nothing good happens when he's happy."

"Stolen? Right in front of everyone?" Professor Hahn took out a pen and scribbled something in his notepad. "Professor Tucker, you are responsible for the safety and security of our guests and the donations. I believe the Board of Regents—"

"Whoa, there, Professor," Bear said, stepping closer again. "Angela was not responsible for the safety and security of the guests and donations. Nor is she responsible for the theft or murder. I had two detectives on guard in the ballroom. Stephanos Grecco's murder was used to someone's advantage and the monies stolen. We'll get them back."

"You had better. This is going to look very bad with the Board of Regents. And in their final selection for the History Chair, too. Now—"

Bear held up a hand. "Did you see or hear anything relevant to this homicide investigation?"

Hahn blinked several times and looked from Angel to Bear. "Well, yes, I did. I tried to tell the other deputy but he thought I was drunk or something."

"What then? Tell me."

"Ah, yes, let me recall a moment. Yes, yes, let me think."

Did I mention W. Simon Hahn was a drama queen?

"Yes, a few moments after the shot, I saw someone emerge from nowhere at the end of the hall and go into the lounge. I went to the lounge door and heard someone talking inside. Just before I went in, I heard a bang—like a door slamming or something."

Bear asked, "And? Did you see who was in there?"

"No one was in there, Detective. I'm trying to explain to you. I went into the lounge and there was no one there. Empty. And I know no one came out—I was at the door."

I said, "How much champagne did he have?"

Angel covered a smile with her hand. "Are you sure, Simon? Are you sure you saw and heard someone inside?"

"Of course I'm sure. I'm not the one talking to myself all the time." He raised his chin and shot Angel a look more sniping than his tone. "Now am I?"

"Just what are you saying, Simon?"

Bear asked, "Why was it unusual for someone to be in the lounge talking? I mean, why do you think it's important?"

"I am not saying it's important, Detective." Professor Hahn jammed his fists on his hips. "I'm saying it was odd. Everyone ran toward the ballroom, except one person who went inside the lounge. Then, poof, no one was inside."

"Poof?" Bear said. "Poof? You're sure?"

"I am not in the habit of telling stories, Detective."

Bear went to a deputy standing in the hall, spoke with him, and returned to us with the deputy in tow. "Professor, go with this deputy. He'll take another statement."

"Now, see here. I have more to discuss with Professor Tucker. After all, with all the complaints I'm receiving—"

Bear pointed to the deputy. "He'll take the complaints, too."

The deputy rolled his eyes and led Professor W. Simon Hahn to the lounge.

Angel said, "Do you think he's telling the truth? About someone disappearing in the lounge, I mean?"

"No," Bear said. "People don't disappear into thin air."

"They don't?" I said. "I can."

THIRTEEN

Angel went off to calm the guests and I followed Bear to Captain Sutter who was inside the sitting room. When we walked in, she waved at Bear. "Bonnie Grecco's resting in a back room. Get her out of here as soon as you can break Spence free, Bear."

"Yeah, okay. It'll be another hour or so—"

The tall oak door creaked open and a deputy ran straight for Captain Sutter. "We have a witness."

"Who?" Captain Sutter asked.

"One of the caterers saw a guest coming down the rear servant's stairway right after Grecco was shot."

Bear asked, "Are they sure?"

"Yep." The deputy explained, "A young gal—Rita-something—is in the kitchen. She remembered because someone yelled into the kitchen something about a guest being shot. Everyone ran to the ballroom to see what was going on. When Rita got to the hall, a guy ran up behind her from the rear servant's stairwell. He almost ran into her. He was upstairs. He could be the shooter."

"Maybe we got a break." Captain Sutter issued orders on her radio. Then she motioned for Bear to follow her. "Let's go speak with Rita."

I followed Bear and the captain to the kitchen. Another deputy stood at a large table cluttered with steaming chafing dishes of food. A young Hispanic girl wearing a white catering jacket was seated at the table. Her dark eyes went big and round when we walked up. She was young—like she should have been studying for high school exams. She was pretty, too, innocent and scared to death. Her eyes darted between Captain Sutter and Bear and her hands trembled on the table.

"Hello, Rita," Captain Sutter said, dismissing the deputy with a nod. "I'm Captain Sutter. This is Detective Braddock. Please tell us again what you saw?"

Rita's voice quivered as she replayed the events—adding a few scattered details from what the deputy had told us in the sitting room. Her voice was low and shy—her heavy Spanish accent and tattered nerves made it difficult to follow at times. She ended with, "*Si*, this man was a big man. Older but not old, you know? He wear round glasses and look very important, very smart, you know? He very nice. Very handsome, too." She blushed and looked down at the table. "He smile when we serve him. He say thank you. Not many do here tonight."

Bear asked, "Do you know his name?"

"No, but the important lady—Professor Tucker, I think—does. He danced with her. She knows."

Every red-blooded man at the gala had danced with my Angel. Beauty was a curse. I had the same problem when I was alive—it was difficult, really.

"Okay, but, can you point him out to us?" Bear asked. "I promise you won't be in any danger. We'll walk around the rooms—you and me. When you see him, tell me. I'll take it from there."

Rita looked down and started shaking her head. "No, no. I cannot. The deputy say he might be the killer. I no want him to see me."

I lay my hand on Rita's and whispered, "Rita, it'll be all right. You can trust Bear. He's a good man."

She didn't budge—not even to pull her hand away. Her face softened as she stared at her hand. A faint, uncertain smile blossomed.

"Rita, I promise." I gave her hand a squeeze. "Trust him."

Her head stopped shaking and she looked up at Bear. "*Si*, I will go with you."

"Good girl, Rita. I promise, you'll—"

"We found it!" Spence ran into the room and held up a clear plastic evidence bag with a heavy object inside. "Got it, Cap."

The murder weapon.

"Cap, we found this upstairs." Spence pointed to the light-framed, .22-caliber pistol inside the evidence bag. He turned the bag over and tapped the over-sized barrel through the plastic. "It's got a homemade silencer and it's been fired—several rounds missing from the mag."

"Good." Bear examined the gun through the plastic. "Where did you find this? In one of the rooms?"

"Yes," Spence said. "The first room at the top of the stairs—just where we thought the shooter had shot Grecco from. It was tucked between the mattress and box spring; jammed inside real good."

Captain said, "Show me, Spence. Bear, take Rita for a stroll."

"Okay, Cap." Bear held his hand out for Rita's. "You ready?"

Rita closed her eyes and I squeezed her hand again. "It's all right, Rita."

"*Sí*, Detective Bear." The thin smile widened and she looked up at him, taking his hand. "I not afraid anymore."

Five minutes later, we finished looking over the guests in the sitting room, den, dining room, and two other large rooms off the main hall. Rita was shy and timid, but Bear eased her along with a soft voice and gentle words. When we stopped at the lounge—I expected to find Vincent Calaprese and the delectable Sassy—but only one guest was inside, sitting at the far end of the bar talking on a cell phone.

At the doorway, Rita tensed and withdrew behind Bear.

"Rita?" Bear turned and put his hand on her shoulder. "Is it him?"

She didn't respond. She didn't have to. The man speaking on the cell phone looked up and gave Bear a quick wave. When he did, Rita crushed tighter against Bear.

"Dear God, no," Bear whispered. "Are you sure, Rita?"

Her face paled and her eyes grew big. She was sure.

The man sitting across the room from us was tall with an athletic build and silver temples. He wore round, wireframe eyeglasses and his appearance was, as Rita had described, older but not old—most called him *distinguished*.

Distinguished. Yes, distinguished is the right word. In fact, I had called him that on many occasions when describing Angel's mentor, former guardian, and uncle.

I groaned and bit my lip. "Bear, there's a rational explanation—you know there is. We've known him for years. He just about raised Angel, for Christ's sake. He's no killer. No way."

Without a word, Bear motioned for a deputy in the hall and sent Rita back to the kitchen. Then he cursed and went to have a chat with Professor André Cartier.

FOURTEEN

"THIS IS ABSURD—ABSOLUTELY ABSURD." André Cartier jumped up from his bar stool. "Angela will vouch for me. And of all people, Bear, you cannot believe I killed anyone?"

"Just relax, André. It's my job." He pointed at the bar stool and waited for André to sit back down. "Funny, a few months ago you thought I was a killer. Remember?"

"Touché," I said.

André sat brooding.

After my murder, vile rumors swirled about Bear and Angel—the kind of rumors that always get stirred up when a dead guy leaves behind a best friend and a beautiful wife. The kind of rumors that hurt. And when the whispers started, André Cartier had his doubts, too.

Funny how indignation has no memory.

"Bear, you know me," he said. "You've got it all wrong."

"I hope so, André," Bear said, sliding onto a bar stool beside him. "A witness saw you come downstairs just after the shooting."

"And tell us what you know of Stephanos Grecco." Captain Sutter said, standing beside Bear with the evidence bag containing the .22 pistol. "Take your time and get it right."

"I didn't kill anyone." André exchanged looks—glares—with Bear and Captain Sutter. "Ask Angela, she can vouch for me."

"All night?" Captain Sutter asked. "She can attest to where you were every moment, Professor Cartier?"

"No, but certainly you remember me, Captain, and—"

"Yes, I do remember you. I know quite a lot about you. But it doesn't change the fact a witness saw you coming downstairs after the shooting."

"No, of course not, I'm sorry." André closed his eyes and took a deep, forced breath. "And of course Angela cannot say where I was all night. I doubt any of the guests—including myself—can restate our exact whereabouts after seeing Steph murdered. After all—"

"Steph?" Bear's eyebrows rose. "Are you two friends?"

"He introduced himself to me as 'Steph.'" André's face fell. "Come on, Bear. You've known me for years. I'm no murderer."

Captain Sutter set the evidence bag on the bar between them. "Then explain this."

"It's not mine. I went upstairs to look around. I've been here once before—helping Angela prepare for this gala. The house intrigues me. A lot of the guests were upstairs during the night. For God's sake, I saw Angel up there, too."

"But not at the moment Grecco was shot." Captain Sutter wasn't asking a question.

"Bad timing, I guess."

"You think?" Bear glanced at Captain Sutter but said to André, "Did you see anyone up there?"

André thought for a moment. He frowned. "No, but I heard someone at the other end of the main hallway. I was in the east wing looking at some antiques in the hall. When I heard the commotion downstairs, I ran down the servant's stairs."

"Why use the servant stairs?" Bear asked.

"They were closer."

I said, "Makes sense."

"And you didn't see anyone?" Captain Sutter asked. "And you claim to have heard someone?"

"Claim?" André started to rise again but Captain Sutter's eyes stopped him. His face tightened and his chin rose. "I did hear something, Captain. A door closed, I think, and someone was walking in the hall."

I said, "Bear, Rita may have seen him but it doesn't prove anything. There's two hundred people here. A lot of them weren't in the ballroom when Grecco was killed."

The lounge doors swung open and Angel pushed her way past the uniformed deputy at the door. She strode up to us and confronted Captain Sutter.

"You've got to be kidding me! André had nothing to do with this."

"Angela, please." Bear patted the air. "Go back to your guests and let us do our jobs."

"Then do them. Go find the killer because he's not in this room."

Bear glanced at Captain Sutter and the telegraph starting tapping away between them again. His mouth tightened and his eyes narrowed—Captain Sutter's temples did the rumba.

"So, Professor Cartier," Captain Sutter leaned forward with an edge to her voice. "Anything we need to know? Anything at all?"

I always had a hard time reading the good Captain. Maybe it was because she played her cards close or because she was a chameleon. Or, maybe it was because she was a woman who could out-cop any of us on the detective squad. Right now, though, it was easy to read her—she was not convinced—guilt or innocence—about André Cartier. None of us were.

None but Angel.

I said to Angel, "It'll be all right, Angel. I'll look after André. I promise."

"You can't keep that promise," she said. When Captain Sutter glanced at her, she said to André. "Tell them, André. Tell them everything."

"I don't know anything, Captain, nothing at all."

"All right then," Captain Sutter tapped the bar. "Tell us about Stephanos and Bonnie Grecco."

"I just met the Greccos tonight. I've never heard of them, although Stephanos claims to be from the Washington circuit."

"DC is a big city." Captain Sutter's voice was curt and direct. "Do you know everyone?"

André bristled. "Of course not, Captain. But I do know most in the philanthropic circuit. He claims to be an antique aficionado. I do many fundraisers throughout the year, and I've never come across him."

"What about Bonnie Grecco?"

André looked at Angel. "I was just introduced to Bonnie Grecco tonight."

"Oh, come now, Captain. Please." Angel stepped forward. "You cannot think he had anything to do with all this. I was up on the second floor tonight, too. Does being there make me a suspect?"

"I don't know, does it?" Their eyes met and Captain Sutter shrugged. "I'm sorry. But, you weren't up near the balcony room seconds before the shot was fired. He was."

"No, I wasn't," André said. "I was on the other end of the house."

"You see? He wasn't there. And, you don't know who else might have been up there. Do you?"

"A murderer won't admit to being there, now will he?"

I said, "Easy, Angel. I'm with you on André, but the captain is just—"

"Doing her job." Angel folded her arms and stared daggers at the floor. "I understand."

André Cartier was a lot of things. He was a professor of history with two doctorates—American History and Anthropology. He was a big shot with the Washington Smithsonian. More importantly, though, he was Angel's uncle and he'd raised her since she was very young. A tragic accident took both her parents when she was a teenager. He'd helped her through the loss of her mom and dad, and then twenty-one years later, the loss of her husband—me. Now, after more than two decades of mentoring, the roles were reversed.

"Bear, Captain, listen to me." André held up his hands. "I have never seen this gun before. I assure you it is not mine. I did not kill Stephanos Grecco. I have not killed anyone in years."

"What?" Captain Sutter cocked her head. "Excuse me?"

"Viet Nam, Captain." André frowned. "I was in the war."

"So you can handle a weapon?" she asked.

"Of course I can. But it's been years."

"Interesting."

"And Bonnie?" Bear asked. "You never heard of her either, right?"

"No, Detective. I have not heard of Bonnie Grecco before this evening."

I reached out and touched André's shoulder, trying to get inside his head. Sometimes, touching objects or people gave me a kind of clairvoyance. Sometimes, a touch showed me what the living couldn't—lost memories, lost lives, even secreted truths buried deep. Often, the simple touch showed me things they didn't want others to know, too.

And sometimes, touching didn't give diddly.

This was one of those times.

André was full of irritation and angst and it started bubbling out. His eyes were tired; his face taunt and defensive. His posture recoiled and was ready for flight. But, I guess if the roles were reversed and the cops suspected me a killer, I'd be worried, too.

Yet, André's gruffness wasn't quite it. It was something else. Something . . . hidden. He said he'd just met Bonnie and Stephanos tonight. Yet, when he said her name, he seemed, well, odd, perhaps evasive, maybe even worried. When Bear mentioned her name to him for the first time, André's emotions pegged my spookmeter into the danger-danger zone. Can a dance and champagne do all that in one night?

Yes, of course it could. How else could anyone explain how the gorgeous and talented Dr. Angela Hill-Tucker was married to me? She once used champagne and dancing to lure me in. Then, I allowed her to fall in love with me.

"Angel, there's something about Bonnie troubling André. Troubling him bad," I said. "But I still think André is innocent."

"Of course he's innocent." She glanced at Bear. "You believe he is, Bear, right?"

He nodded. "We still have to follow the evidence, Angela."

I said, "Anyone could have put the gun under the bedroom mattress. We have to finish interviewing all the guests and see who else was upstairs at the time of the shooting."

She repeated me and added, "I'll speak with my guests and try to calm them a little longer. But they need to go home."

"Yeah, okay Angela." Captain Sutter looked at André. "Professor, mind if we run a gunshot residue test on you?"

"Not at all. Please go right ahead. Do whatever you must."

"Good. And we'd like to check your car, too." Captain Sutter threw a thumb over her shoulder at a deputy standing there. "Right now."

"Of course. Since I don't think 'no' will stop you."

"It won't." She put her hand out. "Your car keys please."

"One moment." André dug into his tuxedo pocket and handed her a slip of paper. "Here is my coat check. The keys are in the inside pocket of my raincoat."

Captain Sutter went to a deputy in the doorway, handed him the coat check, and gave him instructions. A moment later, the deputy returned with a long black raincoat and handed it to André.

As André slipped his arm into the coat, something fell out onto the floor.

"You dropped something.' Captain Sutter bent down and retrieved a black driving glove.

"No, I don't think so." André looked at it. "It's not mine. I didn't bring gloves."

Captain Sutter turned the glove over, then handed it to the deputy. She rubbed her fingers together and smelled them. "Deputy, have the techs check this."

The deputy walked off.

"Captain?" André asked. "Check for what?"

"Later," she said, gesturing toward the door. "After you."

We followed André to a new Mercedes convertible parked inside the mansion entrance in a long row of other expensive automobiles. Captain Sutter issued orders to the deputies waiting there and turned to André. "Very nice car, Professor. I didn't know academia paid so well."

"It doesn't," André sneered. "But being the leading authority on Civil War studies and a historical adviser to the White House does. I've written three books in the past two years alone. If you must know."

"She didn't mean anything, André," Angel said. "Captain, please, can we—"

"Captain Sutter," one of the deputies called, shining his flashlight toward us. "We've got something."

They do?

On the passenger side of the car, a deputy knelt down, searching the front seats and floor. Captain Sutter leaned inside over his shoulder, looking at what the deputy pointed out between the seats.

"Bear, what is it?" Angel called. "What did they find?"

He held up a hand and moved in closer.

I said, "Relax, Angel. It can't be anything important."

Bear stood back and turned toward us. His face was stone.

Captain Sutter stood up, too, slipped on a rubber crime scene glove, and took something from the deputy kneeling at the open car door. She looked at Bear and they both walked back to Angel, André, and me.

"Professor Cartier," her voice was ice. "We found this under your seat. Can you explain it?"

She held a .22 caliber cartridge.

"No, no. Bullets in my car? Don't be absurd," André said in a low voice. "This is all a mistake. Someone—"

"Bear, stop this." Angel took hold of André's arm. "This is all wrong. You know this is all wrong. Someone is framing him. It has to be someone else."

Captain Sutter's radio squawked and she stepped away to talk. When she returned, she was grim and cold. "Professor Cartier, our crime techs found preliminary results of gunshot residue on your driving glove. You do own driving gloves, don't you?"

"Yes, I do. But I told you," he said, shaking his head, "it is not my glove. Mine are in my car." He turned and looked over at Angel. "Angela, I cannot explain this. Not now."

"What are you talking about, André?"

Captain Sutter threw a chin at one of the deputies who burrowed back into the Mercedes. When he emerged, he shook his head.

"No gloves, Captain."

Bear's voice was grave. "André, if you can explain any of this, now would be a good time."

"I cannot. Someone is trying to frame me. You must see it too, right?"

"Maybe." Captain Sutter glanced at Bear and nodded once.

Bear moved around behind André, took a set of handcuffs from one of the deputies, and clasped them around his wrists.

"I'm sorry, Angela. I am." Captain Sutter's voice was all business. "Professor André Cartier, you're under arrest for the murder of Stephanos Grecco."

FIFTEEN

DETECTIVE MIKE SPENCE CLOSED his cell phone and walked over to a deputy standing in the kitchen entrance talking with a young girl in a catering uniform.

"Hospital says Cal will be okay, Woods. Bullet missed the bone and went right through. They put him into surgery and they expect he'll be back to work in a few weeks."

"Lucky man, Cal Clemens," Woods said. "I'll pass the word."

"Where are we on the count?"

Woods flipped through a notebook. "One hundred-eighty three guests, twenty-two catering staff—not counting us—at the shindig."

"It's a gala, Woods. Jeez, a gala." Spence cracked a smile and took the notebook. "How many are left?"

"Twenty-one guests and two caterers to go. Soon as you say, we'll release those we've interviewed. Just say the word."

"Word." Spence flipped a couple pages. "And I want you to match up every interview with the names on the list, okay?"

Woods' eyebrows rose. "Okay, but we got 'em all. They've been corralled in rooms since the killing."

"Humor me. You know the Cap, she'll kick my butt if we miss anything. And I don't want Bear going off on me. Just do it. Then double-check and then you can release 'em."

Woods shrugged, mumbled something, and walked off.

Spence went into the kitchen where a wide powerful man in a tuxedo was hand-chopping the air at an older man in a chef's jacket and checkered pants. "Hey, what's going on? We got a problem?"

The tuxedoed man turned around. He glared at Spence and didn't answer. He was tall and broad and filled the tuxedo like a heavyweight boxer. He smacked the chef beside the head, cursed in some language foreign to Spence, and started to walk away.

"Whoa there, *kemo sabe*." Spence grabbed his arm. "I asked you if you had a problem."

"*Da*." The man yanked his arm free and spat out in a heavy gruff accent, "What you want? This my business, not police business."

"Oh, yeah?" Spence held tight and looked him over in slow, critical snapshots. "It's my business because I say it is. So, stop slapping the staff around."

"Mind your own business. I'm the boss."

Spence was taken aback. "Hey, buddy, lose the attitude. I'm Detective Spence—Sheriff's Office. You are?"

"Peter. I am Festival Catering and Entertainment manager." Peter's voice was heavy and deep, with a Ukrainian flavor. "When we be free to go? You have cost much money and enough of my time."

"Oh, we have?" Spence let the man's arm go and jabbed a pen at his chest. "Sorry our murder investigation has caused such disruption to you and your cook. Now, Peter, let's try your full name, shall we?"

"Cook? Yanni is executive chef. How stupid to suggest—"

"Your name, mister. While I'm young."

Peter was much taller than Spence and stared down at him with powerful arms folded and muscles bulging at the tuxedo fabric. 7

"Stick it, Petya." Spence jabbed the pen again, leaving blue ink marks on Petya's starched white shirt. He put the pen away. "You can leave as soon as we finish interviewing your people. We got a couple to go."

"You stupid man." Petya went to the sink and wet a napkin, dabbing at his shirt. "You'll pay for shirt, yes? And interviews are all wrong."

"Why?"

"Roster the lady professor give you is not right. Kravitz scheduled tonight—he not show. So roster is not good. I already explain to other cop."

Spence lifted his radio, threw a finger in the air for Petya to wait, and walked to the hall. He spoke with Deputy Woods on his radio while keeping an eye on Petya Sergeyevich Chernyshov.

The conversation lasted only a moment.

"Bullshit, Petya. You had twenty-two names on your roster, counting you, and twenty-two warm bodies were checked in by my guys. You replaced Kravitz with someone."

Petya shrugged. "Yes, that is right. I didn't say no, did I? I say Kravitz did not come here. He sent Jorge-someone. I was—"

"Where's Jorge-someone?"

Petya looked at the chef leaning against the sink. The chef shook his head and looked away. Petya said, "We not know. He left. Maybe sick. Maybe other work. Who knows, maybe girlfriend."

"He just left?" Spence smiled like a snake about to strike. "You lost a guy wearing a white dinner jacket and carrying the lobster bisque? How did you lose him?"

Petya stared back and shrugged.

"I need an address and phone. And I need it fast."

"I am sorry. I do not have information you want. I told you, Kravitz send him. We were rushed and I need someone to serve. No papers. I pay cash."

Spence lifted his radio again and spit out orders to check all the guests and grounds for the missing caterer. He peered at Petya. "I guess since there's no paperwork you don't have a description either, right?"

Petya shook his head. "I asked. No one saw him much, you know. No one know him. They say he was Mexican or something. He did not speak but was doing good job. I leave him alone."

"Sure, right. No one spoke. Paid cash. You run a tight ship here, Petya. I'll put a BOLO out for a Mexican-or-something in a white jacket doing a great job. Perfect. You're a big help."

Petya muttered something and made the chef laugh.

"You got something else to say?" Spence stepped forward. "Listen, Petya, you and me are going to go around pretty soon. You—"

"Detective?" Deputy Woods walked into the kitchen. "A minute, Mike?"

"What for Christ's sake," Spence said. "Me and Petya are—"

"Detective, we're missing two guests."

Petya spat a coarse laugh. "Oh, so Detective, it is *you* missing someone? Important someone?"

"Shove it." Spence whirled around at Woods. "What are you talking about?"

Woods had his notebook out. "One-hundred eighty three guests on the list. One-hundred eighty three checked off on arrival. We're doing a name-to-interview comparison, but—"

"What—one-eight-three equals one-eighty-three, right?" Spence shrugged. "If you got 'em all—"

"We didn't." Woods flipped to a page and handed the pad to Spence. "There were two uninvited guests who weren't on the list. So we should have one-eighty-five. We only got one-eighty-three now."

Spence ran over the checkmarks and comments alongside each name. "Who's missing, Woods? Did you count the stiff?"

"Yeah, I counted him. We got some big shot from DC who refused to sign the guest list and some bodyguard who came in with someone else. Both were vouched in by one of Professor Tucker's VIPs."

"One of Angela's friends?" Spence looked up and threw a dagger-eye at Petya who smiled ear-to-ear. "Who, Woods? Who vouched for the uninvited guests?"

"Our suspect, Mike. Professor André Cartier."

SIXTEEN

"No worries, Professor Cartier," Captain Sutter said as André was led toward a police cruiser. "If you're innocent, it'll all be okay."

"Oh, Captain?" André snapped over his shoulder. "The innocent go free? Does it always work so well?"

She didn't answer. She didn't have to. She walked off into the house.

Angel was crying and Bear tried consoling her with a big paw wrapped around her shoulders. It wasn't working.

I stood there, watching and wishing it were me holding her close. But it wasn't and it couldn't be—ever again. Well, not the same way, anyhow.

"Angel," I said, "I'm going to look around the house some more. Bear and I will figure this out. You know we will. André will be fine."

She nodded, pulled away from Bear, and walked toward the street.

I hatched an idea and followed Bear to the rear sitting room that had been taken over as a makeshift command post. Captain Sutter sat at a table making notes. In front of her were three evidence bags containing the .22-caliber pistol, André's driving glove, and the .22-caliber shell found in André's Mercedes.

When Bear and I walked up to the table, Captain Sutter looked up. "Bear, don't start on me. I know he's Angela's family and all. But evidence is evidence."

"No, I get it, Cap. But if you knew him like I do, you'd know he's not a killer."

"Then prove it, dammit. Prove it fast." She stood and stretched. "I'm getting coffee. I'll bring you some. You'll need it—you're not leaving until this thing is wrapped up."

Bear slumped into a chair at the table and watched her walk off. His eyes were red and his temper short. Several times he picked up the evidence bag with the .22 pistol and looked it over, each time tossing it back onto the table as though it were on fire. Frustration was driving him and the ride was getting rougher.

"There's no way André did this. No way."

I looked at the gun sitting in front of him. "Bear, listen to me. Listen." I touched his hand resting on the evidence bag and willed my voice into his head. Even as thick as he was most of the time, he often heard me—especially when things were crazy. If this didn't qualify as crazy, nothing did.

"I need to touch the gun, Bear. Open the evidence bag. I need to touch the gun."

He looked around the room. "Huh? What—Spence, is that you?"

"Open the bag, moron. I know you hear me. Quit being a pain in the ass."

"Let's take a closer look." He grabbed the evidence bag and tore at the corner, peeling back the plastic. The pistol slipped onto the table in front of him. Then he pulled on a crime scene glove from his pocket and held the gun up for closer inspection.

"Bear, what the heck are you doing?" Spence came into the room. "You can't open the evidence up right now. The crime techs are going to throw a hissy fit."

"Let them, Spence, I—"

I couldn't hear them arguing anymore. When my fingers touched the gun, lightning flashed everywhere in the room.

It was happening.

A shower of light and colors swirled around me. It ebbed and flowed, darkness mixing into a rolling sea of light. The electricity finger-walked through me until my entire being was charged and vibrating. And as fast as it began, it calmed and grew dark. Bear disappeared from the table—as did the table, the walls, and the room. Everything was sucked away. Crude stone walls took their place and the remaining light snapped dark as though a doorway closed behind me.

I was in total obscurity.

A musty, dank smell of old stone and stale air surrounded me. I reached out and felt the cold, hard surface of rocks and stones. Somewhere ahead, a faint light flickered on and I walked toward it. The floor was hard—stone or rock too,—a tunnel or cavern that disappeared into the dim light somewhere ahead.

But where?

Hot needles danced in my head like sparks from a fire. It was odd—not that death isn't—but the sparks stirred confusion as disorientation fluttered inside. My thoughts were invaded. Other thoughts raced in and took over; unfamiliar thoughts foreign to me. I was alone, isolated ... alien.

I finally understood.

The .22-caliber murder weapon brought me to the killer.

No, that wasn't right. The silenced gun was in my hand—the killer's hand—and he was me.

SEVENTEEN

ME, A KILLER?

No—never. Yet, at the moment, there and now, the killer and I were one. Strange thoughts consumed me—someone else's thoughts controlled me and kept me focused on keeping calm and steady. I knew I was taking each step, felt the anticipation in the darkness as I moved forward. Someone was ahead. I was meeting them.

Someone I was looking for.

I held the silenced .22 pistol in one gloved hand and a penlight in the other. I followed the tunnel and each step felt comfortable and familiar. Had I been here before? The shooter had. My flashlight beam moved ahead of me and shined where the passage turned left. I followed without hesitation—without angst or concern—knowing the way. Without controlling the body I shared, I followed the passage around another turn. Ahead was a flicker that moved in a slow, upward arc.

A cigarette.

The cigarette glowed and behind it, I saw a man. My penlight bathed him until his hand rose and blocked the light.

"Point the light somewhere else, it's pissing me off." His voice was monotone and curt.

He was in his late forties with a dark, flat face I knew was no friend. His head was shaved and he had no beard or sideburns and thin, almost vacant eyebrows. He wasn't tall but bulky and muscular—no taller than five-eight, and even in the darkness his strength was obvious. His bulk was too much for the fabric of his shirt, and it strained at the shoulders and chest. His cummerbund was crooked and ruffled as though something had been shoved into it. His jacket was slung over his shoulder and his sleeves were rolled up—he was uncomfortable in the clothes, and the tight fit made him edgy.

He was dressed for the evening but he was neither caterer nor guest. I knew this when the light showed the handgun held at his side.

And his gun, too, was a silenced .22 pistol.

Tattoos and prison art peeked out from beneath his rolled shirt-sleeves on his left arm. On his forearm were four one-inch hash marks tattooed side by side. After tonight there would be a fifth one embroidered alongside them.

He wasn't just a murderer, either. The hash marks on his arm told me he was a hired assassin. And he'd killed at least four times before.

He turned away from me—us. "You should have come sooner. I thought I was caught."

Without a word, I slipped a dark leather glove on my gun hand and lifted the penlight into the man's face. His hand rose to shield the light and he turned away from me a second time.

"Put the light down." He waited for the light to shine down to the ground. "Anatoly said you were paying for this yourself. I hope you brought cash tonight; our deal was cash. Imagine, *you* payin' *me*. Who would think?"

I was incapable of stopping. Incapable of speaking. I knew what was about to happen. The plan fluttered into my thoughts; my plan.

My gun rose and my arm leveled the weapon at the assassin's ear.

There was no hesitation. No second thought. No stopping. No remorse.

I fired.

The .22-caliber round, its ballistics quieter and less powerful than other ammunition, was all but noiseless with the silencer—its sharp crack muffled to a mere mechanical cough.

The assassin was dead before he hit the stone floor.

I followed the body down, and, careful to place the muzzle over the exact entry wound, fired a second shot into the man's head.

It was almost a certainty this second shot was unnecessary.

When I stood and turned to escape back the way I'd come, my head spun. I took one step before the killer relinquished me. The whirlpool of lights and electricity took me again and spun me in a funnel cloud, twisting and loosening the killer's thoughts from my head. When it was over, I was woozy and weak—a child after a carnival ride—and it took a moment to regain my own senses.

I was back standing beside Bear, watching him rebag the .22-caliber murder weapon as Spence chided him.

"Bear," I said, dropping into a chair at the table. "You've got another body around here. You have to look for it. Come on, Bear, we gotta find it."

Bear placed the evidence bag on the table. He stared at nothing, an empty expression on his face telling me my words were ringing in his head. He grunted something and rubbed his eyes.

"There are two killers, Bear—*two*. An assassin killed Grecco. Another killer killed the assassin. The assassin was killed in a cellar or some kind of tunnel. The body has to be close. It's here somewhere. It has to be."

Bear stood. "Spence!"

Spence sat across the table and nearly fell off his chair. "Christ, I'm sitting right here. Have you heard one word about the missing people?"

"Listen to me. We have to search the house again. The houses next door, too."

"What are you talking about? We've been over everything twice."

"Do it again." Bear pounded the table. "Then do it a fourth time if you still don't find it."

"Find what? What are we looking for, Bear?"

"Another body."

EIGHTEEN

"Nothing." After two hours, the word was Spence's mantra. "Not a damned thing."

Bear stood across the sitting room command post, leaning on the wall. "If Cartier isn't the killer, then someone got past the deputies around the house. Is it possible?"

"Maybe." Spence rubbed his eyes. "It was rainy, dark—maybe they slipped past. But then again, we didn't find any footprints in the yard or anything. One of our guys thought they saw someone moving around one of the estate houses next door. But, there were no signs of anyone."

"Spence, it *was* raining. There should have been tracks or a sign of something if someone got outside." Bear was sullen again. "Nothing?"

"Nothing." Spence took out his notepad and checked through the pages. "The houses next door were locked up. And there were no tracks, or water, or anything inside or out. I can't explain it. The killer has to be one of the guests or caterers in here."

"Maybe," Bear said. "Then how did he get all the way from the upstairs and outside with no one seeing him and no tracks in the rain and mud? He shot Clemens on the second floor and we chased him down to the first floor before he vanished. The uniforms were right outside the kitchen door. Right?"

"Right." Spence closed his notepad and looked dumbfounded. "Beats me. Unless he mingled back in with the guests and no one noticed."

"One thing, though," I said, "if it was André—and it wasn't—then why return to the second floor? Rita said he came down just after the shooting, right? Then why go back up there later and shoot Clemens?"

Bear looked at Spence with a blank expression. I think he was considering the same thing. "Doesn't make sense. Why go back upstairs?"

"What?"

"Cartier, Spence. Rita saw him come down right after the shooting, right? Then why go back upstairs in time to shoot Cal?"

Spence shrugged. "Heck, I don't know. Maybe to hide the gun?"

"No. He would have hidden it before coming down. And if he hid it already, he couldn't have shot Cal."

I said, "I'm telling you, Bear. It wasn't André. And you haven't found the other body yet."

Bear wandered to a window on the far wall. He peered out with a troubled, angry look. "None of this makes sense. How did we miss him? Where'd he go?"

"I don't know," Spence said. "But we must have—"

"Find out." Bear's voice was curt. "Spence, we're missing some-thing—"

"Detectives?" A voice from the hallway startled us all. It was Captain Sutter standing with a dark-skinned, short woman of about forty-five or fifty. "Detectives, this is Ruth-Ann Marcos from the US Attorney General's Office. Unbeknownst to me, she was one of the guests tonight."

Bear glanced at the woman, nodded, and said, "What's some-one from the Attorney General's Office doing here?"

"Bear," Spence said, "Remember the two guests who never signed in—"

"You?" Bear looked at the woman again. "You weren't on the guest list and Spence says you refused to sign in. What are you doing here?"

"It's Ruth-Ann, Detective," she said as her eyes dissected him into little pieces—perhaps for examination later. "I assure you, Detec-tive, I'm here as a guest only. I thought I would offer any assistance you may need."

"Assistance?" Bear looked from Spence to Captain Sutter. "I don't think—"

"Bear," Captain Sutter said, "she was André Cartier's guest to-night. Give her an overview—it's okay, this is on me." She gestured to a nearby table and everyone sat.

Ruth-Ann took a chair opposite Spence, but her attention was on Bear. Her black, floor-length evening dress was incapable of hiding her strong, full shape. She was short, perhaps only a couple inches taller than Captain Sutter, with wavy, black hair and round, dark eyes. She was elegant in a mysterious, Latina way—simmering and spicy. The expensive jewelry she chose was flattering and her diamond necklace said she didn't need a lot of overtime at the office.

Jeez. When I was a breathing cop, the best I got was Ralph Barone, a dumpy, bald, middle-aged, Commonwealth's Attorney. With me gone, Bear gets Ruth-Ann Marcos?

"Thank you, Detective," she said. "I was present for what happened, so just go over what you have found."

Bear looked at Captain Sutter, who shrugged and waved a "just tell her" hand in the air. He did. He started with the immediate search of the guests and the money found on Grecco's body. Then, he went over his men's search of the estate grounds. He glossed over the missing charity donations and commented he thought it had nothing to do with Grecco's murder—a crime of opportunity. Everyone agreed. Ruth-Ann wondered about the caterers. After all, none of *these* guests would stoop to such unsavory conduct.

Bear ended with André's arrest. He left out the few tidbits I'd implanted in his brain about the assassin's murder—the one from my vision. I'm sure he didn't want to admit what the ghost of his former partner told him, so I said, "there are some other thoughts and theories, but I'll keep those to myself if you don't mind."

Ruth-Ann shrugged. "Not much, is it?"

"No, it's not, Ruth-Ann," Bear said. "Somehow, the killer murdered Grecco and got past us. Our patrols and the Winchester City police are searching everywhere."

"And André is your only suspect?" Ruth-Ann's eyes wandered between Bear and Captain Sutter. "I'm skeptical—but we're friends, too. Any GSR or prints?"

"We're skeptical too, Ruth-Ann." Spence tapped the table. "But we had no choice. André's a friend of—"

"You can call me Ms. Marcos, deputy. And I know André Cartier very well—he escorted me tonight. I've known him since I transferred to Washington, and frankly, I find him above reproach."

"Yes, of course," Spence said. "The coroner will be working up the body first thing in the morning—er—later this morning, I mean."

"Captain, would it be possible for me to see the ME's results as soon as they are ready?" Ruth-Ann looked to Captain Sutter. "And I'd like to see the guest list and the staff lists, if you approve."

Captain Sutter cocked her head. "Why? There's no federal case here?"

Ruth-Ann folded her hands. "Yes, Helen, I'm so sorry. You're right, of course. I am just a guest tonight. But many of your guests are from the Washington circles—as am I. Perhaps I can help. I don't want to intrude. I am very concerned for André, you understand."

Helen? No one ever called Captain Sutter "Helen."

"All right, Ruth-Ann." Captain Sutter nodded. "Maybe you can help."

Spence retrieved a file from another table where notepads and evidence bags lay. He flipped it open and dug through the inch-thick stack of papers. After finding what he was looking for, he slid a three-page printout across the table. "Guests and caterers."

As Ruth-Ann scanned down the columns of names, Captain Sutter caught Bear's eye and shook her head as the telegraph lines sent a clear message—there would be no more information sliding across the table.

"Yes, I know many of these names. Some quite well, too." Ruth-Ann didn't look up. "And you cannot account for a caterer and two other guests?"

Bear leaned forward. "We think the caterer left before the shooting. We're following up. There were two people who weren't on the guest list and didn't sign in—you were one of them. So we're only missing one now."

"Well, how very interesting." Ruth-Ann's head snapped up and her eyes found Captain Sutter's. Her charm and "thank you, yes ma'am" tone was gone. In its place, was an edgy, dry tone. "André was arrested when this man is present?"

Bear said, "'This man' who?"

"Come now, Detective." Ruth-Ann stood up and stabbed her finger on the guest list. "You know full well who I'm talking about. I'm shocked he's even here. Let me see his statement."

Spence leaned over and followed her thin finger to the name. He rolled his eyes. "Ah, his guest is the one missing." He looked at Bear. "Sorry, Bear, I forgot to tell you."

"Who's missing, dammit?" Captain Sutter said, snatching the list from Ruth-Ann's fingers. "If you have a point, make it."

"Nicholas Bartalotta." Ruth-Ann folded her arms. "New York mobster and killer extraordinaire. I assume the other missing guest is his thug bodyguard. Great work, everyone."

Oh, brother. Poor Nic was a suspect again.

NINETEEN

"NICHOLAS BARTALOTTA ISN'T ON our interview list, so he must have left the party before we started," Spence said, reviewing his notes for the third time. "I'm checking on him and I've sent a car to his place."

"Unbelievable." Captain Sutter cringed. "Spence, how the hell did this happen?" Then she turned to Ruth-Ann. "We'll follow this up, but I have to tell you, Nicholas has proven to be a rather upstanding person—at least around here. I know his past—"

"Upstanding? Are you kidding me?" Ruth-Ann's face contorted. "He's a thug and a murderer."

Spence, never understanding the safety of silence, said, "Well, retired thug, I think."

I'm not sure whose look castrated him fastest—Captain Sutter or Ruth-Ann's. It's a shame, really, because while Spence was out of line, he was not wrong.

Nicholas Bartalotta was an aged New Yorker who retired a few years ago to Winchester after a forty-year hiatus. Poor Nic, as he was dubbed by some New York newspaper years ago, has become something of a local legend—part retired gangster who filled hearts with fear and part celebrity who filled charity coffers with cash. Somewhere in there, he ran a couple local businesses, was restoring his family farmhouse—a Civil War historical site—and helped solve my murder.

Nicholas Bartalotta was a man of many talents—or perhaps, many personalities. Some of those you could even talk about without risk of retaliation. And, despite his former life, he was Winchester's favorite, and only, mobster—retired or not.

"Retired?" Ruth-Ann shook her head. "Are you kidding me? He's mob—plain and simple. He's here and you arrest André? Detective, you need my help more than you know."

"Slow down," Bear said. "Let me check with Angela. She'll know the score on Nic." He didn't wait for permission and left the room.

Ruth-Ann said, "He's a friend of Professor Tucker?"

"Now, Ruth-Ann, let me—"

"No, Helen, don't you think you should focus on Bartalotta? If he's around, he's involved."

"Geez," Spence said, snorting a laugh. "Everyone said the same thing last time and he was—" Ice and daggers stopped him. "Sorry, Cap."

"Ruth-Ann, I know how to run an investigation," Captain Sutter said. "So does my team. Thank you for your advice, but we'll handle this. Is there anything else?"

Ruth-Ann stood and walked around the table. Without a word, she scooped up Spence's investigative file and fanned through the pages. A few seconds later, she looked up.

"Yes, there is something. I don't see where you finished canvassing the area—"

"Manpower, Ruth-Ann." Captain Sutter took the case file from her. "This is Frederick County, not Washington DC. We have smaller budgets and only one crime scene team. We've called in assistance from Loudoun County, but it'll be a while."

"I can have the FBI—"

"No."

"No?"

"No, thank you." Captain Sutter threw a thumb over her shoulder for Spence to leave and stuffed the file in his hands. When he was through the doors, she stepped in close to Ruth-Ann. "Listen, Ruth-Ann, it's just us gals now."

"No," I said, "I'm still here, but feel free to slug it out."

Neither cared.

Captain Sutter went on. "Look, you asked for access because of André Cartier. I gave it to you. We're done. There's no federal case here. We can handle this and if we need your help, I'll be sure to ask. But until then, you *are* just a guest."

"All right, Helen," Ruth-Ann looked down. When she looked back up at Captain Sutter, she painted a plastic smile on her face that fooled no one. "You're right, of course. I trust you'll still keep me informed. If Bartalotta is involved, this will be a federal matter. And I want him. We've been after him for years. And Helen, one call to the sheriff and you're washing cars until retirement."

"Yes, of course we'll keep you informed. But Ruth-Ann, the sheriff's up for reelection soon and I'm dating the town newspaper's editor."

She was?

"How wonderful for you. Remember, Captain, we feds decide what we're interested in and what we're not interested in." Ruth-Ann sauntered to the door. "And I choose *interested.*"

TWENTY

It was four thirty in the morning when the last of the guests and catering staff were checked off Bear's list and released. Bear, too, took an instant dislike to the catering manager, Petya, so they released him last. As Petya's catering van pulled away from the rear of the mansion, Bear went room-to-room checking, double-checking, and triple-checking every bit of cop work he could think of.

There was nothing more to do tonight.

"Spence, what's the word on Poor Nic?" Bear said, walking into the kitchen where Spence was draining another cup of coffee.

"Jeez." Spence spilled coffee all over his shirt. "You scared the crap out of me, Bear."

"And what about this Kravitz guy and Jorge-whoever?"

"Bartalotta ain't home and there's no word on Kravitz yet. Our boys are sitting on both places."

"He isn't home? At this hour of the morning?"

"Nope."

"Bullshit, you tell our people to—"

"Bear?" Angel walked in. "What's wrong?"

"It's almost five a.m. and Bartalotta isn't at home." He gave her a quick summary of his argument with Ruth-Ann. "Are you sure Nic was even here last night? I don't recall seeing him."

"Yes, and he donated a very sizable check," she said. "Twenty-five thousand dollars, I think."

"Wow." Bear poured two coffees from a large pot on the stove and handed one to Angel. "Do you remember him leaving?"

Angel thought a moment. "No, but he must have. I don't even recall seeing him after the evening got underway. But then, I was busy and didn't have much time to speak with you or—"

Bear rolled his eyes. "Yeah, I know—*him*."

"Him" would be me. "Your loss, Angel. No worries, I'm making new friends, dear. You can throw fancy parties and make new friends if you like. But so can I. In fact, I already have."

"I was going to say André," she snapped. "But *him* either."

Spence stood up. "I'm going to check the guys again." He said, and walked off.

"Angela, you should go home," Bear said, "We're not through here, but no need for you to hang around." He left in Spence's wake.

I watched him go. "He just won't give in about me, will he?"

"No, and he won't talk about it either."

"He knows I'm here, and he can hear me sometimes, too."

"Yes, he can. I'm sure of it." Angel laughed. "Ever since the day—that was a lot for him. Give him time, Tuck. Give him more time."

"The day," as Angel referred to it, was when Ernie Stuart got justice. After killing me, some of Ernie's victims came back and helped catch him. In the end, at Kelly's Dig where he started his decades of killing with Caroline and Amy, they came back and scared him to death. He died of a massive heart attack. We were all there—Angel, Bear, and even Spence and Clemens. Something happened out at Kelly's Dig. Something no one ever spoke about afterward. Not Bear for certain. You see, there's something about admitting you're seeing ghosts that always makes the room go a little icy. Everyone on "that day" saw me. No one could bring themselves to admit it.

But Bear's coming around. He doesn't have a choice. I'm not easy to ignore.

"I guess I'll leave, Tuck," she said, yawning. "I'll look for you later."

"Sure, go. I'll be home soon." Something tickled my ears like the jingle of a far-away bell. That was my spirit-radar telling me something was afoot. "Or maybe not."

Fats Waller played *It's A Sin To Tell A Lie* and I turned. Sassy stood in the kitchen doorway and walked off toward the hall stairs. She beckoned me with a whistle, and being a former red-blooded, all-American male, I obeyed. "I'll see you at home. Don't wait up."

I walked into the hall as Angel headed for the front door.

Sassy was waiting on the stairs. "Hey, Tuckie, don't be going no-wheres yet. I gotta show you something. It's just the cat's pajamas."

Huh? "Sassy, you're gonna get me in big trouble. What do you want?"

"Come on, Tuckie." She winked and strutted up the stairs. "You'll see. Shake a leg."

I did.

On the third floor, she led me to the mansion's west wing and a bedroom at the end of the hall. There, she flung herself on the huge canopy bed and laughed like a schoolgirl.

"Okay, baby, take a look around."

Baby? If Angel heard this, I'd really be dead. "Come on, Sassy, just tell me. No more fooling around."

"Nope. You gotta play, Tuckie. Look around."

The room was furnished with a few antiques like every other room in the house. There was a small bureau near the windows, nightstands on either side of the bed, and a built-in armoire taking up a third of the wall opposite the bed. Nothing gave off any bells and whistles—just another room in a mega-million-bucks mansion. If you've seen one, you've seen them all.

"What am I looking for?"

She laughed again. "Silly, in there." She pointed to the armoire. "Inside, Tuckie. Look inside."

"Sassy, Vincent's gonna re-kill both of us. I don't think he'll—"

"Tuckie, let me worry about Vincent. He's busy with other stuff." She jumped up and went to the armoire. "Here, silly, I'll show you."

She opened the double-doors revealing an empty cabinet except for a few old hangers and cobwebs. Then she pulled on one of the garment hooks on the side panel. A rear panel opened and revealed a narrow staircase leading up to the attic.

"Hey, how come you can do stuff so easy?" I said. "Open and close things, I mean. I need electricity to help me out."

"I been around longer, that's all. Just pay attention." She went inside and poked her head out. "Come on."

"What's this, Sassy?" I don't generally need to open doors and climb stairs if I don't wish to. But despite the television and movie spin, being a ghost does not make you omnipotent. If you don't know where something is, you can't *poof* to it. Likewise, if you don't know there's a secret room beyond the secret passage door, you can't very well poof to it either.

"Why didn't you just tell me, Sassy?"

She grabbed my hand with schoolgirl enthusiasm. "Come see, Tuckie. You'll be glad. It's one of our old getaways. Coppers could never find me."

"No? I cannot wait to find out why they were looking for you, Sassy."

She nudged me toward the hidden stairs. "Silly, I was a good girl. Honest."

"I believe you." I didn't, but it made her smile.

"You do?" She threw her arm around my shoulder and pushed me up the stairs. "Swell, 'cause Vincent never does. He says he knows I'm lying 'cause my lips move."

TWENTY-ONE

"Sassy, what is this place?"

She stood at the top step and waved her hand around like a conductor leading her orchestra. "In the old days we'd hide our boys up here. Ya know, when the coppers came lookin'. Vincent's place is great for hidin'. Dicks never got wise."

The room was windowless and I guessed we were somewhere in the rear, northwest corner of the mansion. The entire room was little more than ten feet square with a rickety wooden table tucked into the corner opposite the stairs. On it were several gadgets which lighted up and buzzed as we approached them.

"What's all this stuff, Sassy?"

"I dunno. Why do you think I brought you here, Tuckie? I dunno nothin' about it all. I figured you would. All this junk is from your time, not mine."

A small notebook computer sat on the corner of the table and it was on but the screen was dark. Beside it was a small gray plastic device similar to a television remote control. It had one button in the center and five little multicolored lights at the top. Below the lights was a scale ranging from green to red with markings annotating each color. When I reached for the device, the lights flickered and cycled up and down the light scale, whining and chirping.

"What the heck is this thing?"

"Dunno, Tuckie, but it don't like you, does it? It lit up on me earlier." She pointed to the computer. "What's this thing?"

"It's a computer." I touched the notebook's keyboard and it surged energy into my fingertips, sending a jittery flutter through me like I'd just mainlined caffeine. Seconds later, the computer screen turned on.

"A what?"

"A computer, Sassy. It stores information and you can type stuff and go on the internet."

She looked at me like I was an alien trying to make contact. "The inter-what?" This beauty had some catching up to do. "You know libraries, right?"

"Sure, don't everybody?" She folded her arms. "I ain't dumb, you know."

"No, of course not. Well, think of this as a machine with connections all over the world inside. And it can go around the world over the telephone lines and read stuff and talk to people." I didn't try to explain the internet, cell phones, or chat rooms. Her twisted face told me I'd reached her limit. "It connects the entire world."

"The world?" She rolled her eyes. "Sure, sure, whatever you say. What about the other thing?"

The remote device continued to flicker and flash and chirp.

"I have no idea."

The computer's screen was alive and it was divided into four grids. Three of the grids were fuzzy and unfocused, but the fourth was clear and showed a black and white video stream from the downstairs hallway. At the front door, I could see Bear and Angel talking.

"Holy crap, Sassy." I tapped at the keyboard and tried to find the controls to focus the other three closed circuit cameras. "I have to get Bear. Someone's been watching us the entire evening."

"Yeah?" Sassy jammed her hands on her curvy hips and puckered up a cat-call whistle. "Tuckie, what's this stuff gotta do with anything?"

I tugged her along down the stairs. "You better get back to Vincent, Sassy. I don't want you getting into trouble. He doesn't like me much."

"I do, Tuckie. I like you a lot." Outside the armoire, she turned around. "What's all the junk up there mean? Is it important?"

"Very. It means whoever was up there might be a witness to Stephanos Grecco's murder."

"Oh, is that all? I been a witness lots of times—but I ain't no rat."

TWENTY-TWO

"IT'S FOR GHOST HUNTING," Spence said, picking up the gray plastic remote device. Spence had arrived moments ago with Bear and was surveying the devices Sassy had shown me. "You know, for paranormal investigations. This is an EMF meter."

Earlier, after leaving the attic room, Sassy disappeared to wherever she disappeared to and I sought out Angel. I told her what I'd found and showed her the way to the attic entrance through the armoire. She in turn relayed it all to Bear. Before he and Spence climbed to the attic, he sent Angel home for some sleep. She only argued ten minutes before agreeing and leaving them to their treasure hunt.

"Ghost hunting? Are you kidding me?" Bear's eyes lit up. "What the heck is an E and F thing?"

Spence waved the gray remote device around. "EMF stands for electromagnetic fields." He pressed the center button and the device's line of five multicolored lights flickered for a moment. "If it comes into contact with any electromagnetic fields, the lights flash and it buzzes. Each one is a field frequency—"

"Whoa, Spence." Bear held up his hands. "Why do you know so much about ghost-hunting gizmos?"

Spence moved the EMF meter around the attic in an arc, watching the lights. When he turned and pointed it in my direction, all five lights went apoplectic. He looked up at Bear with eyes wide and his voice a little shaken. "Bear, there's something here."

I walked toward Spence and his EMF device glowed and flickered and chirped like a ravenous bird—Spence backed up two steps as his face paled. When I retreated, the lights slowed and stopped chattering. When only one light remained on, Spence's face went from pale white to a not-so-pale white and he breathed for the first time in minutes.

Bear just stood staring at the device. His mouth was clamped tight but he forced out, "Holy shit, Spence. Are you telling me this thing says a ghost is in here with us?"

Spence just nodded and backed up another step.

"Terrific." Bear glanced in freeze-frame glimpses around the room. "Just terrific."

I walked in the device's path again and sent its lights and Spence's heart racing. "Oh, this is fun."

"And you know this how?" Bear asked, grabbing the EMF meter from him and turning it off. He shuddered a little. "You moonlighting on me?"

"I watch all the ghost shows on television. There's a lot of them." Spence seemed happy the meter had gone dark in Bear's hand. "You wouldn't believe how popular ghost hunting is. Some of these guys travel all over the country—even the world—doing this stuff. Do you know how many celebrities have hauntings? Even the White House—"

"Yeah, right." Bear pointed to the computer. "And they use this crap to find ghosts? What's all this stuff do?"

"Somewhere around here, we should find the IR. IR is infrared, Bear; cameras and imaging gear. I bet they have cameras and recorders hidden all over this house. We'll have to search all over again."

"Why would they have it here?" Bear asked, looking down at the computer screen. "Explain it to me. I don't watch television."

Spence dropped into the chair in front of the computer and pointed to the four images still watching the house. Just as I'd found them with Sassy, three of them were out of focus and dim.

"The ghost investigators put cameras all over. Some of them are infrared and some aren't. And they use thermal cameras and digital recorders, too. Then they either sit back and watch the video feed or they take hand-held equipment and search the house. They should be recording everything somewhere."

Bear watched the monitor. On the screen, one of his deputies was talking with Captain Sutter in the front hall, three floors down. "And they see ghosts?"

"No, not really. Not like you think." Spence tapped the screen. "The EMF meter finds electromagnetic fields which could be a ghost because they might give off energy. Most of the time it's just bad wiring and big electrical stuff. The cameras are looking for anything out of the ordinary like blurs, images, shadows, or movement.

The infrared and thermal equipment catch changes in heat caused by a spirit appearing or manifesting. The recorders—"

"Yeah, I get it, Spence. I get it." He looked over the devices on the table again. "Why didn't we find the cameras and recorders when we searched earlier?"

"I don't know, Bear." Spence shrugged. "They must have hidden them pretty good. And, we were looking for guns and people, not tiny cameras and electronic bugs."

Bear rolled his eyes and then he froze. "You said they recorded stuff. Are you sure?"

"They should. They have to collect everything and then analyze their findings afterward. It takes hours to go over all the data."

"So, someone got into this house with all this equipment and has been recording everything going on tonight?"

"Yeah, looks like it, yes." Spence tapped on the computer keyboard and studied the screen. "Except they didn't save the images or data on this notebook. They must have put it all on a flash drive or big external drive and taken it with them."

"Get a computer guy up here, Spence. I want every piece of equipment located and checked. Do whatever you have to do, but find everything these ghost-investigators left behind. Then find them."

"Ah, Bear." I knew the problem before Spence got it. "We better find these guys and fast. They might have recorded the murder—and the killer."

Bear walked back to the center of the room with the EMF meter, turned it on, and waved it around. The lights blinked a little until he pointed it straight at the corner of the room where I stood, then they stayed on and chirped.

"Holy crap." He looked right at me without knowing it. "Spence, if these guys recorded the killer, then they're in danger. The killer may go after them."

"So Cartier isn't our guy?" Spence said. "I knew it."

"I hope not. We just have to prove it. If André killed Grecco, then what about the other body?"

"Other body?" Spence turned around. "Bear, you're worrying me. If you start in about another body again, the Cap is gonna commit you. We haven't found any second body—and no signs of a second shooter either. Where are you getting the idea from?"

"Just find this surveillance equipment and have the computer guys dig into this hard drive. I want to find these ghost-guys fast. And, I hope one of them isn't already the other dead guy."

Spence stood up. "Why do you think there's another body and another shooter?"

Bear pointed the EMF meter toward me again. Its lights danced and the chirping bit everyone's ears. "You wouldn't believe me if I told you, Spence. So don't ask."

TWENTY-THREE

JUST AFTER DAWN, CAPTAIN Sutter sent Bear and Spence home for a few hours of sleep. Neither of them argued. She posted a deputy at the front door, securing the house so even the crime scene team could rest before going back over the house again. Then, she went home, too.

Angel was already home and I'd hoped fast asleep. Her evening hadn't gone as planned—a murder, perhaps two, and a quarter-million in donations stolen. Not the bang-up charity event of the year, although I doubted anyone in Winchester would ever forget it.

I wouldn't.

As Bear drove off, I decided to head home and didn't need a ride from him. I can move from one place to another, like across town to my house or anywhere by just "being there" in my head and "poof" I'm there. I just have to know where I want to go. So, I took the spook-train express. One second I was on the Vincent House's veranda, and the next I was a couple blocks from Old Town Winchester on the front porch of our three-story Victorian. My first stop was my den and I sat behind my antique desk and threw my feet up for a rest.

A man's home may be his castle, but his den is his keep. Mine was no different.

The room was lined with shelves of books, trinkets, photographs, and all sorts of memorabilia. It was as I'd left it last October before my untimely demise. As I walked in and looked around, heavy footfalls bounded down the stairs from Angel's bedroom to greet me.

Hercule P. Tucker—my best pal and companion—jumped front paws first onto my lap to say good morning. His feet fell onto my desk chair, but he wasn't fazed. The big black Lab was used to this little anomaly in our relationship. He twisted in the chair and tried to plant his long, wet tongue on me without success. He didn't care. Hercule was my hero. He took a bullet saving Angel's life the night I was killed—a bullet which could have killed him. It never slowed him down and he was the first to see me back among the living. He also helped connect Angel and me; a simple game of ball led to lots of tears. Tears led to an embrace. All of it led to her connecting back to me.

A red ball with Hercule's perseverance—and she believed.

"Hey, Herc, how are you doing?" I rubbed his ears and sent him to his ritual spot on my expensive leather recliner across the room. "Is Angel asleep?"

Woof. Wag. Woof.

"Okay, boy, where's Doc? Is he around?"

Hercule sat up and turned his nose to the air, searching the room as though snorting out a stash of peanut butter cookies—

Herc was a dog of many talents. His tail went into overdrive and he pointed his nose at the doorway, barked a greeting, and lay back down to finish his fifteen hours of daily sleep.

A tall, broad-shouldered man in his late fifties or early sixties stood in my doorway. He wore green surgical scrubs and had a stethoscope hung around his neck. "Oliver, I've been waiting for you."

"Hello, Doc. Have I got a story for you."

Doc Gilley was a crotchety old surgeon who lived somewhere in the house. I say "somewhere" because like all dead people stuck on my floor, I had no idea where he was when he was not regaling me with his vast knowledge of my faults or his endless wisdom. Doc was my great-grandfather—and the only one of my relatives I'd ever met, albeit after our deaths. Like all grandfathers, he was never short on counsel when I needed it. And more so when I didn't need it.

"It's about time, Oliver." Did I mention he was crotchety? "Angela has been home for hours." Doc's arms were folded and he had a perpetual scowl as permanent as his decades-old scrubs. "Where have you been?"

"Never mind. Do you know a Benjamin? Or how about a place called Quixote's Windmill?"

"Benjamin?" His face tightened. "Why are you asking about him?"

"Because I need to find him and some book he has. It's simple. You know him then, right?"

"I have never met him."

Something wasn't right. "What's with you, Doc? Do you know Benjamin or not? And you never answered me about Quixote's Windmill."

Doc walked over to Hercule's chair and sat on the arm, petting him and ignoring me. This, too, was not unusual. "What makes you ask about Benjamin? What do you know?"

"Nothing. I ran across something at the Vincent House and—"

"The Vincent House? What were you doing there?" Doc got on feet—his scowl had turned more scowly if there was such a thing. "You didn't tell me you were going there."

"Ah, no. I didn't know I was. I didn't know the estate's name, why?"

Doc's eyes, normally a deep blue, were fire engine red. "Well? Answer me, Oliver. What about Benjamin?"

I'm sure I mentioned I hate the name Oliver. "What is it, Doc? You know something about the Vincent House? You're acting—"

When I was a cop, I could judge people pretty well. Well, at least well enough to know if they were going to try to kill me or something. With Angel, I could tell in seconds if I was going to get reacquainted with the couch or showered with kisses. With Bear, I could always tell when he needed a date—which was most of the time. But Doc, he's a different story. He was as readable as braille to a seeing-man—the clues were there but you couldn't quite read them.

"What's with the attitude? You must know Benjamin or you wouldn't be acting like this."

He snorted. "How did you hear about him?"

"I ran into this guy—Vincent Calaprese—who still thinks it's nineteen thirty-something. Anyway, he and this hottie named—"

"Sassy."

"Yeah, Sassy. You know her, too?"

Doc's eyes went far away. "My, my."

"Come on, Doc, tell me."

He nodded but he was years away.

"Doc, who's Benjamin? Vincent was very adamant I bring him to visit. And let me tell you, his bourbon is great. I haven't had—"

Doc stepped forward and threw a finger at me—a teacher about to launch a lecture. He didn't disappoint me.

"Listen to me, Oliver. Listen to me good. People die. Sometimes things happen to them and they stay behind like us; *sometimes*. But, when something happens to us—something bad—it's like dying all over again but much, much worse. It's messy ... and very, very bad."

"Ghosts can die?"

"Don't be a smartass." His eyes drilled holes through me. "Oliver, you have to be very careful with Vincent. Years ago—decades ago—he was a gangster who made Al Capone look timid. He was cunning and heartless. A real bastard. Someone stood up against him. But when they did, he didn't go easily."

"Like this Benjamin guy? You think he stood up against him? You think he wants another crack at him?"

"Yes." Doc returned to Hercule as he became a haze of dust fading from the room. "Of that I am certain."

"So, what happens if I find Benjamin and bring him to Vincent?" I already knew the short answer. "Is it going to get, you know, 'very messy'?"

Doc was just a voice now. "Oliver, forget Benjamin and stay away from Vincent Calaprese and Sassy."

"Why? What are you—"

"He could be the death of you."

The death of *me*?

TWENTY-FOUR

THESE DAYS, I DON'T need sleep. I don't need to eat either, and it's a good thing—I can't. Except that Vincent Calaprese's bourbon was, well, to die for. Next time I visit him—and there would be a next time no matter what Doc said—I'm asking for a rare T-bone, too. That's some of the things I miss the most—eating and drinking. That of course, and, ah, my wife's tender loving care. Maybe next time Vincent has me over for cocktails we can double date.

Maybe.

I got bored watching Hercule snoozing on my pillow beside Angel about eleven a.m. After the night she'd had, I didn't want to wake her or disturb Hercule—he was twenty toes up chasing his ball. Waking him would require a break-in by a brass band or the aroma of the aforementioned T-bone.

I had neither.

Halfway down the stairs a familiar tickle ran up my spine; Bear was on the move. Since this was his first murder case since mine, I figured I'd better go along to keep him out of trouble. During my case, he had a rough time of it. He was suspect numero uno. He got suspended, chased the wrong bad guy, and was accused of sleeping with my wife. The latter was the worst part. Then, he beat the crap out of Detective Mike Spence—that was fun.

Except for Spence; it was a bad week for him.

I did the mind-meld-thing and popped into Bear's unmarked cruiser just as he left Three-A West of the Hunter's Ridge Garden Apartments just outside town—Bear's ah, den as it were. When I landed in the seat beside him, he was talking to someone on his cell phone. He repeated an address, made a U-turn, and sped away toward the county's north end.

"Where we going, Bear?"

He jumped in the seat as his fingers whitened on the steering wheel. He flipped on the radio and tried to find a country station.

"Bear, I have to tell you, we just don't talk anymore. Is it me? Is there someone else?"

Nothing. Nadda. Not even a smile.

"Come on, you big dumbass. I know you can hear me. And I know you believe. So, dig deep and listen for my voice, will you?"

He made a turn four blocks down and headed east on a side street.

"Boo." I leaned over to his ear. "Look out! A dog!"

He jumped on the brakes, swerved the car across the center line, and skidded to a stop over the opposite shoulder. He cursed the entire time through tight lips and big, bulging eyes.

Needless to say, there was no dog. Not even a hamster.

"Oops, my bad."

Bear jumped out of the cruiser and stormed off cursing and spitting up a typhoon. He rambled on and on to no one as he paced back and forth in front of the car. His hands flew in the air and his faced reddened with each guttural foray spoken harsher than at a port bar after midnight.

He needed some alone-time so I waited in the car.

When he returned to the open driver's door, he slipped something out of his suit coat pocket and stared at it—my detective's shield. I'd given it to him just after solving my murder and nailing Ernie Stuart in a strange, not-of-this-world-kinda-thing. That moment, standing above Ernie's body, was the first time he saw me—the first time he knew it had been me guiding him during the case. And it was the last time he ever acknowledged me.

Until now.

"Jeez, Tuck." He slid his hulking body into the driver's seat. "Can't you give me a break?"

"Sorry, pal, I had to get your attention. Can we talk?"

"No. No. No." He closed his eyes and leaned his head against the steering wheel. "Tuck, it can't be you. Don't you get it? You're dead. Ernie killed you. You're gone. It's how it is. You just can't be here. It has to be me—I lost it the day Ernie died. You're not here."

I reached over and took hold of his hand on his leg—my badge still clutched in his powerful grip. When I did, the metal got hot—and so did he.

He jerked upright and tossed my badge into the console between us. "Come on, Tuck. You gotta let me alone. People will talk. The Cap and some of the other cops already think I'm nuts. Spence and Clemens saw things then, too—and they won't talk about it either. I just can't. I can't walk around talking to you and acting like we're still partners. The Department will have me in for a psych and I'll be kicked off the job."

"Yeah, yeah. It sucks. But you need me, Bear. We were a great team—Hope and Crosby, Holmes and Watson, the Captain and Tennille—"

"No."

He looked up at the car roof for the longest time. His eyes reddened and for a second he looked like he would cry. "I miss you, Tuck. I do. But people think I'm nuts—and they are probably right. I could lose my job, and think of what it would do to Angela. No one would believe. No one would understand."

He was right. He couldn't just play along and act like nothing had happened. It was hard enough with Angel to still be her husband and not have a life with her. A voice across the seat and no closer than another world.

I cut Bear some slack.

"Okay, Bear. I get it. So, look, you can ignore me if you need to. But we both know the truth, okay?"

Nothing. He put the cruiser in drive and wheeled back across the road and headed east again.

"Just forget I'm around. Lie if you have to. I'm all in your head." Nothing.

"So where we going, partner?"

"Stanley Kravitz's place. The caterer gave me his ... oh, shit." He grabbed my badge out of the console and stuffed it into his pocket. "Really, Tuck? The Captain and Tennille?"

TWENTY-FIVE

WE RODE THE REMAINING two miles in silence. Sometimes, silence is good for the indigestion. For Bear it was, and for me it was my victory dance in the end zone.

When we pulled into a large apartment complex, Bear parked in the center of three lots and surveyed the area. He tried two numbers on his cell phone, got voicemail for both, and hung up.

The complex had five, three-story brick buildings surrounding a cul-de-sac. Each building had a parking area in the rear. The center building had a sign citing it as the rental office with space available. The buildings were older, but in good shape, and the grounds well kept. There was a playground off to the right of one of the buildings and a pool on the other side. Judging from the cars in the lots—few older than five or six years, nothing up on blocks or looking like the loser in a demolition derby—this was a solid, respectable neighborhood.

I followed Bear to the first building on the right and up to the second floor. It took us two times at bat before we found the right door and he knocked. Well, pounded more like, as anyone on the inside who was deaf, comatose, or dead would have heard him.

"Easy, there, partner. Just because we're spatting doesn't mean the neighbors have to hear."

He grumbled something and pounded again.

"Who's there?" The voice was raspy and meek—a woman's voice. "What do you want?"

"Sheriff's Department. I need to speak with you."

"Why?"

"Just open the door, ma'am. I'm Detective Braddock."

"Prove it."

Bear cursed. "I will if you open the door, ma'am."

A dead bolt clapped open. A second one. Then a chain. The lady fiddled with the knob lock and cracked the door open two inches.

"You have some ID?" The woman was seventy-five if she was a day, and thin, with a full head of white hair hanging to her shoulders. She wore a martial arts gi with a black belt tied around her thin waist. "Quick, too. I'm training."

I said, "Quick, Bear, she's training."

He flashed her his badge and ID wallet, and, after she'd read it three or four times, she opened the door halfway but never budged out of Bear's path.

"Sorry to disturb you." He pocketed his badge and said, "I'm looking for Stanley Kravitz, ma'am. Is he home?"

"No. He's not home. And I'm getting sick of this bullshit."

Bear blinked a few times. "Ma'am? Is Stanley—"

"That asshole doesn't live here and never has. You're the second one today looking for him. I told the other fella, too, I been in this apartment fifteen years. And I don't look like no Stanley Kravitz either."

Bear peered around her. "You sure? He's not in any trouble, ma'am, but—"

"The hell he ain't." She slipped her gi sleeves up to her elbows. "If he shows his mug around here, I'll give him a good whack. I been getting his mail, phone calls, and now you two. Enough. This is my place. My name is Brenda L. Sturges and I'm an old maid. Never had much use for a husband and never had no kids. So this twerp ain't any relative of mine. Leave me alone."

"Yes, ma'am, if—"

Brenda L. Sturges slammed the door and clapped, rapped, and snapped all her door locks back in place. "Go see the manager," she yelled through the door. "I sent the last one of you to him."

I laughed. "Maybe you should recruit her for the Community Police patrol."

We went in search of the manager.

We found Tim something-Swedish behind his computer eating an early lunch of burgers, fries, and a half-gallon of orange soda. Tim was all of 130 pounds and smelled of the pile of cigarette butts in the ashtray just in front of the "No Smoking" sign on the reception desk.

Bear explained what he wanted and ended with, "He works for Festival Catering."

"Hah, those guys." Tim the Swede laughed and gulped down several mouthfuls of soda. "I been fighting with Peter for weeks. And I already been through this once today with—"

"Peter? You mean Petya?"

Tim the Swede shrugged. "Yeah, I don't know. Funny accent, you know, like on TV or something." He munched down on his burger and wiped the catsup up with a napkin. "They all sound the same on the phone."

"Yeah, right." Bear tapped the counter. "Okay, tell me about Petya, Tim—just like on TV"

"Hey, come on, I'm busy here."

"Sure, okay, you're busy. I'll just go door-to-door and roust all your tenants. I'll explain how you were too busy to help me."

"All right, all right. I'm not busy anymore." Tim moved his half-eaten burger aside. "The Kravitz fella never lived here—never. I've been getting mail for him for months. Him and a few other nobodies. Different building addresses but the same story. None of 'em are residents."

"How many?"

"Five, counting Kravitz."

Bear watched Tim with narrow eyes. "So, what's the deal, Tim? What did Petya have to say?"

"Big mistake, he says. Five of his employees just happen to have addresses in our village and all of them are wrong. Big coincidence. Big misunderstanding. Yeah, yeah. And he's going to cater my fourth of July bash to make up for it. Just so long as we keep this between us, you know."

I said, "Jeez, Bear, someone made a big impression on Petya. He's offering restitution without any demand. Sort of odd, don't you think?"

He repeated me. "So, Timmy, what's with all this? What's Petya's underwear all bunched up about?"

Tim slurped long and deep on the orange soda and slid back in his chair. "You guys. Too much heat is my guess. We get mail for those mystery residents every once in a while these past few months. Not often, but now and then. We pile it up and return-to-sender—sometimes. I complained to him before, but this time, he called me this morning all in a panic. Said he was personally going to fix the issue and if anyone asked, just keep it to myself. You know, fourth of July and all."

"Oh, yeah? Did he say why?"

Tim shook his head. "Nope. And I didn't ask."

"Okay, give us the names and addresses of the five then."

"Us?"

"Me." Bear stabbed a finger at him. "Give me the names and any extra mail you got lying around for them."

"Nope." The crooked smile on his face between slurps of soda made it clear Tim enjoyed this part. "Can't."

"Why?"

"'Cause the fella who was here this morning said not to. Said no one was to know and I'm supposed to call him if anyone comes asking. So soon as you leave, I'm calling him 'cause you're asking."

Tim-something-Swedish had no idea how close he was to introducing his orange soda straw to his large intestine. Bear leaned across his desk, grabbed him by the shirt, and dragged him onto his tiptoes so they could see eye-to-eye. Neither of them noticed the half-eaten, catsup-dripping burger ground into Timmy's groin.

"Who, Timmy? Who are you planning on calling? The governor?"

"Ah, better, I think." Timmy dug into his shirt pocket and pulled out a business card. He held it up for Bear to see. "Easy, man. Be cool. Be cool. I'm doing what he wanted."

The business card read "Special Agent James Dobron, Federal Bureau of Investigation," and it listed a Washington DC telephone number.

"What's the FBI want with my missing caterer?" Bear said, heading out the door.

"I don't know." I followed out. "Last night's food wasn't that bad, was it?"

TWENTY-SIX

OUR NEXT STOP WAS a familiar gated two-story Tudor estate some ten miles or so west of Winchester, heading for the mountains. The property was lush and green with manicured gardens, rock landscaping, and an eight-feet high security wall combining old-world charm and modern-day security. The armed thugs patrolling the grounds added just a touch of authentic gangland style, too.

This was the home of the one and only Nicholas Bartalotta. My old pal Poor Nic.

As mentioned earlier, Nic was our resident retired mob boss who made Frederick County his home. Not by chance, though. In the summers of his youth, Poor Nic spent time with his uncle at Kelly's Orchard Farms—the family estate. After some unsavory business split the families apart, as murder sometimes does, Nicholas returned to New York and entered the family business. The family business was organized crime.

Nicholas was very good at the family business. Very good.

Bear and I had called on Poor Nic many times since he moved into the neighborhood. And none of those visits were for expensive cognac or home-baked bread either. None of those times were we well received either. But the last time, at the end of my homicide investigation, Poor Nic became something of an ally.

As we rolled up, a big, burly guard waved us through the iron gate and past two uniformed guards. Two things were apparent—Poor Nic expected us, and Poor Nic was not poor by any means.

The too-bulky guard opened Bear's door the moment he shut off the cruiser. "Good morning, Detective Braddock. Mr. Bartalotta is expecting you."

"Oh, yeah?" Bear said, and stepped out to face Bobby, the butler-driver-bodyguard and senior-henchman. "How come?"

Bobby shrugged and stepped back.

Bobby was six-six and weighed every ounce of three hundred pounds—three hundred pounds of raw meat and pasta. He was taller and fifty pounds bulkier than Bear. All in all, it would be an interesting slug-fest if they ever got so engaged.

"Come on, Bobby. How'd you know I was coming to see him?"

"Dunno, Detective. But go on in. The Boss is waitin' on the patio. You know the way."

"Sure I do, Bobby. How's your probation officer treating you? Okay?"

"Funny, Bear. I'm clean and you know it."

"Do I?" Bear patted Bobby on the shoulder and went in search of the patio with me on his heels.

Any other time, I'd take this opportunity to snoop around. Mobsters, like untrained puppies, often leave piles of shit everywhere when they don't know you're around. Sometimes, accidents lead to bigger, better things. Like evidence and handcuffs. But not this time. Poor Nic knew we were coming.

Poor Nic had changed since my murder. He has been a real upstanding guy around town. He took a personal interest in Angel—not a bad one either—and he has even tried to be something of a close friend to her. I wasn't altogether sure how I felt about it. He'd made some big donations to her foundation, dumped a boat-load of cash on the University for low-income family scholarships, and provided jobs to many of the students needing help to pay tuition.

Poor Nic was acting a lot like Saint Nic. At least on the outside. On the inside, I had no silly notion he was a reformed, retired gangster. No, he was a low-key, semi-retired one. Oh, deep down I figured he had a heart somewhere and wanted to help out when he could. But above all, he liked the power and influence brought on by sprinkling money around town.

When we walked through the French doors onto the stone patio, Bear stopped and stared. I almost ran through him.

Angel sat opposite Poor Nic at a round, wrought-iron table sipping coffee. She looked up and gave us a big smile and a wave. "Bear, we expected you an hour ago."

"Oh, yeah?" He recovered and walked to the table. "What are you doing here, Angela?"

Poor Nic—a distinguished, aged man with a shallow face and big, bright eyes—stood and offered his hand to Bear. He was dressed in slacks, a golf shirt, and a heavy cardigan sweater. His hair was groomed with meticulous care and his manners were old-world and instant. His smile was thin, but warm, and his eyes were a grandfather's eyes greeting family.

"Detective Braddock, I'm so glad you could make it. Please, join us for some brunch, won't you? Coffee or tea?"

"None, thanks." Bear did a passable job of shaking the old gangster's hand but kept his eyes on Angel. "Same question, Angel. What are you doing here?"

"Same as you, I'm sure." She patted the chair beside her and waited for Bear to sink into it. "Nicholas sent a car for me this morning. He wanted to explain about his departure last night and apologize for any issues it caused."

"Yeah, departure—issues." Bear waved off the maid with the sterling-silver coffee pot. "And you're here the same as me?"

Poor Nic laughed and sat back down. "Come now, Detective. We all know the score. The first murder since our dear Detective Tucker was taken from us, and, of course, I am a suspect. It comes with the legacy, I'm afraid. Croissant?"

I said, "Legacy? Sure, it comes with the legacy. Like plague comes with the rats."

Poor Nic spilled his coffee and waved for the maid to bring a towel.

"Well, Nicholas, you were there last night and disappeared," Bear said. "Why?"

"Come on, Bear," Angel said. "You being here is why. Every time there's a crime, everyone looks at Nicholas. That's not fair, is it?"

"Well, sorry, Angela, but yes, it's fair."

It was strange hearing Angel defend the old codger. During my murder investigation, she was pretty sure Nic was involved. Very sure, in fact—serial-killer sure. This morning, they seemed like family and the reason the New York mob sent a hit man to whack him last fall was a misunderstanding. Just a gag among mobsters. No big deal.

"Now, now. I do understand, my dear," Poor Nic said. "Go on with your questions, Detective. I will answer them without benefit of counsel."

"How good of you, Nic," I said. "Surrounded by guns and thugs and you don't need a lawyer. You're really coming out of your shell."

Bear laughed.

Nic looked down at his coffee and smiled. "It's a sign of innocence, Detective."

"Sure, okay." Bear grabbed a croissant from the plate on the table and stuffed half of it in his mouth. "I get it. So, let's talk about last night. Give me the nickel tour, okay? You talk, I'll snack."

Poor Nic sat back in his chair and folded his hands on his lap. "I arrived late, perhaps eight thirty. You can check the sign-in register—"

"I did," Bear said between chews. "You had one of your men with you. You didn't sign him in."

"No, I did not. I offered to sign Bobby in, but since he wasn't drinking and had no donations to make, they agreed to forego the formality. The decision was mutually agreeable."

"Ah, good, mutually agreeable." Bear leaned forward. "André Cartier greased it."

"Yes, I think it was André. And before you go any further, I concur with Angela. You have the wrong man. Professor Cartier is innocent. A man of sterling character."

I said, "Well, I gotta agree, Nic. But, evidence is evidence. Bear had no choice."

Nic smiled. "But you know this already, Detective."

"Sure I do," Bear said, liberating another croissant. This time, he gestured for the maid and waited for a cup of coffee. "But facts are facts and I can't play favorites."

"Which is why he's here, Nicholas," Angel said. "He has to follow up with you just to be fair and thorough. Right, Bear?"

Bear choked on a mouthful. "Ah, no, Angela. André, I would vouch for, but Nic on the other hand—"

"No, of course not, Detective." Nic waved the maid into the house and waited for the French doors to close. He turned to Bear and his dark eyes lost their grandfatherly smile. "I shook some hands and provided Angela with a sizable donation. My second donation, I might add. I was not feeling well, and after a glass or two of champagne, felt tired. Bobby drove me home. I was on the front porch—leaving—when Mr. Grecco was killed. I know this because two of your deputies almost knocked me down charging into the house. They will recall the incident. Bobby was quite irritated with them. I knew what would transpire, so I continued home. I had nothing whatsoever to do with Mr. Grecco's killing."

"Detective Spence tried to reach you all night. Your boys out front told Spence you weren't at home and didn't know where you were."

"I prefer my privacy after midnight. And besides, as I said, your own men saw me outside at the time of the shooting."

Bear looked at him and pondered it all. After a sip of coffee to wash down another croissant, he continued. "You just left? No curiosity? No interest?"

"None. Come now, Detective, if you were me, what different course would you have taken?" A smile broke Nic's face again. "And be honest, I did know I'd be very high on the 'persons of interest' list."

"You sure are."

"As I said."

"Did you know Stephanos Grecco?"

"No."

"Ever do business with him? Know his wife, Bonnie?"

"No and no. I do not do business with those I do not know."

"Ever—"

"No."

Bear tapped the table. "What can you tell me about Festival Catering?"

The question sent Poor Nic's eyebrows up. "The caterer? I own a security guard company, part of a construction company, and some other business assets. I don't believe a caterer is on the list. Why?"

"How about Stanley Kravitz or Petya Cherna … Chernykov … No, Petya Chernyshov?"

"I'm sorry, Detective, no. I have never heard of any of them." Nic threw a chin at the French doors and they opened. The maid headed for the table. "More coffee? We're through here."

"No, I don't think so." Bear snapped forward. "And we're done when I say we're done."

"Bear, please," Angel said, touching his arm. "What more is there to ask? Nicholas doesn't know anyone, he left before it happened, and can't offer anything."

"As Angela said, Detective, I've told you all I can—nothing."

Bear looked at Angel and his eyes narrowed a little. Then he sat back and sipped his coffee, looking out beyond the patio.

I said, "Angel, ask him about Vincent Calaprese."

She glanced over at me—just for an instant—and picked up her coffee cup. "Nicholas, the Vincent House is spectacular. You lived in Winchester when you were younger. Do you know its history?"

Poor Nic threw his head back and laughed. "My dear, Angela. Quite the detective you're becoming, yes? Your question is about Vincent Calaprese, is it not?"

She grinned and nodded.

"I'm an old man, but not too old, my dear. And I can honestly say I have never met the man."

"Not the question I asked, Angel," I said. "Ask him—"

"Come now." Poor Nic held up a hand. "You cannot believe that I commune with one-hundred and twenty year-old wise guys, can you? We don't all know one-another either."

She laughed. "No, Nicholas, but—"

"Angela," Bear said. "Can I have a moment with Nicholas?"

"Yes, of course." She smiled at Nic, stood, and went into the house.

Bear tapped a finger on the table, vibrating the spoons off the coffee saucers. "Okay, Nic. Let's put the cards on the table, shall we?"

"Yes, Detective, please do."

"You've got the attention of the Attorney General's office—"

"Ah yes, Ruth-Ann. Lovely woman—if you like spiders who eat their young."

I said, "That's harsh, Nic."

"Your leaving last night looks bad. André vouching for you is worse. But I get it, I do. And I get you and Angela being friends. But I don't like it much. Just so you know."

"Of course, I understand." Poor Nic patted the air. "Detective, as one of Angela's friends to another, my intentions are honorable. Her husband—the smart-aleck Oliver—was a good man. And despite circumstances, I am sorry I could not have stopped his killer before his death."

"Yeah, circumstances," Bear said, crooking his eye at him. "Whatever. Anyway, here's the deal. You stay 'honorable' or I'll send you to see Tuck, got it? And if you know anything about this Grecco thing, you'd be wise to tell me. The faster Marcos lets go, the better."

Poor Nic nodded and his grandfather smile returned. "I could not agree more. So, in both our best interests, let me give you some advice about these matters." He waited for Bear to nod. "Murder can be a simple magic trick, Detective. If you manipulate your audience, you can make anyone believe in magic. It's all about misdirection. Isn't it?"

"What the heck does that mean?" Bear asked. "If you know something—"

"Do feel free to come see me anytime, Detective—but call ahead. And now, show yourself out, won't you?"

TWENTY-SEVEN

Bear walked to his unmarked cruiser under the scrutiny of one of Poor Nic's thugs—er, security guards. Before he reached his door, a large black four-door SUV careened through the gate entrance and almost ran over the guard attempting to stop it. The vehicle caused quite a stir. Two other guards drew their weapons and charged as it rolled to a stop behind Bear's cruiser.

"No one move," one guard shouted. "Driver, turn off the ignition."

Bear rested a hand on his semi-automatic in its holster. "What's this all about?"

What an entrance. I said, "Bear, it's our new best friend from the Attorney General's office."

"Oh, please. Tell me it isn't." He held his badge up in the air and yelled at the security guards aiming at the SUV. "Put your guns down. Everything is all right. Just relax and back off."

The driver's door opened and a man's arm poked out with a badge and credential in his hand. The voice wasn't happy. "Federal Agents. Lower your weapons. Get away from our vehicle."

One of the guards snapped a glance at Bear, then walked to the SUV and leaned forward to check the driver's credentials. Before he could read the "U" in United States, they were snatched back and the door flung open.

"I said put the guns down," the driver ordered. "And step back."

The guard complied and ordered the other to holster his weapon, too. "You can't just bust in here, mister. You almost hit me."

"I told you—Federal Agents."

"I don't care who you are." The guard held up a hand. "You got a warrant?"

"Step back. Now."

I said, "As much as I don't like some of Nic's entourage, this doesn't look right."

"Everyone just settle down," Bear called, striding over to the SUV. "What's this about, Agent. I'm—"

"Detective Braddock," the voice from the open passenger door said, "what are you doing here?" Ruth-Ann Marcos stepped out. "Is Bartalotta now a suspect in Mr. Grecco's murder?"

"I'm following leads. What are you doing here?"

"Introducing myself, Detective."

I watched Ruth-Ann assess Poor Nic's estate. "Mob retirement seems to suit him, don't you think?"

Two dark-suited men climbed out of the SUV from the back seat and stood behind her.

"One of you stay here and watch these men," she ordered. "No one leaves—except for Detective Braddock."

Bear feigned a smile. "Maybe I should stick around and hear what's happening. After all, Ruth-Ann, this is my homicide investigation. The Feds have no jurisdiction."

"On your case, no, not yet." She headed for Poor Nic's door, flanked by two FBI men. "My visit has nothing to do with your investigation."

I said, "Bear, I'll hang around and snoop. It'll be okay. Trust me."

"Right. Okay, I'll leave you to it." He returned to his car and gave Ruth-Ann a curt nod. "Remember, if you get anything—"

"Of course, Detective," she said with the hiss of a cobra. "I'll be sure to call."

"Bear, give her a ticket for public-bitchiness. She's got a thing about Poor Nic, doesn't she?"

He cursed and slipped into his cruiser, started it, and left black streaks of frustration on Poor Nic's driveway. He, too, almost hit a security guard, but the guard was smart enough to jump out of the way again.

Inside, I missed the opening salutations between Betty-Law and Johnny-Evil. But I knew Poor Nic well enough to know he was taking it all in stride and enjoying the tit-for-tat. Ruth-Ann, however, didn't seem to be. She stood in front of him—he was still seated at the patio table beside Angel—with a scowl on her face hinting she was overdue for a tax audit.

"Please, please," Poor Nic said, gesturing to a seat at his table. "Let us be civil. Sit. Coffee for your men? Tea perhaps for you? Angela and I were just—"

"No. I'm here to ask about a federal matter." She turned to Angel. "I'd like to speak in private, Professor Tucker. Please don't leave the premises. I am curious to know why you're here."

Oh, crap. "Angel, don't—"

Too late.

"I'll wait inside, Nicholas, we'll finish our catching-up afterward." She stood with a glare at Ruth-Ann that could freeze fire. "Ruth-Ann, you can make an appointment with my secretary on campus. I'll make myself available for any *pertinent* questions."

"Angel, go easy. She's a fed, for God's sake."

Ruth-Ann sighed. "Yes, of course, Professor. I'm sorry. Forgive me. But this is a sensitive matter and I'm concerned for the safety of one of our assets. I'll have my office call you tomorrow. If tomorrow is convenient."

"Yes, you do that."

"Professor Tucker," Ruth-Ann began with a faint smile, "perhaps you can answer just one question."

"Perhaps."

Ruth-Ann cocked her head. "How is it you chose the Vincent House for your Foundation work? Is it the Calaprese history? You seem to gravitate to those types, don't you?"

"No, Ruth-Ann, I don't gravitate toward anyone except those interested in helping my foundation—as Nicholas is. You might consider checking your facts before you make accusations."

143

"You still didn't answer my question."

"André Cartier." Angel folded her arms. "André did some government research not long ago about organized crime during the second world war. Vincent Calaprese was a gangster, yes, but he also provided valuable assistance to the government in tracking Nazi, Japanese, and Soviet spy rings. André knew about the Vincent properties and suggested I contact the family to see about transferring the estate into my foundation's charity."

"André?" Ruth-Ann smiled again and I wondered if it were a nervous habit. "I see. Yes, André told me about his research when I first met him. A remarkable man. How convenient for your charity."

"And this will be the end of your interrogation until you make an appointment."

"Yes, of course." Ruth-Ann nodded to one of her agents who opened the patio door. "Please do forgive me for being so rude and—"

"A bitch." Angel just had to say it. She glanced at Poor Nic. "Don't be long, Nicholas." And without another word, Angel walked off into the house.

Did I mention my wife was more than just a university professor and a beautiful woman? She's also a cage fighter. Well, she would be but the competition barred her.

Ruth-Ann pounced. "All right, Bartalotta, tell me what you know about Anatoly Nikolaevich Konstantinova."

Holy Russian mafia, what a name.

Poor Nic lifted his coffee cup and sipped it, looking over the rim at her. "Ms. Marcos, I am not personally familiar with him. But I am, as you are aware, familiar with his reputation."

"His reputation? Come on, Bartalotta, give me—"

"Please, Ms. Marcos, perhaps we can keep a less-hostile tone, no? After all, you arrived here uninvited. You may call me Nicholas. Or you may call me Mr. Bartalotta. Now, I cannot tell you much about Anatoly. But I will tell you what I can."

"Anatoly? I thought you didn't know him." Ruth-Ann's mouth tightened into a prune, and when Poor Nic didn't offer any further comment, she said, "He's making moves in Washington and it seems he's interested in real estate out here, too. What do you know about that?"

"Nothing."

"He hasn't been in contact with you?"

"No."

"Oh, come now, Bart … Nicholas. You mean to tell me he's not reached out to you at all?"

"Yes, of course he has." Poor Nic sat his cup down. "However, you did not ask such a question. I said I have not been in contact with him. He has reached out to me but I am not interested in his kind."

"His kind?" Ruth-Ann cocked her head. "You mean your kind, don't you? The thug-mobster kind?"

Ouch, Ruth-Ann is as subtle as a bullet in the heart. And I should know, I have one.

"Why Ms. Marcos, even the Attorney General's office is aware of the significant difference between my family roots and Anatoly's. And even more aware of the ethics of our two—businesses."

She laughed. "Oh come on, Nicholas. Apples and oranges, really?"

I said, "Nic, she's got a point. Gangsters are gangsters. Even if you're retired."

"Ms. Marcos, you must admit the Russian organizations have a different perspective on life, no? I mean they tend not to honor it at all. They are ruthless. Barbaric at times. And not just to their own either. They solve with bullets and brutality what we Europeans tend to solve with negotiation and—"

"Yeah, you're just a real ambassador, aren't you?" Ruth-Ann looked around at his estate again. "Let me get to the point."

"I wish you would," I said. "You're boring both of us, Ruth-Ann."

Nicholas laughed. "Please do. And did you say 'no' to coffee for your men? Or to at least sit at my table to talk?"

"Forget the coffee, Bartalotta." She dropped her hands onto the back of a chair and leaned forward, glaring at him. "Where's Katalina?"

A wide, silly smile broke across Nicholas' face. He leaned back in his chair and folded his hands on his lap. "Ah, I see why you have come to visit. You have misplaced a federal witness."

"No, a fugitive. How did you know?"

"You would not be here if she were not missing. She is not part of my staff. Is she not part of Anatoly's?"

Ruth-Ann eyed him. "Do you know where she is or not?"

"No."

"You're lying."

"You have evidence of this?"

"I can get a warrant with a phone call."

"Oh, a phone call?" He laughed again. "Then you did not bring one. If you could get one with a phone call, it would be in your possession, Ms. Marcos. So let's not play this game. You are missing an important Russian crime witness. For some reason, you feel she is here or I have somehow inserted myself into Anatoly's business. But, you have no proof or your men would be ravishing my home already."

"Don't push me, Bartalotta."

I said, "Nic, what's she talking about? Who's Katalina?"

He looked over at the agents watching him. Then he stood and wiped his mouth with his linen napkin and extended a hand to Ruth-Ann. "Good morning to you, Ms. Marcos. I'll have my men show you out."

"I'm not through yet." She jabbed a finger at him. "If I find out—"

"If you find something you do not already know, then you'll have enough probable cause to obtain your warrant. And even over your phone, no? Until such time, you may call for an appointment with my attorney—any of the four. Two of them are on K Street in Washington not far from your office. So, it will be convenient."

Ruth-Ann's mouth snapped tight again and she turned to go.

"Oh, and Ms. Marcos," Poor Nic said in a light voice, "I wanted to ask you. Your name, 'Marcos,' it is Cuban, is it not?"

She stopped and turned around. "What of it? My family escaped Castro before I was born."

"Nothing, I'm very interested in ancestry, in particular the history of my friends." He didn't smile but looked at her with hard, penetrating eyes. "And I understand you're forming a campaign for a senate run in the coming election. You can count on my support. I'll have my accountant send over a donation. Please include me on your mailings. But, no need to leave your card on the way out. I have everything I need."

She didn't thank him and almost ran into the glass patio door—and would have if one of her agents hadn't yanked it open at the last second.

Me, I watched her leave and was conflicted. Nic might be a retired mob boss and a ruthless man, but he had helped stop my killer and had saved Angel's life. In the process, he took a bullet that might have been meant for her. Ruth-Ann, on the other hand, made a great target for flying houses and trick-or-treaters. Watching him kick her ass—with a smile—caused a collision between my twenty years as a cop and the satisfaction I felt.

So, while he was a retired gangster, he was my pal-the-gangster now.

What did that say about me?

TWENTY-EIGHT

JORGE-THE-WAITER PARKED HIS MOTORCYCLE on the side street and walked toward Old Town Winchester, keeping an eye open for any curious passersby or a Winchester police cruiser. Neither made their appearance. At the corner, he crossed the street and headed toward the center of town, slipping into a narrow alley a half-block from the Old Town walking mall. There, he ambled another half-block to an old stone building under renovation and went inside.

"Hello?" he called out, looking around the old antique shop. "Anyone here?"

The ground floor was barren of anything but dust and grit. Its walls had been stripped revealing only brick, mortar, and framing. The ceiling was exposed; rough-cut wood beams and a few telltale electric wires remained. There were no lights affixed anywhere and the room was dark except for ambient light filtering through the building's dusty glass picture window. Outside the window, a few bags of mortar mix and an assortment of tools and wood were piled on the sidewalk. There was no one around.

He was alone.

He slipped the thick, manila envelope out of his leather jacket and tucked it behind the ancient radiator on the rear wall. A moment before he retraced his steps back into the rear alley, faint footfalls came from the second floor—at least he thought there were. He turned to go back inside, but thought better of it.

His instructions had been unequivocal. He was to secure the envelope behind the radiator and leave. He was not to speak with anyone. He was not to return to the old antique shop. He was to go to his office and await instructions. Any variance, any lapse whatsoever, and payment would be withheld. More important and more ominous, his name would be provided to the Frederick County Sheriff's Department with a mixture of facts and false allegations which might take weeks to sort out.

Money talked and handcuffs hurt.

He never made it to his motorcycle before one of his two cell phones rang. When he realized it was his burner-phone—an over-the-counter, untraceable convenience store phone—it could be only one person.

"Yeah? What?"

The voice was low and the words sparse. "Where are the drives?"

"Hey man, don't you read the papers? I can't get everything yet. It'll be later today or tomorrow before I can go back."

"Unacceptable. Must I make the call?"

He snorted. "Go ahead, man. Call the cops. You're in this same as me."

"Perhaps. But they will not know me. And you do not know me."

He reached his motorcycle and surveyed the street. "What makes you so sure, man? Huh? How do you know I didn't check you out?"

Silence.

"I thought so."

The voice was cold, stark … menacing. "Based on what? Phone calls and cash? The real question, Victorio Miguel Chevez, is how do you know I have not checked you out? Jorge is not a fitting name for you, is it Victorio?"

Chevez, who preferred the nickname "Chevy" since his younger days at Parris Island, felt a knot in his stomach. "What do you want, man?"

"My disc drives. No more. No less—for now. Soon enough, you can provide me with the recordings, too."

"And I said you'd get it all. It's gonna take time. Just time, man."

Silence. Then, "I want the drives by tomorrow morning. Your first report on the recordings is due in two days. I'll send you the drop information. Oh, and Chevy,"

The mysterious client knew too much. "Yeah, what?"

"Silence is golden. You'll have a lot of money by the end of the month—don't blow it by getting scared."

Chevy laughed. "Yeah, well, you don't blow it by being cheap either."

The call went dead.

TWENTY-NINE

"THIS IS THE WAY we found it, Bear." Spence waved his hand toward the piles of debris in Bonnie Grecco's living room. "The rest of the house looks the same. Somebody was looking for something last night."

"What time did you get here?" Bear asked.

"About seven a.m. Mrs. Grecco didn't want to come here from the Vincent House last night. We put her up at a hotel down by the highway. But this morning, Cap wanted us to look for the letters and for anything else we could tie to his murder."

"Got it." Bear walked around, surveying the mess. "Someone else had the same idea."

There was nothing in the house that wasn't open, torn apart, dumped on the floor, or pulled from shelves and cabinets. The only thing not destroyed was a corner bar made of oak and decorative brass. The three tiers of liquor bottles were largely untouched—two or three were broken and dripping expensive booze—but most of the other bottles and the wine and champagne glasses hanging from a rack and on the rear counter were unscathed.

Whoever had been here either had a passion for good whiskey or was exhausted from the rampage before they reached the bar.

This was no routine breaking-and-entering either. The house sat in rural farm country all by itself south of town off County Route 11. It was a big house, aged, and well kept. There were more luxurious homes all around—newer, with expensive trappings and "look at me" nuances that the Grecco home didn't have.

Someone knew who and what they were looking for.

I said, "Bear, they must have been looking for the threatening letters she received."

"Spence, did you find the letters?" Bear picked up a stack of books and fanned through them. "Anything else left behind? Are we sure it wasn't trashed before last night?"

"Mrs. Grecco said it was fine," Spence said. "Why?"

"Just thinking out loud. But you have to wonder if she had anything to do with all this, right?"

"What are you saying, Detective?" Bonnie Grecco stood beneath the archway leading into the kitchen. She held a tray of coffee and cups and her face was washed with exhaustion and grief. "You think I wrecked my own place? You think—"

"I don't think anything, ma'am—not for sure." Bear stepped forward and took the tray. "I'm trying to look at this from all angles. I'm sorry, but I have to consider every possibility."

"Including me killing Steph?"

"I'm afraid so, yes."

"I shot him through the back while I stood in front of him on the dance floor? In front of all those people?"

I said, "She's got you there. Ask about the letters. Then ask her about André again."

He did.

Bonnie handed out cups of coffee to Bear and Spence and sent two more with a deputy standing by the stairs for the others searching the house. "I have no idea where they are. I told you I gave them to Steph. And if they were here, I guess they're gone."

Spence held a pen over his notepad. "Assuming, of course, the letters are what they were looking for."

"What else would they be here for, Detective Spence?" Bonnie's voice was edgy. "Maybe you think we're drug dealers or something? I'm a murderer and a drug dealer?"

"No, ma'am, I meant—"

Bear held up a hand. "Mrs. Grecco, tell me about your relationship with André Cartier."

"André?" She took a long swallow of coffee and looked around for somewhere to sit. "Dear God, do you think he killed Steph?"

"We are holding him as a suspect." Bear lifted his chin at Spence to keep notes. "What do you think?"

Bonnie resettled a cushion from the floor into a chair across the large great room and sat down. "I don't know. He seems so nice."

"So you do know him?" Bear asked. "How well?"

Bonnie blinked several times and set her coffee on the arm of the chair, balancing it with her hand. Tears welled in her eyes and she fought them back with little success. "No, we met last night. I only know what he told me—something about the Washington museums and his work in, history, right? He's on the charity circuit; he told me as much. And he came with a nasty, rude woman named Amelda Marco."

"Ruth-Ann Marcos," Bear said, smiling a little. "She's with the US Attorney General's office in DC."

I watched Bonnie as hot, sizzling fingers gripped my spine. "Bear, don't let go here. She's not telling us everything."

He pressed her. "Mrs. Grecco—Bonnie—there is something you're not telling me. I need to know it all. Hiding something will only—"

"Enough, Detective." Bonnie's eyes flared and she stood up, sending the coffee cup crashing to the floor among several books and papers littered there. Her right hand flew to her left wrist and gripped her watch—a beautiful European piece. When her fingers caressed it, I knew.

"Hold on a second, Bear. I got something."

I went to her and took hold of her fingers and the watch together. When I did, Bonnie gasped in air and her eyes grew wide with the surprise of a scary movie. She stepped back and faltered, falling back down into the chair with me still clutching her wrist.

It was too late.

The lightning exploded around me and the tornado of light descended. The room swirled and breathed in and out—light, darkness, light … darkness.

And then, from nowhere, my breath caught as the rush of passion seized me—sweat, the sweet taste of wine-moistened lips, and the warm fire of bare skin.

Oh my, how was I going to explain this to Angel?

———

Bonnie Grecco writhed above me, pressing herself deeper and deeper onto me while my hands explored ... *my* hands? She leaned down and kissed my mouth, whispering, "Please ... a little more ... please—"

Well, I stayed this long.

Her body shuddered and released a moment before the one I now shared—she gripped my fingers and let out a low, intense breath just before collapsing beside me.

"You are amazing," she whispered, and rolled out of bed. "I want some champagne. Can we order?"

Order wine? From where?

Somewhere in my head, thoughts struggled for control. I was me—Oliver Tucker, ghost-detective extraordinaire. And I was him, wild, passionate lover. And whoever he was, he was good—amazing, even. Oh, not to say I'm not—wasn't—or whatever. But since my death, this was my first time at bat and, well ... *damn*.

"Sure, hon, I'll order some room service while you grab a shower. Anything special?"

She slipped on a bulky cotton robe—one of those plush, expensive ones the finer hotels put in your room for just such a need. When she turned to face me, the robe was open and the light from the window bathed her. Stephanos Grecco had been a happy man, albeit a tired one. Of course, if he knew about me—er, him—he wouldn't be too happy at all.

"Strawberries and chocolate. Lots of both. And champagne."

"Strawberries, chocolate, and champagne. On the way."

"Now I know why we meet in expensive Washington hotels. It's all about room service."

She giggled and flashed her robe open. "Of course. But you know, I don't want anyone thinking I'm some bimbo after your money and prestige. And—"

"And you don't want me to look like an old fart chasing girls half my age. I get it."

"Half? Hmmm … not even." She raised her arm and admired her expensive watch. "And I just love my gift. Thank you again, it's wonderful."

"I'm so glad you like it." I strode to the window and gazed out at the Potomac. "I guess hotels are best for now. My Georgetown neighbors would have us both on the gossip pages in no time. Besides, I don't have a maid who brings champagne and strawberries."

"Can you hire one?" Her voice was lost when the shower started.

I went to the bathroom and stood in the doorway. This body was a little stiffer and creakier than mine; which might have been the marathon I'd just run before and after my arrival. "So, have you decided?"

"Decided?" She stuck her head out of the shower. "Decided what?"

"About the gala next week. You know, the charity in Winchester?"

Bonnie stepped out of the shower dripping wet—pressing her sexy, hard body against me and running her lips lightly across mine. "I think I've already been rather charitable, don't you?"

Wow, if I had a dollar for every time I heard that at home. "Yes, you have. But they could use the extra support. So, how about it, for me?"

"Ah, isn't the check I gave you enough?" She nibbled my neck—er, our neck. "Do I have to drive all the way out there for moonshine and pigs feet or whatever those hillbillies eat?" She tickled my chin with her lips. "Do I?"

I kissed her and touched my finger to her nose. "They are not hillbillies, Bonnie. There are some wonderful people out there. You know the Vincent House is an important project and the charity needs capital. Look, come on out and bring a date if you're embarrassed to be with me."

"A date?" Bonnie ran her fingers across my back and down. Her lips closed on my ear and she whispered, "Well, okay, but we should talk about it after the champagne, okay? I've got a secret to share." She returned to the shower.

Oh, lord, what a life I was missing. At the sink, I splashed some cool water in my face. "What's the secret, babe? Should I order two bottles of champagne?"

I don't know which was worse—when Bonnie said, "I need to tell you about my husband," or when I looked into the bathroom mirror and watched the color drain from the face of André Cartier.

Lightning.

THIRTY

"ANDRÉ LIED TO YOU, Bear," I said when the sparks subsided and I got my bearings back in Bonnie Grecco's living room. "He and Bonnie are having an affair."

Bear stood across the room watching Spence sort through a pile of books and bric-a-brac lying on the floor. He glanced over at Bonnie who was still sipping coffee. He caught Spence's eye, and nodded toward Bonnie.

Spence readied his pen and notepad.

"You said you don't know Professor Cartier, right?" Bear asked. "You want to think about your answer real careful, okay?"

"Enough." Bonnie's lips pursed and she pointed a finger at him. "I've had it. I'm calling my lawyer."

She stood and headed for the phone across the room.

"Bear," I said. "Tell her you know about the donations to Angel's charity she gave to André at the hotel in DC last week. And ask her if she liked her strawberries and champagne—and her new watch."

He didn't even pretend it was his idea. "I'll have the check by this afternoon, Bonnie. And Cartier won't stay locked up alone for long. You two were playing footsie in DC last week and checks and room service leave a trail. He gave you the watch, didn't he? Cut the b.s. and talk to me."

"Wonderful. Just great." She didn't turn around but replaced the phone on the end table. Then she went to the bar and pulled down an undamaged bottle of gin, poured a hefty three-fingers, and downed it in three long gulps. She refilled it again. "How'd you know? Did he tell you?"

"No." Bear righted a bar stool lying on the floor. He slid it around to her and found another nearby for himself. "But he will. I have a source who told me about your affair. Let's hear it, Bonnie. The truth this time."

Spence scribbled notes. "Ah, Bear. Can you fill me in a little? Seems like I missed something—a lot of somethings."

"Later. Just write."

Bonnie took another long tug of her drink. "It started a few months ago. I met André in DC at a party. He was so great. Nothing like Steph. Steph was fun at first, but he just wanted a trophy—you know—who looked like me. Otherwise, he had no use for me."

"And André?"

"André?" She smiled and raised her glass. "He didn't want anything. We had fun. Dinner, dancing. Drinks. You know, fun. I wanted him more than he wanted me. Least I thought so, anyway."

Bear exchanged looks with Spence. "What do you mean?"

"Oh, come on, Detective. You know. He's an old guy—not too old—but old. He doesn't need anything except some company now and then. He's got money and friends and everything. He wasn't looking for marriage or anything close. At least, I thought so until he found out I was married."

"And?" I asked as Bear's lips moved.

"He flipped. What did he think, I went home to my mom at night?" She chugged the drink. "But, it was Steph who scared me."

"Did he find out?" Bear asked. "Was he abusive?"

"Well, not at first. I told you, we just met on a cruise. But he wanted to live out in this tiny little place—"

"You mean Winchester?" Spence said. "It isn't so tiny."

She forced a laugh. "It isn't Manhattan or DC, now is it?"

Spence shrugged.

"Anyway, he started staying out all night and got angry all the time. He was seeing someone—I know he was—he got calls and would take them outside. I might not be old but I'm not stupid. And he spent money way faster than anyone I've ever seen."

Bear waited for Spence to catch up with his notes. "You don't know anything about his business affairs?"

"No." She shook her head. "He's a deal-maker. That's what he told me. He makes all kinds of deals—business mergers, sales, real estate—for a percentage."

"And now it's all yours." Spence looked up as though he hadn't planned on moving his lips. "Right?"

"Maybe. I never signed a pre-nup. You're asking about it, right? But like I said earlier, I couldn't shoot him from behind on the dance floor, right? I'm flexible, Detectives, but not that flexible."

Boy, was she ever. "Bear, ask her about the thousand-dollar notes in his wallet."

He did.

"Steph liked to flash money around. At least he did until last week."

"What happened last week?" Bear asked, leaning forward to pour another three fingers into her glass. "What changed?"

"He went out and met his lady friend. I know because I followed him. I couldn't see who it was but they went to a hotel. Afterward, he told me we couldn't spend any more money for a while and we were moving—fast. I asked why but he just got mad, he hit me a couple times, and ran off for the night. Probably back to her."

I asked, "How much money are we talking about here, Bear?"

Bear got halfway through the question when the front door burst open and four men in suits strode in. "What the hell?"

"FBI," one of them said.

"Detective, have your men stand down." An average height, thin man in an expensive suit strode in behind the other four. He had heavy eyebrows and a swarthy complexion. "I'm Special Agent Jim Dobron, Chief of the Organized Crime Task Force, WFO."

"WFO?" Bear asked.

To many, "WFO" meant "What the Frig Over," or you can use your imagination. In this case, it stood for "Washington Field Office" of the FBI—Fed central in these here parts. But often, especially to us local cops, the two definitions are synonymous.

"Now, just hold it a minute." Bear held up a hand to stop the four men moving toward him from the doorway. "I'm Detective—"

"Theodore Braddock, Frederick County Sheriff's Office, Chief of nothing. Yeah, I know," Agent Dobron said. "Thanks for baby-sitting—I'll put in a good word with your captain. We'll take over now." He waved two of his agents toward Bonnie.

She tried to pull away when they latched on. "Detective, what's going on? I don't understand."

"Neither do I."

Dobron held up a hand at Bear to silence him as he walked up to Bonnie. "Bonnie Grecco—or shall I call you Bonnie Long, Wiseman, or DeFleur? You're under protective custody as a material witness in a Department of Justice RICO Probe."

No, RICO does not stand for "Really Innocent, Cooperative Old-guys," it meant "Racketeer Influenced and Corrupt Organizations—mobsters, gangsters, organized crime families, thugs, thieves, murderers, et cetera, et cetera.

Bear looked at Bonnie. "What haven't you told me, Bonnie?"

There must be a few things Bonnie held out on us. Although she didn't hold out much on André, or me, earlier.

"I'm not saying anything more. Help me, Detective. Help me and I'll help you."

As Dobron's men whisked her from the room, I couldn't help but wonder what else she was hiding from us. I also couldn't help but think about the few moments I'd been André.

Is it cheating if you have a girl like her while you're possessing another guy's body?

Nah, can't be.

THIRTY-ONE

CHEVY CHEVEZ—THE FORMER JORGE the waiter—snapped three photographs of the luxury sedan pulling out of Nicholas Bartalotta's estate. Chevy sat on his motorcycle parked down the street, secreted behind some trees, watching. The distance to the gate wasn't a problem for his telephoto lens but, just in case, he snapped four more as the Lexus passed him heading toward Winchester.

The driver didn't notice him. So far so good, considering Bartalotta's men had a reputation for disliking cameras. So, Chevy waited until the car was well ahead before pulling out and following.

It took about fifteen minutes to reach the three-story Victorian sitting on a side street a few blocks from Old Town Winchester. The driver knew the streets well and negotiated an alley a block north of the house in order to avoid construction and arrive with the passenger's door along the sidewalk at the gate.

Chevy made it to the top of the hill overlooking the house and snapped three more photographs as the thirty-something history professor climbed out of the sedan, thanked the driver, and headed inside. He watched her check her mail on the front porch and snapped two more shots while she searched for her keys, keeping his eye on the viewfinder a little longer than he needed, admiring her auburn hair and sexy figure. During his time on campus, she turned as many college-boy heads as any campus coed.

"Oh, my, Angela, you're sure fine. And no husband either. I might have to take some of your classes."

Chevy moved his motorcycle around the corner a block from the Victorian. He dismounted and changed the telephoto lens for another, more compact one from his backpack. Then he made his way back along the sidewalk to the rear of the Victorian. There, he slipped behind a tall oak, swung up on a limb, and easily negotiated the four-foot wrought-iron fence. He dropped into the side yard among overgrown, bushy evergreens and shrubs which provided him ample cover to penetrate the property unobserved.

Chevy knelt, readying his camera at the side of the Victorian's rear sun porch where the shrubs concealed him from the street. He checked the rear and side yards, confident no one could see him unless they pulled into the small driveway at the rear of the house. He would hear anyone turn into the drive and he could retreat before being seen. If surprised, he was ready with a cover story—business cards and desktop published literature for "Good Neighbor-Scapes Landscaping." A pleasant smile and ready handouts fooled 90 percent of wary observers.

So far, so good.

He tried the sun porch door. It was locked. His pocket knife and practice got him through in seconds. Inside, he went to the inner windows. One gave him a view down the Victorian's long hallway bisecting the first floor; one window viewed into the kitchen; and another the dining room. From where he was, he could get some good photographs.

Dr. Angela Hill-Tucker was nowhere to be seen.

He knelt down and adjusted his camera for a few low-light shots. He took a chance and stood, lifted his camera, and froze.

Staring back at him through the window was a large, black, furry face the size of a concrete block. The huge beast was eye-to-eye with him, standing on his rear legs with front legs braced against the window frame. The animal watched him—unblinking, dark eyes—rigid and powerful. His mouth opened and a low, rumbling sound started rattling the window glass.

"*Madre de Dios.*" Chevy remembered the photograph on the professor's office shelf. The big Lab was 115 pounds or more. He was a powerful animal whose breed reputation as playful and loving was lost somewhere behind bared teeth and target-locked eyes.

"*Madre de Dios.*"

The Lab's tail snapped straight out. His powerful jaws opened to bare shiny, white, *large* teeth. When he barked, the sun porch windows reverberated and the alarm was unmistakable. A powerful paw hammered against the window frame as the wooden blind fell from its hanger and crashed onto the floor inside.

Chevy fell backward and dropped his camera.

Before he could retreat through the sun porch door—he'd closed it behind him—the interior door swung open and the huge Lab charged.

"No, hell no—"

Someone yelled, "Freeze! I've got a gun."

Chevy wasn't worried about guns. He didn't stop. He scrambled for the door and dove head-first toward the shrubs. He didn't make it alone.

The dog was on him.

"Hercule, hold him."

Hercule tackled him around his waist and drove him through the door, over the outside railing, and down into the shrubs. The Lab's powerful jaws clamped around his arm and twisted—yanking him back and whiplashing him around like a ragdoll. Then, Hercule settled over his mid-section and chest with all fours pinning him to the ground, half in, half out of the evergreen shrubs.

"Get off me! Whoa, boy, easy."

"Hercule, back," a voice shouted from the porch. "Come on, boy, back."

Hercule bore down with powerful jaws and growled a deep, guttural warning on the "no trespassing" rules he was enforcing. After one last clamp of his jaws, he released Chevy's arm and backed up onto the sun porch stairs.

"Don't move." The voice said from inside. "I've called the police. I have a gun."

"Screw you, lady." Chevy crawled backward deeper into the bushes. He rolled over, scrambled to his feet, and bolted over the fence.

He never looked back.

A city maintenance truck rounded the corner and slammed on his brakes when Chevy darted across the street at a full run. The driver laid on his horn and cursed out his window. Chevy never missed a step and sprinted down the block, disappearing around the corner. Out of breath, he eased farther on and settled into a brisk walk, taking the time to check over his shoulder and listen for any sound of police sirens or charging hooves approaching.

No one gave chase. No one approached. There were no sirens.

And he was empty handed.

"Oh, shit." He left his camera behind. "*Mierda que pendejo.*"

He dug his cell phone out of his pocket. He cursed again as he walked up to his motorcycle and found a ticket tucked into the handlebars—he was parked in front of a fire hydrant. He hit a speed dial number.

The call went to a voicemail only identified by its number.

"Man, you better call me back, pronto. We got trouble. You don't pay me enough to get eaten."

THIRTY-TWO

Poor Nic looked up from the papers on his mahogany desk as Bobby opened the heavy doors and led a young woman in. He gestured to a chair in front of the desk, waited for Poor Nic to nod, and left, shutting the doors behind him.

"Ah, my dear, I trust you slept well?"

The woman was young—perhaps twenty-eight or nine—with long, curly black hair pulled back behind her ears. She was pretty with big, round eyes and a full figure—not fat—but curvaceous and not slight at her bosom. She sat opposite Poor Nic and watched him. Her eyes were red and tired, her face drained of color, and her fingers gripped the arm of the chair as though fearing she would have to flee.

"No, I do not sleep. Maybe later."

Poor Nic's voice was smooth and warm. "There is nothing to fear here, Katalina. You have my word. Bobby will be with you at all times. Even in the house—he is right outside the door."

"Yes, Nicholai, thank you. But—"

"Anatoly cannot reach you here, my dear. I assure you he cannot."

"If he know where I am, he reach me."

"No. But only time will convince you." He stood and moved around his desk and sat in the chair beside her. He crossed his legs and folded his arms, bathing her in confidence. "Now, my dear, please tell me what brings you to my home."

Katalina's eyes flushed and the terror made a dark stream down her cheeks. She stared at her hands, her knees, and to the floor. When she looked up and over to Poor Nic, she steeled herself as her chin rose. "Anatoly Nikolaevich Konstantinova. He owns all of us from New York to—"

"Not all of us, Katalina," Poor Nic said with a slight, confident smile. "Anatoly controls all things *Russian*. He is a very dangerous man. But even so, of the things Anatoly is willing to do, entering my home is not one of them. I will protect you."

"Dmitry, he say he will help. He will protect me."

Poor Nic nodded. "Ah, but you do not trust him?"

She shook her head.

"And why is it that you do not, my dear?"

Katalina looked away and her fingers whitened on the chair arms. "I must do things—listen and learn what Anatoly do and say. I must do these things for Dmitry. But I am so fear … afraid. I tell him many things—then, Anatoly, I think he knows."

"I see. You believe Dmitry is working for Anatoly?"

She shrugged.

"What is it you learned, Katalina. What is so important?"

"Nicholai, I know this book." She cleared her throat. "I know Anatoly's people. And I know what book will bring—very bad things."

"Ah, yes, the book."

Katalina leaned over and touched Poor Nic's hands. "Nicholai, for what I know of book, Anatoly and others kill me."

———

"You're sure you are okay?" I asked Angel from across our kitchen table. "I'm so sorry. I usually pick up on things when you're in trouble. I don't know how I missed it."

I was lying of course. Oh, not the part about picking up on Angel being in trouble—that was true enough. Whenever she was in danger, her fear found me and brought me to her. It was weird. Uncanny. Spooky if you pardon the pun. And it never failed before. No, the untrue part was me not knowing why I'd missed her peril this time. It was my philandering with the sexy Bonnie Grecco—as André Cartier of course. After all, I couldn't be getting signals from two women at once, could I?

"Yes, I'm fine. I told you, he never got close to me. Hercule was here." She sat at the table with a Walther .380 semi-automatic on the table between her and Bear. And, after thirty minutes of questions—the same ones over and over—she was more irritated than upset.

"I should have been here sooner, Angel. I'm sorry."

I didn't know what had happened until Bear got the call at Bonnie's place. Then I caught the spirit-train here presto-chan-geo-quick. But I was too late. Whoever had been here was gone. He was brazen, too. He made a move on the house in broad daylight. But brazen was also dumb. His mistake was thinking there was no man around the house. He hadn't counted on Hercule—who was more beast than man but smarter than most men. And braver. And more protective. And he bit harder, too.

"You're a hero again, Hercule," I said to him across the kitchen. "How can I reward you this time? Cookies? A belly rub?"

He flipped his head and tossed his big, red ball across the kitchen where it landed at my feet.

Woof.

Bear looked down at the ball and over at Hercule staring at it. "Jeez, even the dog does it. Can't you get him to stop playing ball with no one?"

Woof. Wag. Woof.

"He wants to play with Tuck," Angel said. "You know he's here, Bear."

"Fine, yeah, okay." Bear changed the subject. "You never saw his face? Any description? Anything at all?"

"No. Nothing." She shook her head. "When Hercule went for him, I ran inside for my gun. When I came out on the porch, Herc had him in the bushes but I couldn't get a good look at him. I called Herc off and he ran."

"Any idea who he was or why he'd be following you around?"

"Following me around?" She cocked her head. "What do you mean? Isn't this just some perv or something?"

"No, I'm afraid not." Bear picked up a large evidence bag from one of the kitchen chairs. In it was a digital camera. He found it lying behind the rocking chair on the sun porch when he arrived.

"Angela, I don't think this was an ordinary peeping-Tom or break-in. I think it's a bigger problem. And since you're keeping secrets these days—"

"I'm not keeping secrets." She pushed back on her chair.

"You never told me why you were at Nic's house this morning. Maybe the two incidents are connected."

"Two incidents? I told you, I went to Nicholas' about the party last night. I'm trying to find out what happened and prove André's innocence."

"This investigation is my job."

I said, "And this changes things how, Bear? You know she's going to play detective."

Angel's face twisted. "I don't play detective. I did pretty well last time."

"And almost got yourself killed." I hate to say it, but she was right. She'd chased down several leads on my murder case which proved invaluable. But I was right, too. The leads almost got her killed. "Angel, you have to be careful. No investigating without Bear or me. Okay?"

"Fine, but you two weren't around." She looked at Bear. "And why do you think they could be connected?"

"Because whoever he is, he's been watching you for days," Bear said, laying the camera on the table. "Including going to and from Nic's house—I looked at the shots on the camera's memory stick. He was outside Nic's and followed you here."

"Why? Why would anyone want to follow me?"

Good question. "I don't know, Angel. But you know what happened the last time someone took a strange interest in you."

"Yes, I do. He killed you."

True enough. Old Ernie came to our house to kill her and retrieve evidence against him. But he screwed up and put a hole in my heart—right down the hall—and ended my life.

"Look." Bear fumbled through the evidence bag with a couple buttons on the rear of the camera—the plastic made manipulating them difficult. He hit the right sequence and the display screen lit up. He showed her the hundreds of digital pictures. "Whoever he is, he's up to more than some perv-shots. I better find him fast."

"Yes, Bear, fast is good." Angel watched the display screen and with each photograph, her face paled more until she turned away. "I don't want to see any more."

The photographs began with shots of our house—early morning and late night when only lights were on in our upstairs bedroom. There were photographs from all angles. Shots of her Explorer coming and going in the driveway, too. The next series was at campus; shots of her parking, walking to and from the car to her office. Shots around campus at lunch, sitting outside the cafeteria with friends and colleagues. There was even a shot of her lecturing—the creep had taken photographs through the door windows in the back of the lecture hall. The worst ones—the ones that unnerved all of us—were a series of her talking to me on campus and in our back yard one night she'd cooked out. Well, not talking to me per se. She was sitting at the picnic table or standing over the grill having an animated conversation with, well, no one. Many were high-speed shots catching the moments very well. Too well. She was a crazy woman—talking and making a point to me with

174

her spatula. Sharing a laugh. Even a warm moment when she sipped some wine.

Anger flooded me. Our property was not unprotected. During my murder investigation, my killer and an assassin found it too easy to enter and make their way around our home. Later, Angel was kidnapped from our house. When the case was closed, Bear upgraded our security—a new alarm system, repairs to the wrought-iron fence around the front and side yards, a higher privacy fence around the rear yard, and reinforced locks on all the doors.

This stalker wasn't deterred by any of those steps. Two things about him scared me—he was stupid and gutsy. He braved our security and ignored Poor Nic's beefy bodyguards. Hercule was nothing compared to them. Yet he took the photographs anyway.

"Bear, this guy's stalking Angel," I said. "He's dangerous. He was trying to get into the house and he knew she was home, too. If not for Hercule, God knows."

Bear grumbled and continued looking at pictures. "There has to be something on this memory stick to ID him. I'll have the techs go through it. Maybe they can find something erased that'll give me a lead."

"Angel," I said, looking at shots of her talking to me outside the Vincent House last night. "You gotta be a little more careful around me. You look a little, well, nuts, babe." She sat behind her steering wheel in a couple telephoto shots, turned facing the passenger seat, talking to no one; talking to me. I had complimented her dress—her black evening dress, my, my—and she was lecturing me on my dinner etiquette.

Now, the photograph made her look like she was lecturing her second grade imaginary playground friend. It was not, to say the least, a flattering shot.

"I see," she said. "I never considered any of this before. I'm used to having you around and forget."

Bear said, "I'll find this guy, Angela. But he's right, you do need to be more careful."

She looked up and smiled, taking Bear's hand on the table. "See, you do hear him. When did you decide to give in and admit it?"

"I admit nothing." The thinnest of smiles tried to hide the lies on his lips.

"Of course not." She looked out the kitchen window at a crime tech packing up his van. "I guess your people are done."

"Yeah, no prints on the glass, nothing. But we have the camera. I'm taking this to the lab myself."

Angel stood and went to the refrigerator and took out the makings for sandwiches. She busied herself at the butcher block across the room. "Do you think there's any danger? I mean, why would someone be following me around?"

It was the million-dollar question.

"I don't know. I'll have someone watching the house and I'll alert campus security. Don't go anywhere without telling me—and pack your Walther. With any luck, we'll have this creep by morning."

"Yeah, by morning," I said as Angel made a sandwich for Bear. "Mustard or mayo, partner?"

"Mayo—Jeez, I did it again."

Angel grinned. "Just give in, Bear. It'll be easier."

"Whatever." He stood up and went to the refrigerator. "Got any beer?"

"Bear? You're on duty," she said. "And it's only one-thirty in the afternoon."

"Is it that late? Maybe I need bourbon."

THIRTY-THREE

Detective Mike Spence sat at his desk with stacks of yellow legal pads in front of him. He was just hanging up his phone when Bear and I walked in. His face brightened—as much as his ever did—and he did the drumroll and cymbals-thing that grown men should never do in public.

"Bear, Cal's doc was on the phone," he said. "Cal had some problems this morning but they've got him stabilized. He'll be laid up longer than they thought, so it's you and me for a couple months."

Bear rolled his eyes. "Terrific."

"Oh come on, Bear," I said, "Mikey isn't so bad. He used to be a real jerk but you and he bonded over my case, remember? And he's been doing all right this time. Cut him some slack."

He grumbled something and found comfort in his office chair.

Spence looked on while he sorted through a stack of folders. "I could use some help with these witness statements. And the coroner called—she confirmed it's a .22 caliber and the gun we found at the Vincent House was the murder weapon."

"What about Clemens' shooting?"

"Same .22 caliber, but the slug was mangled too much for a positive ballistics match with the murder weapon. They found a couple spent shells on the second floor, too, where Cal was hit. No prints."

"Same gun. Has to be." Bear gave Spence a brief overview of Angel's stalking and his run-in with Ruth-Ann Marcos. Then he said, "What'd you find out about Bonnie Grecco? Any word on what the Feds are up to?"

"Nope, nothing. Captain Sutter went nuts when I told her. She's been on the phone with the Commonwealth's Attorney since I got back."

"Great." He shook his head and looked around his desk like something was missing. "Crime Techs are checking the camera for fingerprints and downloading everything onto a drive for us. We gotta nail this perv. Angela's had enough problems."

"Yeah, okay, but with Clemens out, I'm buried." Spence tapped the top of the foot-high stack of yellow legal pads. "I got over two hundred witness statements to go through."

"Did anyone see anything?"

"Nope."

"Does anyone know anything?"

"Not so far."

Bear leaned down on his desk. "Does anyone even know Stephanos Grecco?"

Spence shook his head.

"Then don't waste much time re-reading those statements." Bear picked up his phone, dialed, and spoke with someone. Afterward, he retrieved a cup of coffee from a half-full pot by the doorway, and dropped back into his chair. "I'm putting a uniform on Angela's house. Then I'm going back to the scene to find what we missed."

"Maybe we didn't miss anything."

"We did or we'd have a lead by now."

"I get it that it's Angela and all, but listen—"

"You don't get anything." Bear jabbed a finger at Spence. "We need leads, not talk."

I said, "Whoa there, Bear. Ease up."

Spence stood up and grabbed his jacket from behind his chair. "And I get it you are still wound a little tight since Tuck's murder. But get off my ass, okay? I don't like partnering with you either. And if you haven't noticed, Cal was shot last night. So we're sort of in the same frame of mind."

"No, we're not." Bear dropped his coffee cup on the desk so hard it spilled. "Cal's not dead, Spence. It's not the same."

"He almost was." Spence headed for the door. "When's the last time this county had two cops go down—let alone back-to-back? Cal could have been killed. It could have been you or me, too. Just—"

"He's right, Bear," I said sitting on the corner of his desk, "scary as it sounds. Ease up on him."

Bear stood up and headed for Spence.

"Whoa, partner ... easy."

Just as it looked like Bear was going to knock him on his ass—he'd done it before—he did an incredible thing. He stuck out his hand.

Spence, of course, fearing *deja vu*, ducked and stepped back. When he realized Bear's meaty paw was a peace offering, he stared at it and slinked back to him.

Bear said, "You're right, Spence. I'm sorry. Cal is a good guy. And I know how you feel—I do. I'm just, well—"

"Sorry to interrupt this love-fest, Detectives," a voice said from the doorway, "but we need to talk, Braddock."

FBI Agent Jim Dobron stood in the door—he has a thing about making an entrance and standing in doorways. Maybe he was waiting for trumpets or a drumroll. Or maybe he was a vampire and waiting to be invited in so he could suck the life out of us.

Can a vampire hurt a ghost?

"Who are they going to steal from us?" I had the wrong question. It wasn't "who" but "what."

"I came for the witness statements, evidence, and any guest video you found from last night," Dobron said. "And anything else you got. And I want—"

"You want?" Bear said, as an angry color washed over his face. "I'm lead on the Grecco case."

"Not anymore, Detective." Dobron strode into the room. "I guess you didn't get it earlier. The FBI is taking this case. You're in support—just support. But we're all on the same side."

When the FBI stole your case, they always said, "We're all on the same side." This was true, of course, provided your side was doing all the cop stuff and their side stood in front of microphones taking the credit. Then sure, we're all in it together.

Bear folded his arms and leaned against Spence's desk. "Says who?"

"The Attorney General's office—Ruth-Ann Marcos. But, I don't need anyone's permission. And you know I don't. She's already spoken with your Commonwealth's Attorney. It's settled."

"What does she want with this case? I thought we got all this straightened out last night."

The FBI man cocked his head and removed his round, wire-rimmed glasses. "You thought wrong, Detective. Now, I want a complete inventory of all the evidence you took."

"Hold on. You didn't answer my question. What's Marcos want with a homicide?"

"That's classified." Dobron picked up a stack of witness statement pads from Spence's desk. "I'm taking over. That's all you need to know. So—"

"Based on what—exactly? It's a homicide. Last I checked, the FBI didn't investigate local homicides—"

"We don't. But this isn't a simple homicide you'd be able to handle."

"Screw you," Spence said.

"Why Mikey," I said, "how apropos."

Bear smiled but it didn't last long.

Agent Dobron sifted through files on Spence's desk. "This is a federal racketeering case. We're in. You're out."

"Just like that," Bear said.

"Just like that. Are these all the statements?" Agent Dobron looked at Spence. "Get them boxed up and sent over to my office. We're at the county courthouse."

"Bear?" Spence asked. "You want me to—"

"No, you were on your way to the morgue. Go."

Spence nodded, flashed a big, fake smile at Agent Dobron, and left.

"Detective Braddock, I don't find this amusing," Agent Dobron said. "I want—"

Bear laughed. "It's your case. Box all this up yourself. And carry them to your office yourself. But sign the evidence releases first or you don't get diddly."

Dobron ran his long, slender fingers over his face and thought.

He had an expensive—like the price of a luxury car expensive —gold watch on his wrist. He also had a diamond ring on his pinky finger. How did FBI government guys afford so much bling?

"So, is this the way it's going to be?" Agent Dobron slipped his cell phone out of his suit pocket.

"Yep," I said.

Bear repeated me, adding, "Sign the evidence log and it's yours. But, move it yourselves. We're cops, not bellhops."

"I could have—"

"Yeah, yeah. You could have my badge," Bear said with a snort. "I've heard it all before." Then he went and refilled his coffee cup while Agent Dobron watched him from Spence's desk. "Where is Bonnie Grecco? What are you doing with her?"

"It's classified."

"I saw the movie, too. Try again."

Dobron stared at Bear for a long time. Twice he started to say something, and twice he stayed silent. He retreated to the door- way and spoke on his cell phone, then returned and stood in front of Bear.

"Okay, have it your way, Detective. My men are on their way over. I expect one-hundred percent cooperation."

"With what? I have no idea what is going on, Dobron. You storm into Grecco's house and whisk Bonnie Grecco away. Now, you're storming in here stealing my case. Look, if you want help, a little less storm-troopin' and some manners would go a long way. Until then, I repeat what my esteemed colleague said, 'screw you.'"

"Esteemed colleague?" I said. "Wait until Spence hears about this."

Dobron held up a hand as his eyes read over the evidence list Bear gave him. "Whoa, there. Not so fast. There's a camera listed here you seized today. I wasn't aware. What's this about?"

"Nothing you need," Bear said, returning to his desk chair. "A local matter. I'll take it off the list."

"Answer me, Detective."

Bear hesitated just long enough to send striations of anger raging over Agent Dobron's face. Then, just when I thought Agent Dobron would explode, Bear gave him a thin summary of the incident at Angel's house. He left out the photographs involving Poor Nic. "See, just a local thing."

"Right, a local thing." Agent Dobron eyed him. "All right, Detective, so what are you holding back?"

Bear winked. "Sorry, it's classified."

THIRTY-FOUR

I ARRIVED HOME LATER in the afternoon to find Angel slipping on a spring jacket at our front door. She was on her cell phone but hung up as I popped in.

"We going somewhere? I wanted to talk to you about Poor Nic."

"I have to go over to the Vincent House." She waved her phone in the air. "I've been trying to reach the caterer and can't. We're supposed to meet to go over the bill from last night. I'm running a little late."

"Okay, I'll tag along. So, about Nic—"

She frowned. "Tuck, I went there to see what he knew about Stephanos Grecco. He knew nothing. I also wanted some history on the Vincent House. He had it in his library and he'd find it and send it over. We were discussing the estate when you and Bear showed up."

"Good, I'm interested in what Nic knows about the place. It gives me the creeps. Not just because Vincent is still there either."

"Oh? Ghosts give you the creeps? So, the Vincent House is haunted, right?"

"Sure is. And haunted houses are creepy."

"Our house is haunted."

"Sure, but just by Doc and me. I'm lovable and Doc is well, not so much—but he's quiet and doesn't throw loud parties. Hercule likes him, too." I looked around. "Speaking of Doc, I want to talk to him before I run into Vincent again."

Angel was halfway out the door. "Vincent? What about your new friend, Sassy?"

"Sassy? Oh, her. I can handle her."

"You know, Tuck, it's hard enough understanding *you* being back—but others, too? And some flapper with great legs and boobs—"

"Huh? I never said she was a flapper. But the rest—"

"Watch it. Two can play the same game."

She was right. And she could play a lot easier than me. "You know, Vincent is a little rough around the edges, but his bourbon is good. As long as I can find Benjamin and some book, I think he'll let me come around now and then for a drink."

"Wonderful. Maybe we can double date."

"Hey, I thought the same thing."

She rolled her eyes as Hercule trotted in carrying his leash in his mouth. "No, sorry, boy. You have to stay here and guard the house."

Moan.

Doc walked out of my den. "Oliver, a word please."

When anyone else called me "Oliver" I corrected them—Doc was futile. "I'm heading—"

"To Vincent Calaprese's house. I know. The Vincent House is what I wish to speak with you about."

"Can't it wait until I get back?"

"If it could, I would not be standing here, would I? Use your head, Oliver."

Doc was such a kidder.

"Okay." I turned to Angel. "Go on ahead, I'll catch up."

She dialed her phone again, nodded, and left.

Doc summoned me into the den. "Oliver, I think it's in everyone's best interest—in particular yours—if you did not return there. Ever."

"Ever? Look, if the Vincent House is dangerous, I can't let Angel go alone. Now can I?"

He thought a moment, adjusting the stethoscope around his neck. "You are correct. Don't let her go. It is a dangerous place. I warned you before and you're not listening—as usual. Too much has happened there. And I'm not talking about last night."

Oh? "Then, tell me, Doc."

"I don't wish to."

"I'll ask Sassy—"

"No, I forbid you."

"Forbid me? You tried to forbid me once before. How'd it work for you?"

"Oliver, don't cross me on this." He pointed an aged finger at me and his eyes narrowed like a great-grandfather about to scold me. No, not like—*exactly*. "You listen to me, Oliver. Listen good. Vincent Calaprese is a very dangerous man. He was a thug and a killer back in my day and he is far worse now. Don't let his smiles and pleasantries fool you. If he contacts you, it isn't to share his liquor and Sancho Panza's—"

"Those were Cuban cigars? I could get used to those. Although I don't smoke. But—"

"Dear God, focus, Oliver. Focus." He rolled his eyes. "If he contacts you it's because he wants something. And he won't take 'no' for an answer. He's dangerous, even to us. Stay away from him."

Doc never acted like this before and it bothered me. Oh, he'd warned me about things here and there—like not focusing and using my spirit-tricks too much—but he had never been so agitated and ornery. And never, in the months I'd known him, had he ever wanted me to hide from anything.

"Look, Doc, you gotta tell me what you're worried about. Tell me what's going on. What has your stethoscope all twisted?"

"You, Oliver. You're too impetuous and you don't listen."

"Other than the obvious?"

"You failed the last time I warned you, remember? Think of your failures when you went about investigating your own murder."

He was referring to the time I figured out a way to do battle with an assassin trying to kill Angel. I overdid it a little—well, a lot—and disappeared for days. It sucked the energy and spirit right out of me. Almost killed me for good. I didn't know it, of course, but he did. It was just one of those things, like parachuting out of your window with a bed sheet or a teenage drinking game gone bad. Okay, maybe worse.

"Hey, lighten up, Doc. Just tell me the truth."

Doc thrust his scalpel-finger into my chest and it hurt. "Oliver, I told you. Vincent Calaprese was a dangerous man and is an even more dangerous spirit. We cannot afford to cross him and we can less afford to help him."

"You've already given me the hokey 'he's a dangerous man and ghost' speech. You sound afraid of him."

"Yes, afraid." Doc's image was losing focus and fading into nothing. "And Oliver, one more thing. It's the most important thing, too."

I thought everything he said was the most important thing. "What?"

"The book, Oliver." Doc was just a voice. "We have to protect the book."

THIRTY-FIVE

"WHAT BOOK, TUCK?" ANGEL asked, driving across town to the Vincent House. "What's Doc talking about?"

"I don't know. Vincent told me to find Benjamin and something about a book. Maybe it's a cookbook. I don't know."

"A cookbook?" Angel's words dripped with sarcasm. "A dead mobster comes back to haunt you over a cookbook?"

Well, it didn't sound so stupid when I said it.

We arrived at the Vincent House just as the sheriff's crime scene van pulled out. There was one remaining sheriff's deputy standing on the front veranda and no other police cruisers or officers anywhere in sight.

The deputy stopped her at the front door. "Sorry, Professor Tucker, no one goes in anymore without an escort. Captain Sutter's orders."

"All right, I understand. Has the caterer, Petya Chernyshov, been by yet? He's supposed to meet me."

The deputy looked over a list on a clipboard. "No, ma'am. Detective Spence was by earlier, and the crime techs just left. Everyone else left about lunch time. Sorry."

Angel returned to the car. "Petya said he'd meet me here. He was returning two hours ago to check the clean-up." She pulled out her cell phone and dialed. It rang several times and went to voicemail. "He's still not answering."

"You keep trying, Angel," I said. "I'm going inside to take a look around."

"Okay, I'll see you later. I'm going to the office to check some work and then home. I didn't get much done yesterday with the gala, so I want to catch up today."

"You're leaving me?"

"It's not like you have to walk home."

"True."

I walked past the deputy on the veranda—he, of course, never noticed me—and went in search of the delectable Sassy and her menacing companion, Vincent Calaprese.

I knew they were around when Billie Holiday's *Blue Moon* began playing in the foyer. Visiting Vincent and Sassy was not only educational, it was a great tour of swing and big band tunes, too. Oh, and the bourbon was worth tiptoeing around Vincent's wrath.

Vincent stood on the second floor landing looking down at me. He had a wide smile and smoked a cigar—a Sancho Panza if Doc knew him at all.

"Oliver, I trust you've brought me good news."

"Ah, no, sorry, Vincent." Bad news to a gangster wasn't the way to start a conversation. "How about a drink? We can talk."

"Ah, yes, of course." Vincent descended the stairs and led me into the lounge. "But, not too much. It isn't good for you."

"What's it going to do, kill me?"

He slapped me on the back. "You have a sense of humor. Good. Now, tell me about Benjamin."

I waited for him to pour two drinks, raised mine in customary salute, and took a long sip. "Nothing to tell, I'm afraid. I don't know who he is. Tell me more about him and about this book you want. And most important of all, tell me why you're talking to me."

"Certainly you know by now you're unique?" He drained his glass in one gulp. "Not all of us can do what you do—work with the living. Most are, well, not able. If we were, things would be very different. Tell me about Benjamin."

"I told you, I have no idea who he is. I'm not fibbing either."

Vincent poured himself another drink and leaned on the bar facing me. His face was dark and brooding—not unusual for a mean-hearted spirit I'm sure. "Do not toy with me, Oliver."

"I'm not. But if you know where he is and how I can find him, tell me."

Vincent stared at me. "You know, today is not so different than my day—1939, I mean. You got the good guys and the bad guys and some of the bad guys are good. You understand?"

"No."

"Sure you do." He refilled our glasses. "I can be a good guy, Oliver. Or I can be a real, real, bad guy—like the old days. Play your games if you must."

"I'm not playing anything, Vincent. I don't know Benjamin."

His eyes narrowed on me. "Here's the way things are—you bring me Benjamin and the book or I'll put the hurt on your long-legged beauty at home."

I stood up and pushed my glass across the bar. "Don't threaten me, Vincent. And don't threaten Angel. She's not involved in this."

"Of course she is."

"No, she's not." I slammed a hand on the bar and it only made him laugh. "Tell me where to find Benjamin and this book—give me something to go on—and I'll do what I can. But don't—don't ever—threaten her again."

He laughed again, this time, letting a good belly laugh taunt me. When he was through, he leaned forward and shot a bullet-finger at me. "No, *you* listen, Oliver. You may have been a hotshot copper once, but not no more. In this world—our world—you're nothin'. You're just a smart-ass rookie who doesn't know the score."

"How do you say, 'screw you' in 1939?"

"See, a real wise guy." Vincent yanked his .45 semi-automatic from beneath his jacket and jammed it into my face. "The book is mine. It is, shall we say, insurance. The book has the key to my enemies in DC. They were a bad bunch, them commie-bastards. A bad bunch. I want it back."

"Commies? As in Russians?"

"Yeah, damn Ruskies." He prodded me with his gun again. "And somebody whacked me for it. I want it back before it falls into the wrong hands again. See, Oliver, times change and the date changes, but people don't change. And families get bigger and stronger. Mine and theirs, too. You gotta find the book before the wrong family gets their hands on it. I gotta have it."

"Why? What could be so important in a seventy-five year old book?"

"Because there's more at stake than you know. Them commie-bastards are making a move nobody is gonna see coming. What they started back then is about to pay off in a big way soon. And I gotta stop it."

"And Benjamin?"

He looked at me eye-to-eye and tucked his .45 back into his shoulder holster, patting his jacket over it. "Benjamin owes me, big time—Benjamin tried to steal my girl."

"And you want him to pay after all these years?"

"No." He puffed on his big Cuban. "He already paid. No, Oliver, he knows about the book. And I know all about him. Benjamin is the key to finding the book and stopping them commie-bastards."

Holy Joe McCarthy. "You do know we won the war, right?"

"Did we? Or did things just change?"

Good point. But he missed mine. "You're talking about communists and whacking people seventy-five years ago—this is 2014. I don't see the—"

"You will. Benjamin can explain it all. Bring him, Oliver. Bring him soon before things go too far—for them commies and for your gal. Don't make me hurt you, Oliver. I like you. But if you fail me, I will hurt you bad."

His eyes watched me like a hawk about to swoop down for the kill—distant, but cunning and all-seeing. Vincent Calaprese, of the New Jersey Calapreses, wasn't fooling around.

"Okay, Vincent. You win. If the commies are involved, I'm in. After all, I'm a red-blooded American. But you leave my Angel

194

alone or I'll find the book and you'll never get it. So, how can I find Benjamin?"

He blew a cloud of Cuban smoke into my face and drowned the cigar in my drink. "His name is Benjamin Gillen Tucker."

What? No way...

"You call him 'Doc Gilley.'"

THIRTY-SIX

"And you're involved with a murderer." W. Simon Hahn—
"W" for worm—stood in Angel's university office, in front of her
desk, shaking his finger at her like a student caught cheating on a
test. "It's been bad enough you've developed a reputation—"

"A reputation?" Angel's voice rose in both octave and volume.
"What does that mean?"

I walked in just in time for the "involved with a murderer" comment. "Angel, are you cavorting behind my back? You're not moonlighting at the bingo games again, are you?"

"No." She flashed me a look.

It was ill-timed and all my fault.

"See what I mean, Angela?" Professor Hahn's eyebrows raised
as he followed Angel's gaze to me—where he saw and heard nothing. "There have been rumors and gossip about you for months.
And I'm afraid to say it's reached the Board of Trustees, too."

I said, "Toss this weasel out, Angel. You don't need this crap. He's talking about André and me and—"

"Oh, the board has heard, has it?" Angel walked around her desk and confronted Professor Hahn as he took a "polite" step back from her. "What have you told them, Simon?"

"Me? What makes you think it was me?"

"Because I've heard rumors and gossip, too. You want Ernie's Department Chair and you don't like the fact I'm in it."

He lifted a finger in the air. "Ah, yes, but only on a temporary basis until the board decides on a permanent hire. There are several in the running."

"Yes, perhaps. But we both know it's down to you and me." Angel examined him with x-ray eyes. "What did you tell them?"

"I told them nothing. However, I do understand they have heard you have been observed talking to yourself repeatedly. They also heard about you taking your lunches alone in your office and having lively conversations—with no one. And—"

"They heard or you told them?"

This was my fault. "Angel, it's because of me. I won't come to the campus anymore, promise. I'll hang with Bear and ruin his career instead."

Angel looked down and returned to her chair behind her desk. "Did you ever consider I am still grieving? I do talk to myself—to my husband, too, sometimes. It's normal and its therapeutic. Simon, you must understand?"

"Yes, yes, of course I do." Simon's mouth said the words but his beady little eyes were lying. "It's the board, Angela. And this position is too important. Perhaps you should take some time off."

"I am fine, Simon. The job isn't a problem. My life is getting back to normal and the department is in fine shape." Angel sat down. "But if you have other opinions, I'd be interested to hear them."

He had one and it was a spear to her back. "Your gala was a disaster. You lost a quarter-million dollars in donations. And your friend the Mafia Don was present. And the murder! What do you think the board will say?"

As serious as Professor Hahn was, I couldn't help but laugh. "Okay, Angel. Turn on your desk lamp and let me juice up a little. I'm going to introduce myself to him. He deserves it. Quick."

"No," she said, throwing another look at me. Then, when he followed her eyes, she looked over at him and let a thin, sarcastic smile escape. "What's the matter, Simon, you think my husband is here? If he is, he's upset with you for stirring up trouble."

"Why, no." He looked to his right at the corner of desk, then looked to his left. "Of course not."

I blew in his ear and flicked his lobe, making him grab it as he tensed to pucker-factor nine.

His voice cracked when he said, "But the board—"

"No, Simon, the board will understand. There's some cash still missing but I'm not concerned. The majority of the donations were checks. The guests—I've spoken to all of them—are more than generous and understanding. They have all committed to replacing them."

"I see. And what of the Mafia—"

Angel laughed—I would have slugged him, but she always was the reasonable one of the family. "Nicholas Bartalotta has contributed a great deal to this university. He has granted the university annual scholarship funding and provided numerous jobs for student work programs."

Professor Hahn straightened and folded his arms. "Oh? I did not know. You should have informed me—"

"It's in the minutes of the last staff meeting—you weren't there. In fact, you've missed the last several." Angel leaned back in her chair and watched the redness tie-dye his face. "Perhaps you should go to the board with your complaints about Nicholas. They'll be interested to speak with you. After all, I had lunch with Nicholas and the Dean earlier this week to discuss his job initiatives and financial contributions. And he has insisted on covering the missing cash from the theft should the police not recover it."

"I see." Professor Hahn looked down and contemplated her desk clock. Then he lifted his chin up and took another swing. "And the complaints? The murder?"

I said, "He just won't stop, will he?"

"You cannot think I had anything to do with all this? And I assure you, neither did André Cartier. His credentials are above reproach."

"If they were, he wouldn't have been arrested."

Angel's face darkened and her lips lost their color. "What do you want, Simon?"

"Let me be clear." He cleared his throat and looked at her eye-to-eye. "I've received complaints on your performance at the gala. Several of them—the things people saw are disturbing." He folded his arms with a thin, "gotcha" smile. "I have no choice but to—"

"Good," she said, taking her cell phone from her purse. "I'll call Detective Braddock. You can provide the names and information to him. No one came forward at the crime scene, and since they confided in you, he'll want to speak with them again—he'll be sure to mention you provided their names."

Professor Hahn's smile evaporated and I could hear his ass snapping closed like a clam under attack. "What? No. They spoke to me in confidence. I cannot disclose their information."

I said, "Do you know what obstruction of justice is, asshole?"

Angel repeated me word-for-word, adding, "And falsifying information is, too. Let's ask Detective Braddock—"

"No, no, wait." He held up his hands in surrender. "W" was for "withdraw." "Perhaps I've exaggerated a bit. I'm upset. Please, Angela, forgive me. I'm—"

"What?" she demanded. "What is it, Simon? You're being very difficult."

His face dropped. "I'm worried about you. Really I am. I know you're grieving for Oliver."

"My friends call me Tuck," I said, reaching down and taking hold of Angel's cell phone for a little electric pick-me-up. "You can call me Detective Tucker. Or sir. Yeah, I like sir."

Angel smiled.

"Angela, I am worried for your health. You should take some time off and leave the department to me for a short time. I'm sure the board can postpone the decision a few months. Take the time you need and when you're ready—"

"No need for me to take time off. I am ready, Simon. I'm as ready as I can be." She waved him toward her office door. "And if you don't mind, I have work to catch up on."

He tried to smile but only formed a feeble-looking grin. Maybe it was his best work. "All right, Angela. But you will call with any news on the gala or if you just want to talk, right?"

"Of course I will, Simon."

"When she's ice skating in hell." I couldn't resist.

W. Simon Hahn went the door and hesitated, looking like he was about to return for more ass-whooping. I beat him there and grabbed hold of the door handle. I was still tingling from Angel's cell phone and it gave me a little "oomph." As he tried to open the door, I held it tight. He couldn't budge it.

He tried it again. Nothing.

When he stepped aside and looked at Angel, I swung the door open. It startled him and he jumped. But as he reached for it again, I slammed it closed and flicked his ear.

"There, asshole, explain that to the board."

He wouldn't, of course, because he might have to explain the stain I swear formed in his pants when he left.

"W" was for wussy-boy.

THIRTY-SEVEN

AFTER PROFESSOR HAHN LEFT, Angel and I went home. I didn't tell her about my encounter with Vincent earlier. Instead, I lied and told her I hadn't found him. She had enough on her mind without wondering why he was threatening her—on top of some nut-case stalking her. I wanted to get things square with Doc first. That was impossible as Doc must have taken a vacation and disappeared for a while.

It bothered me that Doc lied. I asked him point-blank about Benjamin. Why didn't he tell me it was him? What was he hiding? And why hide it from me?

I pondered this and many mysteries of the universe—not really—until Bear arrived a little after six in the evening. He wandered in, relaxed onto our couch like he owned the place, and laid back to take a nap.

Before my death, he was my partner and best friend—more than a guest in our home. Since then, he had become a more permanent fixture. While it wasn't until today he admitted I was still around, he had been a rock for Angel for all facets of life without me.

Angel came in from the kitchen and handed him two-fingers of my best bourbon. She slipped into the over-sized chair opposite him and curled up. "Any luck, Bear? Did you find anything on Bonnie or Stephanos?"

"Not a darn thing." He drained half the glass. "The FBI is blocking me every step of the way. They took the case away from me."

"Can they do that?"

"They can and they did." Another glug of bourbon. "But the stolen donations and your stalker are still my cases—and I'll use them to my advantage. I'm meeting Spence over at the Vincent place in a little while. We're going to stake the place out."

"What for?"

He winked. "Coincidences."

"I thought you didn't believe in them."

I said, "He doesn't, Angel. That's the point."

Bear emptied his glass and went to the bottle on the fireplace mantel and refilled it. "The money was stolen and there's another body out there somewhere, too."

"The one Tuck saw?" she asked, gesturing at me sitting in the leather recliner beside her. "The one he says he killed—or, well, was inside someone and killed him?"

"The word is 'possessed,' dear," I said. We both love old horror movies and spook flicks. Our favorites are those when the devil and evil spirits possess people and run amuck. Now, it's not quite as fun. "You can say it."

"Yeah, possessed." Bear followed her gaze to my leather chair, tipped his glass toward me, and took a sip. "Whoever has the house wired up left a lot of weird surveillance gear in the attic. And the same someone is following you around—one plus one is two. They have to be connected."

"You're sure?"

"Yes. Some of those photos of you were at the Vincent House. And they could be the key to this case." He sat back down. "Someone had the entire house under video cameras. Our techies haven't found any recordings yet so whoever did it must have them. They might have the killer on the recordings—or—"

"He's the killer," I said. "Even odds."

Angel nodded. "Who do you think the killer is? That man stalking me?"

"I'm not sure—but he's dangerous."

"How do you catch him? Your stakeout?"

"Yes, we wait at the Vincent House. He's bound to come back for his equipment. It's too expensive to leave behind. We didn't report any of that in today's paper and didn't tell anyone else—not even the FBI or any of the guests. He hid the stuff well so I'm hoping he thinks we haven't found it. With any luck, he'll come back to get it and we'll have him."

"What about the body I saw?" I said. "What about Kravitz and Jorge?"

"I don't think there is a Stanley Kravitz." He looked at my leather chair. "I don't think there's a Jorge-the-waiter either. I think it's all just one guy—your stalker. He might be our killer, too."

Even I didn't connect those dots.

Angel eyed him. "Why do you think he's the killer?"

"There's no record of a Stanley Kravitz in this county or the surrounding counties. Petya Chernyshov is cooking his books. He's using addresses and fake names to bolster his employee roles for his boss. Then, he pays the bogus wages and pockets the money himself. When he needs the extra hands, like last night, he hires some hourly stiff to work for cut wages. He makes out all the way around."

Clever. "And how did you come to this conclusion, Bear?"

"Well first, today the old lady and building manager never saw Kravitz—they get mail and all, but he's fictitious. Then I checked the roster of employees and surprise—a dozen fake names and socials—but they're cashing checks every two weeks. It's got to be Chernyshov. I'm going to bring him in tomorrow and find out."

Angel asked, "Okay, so how does it all fit in with my stalker and Grecco's murderer?"

I knew the answer. "Whoever Jorge was last night is the wild card. He must have figured a way to work for the caterer to get close to Grecco. He's a surveillance-wiz, I'm betting. He's the only one unaccounted for. And it makes sense he is your stalker, too, since the chances of two surveillance wizzes at the same time doesn't add up."

Bear nodded. "Tuck's right—as tough as it is to say, I mean, to have this conversation with him."

Angel stood up and went to look out the window. "Bear, why me? Why would Grecco's killer be stalking me, too?"

"Maybe because you're the only one at the party who knew him at all before the party. Maybe because you've got something he wants. Maybe something else."

"And André?" She didn't turn around. "If you think this Jorge or Kravitz or whomever killed Grecco, why is André still in jail?"

"He's not." Bear stood up and placed his glass on the coffee table in front of him. "The Circuit Judge released him after lunch. Ruth-Ann Marcos pulled some strings and got André out on his own recognizance. She's really sticking her neck out on this."

She sighed. "Thank God she is. I don't know how anyone could even think André could be involved with any of this. What would be his motive?"

Uh, oh—can a gentleman kiss and tell when it's a murder case?

"Angel, perhaps there's something I should tell you both."

She looked at me. "What is it, Tuck?"

Here goes. "André knew Bonnie Grecco better than you think— much better." I told them about my little escapade with André Cartier and Bonnie. I left out the juicy parts and sort-of let them think it was all innocent and nice-nice. I ended with, "He's been having an affair with her, Angel. I wouldn't believe it if I hadn't, um, seen it first hand—very first hand. Anyway, during one of their trysts, she told him about her husband."

"André had an affair with her?" Angel's eyes closed. "I can't believe it."

Bear said, "Yeah, I know. And, that makes things worse. He's been lying to us. And if Stephanos found out, maybe the shot was meant for her. Witnesses said a second before Stephanos was hit, Bonnie was standing in the same spot—or pretty close to the spot—on the dance floor. So were you, Angela."

"And, Bonnie got those threatening letters." I said. "Maybe she's broken other hearts before."

"We can't confirm the letters." Bear stared at the floor. "No one seems to know Stephanos or Bonnie. And if they don't know them, how could they know they were going to the gala last night?"

"Someone's lying. Maybe André." Angel's voice was a whisper. "Oh, God, he lied about the affair. It's going to look like André wanted Stephanos out of the way. This looks like—"

"Bad news," Bear said, reaching for his bourbon. "André Cartier has the oldest motive in the world for murder."

THIRTY-EIGHT

BEAR LEFT TO MEET Spence for their stakeout of the Vincent House and Angel disappeared upstairs. I went in search of Doc again, hoping to have a few quiet words about Benjamin and this mysterious book.

"Doc? Come on, quit hiding. Come out and talk to me." He was starting to irritate me. "You're acting like a baby."

Nothing.

"Doc?" I wandered the house for ten minutes and he was nowhere. Of course, for the ghost of a surgeon long dead, nowhere could be anywhere—or really *nowhere*. He could also be walking behind me and I wouldn't know. I relied on Hercule to warn me if he was. Hercule followed me on my first patrol around the house. Halfway through the second, he disappeared and I found him in my den napping.

"You avoiding me, Doc?"

Angel returned from upstairs. "Who is avoiding you? Hercule?"

"No. Doc." I told her about my meeting with Vincent.

"He wants Doc?" she said. "What did he do to Vincent?"

"I don't know, Angel. I want to hear from Doc. He knows all about the book, too. Doc's involved up to his stethoscope with Vincent Calaprese of the New Jersey Calapreses."

"Maybe it's not just about Doc, but the Vincent House, too." Angel went into the kitchen and returned with two large photo album books and several long, rolled-up documents. "Nicholas' driver, Bobby, dropped these off earlier."

"Did you offer him tea or a safe to crack?" She ignored me so I asked, "What are they?"

"Something that might help."

She unrolled one of the documents and spread it out open on my desk, using items on my desk to hold down the corners. They were architectural drawings of a huge building and three surrounding structures. The building plans were old and worn and the legends faded and hard to read. But I didn't have to read them. I knew what the plans were on sight.

The Vincent House estate.

"Nicholas told me the estate was built back in the late 1800s." Angel turned on the desk lamp to brighten the faded plans. "When the Calaprese families moved in and took over the block, they did a significant amount of renovations."

"They bought the entire block?"

"Most of it." She opened one of the large photo albums and flipped to some early twentieth-century photographs. "Remember, it's in the old section of town. Those are antebellum homes with large lots. There used to be a narrow street running between

209

them, but it was lost when the properties were combined into one large estate compound."

"Did Nic say why they combined them?"

"Yes, he had some ideas. They purchased two properties and combined them into the one main estate called the Vincent House. The property spans about a half block. They also purchased two other homes beside it to take up the majority of the remaining block."

One of the photographs was a map of the area on which someone had sketched the placement of the Calaprese properties. There was the main Vincent House on the west side of the estate, a carriage house just to the east of it, and two other large homes farther east of the carriage house along the eastern-most estate wall. The culmination of the properties formed a virtual fortress.

"The properties are surrounded by stone walls and iron fences. It's a fort."

"It was all about business." She tapped her finger on the second photo album and opened it to a page she had bookmarked. It was a family photograph from 1933. There were at least twenty family members all standing around the Vincent House's front veranda. The women wore long, elegant dresses and hats. The men were in expensive, wide-lapelled suits and fedoras. At least ten children knelt in the front row. Everyone was centered around one man sitting in a tall-back chair in the center of the veranda.

Vincent Calaprese.

"Where did Poor Nic get these, Angel?"

She shrugged. "They've been in his library for years—passed down by family. He never explained."

"So, this was their mob-vacation home," I said. "Nifty."

"Well, not a vacation home, although Vincent's family came here a few weeks a year. It became the Calaprese's main headquarters. It was out of the way but still not too far from DC. A good, rural area where they could be safe and away from the city. Nicholas told me Vincent would bring his family here a few times a year by hiring two entire Pullman cars from the railroad—one for his family and one for his men."

I studied the photograph. "Nice, if you go in for goons and guns."

"Yes, a very safe hideout." She ran her finger over the plans. "The families lived in two of the homes, Vincent and his gang used the others. When the families weren't around, they used the homes as a retreat for other mobsters."

"Club Thug? I bet the towels and bathroom soap were stolen."

"And it didn't come cheap. He charged big money for a night at his estate. Big money—and the guests paid. Nicholas said it was a very profitable operation."

Vincent didn't look like the bed and breakfast kind of guy to me. "What else did Poor Nic tell you? There has to be more."

She pointed to sections of the building plans where parts of the floor plan were void of details or architectural annotations. "See here, where there are no draftsman's marks?"

"Yes, so?"

"Nicholas says the missing information is on purpose. Vincent renovated the homes like speakeasies and didn't annotate any of the changes. He obtained the original blueprints and changed them to hide the details."

"Speakeasies? Like the secret bars and joints from the roaring twenties?" I knew Vincent had some class. "I like it. We should do that here."

She rolled her eyes—she must have dust in them. "Yes, hidden entrances, secret escape routes, hidden rooms. All of those." She slid another drawing out. "The local police and FBI often watched the property. When they raided the houses—and that was rare—they were never able to find anyone they were looking for."

Disappearing gangsters right out from under the copper's noses? Hmmm, sounds familiar—like Stephanos Grecco's murder.

I looked over the building plans again one-by-one. The drawings of the attic and basement levels were similar to the other floors—the standard draftsman annotations for plugs and wiring and even the doors and windows I knew to be there were missing. In fact, other than the outline of the rooms, there were no other architectural annotations recorded. The last document was a county planning map of the entire estate.

"Angel, who owns all the other parts of the properties today? I mean, your historical foundation bought just the Vincent House, right?"

She nodded. "Yes. The carriage house and the other two connecting properties are still held in trust."

"The Calaprese family trust?"

"Yes, and the trust is under the control of the elderly matriarch of the family, Frannie—as in Francesca Calaprese-Masseria. She lives outside Charlottesville in a retirement community. I met with her over the sale of Vincent estate grounds and to purchase many of the original antiques for the home."

"Antiques?"

"The house had sat empty for a very long time. She was in the process of selling off the antiques and valuables when I approached her for the Foundation. She'd had some trouble on the grounds—"

That sounded interesting. "What kind of trouble?"

"Vandalism and some break-ins," Angel said. "A few months back, she had several break-ins. The last one was terrible, someone smashed antique furniture, broke up the hardwood paneling in two of the rooms, and slashed the backs of three portraits hanging in the dining room. When I heard about it, I arranged for private security until we could complete the transfer to the Foundation."

Vandalism? Break-ins? Someone was looking for something. "All this started around the time you were buying the estate? You stirred something up."

"Like what? You can't think my Foundation's interest in the Vincent House caused Grecco's murder."

Maybe yes. Maybe no. "I think we may have to go see Frannie. But we better check with Bear first. There's something about the Vincent House that's about more than just Grecco's murder and your missing money. Vincent Calaprese is all fired-up and someone is vandalizing his home. Then, there's a murder in it. Too coincidental."

"You think it's about the house?"

Was it? "Well, every gangster movie I ever liked had some hideout where the bad guys hid loot and secrets. And every ghost movie I ever saw had a haunted house with some secrets. This case has both."

"Okay, Tuck, gangsters and haunted houses." She rolled her eyes. "Just remember, you live here. And there's no hidden treasure or secrets here."

"How do you know?"

"Your imagination is getting carried away." She opened one of the photo albums and began flipping through the pages. "And don't get me started on Doc."

I looked over her shoulder. "And Poor Nic had these lying around for no reason?"

"Yes, he said as much."

"He's lying."

She shook her head. "Why do you say that?"

"Because he said they were just lying around for no reason."

She shrugged.

In several old, scratchy black-and-white photographs, dozens of workers were posing with pickaxes and shovels. In one shot, a large, early-model bulldozer was parked beyond the estate wall almost out of camera shot.

"What kind of renovation requires so much digging and heavy equipment? The property didn't have a swimming pool and didn't add any buildings, right?"

She studied a few photographs. "None I know of. What are you thinking?"

"Look at all these workers and the layout of the properties." I tapped the drawing which showed the positions of the Vincent House and the surrounding properties. "You don't need a lot of manpower like this to do normal renovations. And back then, using a bulldozer was still very new—and expensive."

"Maybe you're right."

"Poor Nic said they renovated it like a speakeasy, right? Maybe they were putting in escape tunnels. You know, in case any G-men came-a-knocking, they could scram."

"G-men? Scram?" She flipped the page. "You sound like Elliot Ness."

"No, not quite, Angel—Elliot Ness was after bootleggers." I looked down at another hazy photograph of construction around the Vincent House. "Vincent says it's all about the Ruskie spies."

THIRTY-NINE

"Are you sure this is a good idea?" I wasn't. But then again, Angel didn't ask me. She just packed up a small knapsack, grabbed the building plans for the Vincent House, and headed for her Explorer with Hercule trotting behind. "Shouldn't you at least call Bear, Angel?"

"No." She opened the rear door and waved Hercule into the seat. "He'll just tell me to wait until tomorrow."

"It's almost ten at night. Bear's on a stakeout with Spence at the Vincent House already. You need to call him. You can't go blundering into his stakeout."

"I'll call when we get there." She started the engine and I popped into the passenger's seat. Hercule was in the back. "Besides, we're not going to the Vincent House. We're going to the other homes on the estate to look around. If we find anything, I'll call him. Okay?"

"No."

"You've turned into such a worrywart since you died."

"Do you know how ridiculous you sound?"

Woof.

"See, even Hercule agrees with me," I said. "He thinks you should call Bear."

She huffed and hit a speed dial number on her phone. She waited about three seconds and ended the call. "He's not answering."

I wondered if she called his speed dial or my old phone in our kitchen drawer. "Okay, but I'm going to find him when we get there. You know, because I'm dead. Not because it's the smart thing to do."

A half block from the Vincent House estate, Angel pulled up to the curb beneath some monstrous oak trees. If I recalled the building plans, we were outside the estates' second home on the southeast corner.

"All right, Angel. Now what?"

She gathered up her knapsack and the plans. "No one has lived in these homes for decades. Let's go exploring."

"Go where ... wait, look." Someone emerged from the darkness a hundred yards ahead walking toward us along the sidewalk. "Maybe it's Bear."

"He's too thin to be Bear," she said. Then, her face flashed surprise. "I don't believe it."

André Cartier crossed the street twenty yards ahead of us. Angel rolled down her window and called out. "André, what are you doing here?"

For a moment, he froze and stared back. He looked behind him down the block and then jogged over to us, stopping at the passenger's side door where Angel rolled the window down.

"Angela," he said out of breath. "Thank God I found you."

"Found me?"

"Yes, of course." He opened the passenger's door and slid in. I vamoosed to the back seat with Hercule. I liked André, but not so much I'd let him sit on me. "I've been looking for you."

"I thought you'd be home in DC. Bear told me you were released today."

"Yes, thank God. I don't know what Bear was thinking—"

"What Bear was thinking? Are you kidding me?" Angel jabbed at him with an accusatory finger. "What have you been thinking? My God, André, you're having an affair with Bonnie Grecco. And you lied to us."

"Yeah, André," I said, leaning over the seat. "And she's not even half your age. Any other time, I'd congratulate you. But murder sort of rules out a slap on the back."

"Angela, listen to me—"

"You lied to us, André." Angel's voice was curt—part anger and part hurt. "You told us you met Bonnie the night of the gala. Now, you're a murder suspect. I think I have an explanation coming, don't you?"

"I didn't lie to you, Angela. Not really." André's face was sad. His eyes showed pain. "I hadn't met Bonnie Grecco before the gala. She told me her name was Bonnie Chase. So, I wasn't lying—"

"Semantics? Come on, André, do you hear yourself? You're having an affair with her—Bonnie Grecco or Bonnie Chase, it's the same person."

"But I didn't know." He looked up at the car roof and closed his eyes. Then, with slow, deliberate effort, he turned in the seat to face Angel. "It wasn't an affair, Angela. Not the way you think."

"Oh? Either you're sleeping with a married woman half your age or you aren't."

"No, no, you don't understand. I was dating her over a month before I learned she was married—I swear to you. So, what was I to do?"

Angel didn't have to think. "End it."

"I tried, but—"

"But what?"

His face fell with the weight of embarrassment and defeat and I wasn't sure which was more painful to watch.

"I was in love with her, Angela. I tried to end it, but I couldn't." He reached across the seat and tried to take Angel's hand but she withdrew it. "Angela, please. Listen to me. There's more—something I cannot tell you—not yet. You just have to believe in me. I'm involved here, yes, but I didn't kill Stephanos. Please. Give me time to prove it to you."

There's something he can't tell us? "Angel, what's he holding back?"

She asked him.

"I can't say anymore. Please, just trust me."

"Trust you? You refuse to explain yourself and you want me to trust you?"

I said, "Angel, I'm pretty sure Bonnie lied to him about Stephanos at first. We'd just gotten out of bed and I remember the look he had when she told him she was married."

"Excuse me?" Angel ignored André and snapped her head at me. "Just gotten out of bed?"

Oops.

"Angela? You're not talking to him again, are you? Please, I don't have the patience for your silliness right now."

André was not a believer.

"All right, André, then tell me what is going on. Start with what you're doing here."

"I came looking for you." His face lightened—no doubt thankful to be off his affair with Bonnie Grecco. "I wanted to clear the air with you before I returned to DC. I'm headed home tonight and I had to speak with you. I knew you'd be worried."

"I am worried, André." She threw a death-ray into the rearview mirror and turned to him. "And you thought to look for me here?"

"Yes, I saw you drive away from home and I followed you here. I parked around the block."

I said, "Around the block?"

"Why around the block?" Angel pressed. "No matter. You found me."

His eyes dropped. "Does my sleeping with Bonnie change your opinion of me? Do you think me a murderer, too?"

"I don't know what to think." She held his eyes for a long time—hard and angry static crackled between them and no words were needed. When he looked away, she breathed a heavy sigh, reached out, and took his hand. "No, no, of course I don't think you killed Stephanos. But you should have told us—Bear and me—about Bonnie. It makes you look guilty. You're in love with a much younger woman and her very rich older husband is murdered."

"I would have told you if I thought Stephanos was the target. Angela, I'm certain the bullet was meant for Bonnie."

"Maybe it was. Although Bear never found the threatening letters. The shooter could have been aiming for her on the dance floor."

He shook his head. "My God. You know, after she confided in me about Stephanos—telling me she was married—she told me about the letters. She said Stephanos was handling it and she wanted me to stay out of it. She was afraid if the police got involved, we'd be found out, too."

I asked, "Was she going to leave Stephanos for you, André?" Angel asked him.

"We hadn't thought that far ahead." He shrugged. "There was something else going on with them—something bad. At first, I thought she married him for his money and it bothered me. But after I got to know her, I found out the truth—and money wasn't important anymore."

"How do you know? You've got money, and she moved onto you pretty quick, too," Angel said in a dry voice. "I like Bonnie. I do. But if she played you for a month, maybe she was trying to lure you in with more lies."

"No," he turned and looked out the window. "I don't believe she did or would. What happened between us was not our fault. We met at a fundraiser and hit it off. She was very interested in charity work and history—just as I am. I told her about you and your work at the University. One thing led to another and she asked for my help in finding historical pieces for herself. It was very accidental."

Angel looked at him and I could see the sympathy softening her face. "All right, André, all right. What about—"

"Ask him what historical pieces she was interested in, Angel." I had a hunch. "Ask him if it was a book."

She did and his answer sent jagged fingernails screeching down the blackboard.

"Yes, she wanted books—but most collectors do. I located several other items—some paintings and portraits—even some old county photographs. But it was the books she wanted most. Why, is someone else interested in the gangster's old books?"

Oh yeah, you could say so, yes.

FORTY

ANDRÉ CARTIER BEGGED ANGEL to allow him to help investigate the Vincent estate, but Angel knew it was a bad idea. She sent him home. He was in enough trouble and his presence with us as we broke a half-dozen laws sneaking onto the estate would make things worse if we were caught. Bad for us. Worse for him.

"Something is off about him, Angel," I said as we watched him walk off into the night. "I've never seen him so, so—"

"Nervous?"

"Yeah, nervous."

"Well, it's nearing midnight outside the crime scene where he's accused of murder. His married mistress is in FBI custody, and he's a murder suspect. Maybe that's why."

"Maybe." I wasn't so sure that was all of it—although it was a lot. "I'm just not sure."

Angel let Hercule out the rear door and onto the sidewalk. He stopped and gave the darkness a thorough inspection, sniffed the air in long, slow nose-fulls, and sat down. He moaned his report—the area was secure and ready for trespassing.

The Vincent estate was surrounded by a six-foot high stone wall. We were around the corner from where Bear and Spence should be sitting so we looked for a way inside close by. There was a wrought iron gate a dozen yards down the street and Hercule and I followed Angel there.

"Someone has been here already," she said, lifting the heavy iron hasp on the gate. "The chain and padlock have been removed."

"Now is it time to call Bear again?"

"No." Angel opened the gate eighteen inches or so and waved Hercule in, then slipped through after him. She closed the gate behind her. "And if you tell me to call Bear one more time, I'm sending you home."

"Don't yell at me later when this goes bad." I patted Hercule on the head and pointed into the darkness ahead of us. "Check it out, boy. But be quiet about it—doggie jail is not as plush as my den."

Moan. He raised his nose, sniffed the air again, and trotted off down the driveway toward the carriage house almost straight ahead of us.

"Okay, Dr. Tucker." I turned my spirit-radar on full force. "This is your expedition. Where to?"

"I want to find out if there are any tunnels connecting the houses. If I were going to make tunnels to escape the police, I'd want them coming from all the houses just in case. Nicholas' photo album showed crews digging outside all the houses. The carriage house is the perfect point to converge them, too. And the house on the northeast corner sits closest to the compound wall—maybe there's a way out of the compound there."

Good logic. "You know, doing this sort of makes us the Tucker gang. And you're our gang boss. How about a gang nickname?"

"No." She followed Hercule into the darkness.

I followed. "How about Angel the Knife?"

"Shut up, Tuck. Please."

"Boss Tucker? No, wait, how about—"

"Stop. I mean it."

"Angelface—you know, like Scarface."

Woof.

"Angelface it is, Herc. And you can be Twenty-Toes Hercule."

Woof. At least he had a sense of humor. I patted his head. "All's clear, Angel Face. Did you bring your heater?"

We weaved through the estate's trees and overgrown gardens to the two-story Victorian sitting in the northeast corner of the estate. At the rear door of the house, Angel opened her backpack and took out a flashlight and her Walther .380.

"It's locked," she said, checking the door. "Can you go in and look around? Maybe find us a way in?"

I did my best Bogie imitation. "Whatever you say, sweetheart," and slipped through the door. I didn't have to look back to know she was rolling her eyes. It must be the dry night air.

The house was empty, with no signs of anyone having been there for some time. Old furniture was still covered with dust covers—what little furniture there was—and the doors and windows were locked and appeared untampered with. There were no signs of any killer or bad guys. A cursory check failed to reveal a tunnel entrance or secret anything, too.

I returned to Angel. "Nothing, Angel Face. No signs of anyone. And there's no power. We'll have to break through a window or pick a lock."

"Okay, let's go around back."

"You're not seriously going to break in, are you?"

She winked. "Isn't this why we're here?"

"I don't recall breaking and entering on our to-do list. I thought we were just checking the grounds."

Hercule lowered himself and let out a low, throaty growl.

"Herc? What is it?"

Behind us, across the gardens on the other side of the carriage house, the faint groan of the iron gate came through the night.

"Angel, someone's coming. Scram and hide."

She ran across the yard to some tall, brushy evergreens and dropped down on the ground. Hercule lay beside her, ears up, tail straight back—ready for action. Me, I waited on the stoop and watched. Surveillance for me was far less stressful and much cleaner.

But all the running and hiding wasn't necessary after all.

Without lights to betray it, a vehicle rolled through the gate and pulled up beside the carriage house. It was a dark-colored panel van. The driver's door opened and a figure slid out and went into the carriage house through the side door.

"Angel, someone just went into the carriage house. I'm going after them."

"I'm coming, too."

"No, let me see who it is first. Twenty-Toes, keep her here, boy."

Hercule moaned and wagged his tail. He liked his gangster name.

I ran for the side carriage house door and passed through inside. The barn-like structure was a large, four-car-sized garage. It was a cavern with a poured concrete floor and wood plank walls, heavy, hand-honed timber framing and a rough-cut beamed ceiling. There were no cars—or carriages for that matter—with only a few remnants of working life left behind—two or three pieces of old furniture, some storage boxes, and a few old garden tools hanging on the walls.

I looked around but found no one.

The side door creaked open and Angel and Hercule came inside. Hercule took a look around, sat down, and yawned.

"Tuck?"

"I don't know where he went. I think your tunnel theory is looking pretty good. Herc?"

Hercule was already nose down and searching. It took him just seconds. He began his search at the side door and followed the figure's scent across the carriage house to the far side wall. There, obscured in the darkness, was an old horse stall about five feet square—it was, of course, void of equine and empty.

Hercule faced the stall and moaned. Then he looked up at me, wagged, and sat down.

"Angel, he went in the stall but he's gone."

She shined her light around the stall but found nothing. Then she ran the light down the carriage house wall in both directions.

"There's no other door and no place to hide. Herc, look again, boy."

"No, wait." I followed her light beam to the rear corner of the carriage house wall. There was a window hung tight into the corner. "See the corner window? It's not right. Who builds a window so close into a corner? The other windows are three feet out of the corners. There's a false wall or something there."

She lighted the stall again.

"There, Angel," I said, pointing to the side stall wall where the wood planks were irregular and misaligned. "The wall boards don't line up."

Three of the wall planks didn't sit flush with the others and their edges were misaligned against other planks. Angel shined her light on the plank as I walked over to it.

"Okay, Angel Face, if I'm not back in—"

"Just go, Tuck. And stop with the nicknames."

See, no fun at all. I slipped through the wall and was gone.

Hercule was right. The stall wall concealed an entrance to a narrow passage the length of the building. At the far corner of the passage, I could see a faint light and went to investigate. The light emanated from a stone stairwell that led down below the floor into a subterranean corridor. I descended the stairs—at least twelve feet down—and found the entrance to a tunnel heading toward the center of the estate grounds.

The tunnel floor and walls were stone and brick. There were single-bulb lights affixed to the tunnel roof every thirty feet or so but they were dark. The air was damp and stale and smelled of musky dirt and old stone. I followed the tunnel to an intersection—a wheel hub of sorts—somewhere in the center of the estate grounds. There were three other tunnel-spokes heading away from the hub. While there were no markings, I assumed the largest tunnel led to the Vincent House, and the other two led to the other two houses on the east side of the property.

These were Vincent's escape tunnels.

As I started back to the carriage house, Angel and Hercule emerged in the darkness. Angel followed her flashlight down the dark corridor heading for me. Hercule was on her heels.

"Angel, what are you doing? How did you get in here?"

"I found a loose board, pulled it, and a door opened." She shined her light around at the tunnel hub. "If you can do it, I can."

Now she was getting cocky. "And what if someone is headed toward you?"

She lifted her gun. "Then I'd make an arrest."

"An arrest? You're not a cop."

"A citizen's arrest."

"Of course you would." I showed her the other three tunnels off the hub and theorized where they led. She agreed. "Did you call Bear before you followed me? He should know where we are."

"Ah, yes." She passed me and headed down the tunnel we assumed went to the Vincent House. "He didn't answer."

"Oh, really, Angel?"

Several yards ahead, there was another intersection and a new tunnel turned left, heading away from both the Vincent House and the carriage house. I had no idea where the tunnel might lead.

"Which way, Tuck?"

I tried to look thoughtful and decisive. I failed. "I have no idea. But let's just continue straight."

Grrrrr. Hercule stopped and his tail snapped into a saber.

"What is it?"

"Shush," Angel said.

Shush? "You're the only ones who can hear me."

"Hearing you is the problem—so shush. I want to hear."

Hercule lowered himself and crept in front of Angel, blocking her from continuing forward.

Something tickled my spine. "Angel, get back to the hub and take a side tunnel. Move."

We made it to the tunnel hub just as a dim light fluttered in the darkness from where we came. The light stopped moving.

Crack! A shot whistled down the tunnel.

"Angel, get down the side tunnel. Hurry."

Hercule jumped on her, pushing her back into the darkness of a side tunnel. He continued pressing her until she'd retreated fifty feet or more.

"You stay put. And I mean it, Angel. I'm going to see who it is."

"No. I've got a gun."

"No one can shoot me, but, they can you two. Keep her here, Hercule."

Moan.

As I started back to the hub, a light bounced and jiggled ahead of me beyond the hub intersection. Then, another shot rang out from down one of the other tunnels and the light ahead of me snapped dark.

Another shot.

I ran on and, when I reached the hub, I turned right and headed for the carriage house. A fourth shot startled me—the bullet passed through my chest and skipped off the stone walls behind me. A hot poker of fire singeing through me.

I've been shot... *again*. This time, it hadn't taken my life—just a sharp, fiery spear sending bolts of energy surging through me; brilliant bolts of power and heat. I ran forward and reached the stone steps, bounded up and out into the carriage house.

No one.

I ran to the door and peered out. The panel van was still there.

Something stabbed my thoughts. "Oh no, they double-backed through a side tunnel... Angel—"

I tried my ghost-express to return to Angel and Hercule but it didn't work. My bearings weren't connected well enough and I never left the carriage house. So, I bolted for the hidden stairs and down to the tunnel. Before I reached the bottom step, another gunshot cracked ahead of me.

An icy stab to my brain.

"Angel!"

FORTY-ONE

"DON'T MOVE," ANGEL YELLED. "I've got a gun and I'll shoot."

Crack! I reached her just as the next shot whistled past her and struck the tunnel wall. "Stay back, Angel. Get down."

Hercule barked but stayed around the corner of the tunnel out of the line of fire as Angel knelt on one knee. She peered around the corner trying to see down the main tunnel. "Someone came running up the tunnel. I heard him but I couldn't see anything." She leaned back against the tunnel wall and gestured with her Walther. "I was standing here and turned around. They fired but I couldn't get a shot off. I think they moved back beyond the hub."

"Could you see who it was?"

"No. It all happened so fast and I cannot see anything in the dark without my flashlight. I didn't dare turn it on."

"Did you hear anything?"

"Just running feet. I think they have gone back down the tunnel to the Vincent House."

"Whoever it was must have double-backed on me. There was no one at the carriage house. Let me check ahead."

I left them on the side tunnel and moved toward the Vincent House, careful to listen as I did.

Nothing.

"Come on, Angel, it's clear."

She kept her flashlight low and obscured the light with her other hand.

When she reached me, I said, "Keep Hercule close. I'll go up ahead around the corner and clear the way. Wait for me to call for you before you move up. And for crying out loud, stay low in case someone shoots again."

"Be careful."

"Why?"

I could see her smile even in the darkness. "Old habit, I guess. Just hurry."

The tunnel was empty for another two-hundred feet. There were no noises. No lights. Nothing. Since bullets and bad guys don't faze me, I jogged along until I found another sharp bend. There, I made the turn and reached an antechamber at the end of the tunnel— the dead-end of the tunnel. Facing me was a stone wall and in the center of it was a narrow, heavy wood plank door secured by rusty, iron hinges.

Moving closer to examine the door, I found what the shooter was trying so hard to escape. Dead bodies.

Two bodies lay beneath an old canvas. The first I recognized from my vision. It was the tuxedoed assassin I'd met the night of Stephanos Grecco's murder. Now though, his tuxedo was tattered and dirty and his cummerbund lay torn beside him and his jacket balled at his feet. His white corsage was dead and crumbled on his tux lapel. I recalled smelling the sweet scent of the flower the second before I pulled the trigger and killed him—well, uh, killed him in my vision.

The other body was easier to identify. It was the catering manager with the heavy, Ukrainian accent—Petya Sergeyevich Chernyshov.

Vincent Calaprese warned me about Ruskie Commies back in his day. I wonder if Ukrainians fell under his definition of Ruskies now?

They did mine.

FORTY-TWO

"PETYA," ANGEL SAID, SHINING her cell phone light around the antechamber. "The caterer. Poor man. Who is the other one?"

"I think he's Stephanos Grecco's killer."

She shined her light over the body. "Then who killed him?"

"Me."

"What?" She looked at me with crazy eyes. "Oh, yeah—in your vision. But it wasn't you. Is this where he was killed?"

"I'm not sure, maybe. Or another part of the tunnels and they moved his body. The question is, who was I when I killed him?"

"My guess is whoever shot at me just now." Angel walked around the antechamber examining everything her light fell upon. "He must have been trying to move the bodies. We interrupted his plans."

"Maybe."

Angel knelt down and unwrapped part of the canvas covering the two bodies. A dark-colored backpack lay between them.

"Tuck, what do you make of this? Should I open it?"

I knelt beside her. "We shouldn't touch any of this. It's evidence. But, if we peeked at the contents, I think Bear would understand— when you call him."

Angel used her shirt sleeve to manipulate the zipper on the top of the backpack without leaving fingerprints and guide it open. What we found inside surprised us both—dozens of checks and a pile of cash.

"It's the stolen donations from the gala," she said. "The killer just left this here?"

"Maybe the killer didn't want anything leaving a trail."

Angel rooted through the pack. "I think it's all here. Maybe Petya stole the donations. And the killer killed him because he interfered with Grecco's murder? Or, maybe Petya was down here hiding the money and stumbled on the real killer."

"Too many maybes. This guy beside Petya killed Grecco. I know he had a boss—because I was in him. The boss killed him in this tunnel. Afterward, the boss tracked down and killed Petya—either because he was also an accomplice or because he was in the wrong place."

Angel agreed. "Jorge-the-waiter could be the killer or an accomplice, right? And if he's not—the killer may be after him because of his video recordings."

"We have to get you out of here, Angel." I knelt down and looked the bodies over again. "Bear and Spence are outside somewhere. They don't know about these tunnels so they'd never be expecting anyone to get into the house this way. Jorge may have come through here to get his equipment he left behind. He knew about the hidden stairwell and secret attic room, so it makes sense he knew about these tunnels. He must have been the one shooting at you."

"Now what?"

"We get Bear."

"It'll take too long and Jorge might still be down here—or might return." She shined her light on the old door built into the brick wall. "There has to be a way through."

"You look for a door release. I'll go inside and see where the door leads and make sure it's safe."

Hercule went to the door and ran his nose along its frame. He backed up two steps and sat down, looking at Angel and woofing. It was safe.

"Good Herc," I said, "but let's be sure."

Moan, grumble. He *was* sure.

I passed through the door and stepped into a small room off the Vincent House's basement. The dank room was dark and ominous. On Angel's side was a door, but on this side there was just a tall rack of wine racks and storage shelves running the entire length of the room. I couldn't see any discernible door or entrance. I searched the remainder of the basement where I found several smaller rooms off to the left side and in the center of the basement were three large, ancient steel furnaces covered in cobwebs, dust, and a rats nest of old, frayed wires. Behind the old furnaces were two new furnaces and a row of other mechanical equipment my meager mechanical brain filed under "basement junk." Nothing I saw raised any alarm.

One thing I was certain of, though—there was no killer hiding nearby.

I returned to the shelves where I had entered from the tunnel. There had to be a door somewhere.

"Angel, push on the door. See if you can move it."

The shelves didn't budge so I returned through them into the antechamber. Angel stood beside Hercule shining her light at the door.

"What," I said, "can't you do that?"

"Funny."

She showed me a round iron ring affixed to the brick wall on the right side of the chamber.

"I think it's a release for the door. It's jammed and won't budge."

"Let me check the other side again."

Back in the basement, I examined the shelves closer and found the problem. Someone had taken a heavy iron bar and wedged it under the center shelf, preventing it from pivoting open. I was helpless to remove it.

Situations like this irritated me. Being a ghost has its perks, mind you, but moving objects—in particular ones requiring more than finesse—is not easy. Oh, a piece of paper here or a pencil there is one thing, but unjamming an iron bar from beneath a heavy oak shelf is a another. Without juice, of course. If there were an electric light or plug nearby, the power would change things. I could grab hold and charge up a good few minutes of strength and dexterity. I might even be able to go a few rounds with the killer. I did that once and saved Angel's life.

Not now. There was no power. No electric light. No juice. I was just a 185-pound weightless poof of air and dust. All brains and no brawn. How embarrassing.

"Angel," I yelled through the shelf. "Stay where you are. I'll go find Bear. The entrance is jammed closed."

Her voice was faint. "Hurry. I tried calling. No signal."

And I was off.

I checked the first floor and didn't find anyone. Outside, I found Bear and Spence's unmarked cruisers parked on the street, outside the stone wall on opposite sides of the Vincent House. Both cars were empty. I was just returning to the ballroom when faint footfalls touched my ears from the rear servant stairs by the kitchen.

"Bear? Hey man, is that you?" Spence appeared behind me at the foot of the stairs with his weapon drawn. "Spence, you have to, Spence. Please."

He stopped and lifted his weapon, peering around the hallway and into the ballroom. "Bear?"

"No, Spence. It's me." I moved close and touched his shoulder. "It's Tuck. Listen for my voice. Angel's in trouble."

His eyebrows rose and he swatted at this shoulder like he was brushing away a bee. He took a step back and flattened himself against the hallway wall, looking around as his face went ash-white. "This place is freaking me out. Where are you?"

"It's all right, Spence. It's me, Tuck. Can you hear me? Please, go to the basement."

His eyes dropped to the floor as he listened. Then he looked up and around the hallway again. This time, he slipped into the lounge—was gone only a few moments—and reappeared.

"Spence, come on—"

A gunshot cracked from somewhere near the kitchen. I didn't see where it hit—but it was close and it sent Spence diving for the floor. He hit, rolled left, raised his gun, and squeezed off two shots. They slammed into the kitchen doorframe.

"Sheriff's Department! Drop your gun!"

Heavy footfalls ran through the kitchen and stopped. A door banged and glass rattled. Old hinges creaked. A door banged again.

"Go, Spence, go!"

He jumped to his feet and made chase.

We met Bear storming through the rear kitchen door, gun drawn, and anger tight across his face. The moment Spence burst into the kitchen, Bear's gun snapped up.

"Whoa, Bear, it's me."

Bear's gun lowered. "What are you shooting at, Spence?"

Spence was out of breath. "Someone shot at me. I shot back. He came through here."

"He didn't go outside. The door was open but I was out back. I would have seen him."

I said, "Bear, the basement," I pointed to the basement door across the kitchen. "Get down there. Angel's in a tunnel connecting to the carriage house. She's trapped inside. She's in trouble."

"Angela?" Bear grabbed the basement door, yanked it open, and rushed down the stairs. "Let's go, Spence."

"Where? What are you doing?"

"The basement. Angela's down there and she's in trouble."

Spence fell in behind him. "How do you know?"

"Didn't you hear him?"

"*Him?*" Spence's face twisted. "Damn you, Bear. Cut it out."

Across the basement in the far corner room where the tunnel entrance was, a man's voice screamed, "Get him back. Get back or I'll shoot."

Hercule's ferocious bark echoed like a wild beast from an old horror movie. Then the man shouted something I couldn't understand—Hercule's bark turned to a demonic growl.

A gun shot.

Angel yelled, "Don't move."

Hercule's bark became erratic and frenzied. The man cried out. The cacophony of the big dog thrashing about mixed with more cries and gnashing teeth.

Silence.

I beat Bear and Spence to the room where the secret shelf-door was open.

A dark-skinned Hispanic man lay on his back with his hands and face smeared in blood. Hercule stood atop him with all fours planted firm and the man's right hand twisted and clamped in his powerful jaws. A gun lay on the floor beside them. Each time the Hispanic tried to grab hold of Hercule, Hercule growled and jerked the hand clamped in his teeth, wrenching it to and fro.

"Get him off, lady. Get him off. I give. Please. Stop him—he's breaking my arm."

Hercule stared down, eye-to-eye. His mouth secured on the Hispanic's wrist, his growls sending a clear message—resistance was futile.

Angel emerged through the open passageway door, gun first, aiming at the Hispanic. "Good boy, Hercule. Keep him there until Bear and Daddy get here."

"I'm here, Angel," I said. "Bear's coming."

"Daddy?" the man said, daring a glance at Angel. "I thought you were widowed?"

"Oh?" Angela leveled her Walther at his head. "And how do you know I'm widowed?"

He didn't answer.

Bear and Clemens edged into the room. Spence flipped on a flashlight, shining it down on Hercule's captive. "Sheriff's Department. Don't move."

"No kidding man," he cried. "Get this beast off me. I was just trying to get my stuff. The lady almost killed me. This mutt—"

Hercule's jaw tightened. He shook and wrenched the man's hand in painful twists.

I said, "He doesn't like the word 'mutt.'"

"Don't piss him off," Bear said. "What's your name?"

Spence tugged a wallet from the man's jeans and flipped it open with one hand. "Victoria Chevez."

"Victorio, man. Come on, do I look like a chick?"

"What kind of name is Victorio?" Spence asked.

"I'm half-Mexican, half-Cuban, and all-American. What of it?"

I stepped closer and looked Chevez over. An EMF meter hung on his belt—identical to the one we found in the attic—and started vibrating and blinking. Chevez glanced down at it as Angel pulled Hercule away. "Come on, man, get me outta this crazy place. Come on, arrest me. I give you permission."

"Permission?" Bear forced a laugh, moved Hercule over to Angel, and dragged the man to his feet. "You're under arrest. We'll start with criminal trespass and assault—"

"He shot at me, Bear," Angel said, soothing Hercule with a good head rub. "In the tunnels, just a little while ago. And there's two bodies just inside the entrance—with the stolen gala donations."

"Angela," Bear said with an edge to his voice. "We saw the van pull into the property and figured it was this guy coming to retrieve his equipment. But, what are you doing here?"

She threw a thumb toward the tunnel entrance. "We figured out about the tunnels and came to see if we could find them. We were going to find you when we were done."

"We?" Chevy glanced around the basement. "You and who else lady?"

"Hercule," Angel said as Bear tried to hide a smile. "He tried to kill me, Bear."

"No, lady, it wasn't me."

"You're in big trouble, amigo." Bear snapped handcuffs on Chevez and shoved him toward Spence. "Make your charges criminal trespass, assault, and attempted murder for starters—just starters."

"No, no. This ain't right, man." Chevez pulled against Spence's grip on his arm and tried to look into the tunnel. "You got it all wrong. She was shooting at me. I swear, man. Let's go to your office and talk it through. I wanna get out of here."

Spence read him his rights and Chevez calmed.

Bear eyed him. "Did you kill Stephanos Grecco? How about Petya, the caterer, or Grecco's killer? Or did you do all three?"

"What are you talking about? Oh, hell no, man. None of the killings was me. Come on, get me out of here."

I sized him up. "Chevez, huh? He's also Jorge the waiter and maybe Stanley Kravitz or both, Bear. And he's your ghost investigator, too. Look at his belt."

The EMF meter on Chevez's belt was still flashing and buzzing. As Spence patted him down, something buzzed in his jacket pocket and Spence pulled out a square electrical meter. The meter resembled an electrician's volt meter with dials and lights and a needle wavering back and forth over a numeric scale.

"This is a tri-meter, Bear," Spence said, turning the meter around for Bear to see. "It measures—"

"Yeah, yeah," Bear said. "Ghost farts or something."

"Neat toys, Chevez." I touched the device and the lights went apoplectic. "I hope they're worth life in prison."

Chevez looked from the device on his belt to the one Spence held. His eyes were wide and frightful and his voice broke with each word. "You gotta get me outta here. Now, man."

"You in a hurry to go to jail?" Angel asked. "You almost shot me in the tunnel. Why?"

"Shot you? You shot at me, lady. You hit me, too." Chevez turned and pushed his elbow out. There was a ragged hole though the lower sleeve of his denim shirt. "Almost killed me, lady. That ain't cool. I didn't do nothing to you."

"Oh? I never fired a shot." Angel handed her Walther to Bear. "Not one."

"She reloaded then." Chevez twisted but Spence held him tight. "I didn't know you was dangerous. You tried to kill me. The man didn't say you was dangerous."

"What man?" I asked, and the electronic gadgets danced away.

"What man?" Bear repeated. "Who are you working with, Chevez?"

"Nope. No way, man. I ain't sayin nothing until—"

"Until you get a lawyer," Spence said, shoving him out of the room. "Let's go."

"Screw the lawyer, man." Chevez pulled Spence toward the stairs. "I ain't sayin' nothing until you get me outta here. There's supernatural mumbo-jumbo going on—real stuff, too—and I'm in handcuffs. Man, just get me outta here. I don't need no lawyer."

FORTY-THREE

"ONE MORE TIME, CHEVEZ" Bear said, placing a fresh cup of coffee on the interview room table. "From the top. And leave out the bullshit this time."

Victorio Chevez reached over the stacks of electronic meters and camera equipment Bear laid on the table and picked up the coffee. He took a long sip and spit it back into the cup. "Come on, man, I asked for sugar. Lots of sugar. I know my rights."

"Your rights don't include sugar," Spence said, leaning on the wall behind Bear. "Detective Braddock is getting antsy, Chevez. And you don't want him antsy. He rips telephone booths in half— not books, Chevez ... *booths*. So maybe focus a little."

I watched from the corner of the room and had to smile at Spence. He was turning into a real detective—surprising since in the past, he seemed more fitted to selling shoes or working at a car wash.

"All right. All right." Chevez leaned back and folded his arms, exchanging vampire-eyes with Bear. "Everyone calls me Chevy—"

"I thought you rode a motorcycle?" Spence asked

Okay, maybe Spence still had a job at the carwash.

"Ah, you're kidding me, right?" Chevy's eyebrows rose and he cracked a smile. "Hey, Braddock, he slow or something? And you guys turned down my application to be a cop? Go figure."

"This guy's a real smartass, Bear." I sat on the corner of the table and made Chevy's EMF meter blink and whine. "Less jokes and more answers, pal. Or I'll haunt you for life."

"Oh, come on, man." Chevy's eyes fixed on the flickering lights as he slid his chair back from the table. "What's goin' on here? The EMF meter never goes this nuts."

"It's my old partner, Tuck," Bear said as he pulled Chevy back to the table. "But you know him by his full name, Oliver Tucker." He watched Chevy's eyes explode. "Right—Angela Tucker's husband. He's watching out for her."

Chevy pushed back from the table again. "Don't screw with me man. You don't—"

"He's upset because you tried to kill Angela."

"I told you, man, I was defending myself. She shot at me and I shot back. I was just in the house to get my gear. This stuff costs money, you know? I was coming in through the tunnel she was in. She shot at me and I shot back. Just to scare her off."

Bear leaned over the table and went eye-to-eye with Chevy. "Listen to me, you twerp, Angela Tucker didn't fire a shot. But you did—several—and we'll have ballistics tomorrow. If they match those two bodies, you're in deep trouble. So, who's your partner? Who drove the van?"

"Van?" Chevy's face twisted. "What van, man? I ride a motorcycle. And I work alone."

"The van we towed from the Vincent place was stolen in West Virginia yesterday. You know the one." Spence leaned over Chevy's shoulder from behind. "Who are you working with, Chevez? Make a deal with us before we find your partner and he makes a deal."

"I work alone. Don't you listen?"

"Somebody drove the van outside. Who?"

"I told you—I have no idea." When Bear's teeth bared, Chevy added, "I don't know nothing about any van, okay? I got an email hiring me for this gig. Cash left at my office. They paid me five grand for two weeks. Cash is king."

I said, "What about this equipment, Bear?" The EMF meter lighted up again and its needle wavered back and forth with each inflection of my voice.

"And all this electronic crap?" Bear asked. "What's it for?"

"I told you. I'm a private investigator. You got my ID and license. I'm legit. I also do ghost investigation stuff on the side, you know, for extra cash. I record everything I find and if I get anything cool, I sell it to a ghost show on TV."

"Did you?" Spence asked. "We know about the remote cameras and night vision, too. And this EMF meter and—"

"You a fan, man?" Chevy asked, smiling. "You know about this stuff?"

Spence nodded.

"Then you get it. I'm a paranormal investigator."

"A paranoid investigator?" I tapped the EMF meter and made it convulse. "There's money in it?"

"Paranormal," Bear corrected and drew an awkward glance from Spence. "Where's the rest of your equipment?"

Chevy raised an eyebrow. "Rest of what? You got my cameras and meters and recorders. And I want them all back. What else is there?"

"The recordings," Spence said. "Your video and audio recordings, Chevez. You're looking at some serious time for murdering those two stiffs in the tunnel. We haven't even talked about Stephanos Grecco's murder yet."

Chevy jumped up, crashed into the table, and knocked two of his cameras on the floor. "Murder? No man, no way. You can't hook me on no murders. No way. No." Bear grabbed his arm and pulled him back down. "Come on, detectives, I'm just trying to make a livin'."

"Oh, yeah? You worked the gala under an assumed name and sneaked out after Grecco's murder." Bear jabbed an iron finger into Chevy's shoulder. "Then you attempted to break into Angela Tucker's house and did God knows what we haven't found yet. Tonight, you shot at her, and we had two bodies at your feet when we found you." Bear turned to Spence. "What do you think, Spence?"

Spence smiled. "The needle for sure."

"Needle? Come on, man, no." Chevy dropped his head into his hands and sat thinking for a long time. When he looked up, his eyes were red and his dark skin pale. "Look, I didn't kill anyone—nobody. I don't even know the Grecco-dude. I was hired to wire up the house and keep tabs on everybody. Since I was there, I added a few tricks of my own for the ghost-chasing TV show—big money maybe. But I had to get my stuff back. So, tonight, I went into the house through one tunnel and went back out through another. I didn't see any bodies. And I told you, the lady shot at—"

"No," Bear slammed his hand on the table so hard the ghost meters bounced and started chirping. "Her gun wasn't fired. There are two bodies and the stolen donations where we found you. You know an awful lot about the tunnels and secret rooms that no one else does. It's murder, plain and simple—"

"No, no ... okay. Just wait."

"We're listening." Spence leaned over his shoulder again. "But not for long."

"Look, I'm a vet, man—a Marine. I did my time in the sand and in Afghanistan. I ain't gonna kill anymore. I was doing this job for this guy and things went bad. I got caught up in it. Help me out, man, help me out."

"Help you out? Help yourself out, Chevez. We have three bodies and your name is on them. The Commonwealth's attorney will go for capital murder—the needle, Chevez."

The words "capital murder" caught Chevy's breath and sent a wave of angst across his face. He gripped the interview table until his knuckles turned white, looking from Spence to Bear—mouth open, trying to summon words that weren't forming.

When resignation restored the color to his face, he said, "See, this guy, a smooth-talking dude, hired me to watch Professor Tucker."

Bear beat me to the punch, "What are you talking about? What guy?"

"A guy, man. Just a guy." Chevy shrugged. "It's about Professor Tucker, man. I wired her office and house and watched her everywhere she went. You know, to get everything on camera. Four grand down, four more when I'm done."

"Who?" I yelled. The EMF meter erupted. "Who's after Angel?" Bear pounded the table. "A name."

"I dunno who, man, I swear. Emails and cell calls. Nothing else."

"Bullshit," Spence said. "You took four thousand over email?"

Chevy tapped the table beside his cell phone. "Check for yourself. He's using a burner phone. I don't like taking jobs blind, but I need the cash, man—bad. The PI biz is slow and I'm hurting. The ghost-chasing show offered me some fast money if I got video inside the Vincent place. So I double-dipped. The other guy—the one wanting Professor Tucker followed—he'd never know."

"He's using a burner phone?" Spence grabbed Chevy's cell phone and left the room. "You better not be lying, Chevez."

"Check my computer, too. You'll see, I kept the emails in case I got jammed up."

"You're not as dumb as I thought," Bear sneered.

"You're funny, man, but I ain't laughin'." Chevy took the rest of his coffee in one gulp and stared at the ceiling for answers that weren't written there. "I checked the dude's IP address. It's a dead end. Maybe you can get more. And yeah, I was at the Vincent House when the Grecco dude was hit. When all that was going down, I went to the attic, grabbed a couple flash drives and hid out. Soon as I could, I split. Then I went to the university while the Tucker lady was still at the party."

Bear asked, "You bugged her office? What's all this about?"

"The man didn't say. All he said was he wanted everything I could get—leverage or something. For eight grand, I don't care why."

"No? What if it's about murder, Chevez?" Bear said. "You're messing with my friend and Tuck's wife. He won't be happy."

I put a hand on Chevy's EMF meter and it went off the charts. "I'm not happy, Chevy."

"Don't be talking angry spirit stuff, man. Ghost chasing is just about money. I never got any evidence before this. I didn't even believe in ghosts. But, watching the lady professor ... she's a believer, I can tell. You all are spooky, man. Just too spooky."

"Is that why you went to her house?" Bear asked.

"Yeah, I was trying to get some video of her in the house, but her big ferocious dog almost ate me."

"Hercule is funny about burglars. You're lucky."

"Lucky?"

"If I had been there, I would have let him have you." Bear stood up and went to the door. "Where are the videos?"

Chevy's face tightened. "I gave some to the guy."

"Some? How if you don't know him?"

"I left them at a dead drop in Old Town. He was there but I never saw him. He called me after I left and said he wanted more info and wanted the rest of the recordings, too."

I said, "Bear, he made copies. I'm sure of it. If he's an abnormal investigator—"

"Paranormal," he corrected.

"Yeah, paranormal. If he is, he needed copies to sell to the TV show."

Bear repeated my thoughts and watched Chevy from the doorway. "Where are the copies?"

"I got copies, sure, of course," Chevy said, folding his arms. "And other stuff, too. Recordings, photographs, before and after the party. It's gonna cost you. You know I ain't lying, Detective. And you know I didn't kill nobody. So, it's gonna cost you."

Bear never touched the ground until he landed on Chevy. He ripped him out of his chair, slammed him against the wall, and pinned him there, dangling a foot off the floor. "You want a deal? You little turd, I'll give you a deal. You tell me everything or you're going down for capital murder—after you get out of the hospital."

"Immunity, man. I want immunity for anything I did at the house and with the professor lady." Chevy's eyes were round and his face ash. He grabbed Bear's wrists and tried to wrestle himself free—he failed. "I can't lose my PI license, man. I can't. Just give me a pass."

Bear let go and Chevy crashed to the floor onto his knees. Bear smiled, extended his hand to help him to his feet, and said, "Oh, heck, I think I can work that, Chevy. Let's hear what you have to trade?"

"Come on, man, you're crazy."

"Talk."

Chevy stood but stayed close to the wall. "I'll help you catch this guy, okay? I'll lure him into a trap or something. And I'll give you the originals of what I recorded at the Vincent place, too. But I want my cameras and recorders and everything back and I keep copies of the house video for the TV show—not the lady professor, but the other stuff."

"Maybe. What about the van and the bodies?"

"No, man, no—I ain't involved with no bodies. I saw you guys watching the front and rear of the Vincent House, so I came in through one of the other houses by a tunnel—they're all over the place down there. Then, when I reached the Vincent House, I heard somebody inside so I ran to the basement and tried to get back out. The professor-lady was in the other tunnel—I heard her—and when I opened the basement entrance, she shot at me. I shot back and ran upstairs. But, you guys were there and I had no choice and went back down. I never saw the bodies and no money until you told me they were there. Honest. I swear."

Bear took it all in and studied Chevy, looking for the lie. So did I and neither of us were sure there was one. I said, "Bear, I think he's telling the truth. It would make sense. He was in the house ahead of us. The van came to the estate later and whoever was in it was down in the tunnels between Chevy and Angel. If the van isn't his or a partner's—and I don't think it is—then he didn't kill anyone."

"How so?" Bear ignored Chevy's stare. "Maybe he and a partner were moving the bodies?"

"No man, I told you, not me."

I said, "I think he's telling the truth. Whoever killed Petya and Grecco's killer came in the van to move the bodies. Chevy and Angel got in the way. That's who shot at them."

"Yeah, Grecco's killer—we gotta ID him." Bear went to the interview room door and opened it, turned back, and aimed a finger at Chevy. "I'll get you some more coffee with lots of sugar. And maybe some breakfast, too. You start writing down every little thing you forgot. We'll go through this one last time. And if there's a comma out of place, it's eggs and capital murder for you. Got it?"

Chevy nodded. "Extra bacon."

"Right."

"And pancakes—lots of syrup."

Bear slammed the door behind him.

Chevy breathed a heavy sigh and sat at the interview room table, checking his cameras and equipment. He picked up a small, thin, digital recorder and flipped it on. "You guys better not have busted my stuff. Testing, testing—"

"Boo, Chevy," I said, leaning in close and making the EMF meter dance and flicker. "I'm watching you, *amigo*."

"Testing, one, two." He flipped the device to replay mode and turned up the volume. "... *better not have busted my stuff. Testing, testing ... Boo, Chevy, I'm watching you, amigo.*"

"*¡Hijo de puta!*" He threw the recorder across the table and shoved himself back from the table against the wall. "*Madre de Dios,* it can't be."

FORTY-FOUR

"SORRY ABOUT THE BREAKFAST." Agent Jim Dobron stood across the room pouring coffee from a cardboard carafe. "This is the best I can offer for a Sunday morning to-go order."

Bonnie Grecco sat at the small dinette table watching him. She snapped her arms folded and huffed, frustrated at the FBI man's casual attitude. She'd been sequestered in the hotel for a day with around-the-clock FBI men hovering nearby. She was tired, fed up, and scared. The one thing she was sure about was they hadn't gotten to the point yet.

"Look, Agent Dobron, I've been here since yesterday morning. All you've done is ask about Steph's business. I told you—I didn't kill him and I don't know anything about his business. When can I get out of here?"

"When we get to the bottom of his murder, Mrs. Grecco." Dobron stirred sugar packets into his coffee. "And when you help us with a few business matters, you'll be moving on even faster."

She jumped up. "How many times do I have to tell you? I don't know anything. He didn't tell me anything. I didn't learn anything. And I didn't see anything."

"Yeah, you said that."

"Then what else do you want from me?"

Agent Dobron returned to the small dinette table and took a chair. He looked across the hotel suite at the other FBI man sitting in an armchair beside the door. "Mike, get some air, okay?"

The agent nodded, stood, and left the room. A second later, the door lock clicked.

Bonnie took a breath and sat down. "Now what?"

"A little talk." Dobron smiled. "Bonnie, it's just you and me. No one is listening. So here's the deal—I want the book. Stephanos knew about the book. I want it."

"What book?"

"The book your husband had up for sale. The book every mobster on the East Coast wants. You know the one. Give me the book and I'll still put you into witness protection and give you a new life somewhere nice."

"How nice?"

"Nice."

"The book?" She framed her best poker face. "The book is what this is about? I thought—"

"Sure, sure, I know." Dobron patted the air. "We want his killer, too—of course. But if we get the book, we get the killer, too. Right?"

She shrugged.

"So where is it?"

"I don't know. I don't know anything about it. Everyone wants the book and I don't know why. I asked Stephanos and he hit me—he hit me good. If I'd found the thing, I would have burned it. He was a bastard."

Dobron watched her over his paper coffee cup. "Where'd you look for it?"

"Around our place a few weeks ago. I didn't find it. I knew it was important because of the way he talked on the phone—secret and hush-hush."

"What did you hear—exactly?"

She folded her arms and looked at him. He seemed interested in what she had to say. He wasn't asking the same old questions and looking bored or indifferent. He wanted to hear her—wanted to hear about the book.

It was always about the book.

"Well, let me think." She played it slow. "A couple weeks ago, I heard him talking on the phone. He said he had the book—like everybody in the world knew what the book was."

"Talking to who?"

"I don't know. He said it could make them rich and they wouldn't have to worry about anyone anymore. For a price, of course."

"Come on, Bonnie, quit screwing around. Your Caribbean beach house is waiting for you."

"I could live there—beaches, fancy drinks." She picked up her coffee and played with the cup. She took her time; she liked the way it irritated him. "They must have asked him for proof he had it because he said he had some old notes to prove it. He would bring the notes to the party."

Dobron narrowed his eyes. "Angela Tucker's gala?"

"Yeah, that party."

"Notes?" Agent Dobron went into one of the two bedrooms and returned with his briefcase. He opened it and took out several pieces of paper, handing one to her. "This kind of note?"

She looked down at a photocopy of Grover Cleveland's face on a one-thousand dollar bill. "I never thought of those. He had a lot of them, too."

"Oh? Where's all the money, Bonnie? Where does he keep it?"

"I don't know. I only saw it all once. You never asked me about it before, why now?" She leaned on the table. "What's this about, Agent Dobron? You're more interested in the book and the money than in Steph's murder."

"Oh yeah? You aren't very broken up about his death either."

"I cried it all out yesterday. I'm grieving inside." He was fishing so she cast some bait. "You want to make a deal? No lawyers, no Ruth-Ann Marcos—nobody else, right? Just you and me?"

"A deal?" Dobron took the photocopy out of her hand and slipped it into his briefcase. "What kind?"

"The kind of deal where you get a lot of this old money and I get some money and I get to go away. Everybody wins, right?" Bonnie ran her tongue along the rim of her coffee cup and smiled when his eyes followed it. "But I get a free pass on anything Steph did."

"Maybe. But it depends." Dobron refilled her cup, taking care to hold her hand and steady the cup while he poured. "What kind of illegal things did your husband do, Bonnie?"

"I'm not sure. But if I'm in this lousy hotel with you, it must be big, right? And you're asking about the book and stash of old money, too. I know he didn't get it making business deals. Who pays off in old thousand-dollar bills?"

Dobron picked up his cell phone, stood up, and walked across the room. "It's me. Bonnie Grecco and I are talking. She has a lot to tell me I think—so, we should talk later." Silence. "All right. But I can't get anyone else out here for an hour. Sure, send them. I'll meet you in thirty."

When he tapped off the call, Bonnie asked, "You going somewhere, Dobron? I thought we were going to talk about a deal?"

"We will," he said, slipping on his suit coat. "I have to go talk to someone first. You sit tight with Mike. I've got more agents coming out and there's a West Virginia State Trooper in the parking lot. You're safe."

"I better be." She stood up and went to her bedroom door. "Look, you have to take me to my house later. I want to get some more things. And I have to make arrangements for Steph's funeral, too."

"Don't worry about the funeral. I'll take you when I get back. Stay away from the windows until I do. And no calls out, okay?"

She nodded and went inside her room, shutting the door behind her.

Bonnie lay on her bed, listening as Agent Dobron spoke to the other FBI agent, Mike-somebody. Mike was young and athletic and she had caught him eyeing her several times already. Maybe she could talk Mike into getting something other than bad coffee and egg sandwiches for breakfast. Maybe Mike would be nicer to her.

She had a way with men.

She checked her overnight bag, sorting out the two changes of clothes and cosmetics Dobron let her gather after swooping her away from Detective Braddock. The few things just wouldn't do. She needed to get back home and get to the basement safe; the safe the FBI didn't know about. The safe with Stephanos's hidden loot.

Strange how Agent Dobron wasn't interested in the money. Did he know there was almost a quarter of a million dollars? If he did, then the book was far more valuable than the money. The book must be all he wanted.

It's all everyone wanted.

FORTY-FIVE

It took Chevy a while to calm down after listening to his recorder—he almost wet himself and accused Bear of trying to intimidate him into a false confession. Spence convinced him there was no trickery and a hot breakfast and a deal with the Commonwealth's Attorney soothed him the rest of the way.

"So, you were ghost chasing while you gathered information on Angela Tucker for your mysterious client?" Bear watched Chevy devouring a plate of eggs, sausage, and hash browns. "For a guy who is afraid of the dark, ghost hunting seems like a strange occupation."

"I'm a PI and I ain't afraid of the dark," Chevy said before taking a long mouthful of coffee. "I got into this ghost thing to make some extra money from the videos. I got a friend who knows a guy—"

"Yeah, yeah," Bear said, "who introduced you to the producer on the *Ghost Walk* TV show. You have haven't explained how you found the tunnels and secret rooms at the Vincent House. Did the ghosts show you?"

"No. I don't—I didn't—believe in ghosts. Whenever I get a gig from the show's producer, I do research on the place. You know, like the building plans, city and power lines, and sewer access. The whole history of the place."

Bear wasn't taking notes. "And it's all for the cameras, huh?"

"Heck yeah, man, it makes good video and I ad-lib a lot. The producers love it when I talk about a building's history and stuff that happened in it. And man, they go nuts when I 'uncover' some old wine cellar or underground city tunnel. Sometimes—and man, don't tell no one—I talk it up like I just discovered it—but I knew it was there from my research. It's all for show."

I asked, "And he found the Vincent House's tunnels through research?" Bear knew Angel and I found them the same way. "Makes sense, Bear."

Bear started scribbling notes. "That's it?"

"Most of it. There were old sewer lines running through there around the turn of the century. They followed an alley that split the Vincent estate property in sections. But Vincent bought it all up. I figured the sewer lines were converted into tunnels. Just like up in New York—"

"You know a lot about escape tunnels in New York?" Bear asked. "How?"

"I told you—research." Chevy sipped his coffee. "Anyway, one night I was checking the place out—last week—and I got some strange readings on my tri-meter so I lit the place up with my IR camera."

"What?" Bear stopped writing and looked up. "Let's pretend I live in the real world, Chevy. Explain all the electronic junk."

Chevy put his coffee down. "Junk? I paid three grand for the infrared camera gear and almost two for the tri-meter. The tri-meter system detects any radio and microwaves, electric and magnetic fields—they say spirits and paranormal phenomenon disrupts electric and magnetic fields and gives off readings. The stronger the reading, the more energy is around. You know, energy equals ghosts and other stuff. And the IR—"

"You can see ghosts?"

Chevy shrugged. "Well, kind of—the equipment can. But you know, I never have before. Except that night—oh, man, I gotta say, it scared the crap out of me."

Bear was about to laugh when I said, "He's not lying, Bear. His equipment knows I'm around. And he could have seen something in the house—there's plenty there to see, trust me. Wait until I tell you about Sassy—"

"Detective, I'm telling you, the night we're talking about, I was in looking for the tunnels and hiding my cameras. All of a sudden my gear goes wonky. I saw something moving around first floor at the bar. I kept getting tri-meter readings, too, so I turned on the IR camera in the lounge and watched from the attic."

"And?"

"Plenty." Chevy pushed his empty plate across the table and poured himself more coffee. "The hot spot on my IR disappeared behind the bar into the booze closet."

"Disappeared? Like, vanished?"

"I can prove it."

"Then prove it," Bear said. "Now."

Chevy cracked a thin smile. "Okay, I'll give you a little taste. But if you like it, we make a deal. Okay?"

"Sure. Prove it."

Chevy nodded. "Under my bike's saddle is a pouch for my insurance card and papers. There's a flash drive inside. Get it."

"Your bike is sitting on a truck out back." Bear stood up and headed for the door. "You better not be lying, Chevy. If you are, you're going down for murder."

Bear stuck his head out of the interview room door and issued orders to a uniformed deputy. Ten minutes later, the deputy returned with a notebook computer and a small computer USB memory drive.

Bear placed the computer on the table. "Okay, Chevy, impress me."

Chevy took control of the computer and banged away on the keyboard. Twice he had to log into websites to access software he needed. Ten minutes later, he brought up a video program and inserted the USB drive into the notebook.

"Ready?" He turned the screen around to face Bear. "When I saw this IR image disappear behind the bar, I went down and checked it out." Chevy tapped the keyboard. "One of the booze racks is a secret door. Watch what I found."

First, Chevy played a video clip showing the Vincent House's lounge and bar. The camera pointed down from the corner of the room. In the center of the view, a distorted red and yellow blob of light moved in front of the bar. The image looked like a grotesque shape without features or a fine outline. Instead, it looked more like a person made of gelatin and radiating reds and yellows. After a few seconds, the image moved behind the bar to the far corner wine closet. The image bent over and disappeared.

"See, man, the ghost went through the wall. Watch what I found when I went down there myself. I was holding the camera going through the house."

This video began in the second-floor hallway and descended the stairs. It bounced and jiggled as he descended the stairs and walked down into the bar. He steadied the camera as he walked behind the bar. There, he set the camera down and entered the screen view, poking and probing behind the bar for clues. He opened a small closet door and revealed a liquor and wine storage closet with shelving on all sides still laden with old, dusty bottles. He picked the camera up and went inside. It took him several tries probing the shelves before he came to the center one—he tugged on the shelf and the bottles shook—another tug and the shelf pulled open.

"See." Chevy tapped the computer screen. "There are stairs inside leading up to the second floor. They come out in one of the bedroom closets at the top of the stairs. When I went back and checked the video for the bedroom, I saw the same ghost-hotspot there, too."

Bear laughed. "And you think the blob of light was a ghost?"

"Yeah, why not?"

"Why would a ghost use a secret passage? Don't they just poof to where they want?"

"I dunno. But you saw what I did, Detective. We got a deal?"

I had an idea. "Bear, he's got something. Maybe the killer was there, too. We know the shot came from one of those bedrooms on the second floor. Maybe the killer was setting up, too, just like Chevy."

Bear asked, "Chevy, what night did all this go down?"

"Monday, late. I sneaked in around midnight, maybe a little after. I had a key, so—"

"You had a key?" Bear almost came out of his chair.

"Yeah, I told you, the guy who hired me put a key in one of my payments at the office."

"You forgot to mention that."

"Oh, sorry. Yeah, I had a key. So, we got a deal?"

"Anything else you forgot?"

"Deal first, Detective." Chevy turned off his video program. "Oh, and did I mention I'm making another drop of recordings to-night—at midnight—in Old Town?"

"No, you little turd, you didn't."

Chevy smiled a big, evil smile. "Oops."

The knock on the door kept Bear from twisting him into a pretzel.

Captain Sutter leaned in the doorway. "Bear, a minute outside please." Her voice was irritated and her face tight like she just lost her mortgage payment on the ponies. "Now."

"Sure, Cap," he said, following her out.

Next door to the interview room, standing beside Captain Sutter in front of the one-way glass in the observation room, Agent Jim Dobron lifted his chin as Bear walked in. "Just what are you doing with this witness, Detective?"

"Interviewing him."

Dobron's tone was edgy and curt. "Don't you get it yet, Brad-dock?"

"I get it just fine. Do you?" Bear looked at Captain Sutter. "I'm sure the Cap has already told you, Dobron, I'm following up on Angela Tucker's stalker. Why? What brings you here this morning? You already stole all my crime scene evidence."

"Stole?" Dobron stepped close to him. "You're still chasing the Grecco murder. I told you it was an FBI case."

"Yeah, you did." Bear forced a laugh. "But since then, somebody tried to break into Angela Tucker's house. They broke into your crime scene, too, and now, two more bodies are lying in the tunnels beneath the estate."

"What? Why wasn't I informed?"

Captain Sutter raised a hand. "We tried, Agent Dobron. I called your office and they said they would relay the message to you and Marcos. They said you were together."

"We weren't. My meeting got cancelled. But that's not the point. Why were you at my crime scene?"

"I was pursuing *our* stalking suspect and he led us there."

"He led you there?" Dobron looked through the one-way glass at Chevy. "Bullshit, detective. You're lying."

Bear closed on Agent Dobron and jammed a steel finger into his chest. "You listen to me, Dobron, our suspect dropped his camera outside Angela's house. There were photos on it proving that he stalked her at the gala and photos proving he had been inside the estate. He also left several thousands of dollars of equipment at the Vincent House."

"You should have informed me—"

Bear jammed his finger deeper. "If you had bothered to look over the case file and evidence you stole from us, you'd know about the surveillance gear left at the house. We staked the place out to catch him trying to recover it. And as you can see, we got him. Back off."

"Easy, Bear." I patted Bear on the shoulder. "Like it or not, we're all on the same side—I think."

Captain Sutter threw a thumb at Bear, making him step away. "Seems we have an impasse, Agent Dobron."

"Yes we do, and it's because you can't control your detectives, Captain."

She laughed. "You should have seen his partner."

"Then I suggest—"

"No, I have a suggestion." She patted Bear on the back. "I'll assign Detective Braddock—temporarily—to your team as a liaison. He can muck around in your investigation in an official capacity and you don't look stupid for missing what he won't."

Agent Dobron looked from Captain Sutter to Bear. When he caught Bear's eyes, he tried to stare him down and failed. He faced Captain Sutter. "We need local support anyway. But he answers to me."

"Terrific," Bear said in a snarky tone. "But keep your Feebie geniuses out of my way. We work alone."

"We, Detective?" Dobron asked. "I'm only signing up for you, not Detective Spence."

"Whatever." Bear pointed to Chevy through the observation glass. "And he's my witness, not yours."

Dobron's mouth tightened. "Fine. What did he give you?"

Bear briefed him on the discovery in the tunnels of the missing donations and the two bodies—one we presumed to be Grecco's killer and the other, Petya Sergeyevich Chernyshov. He didn't share many details but did give him the highpoints of what we'd learned from Chevy.

"You know what I do," Bear said, wrapping up. "More or less."

Agent Dobron looked at the floor for a moment and then up at Bear. "And my men missed all this?"

"Could have happened to anyone," Bear said, "in the FBI. We simple sheriff's detectives caught it all."

"Agent Dobron," called a dark-suited man from across the detective's bullpen. He ran through the office toward us. "Sir, it's the West Virginia State Police." He handed Agent Dobron his cell phone. "Our back-up team arrived at the hotel safehouse a few minutes ago. They found Agent Mike Childs unconscious. He's being medevac'd to the Charles Town Hospital."

"What happened?" Agent Dobron's face flashed red. "What about Bonnie Grecco?"

"We don't know much yet, sir. We're only getting bits and pieces from Childs."

"What about Grecco? Where—"

"Unknown, sir," the agent said. "The state boys didn't find her. She's gone—someone took her."

FORTY-SIX

AGENT DOBRON PACED THE bullpen with the intensity of a caged bull. He stopped just long enough to curse and shout orders into the cell phone before taking up his patrol again. When he clicked off the phone and turned to Bear, his face was stone.

"No sign of Bonnie Grecco. Every badge in two states is hunting for her. So far, nothing. She's gone."

I asked, "Any signs she was injured? How'd they take her?"

"Your man see anything?" Bear asked. "How could she have just vanished?"

"My man went down to the front desk for more coffee. When he got back, someone was waiting for him. They took him from behind and it was over before he knew."

"And Bonnie?"

"He didn't see her. He opened the door, walked in, and wham—down he went. He came to when my other agents arrived twenty minutes later. She was gone."

Bear looked across the bullpen at the interview room where Chevy was. "I'm going to follow up on Chevy's story. I'm taking him to his office to see what recordings he has."

"You are, huh?" Agent Dobron stopped pacing. "Don't you mean you're requesting permission to go?"

"I don't need your permission."

"Yes, you do. You're assigned to me, remember?" Agent Dobron looked over at the other FBI man who shrugged. Then, Agent Dobron nodded to Bear. "Okay, Braddock. Permission granted. But first, who do you have at the Vincent House?"

"Mike Spence. He's a pain in the ass, but not a bad cop. He's there with my crime techs. They're looking over the body dump in the tunnels and trying to find any more passages or rooms in the houses we missed."

"Good. My men are there, too."

Something wasn't sitting well with me. "Bear, does this sound right to you about Bonnie? I mean, if someone intended on killing her, why abduct her first?"

"Dobron," Bear said, taking it all in. "Abducting Bonnie doesn't make sense."

"No, it doesn't," he said. "Unless it doesn't have anything to do with Stephanos's murder."

Bear had never told him about André's affair but he did now. "André Cartier was—"

"He was involved with her. We've known for a week."

Bear cocked his head. "A week? Before Stephanos's murder?"

"Oh, did my boys one-up you?" Agent Dobron waved in the air. "We've been investigating the Greccos for weeks. Cartier's involvement doesn't change anything. As bad as he looks, I think someone is trying to frame him."

I sighed. "They've done a good job."

Bear agreed, said so, and added, "Chevy is picking up payment at a dead drop tonight in Old Town."

"You and your people handle him." Dobron started pacing again. "But remember, Braddock, this is my operation—you share everything."

"Sure." Bear smiled a big, broad, plastic smile. "I'm just a dumb local cop trying to help you big-Feebies out."

A uniformed deputy walked into the bullpen and handed Bear a file. "Detective," the deputy said. "BCI in Richmond just sent this over. It's the IDs on the two bodies you found last night."

"Great, let me—"

Agent Dobron snatched the file from his hand. "Let me have that." He opened the file and read. "How did this happen?" He handed the file to Bear. "One of the corpses is Petya Sergeyevich Chernyshov—"

"We know about him. Who's the other?" Bear's eyes flared as he glanced down at the header, which read, "Department of Justice."

"Petya isn't any caterer." Bear's voice went cold. "He's an outlier for the Russian mob in DC. But you knew, right, Dobron?"

"No, I didn't."

Neither did I, but I knew the next part. I remembered it from the man's tattoos on his arm. "Look at the other one, Bear."

He did. "The other slug—Viktor the knuckle-dragger—I can't even pronounce his name—is a Russian mob enforcer. And he shouldn't be in the Vincent House's basement at all."

"No, he shouldn't. He's supposed to be in Lee County, Virginia." Agent Dobron cursed again and punched the side of a filing cabinet sitting innocently against the wall. "At the federal prison where he was two weeks ago."

FORTY-SEVEN

"I MISSED YOU AT THE party, Bonnie. Soon you'll be dead, too." It was a man's voice—hushed and disguised.

Angel leaned across the truck stop table, took Bonnie Grecco's phone, and replayed the voicemail. "Bonnie, we have to get this to Bear."

"No. I don't want the police involved anymore."

"Then why did you call me? What can I do?"

"They're gonna kill me. I received this message just after Dobron left the hotel room where they were keeping me. Then someone broke in and I ran."

"You're not telling me everything, Bonnie. No more lies."

Bonnie's face was pale and her hands trembled. Every movement nearby—every customer who walked into the truck stop café—sent her closer to the edge of her seat.

"Angela," Bonnie's voice cracked as she spoke. "I am so sorry to drag you into this, but I have no choice. I don't trust any of them.

No one. I had no one else to call and I knew you had the right friends to help me."

"The right friends?" Angel watched a trucker drop into a booth three down from them. "What do you mean?"

"I mean I don't trust the cops. Not that bitch Marcos. Not the FBI. No one. I need protection, Angela. I need your friend's protection."

Angel lifted her cup and watched the steam rise, taking the time to try to sort fear from fiction. So far, Bonnie had lied about almost everything she thought to be important—her relationship with André Cartier at the top of the list, and her revelation a few moments ago about Stephanos Grecco's life.

"Bonnie, why did you run away from the FBI? They were protecting you."

"I don't trust them. You have to understand—"

The café door opened and Bonnie's head snapped around. When a short, round man dressed in dirty jeans and work boots ambled in and sat at the counter, she closed her eyes and sighed, dropping her head to her hands.

"Angela, Steph was not a good man. He was, well, a crook. And hey, I'm not up for sainthood either, but Steph was a real beaut. He was always running scams and wheeling and dealing. He'd get rich people to put up money for some scheme and he'd skim it off before anyone knew. Sometimes—like last year down in Florida—he had to run because he cheated the wrong people."

"And you met him after he ran?"

"Uh, huh. And I figured out real fast what he was all about."

"And you stayed?"

"Yeah, I did." Tears trickled down her cheeks. "It was too late. I was in love with him. And we moved up here and I met André. I thought he could get me out of it all and away from Steph."

"The FBI, Bonnie." Angela tapped the table. "Why did you run from them?"

"After Steph and I met, these guys started coming around all the time and he made me leave. I thought they were the mob or something, but they weren't. They were the Feds. Steph was working with them all along—he told me so—but I wasn't supposed to know. He said he was on their team and they were looking out for him. After he got killed, why should I trust them?"

Angel's eyes flared. "Stephanos worked with the government? He was an informant?"

Bonnie shrugged. "He said he was an 'asset,' yeah, an asset. We kept moving. Every time he got into trouble with a scam, these guys would show, there would be a big fuss, and we'd be moving again. It's been the same way for six months. I've moved six times."

"Bonnie, just because he was somehow working with the FBI doesn't mean they're responsible for his murder."

"It doesn't mean they're not."

"Be reasonable."

"He's dead, isn't he? Dobron and his guys had me in the hotel. Never once did Dobron tell me he was working with Steph. Not once. Why not? I'm his widow, for Christ's sake. Steph was about to make a lot of money—enough to get away for good—and then he's dead." Bonnie's eyes followed the waitress around the room with the coffee pot again. "So you tell me, Angela. They're protecting me and still somebody leaves me a threatening message and tries to grab me? Why should I trust any of them?"

Angel knew no matter what she said, Bonnie wouldn't buy into it. Instead, she changed the topic. "Tell me about this book."

"The book?" Bonnie's face paled. "You too? Great."

"André is my uncle," Angela reached across the table and took one of her hands, pulling it to the center and holding it tight. "He's been a father to me. You told him about it, and now, he's a murder suspect. So, tell me about the book."

Bonnie looked out the window and her eyes fixed on a large, black SUV pulled up to the gas pumps yards from the café window. "Later. Get me out of here, Angela. Get me to your friends and I'll tell you whatever you want. But get me out of here."

Angel followed her eyes to the SUV. The driver gassed up and two other men—both in dark jeans and leather jackets—stood nearby talking on cell phones. A fourth was headed for the café door.

"What friends, Bonnie? Who do you think can get you out of this mess?"

Bonnie stood. "I'm going out the back. If you want to know about Stephanos's book, pick me up there."

FORTY-EIGHT

CHEVY'S OFFICE ALARM WAS flashing when Bear nudged the rear door open and led Chevy inside. The red light on the alarm panel blinked every ten seconds and the screen read "Alarm Activated—0846." Another tiny red light on the side of the panel flickered —the system was on battery backup.

I looked at Bear's watch. "The batteries kicked in three hours and ten minutes ago."

Bear dialed the Sheriff's dispatch and spoke to an emergency operator. When he tapped the call closed, he looked at Chevy. "Why didn't the alarm company call our office? Didn't you pay your bill?"

"Too many false alarms," Chevy said, looking around his three-room office. "The past couple weeks I've had so many false alarms the cops said they'd fine me over the next one. I told the alarm company to contact me instead."

"Did they?"

Chevy slipped his cell phone out of his jacket pocket and nodded. "Yep, I had two texts at eight-forty-seven and one ten minutes later. You guys had my phone and turned it off, man. If I'd had my phone—"

"You would have if you hadn't broken a dozen laws." Bear flipped the wall light switch but the lights didn't come on. "Power's out." He crossed the office to a small, imitation-wood desk and picked up the telephone. "Phone, too."

"*Muy bien,*" Chevy said, "someone must have shut the power off in the electrical closet down the hall. Maybe they thought it would stop the alarm. The alarm panel is on battery backup."

"Or maybe you didn't pay your electric bill either." Bear opened the plastic window blinds for more light. "We'll check the electric boxes after you find the evidence you promised."

I surveyed the dreary office. "Remind me never to be a PI in this town. And I think being dead is sometimes depressing."

The office of "Victor & Associates" was unimpressive—to be polite. The main office had Chevy's cheap desk, a beat-up filing cabinet, equipment cabinet, a small, dilapidated couch against the far wall, and a coffee pot sitting with three mismatched coffee mugs on a rickety table in the corner. Adjacent to the coffee maker was a tiny bathroom with a shower. Off the rear wall was a short hall leading to a back door and a second office used as a bedroom. Inside were an unmade twin bed covered in a ragged blanket and pair of old blue jeans, a dresser against the far wall, and a narrow folding table covered with photo equipment and assorted electronic devices similar to what we'd found at the Vincent House.

"Very homey, Chevy." Bear watched Chevy settle behind his desk, then went over to a small bulletin board beside the bathroom door and read the business license. "Victor and Associates? Do you have any associates?"

"Nope—unless you count the landlord's cat who comes around for scraps."

"You're Victor?"

Chevy nodded. "Right again, Detective. Nothing gets past you."

"Watch it, smartass." Bear never liked my snappy comebacks either. "Isn't your name Victorio Chevez? That's false advertisement."

"Who's gonna call a Latino PI around here?" Chevy slammed the top drawer and went to his filing cabinet. "I gotta get them in the door first, you know, 'cause once I get them face to face, I can talk my way into any job. It's all about confidence. And people like me, Bear. They like me a lot."

"I'm starting to like him, too," I said, "when he's not stalking my wife, of course. Other than his bad habits, he's a good guy."

\ a little and he went into the bathroom. There, he tried to close the bathroom door but Bear jammed his size thirteen in the way.

"No secrets, Chevy. If you want to walk on the stalking charges, I get to see you with your pants down."

"Okay, Detective." Chevy gripped the medicine cabinet door atop the bathroom sink and pulled. The cabinet swung open revealing a storage area behind it. The cavity was about eighteen inches square and eight inches deep with three shelves lining it.

I said, "Does everyone have secret passages and hiding places these days?" I peered over Chevy's shoulder as he dug around inside. "I gotta get one of these."

"They got one here, too." Chevy turned to Bear. "Ah, you aren't gonna believe this, but—"

"But what?" Bear said from the doorway. "And don't give me any lies about being robbed either."

Chevy lifted a manila folder from the bottom shelf and beneath it was a .38 snub-nosed revolver.

"Gun!" I yelled.

Bear's hand snapped to his handgun beneath his sport coat as he lunged into the small bathroom. He grabbed Chevy's shoulder in a powerful grip. "Don't even think about it."

"Relax—it's for emergencies." Chevy held up his hands and stepped back from the cabinet. "How'd they know my stash was in here?"

Bear nudged Chevy out of the bathroom and looked into the cabinet. He withdrew the .38 revolver and tucked it into his belt. "Let me guess. All your supposed-evidence is gone, right? Your supersecret hiding place is empty? And only you knew it was in there. How am I doing?"

"It was here, Detective. I swear, man. You gotta believe me. Give me a polygraph, man."

Bear took Chevy by the arm and shoved him toward the front door. "I don't need a polygraph. My bullshit-meter is pegged. Let's go back to the office so you can file a police report on this alleged break-in while I book you on a dozen felonies."

Chevy turned around and threw up his hands. "No, no, man. I got proof. I do. Take me to the Vincent place. I got more evidence there, man."

"No. Let's go, Chevy." Bear pointed at the door. "Don't make me handcuff you, *man*. We're just starting to like you."

"We?" Chevy glanced over his shoulder. "Ah, come on. Just one fast trip to the Vincent place. It'll prove me righteous. I swear."

I said, "Bear, let's do it. I think he's telling the truth. Besides, if we go and you're a good boy in the car, I'll introduce you to Sassy. It'll be worth it."

"Let's go, Chevy. Move." Bear reached behind his back for his handcuffs. "Turn around, Chevy. I didn't want to do this but—"

"No. You're not takin' me in yet."

Bear grabbed his shoulder. "Chevez, turn around and get against the wall." He stepped in close.

Neither of us saw it coming.

As Bear reached for his handcuffs behind his back, Chevy pivoted to his right. He grabbed Bear's arm, twisted and jerked it up, stressing his shoulder, elbow, and wrist all at once. "You gotta listen to me, Detective."

Bear growled in pain but couldn't get free—his size and power couldn't overcome Chevy's arm lock. "Chevez, you're going down for murder and I'm adding assaulting a cop." Bear tried to turn and snapped a punch at him.

Chevy blocked the punch, drove his leg behind Bear's knee and swept his leg out from under him. He followed the leg-sweep with a hard elbow into Bear's back, driving him down to the floor as

Bear fell off balance. As he fell, Chevy threw a leg over him and bronco-rode him onto the carpet.

"Don't fight me, man, I don't want to hurt you."

"Hurt me?" Bear raged. "I'm going to break you in half, you little turd."

"You just don't listen, man." Chevy tugged Bear's handgun from its holster and tossed it away, then grabbed his own .38 from Bear's belt. Next, he took Bear's handcuffs and snapped one cuff around Bear's wrist and the other onto the old radiator beside them.

"Sorry, Detective." He fished around Bear's jacket pocket and pulled out his key ring with the handcuff key dangling off. "I'm outta here, man. I gotta take care of myself."

Bear lay on his side, struggling to get to his knees, glaring a death wish at Chevy. "You just racked up three more felonies. Unlock these cuffs and I promise not to shoot you right here."

"Later, man." Chevy found Bear's gun and unloaded it, dumping the weapon and the full magazine into the toilet. Then he went to the back door and looked outside. "This is your fault, man." He slipped out the door and was gone.

I sat in Chevy's wobbly office chair watching Bear struggling to sit up. "Holy crap on a peanut butter sandwich, Bear. I wish I had a camera. Angel won't believe this. And wait until Spence hears—"

"Get me out of this," he yelled, kicking at the radiator. "He took my keys, Tuck. Do something."

"Tuck?" Twice in one day Bear spoke to me. "You've been ignoring me for months and now it's 'Tuck, do something?'"

"Dammit, cut the lip and get me out of this."

I walked over to him. "Sorry, can't help you. I'm not good with handcuffs unless I'm all juiced up. And you said yourself, there's no power in here. I can't do anything to help you. So, I'm going to the Vincent House. I'll fill you in later if I find anything."

"What?" His face was on fire. "You nag and nag and drive me insane. I pretended you weren't around, but no, you just had to hound me. Now I need you, and you're running off?"

"Sorry, Bear." At the back door I watched Chevy drive off in Bear's unmarked cruiser. "I need a good stiff drink."

FORTY-NINE

"THE BOOK IS THE key to the war between the Calaprese families and the Reds." Poor Nic stood behind his antique mahogany desk with his grandfatherly smile directed at Bonnie Grecco. "Or I should say, Soviet Intelligence in Washington—well before the KGB or the thugs operating today."

Angel glanced over at Bonnie and noted she didn't seem surprised at Poor Nic's revelation. She and Bonnie had arrived at Nicholas' an hour ago after escaping the roadside truck stop. Angel secreted Bonnie out of the rear parking lot after she was convinced the large, black SUV was there for her. Angel drove straight to Nicholas' house.

"Spies? Vincent Calaprese was involved with Soviet spies?" Angel asked.

"No, no, not the way you think, my dear," Poor Nic said. "Vincent Calaprese was, shall we say, a business man who preferred to operate outside the normal restrictions of the law."

"They were gangsters," Bonnie said in a flat voice. "Mob. Like you, Nicholas."

Poor Nic let his smile settle the awkwardness Bonnie's words lay between them.

Angela shot her a "you're a guest—behave" glance, then she asked Nicholas, "What did he have to do with Russian spies?"

"Ah, yes. You see, it was the late-thirties and the second world war was starting to churn. German and Japanese spy networks were already operating in our country. Little do many people know, but so were the Soviets—many worked through the Communist Party of the United States. Oh, the party was a legitimate group, mind you, but some were also Soviet spies and sympathizers."

"Yes, I know the history," Angela said. "Those were confusing times, here in the States. The Soviets and us were allies against the Axis but the Soviets were an ally in name only. We had a common enemy—Hitler and the Japanese—and while the Soviets were aligned with us, both our governments knew it was not a true alliance. We were destined to clash—we planned for it as did the Soviets. They developed spy networks here. Everyone's focus was on the Nazis and Japanese so they went almost undetected for years."

Nicholas gave Angel an approving wink. "Ah, I sometimes forget you are a historian. Yes, you are correct. Those were dangerous days. Very dangerous."

"How was Vincent involved, Nicholas?" Angela asked, glancing over at Bonnie who looked bored and was wandering around Nicholas' den. "What does he have to do with the Soviet spy rings and what's this book have to do with either?"

"Yes, yes, the book." Nicholas watched Bonnie for a moment before turning back to Angela. "Various entities—the other New York families—were trying to muscle Vincent out of New York. He was a smaller player so he decided to concentrate his enterprises in Washington and Baltimore—although he kept his hand in New York where he could."

"How did he stay clear of federal scrutiny in DC?" Angel asked. "I know some organized crime figures were reported to have worked with the FBI and intelligence in support of the war. Was Vincent one of them?"

Poor Nic nodded. "He was. Vincent was interested in the same enterprises as his New York competitors—liquor, gambling, black-market goods. But he recognized there was another service to parlay—information. He used his enterprises to collect information about the German, Japanese, and Soviet organizations—among others. His information was very valuable to the US authorities."

"And he kept it all in his book." Angela saw it. Vincent Calaprese turned his muscle and street organization into his own intelligence agency. "Were there Russian mobsters here then?"

"Of sorts, but not like today, my dear. There were some Russian immigrants who formed dangerous gangs and other organizations cent's Washington network was quite successful against the Nazi rings, Japanese sympathizers, and Soviet operations. His network was second to none in DC—including the FBI's. Hoover's men relied on him for information they could not get. Imagine, the FBI coming hat-in-hand to the Calapreses."

Angela watched Nicholas reminiscing in the nostalgia—she heard the melancholy tone of his voice and watched his eyes seeing life in past years. In the months she'd come to know him, she'd grown fond of him; a strange relationship given he was a man cloaked in a lifetime of crime and corruption. Yet, since arriving in Winchester, he was a different man. At least, to her he was.

Angel asked, "Vincent used the information to keep the Russian gangs and others away? And keep the authorities at bay, too?"

"Yes, my dear, very good. He provided the authorities with information on the Nazi and Japanese activities, and kept the rest for his own use. If the other crime families left him alone to make a living, he would not disclose what he had collected."

"And he kept all this in this book, right? A ledger or journal?"

"Yes. The content of the book is worth many millions today—and many lives. It holds the roots of several prominent businesses today, many of which are rooted in Soviet spy networks operating in Vincent's day. And some still operate today; at least, that's the belief. Vincent was a very influential man. His influence, back then, is still worth a fortune and power today."

Bonnie wandered back from her tour of Nicholas' den. "He sounds a lot like you, Nicholas. Which is why I asked to see you."

"Perhaps." Poor Nic's eyes rested on her. "Please, tell me why you are here."

"My life is in danger and I had nowhere else to go," Bonnie said. "I need your help."

"Ah, I see." He watched her with a calm, quiet gaze. "But why and how did you come to know to ask for me? After all, you were under the FBI's protection, were you not?"

"Yes, I was." Bonnie looked down. "Steph was trying to make a deal with them for more protection and someone killed him.

They're trying to kill me, too—someone came to the hotel where the Feds had me. I barely escaped. I can't trust anyone. I need protection, Nicholas."

"But why me?"

"The party." Bonnie sat back in the chair beside Angela. "You were quite the talk of the party, Nicholas. Everyone said you were Angela's godfather—I'm sure they meant it in fun."

"Of course." Poor Nic smiled and nodded.

"And one of the women mentioned that you did much for the community—even helped solve Angela's husband's murder. She said if she were ever in trouble, you'd be the one she'd turn to."

"Really? How interesting." Poor Nic clasped his hands. "It seems the town has grown to accept me." He winked at Angel. "At least, some of them have."

Angel said, "Play him the voicemail I heard at the truck stop, Bonnie."

She did. *"I missed you at the party, Bonnie. Soon you'll be dead, too."* She played it a second time, and on the third, she started to cry but wiped the tears away and hardened herself. "You see, I'm in danger."

He shrugged. "Tell me, why was Stephanos murdered?"

"I don't know."

"You're lying."

"What? No!"

Poor Nic's voice was flat and cold—his grandfather-smile was gone, too. "My dear, you cannot expect me to believe you do not know. Tell me the truth."

"Bonnie?" Angela looked at her. "Tell us what you know. Please. You asked for our help. You must tell us what's going on."

Bonnie stood and walked to the large bay window on the far side of Nicholas' den. She stood at the window staring out—the grip of a decision holding her there. "Steph discovered the history of the book several months ago. I don't know how, but he did. He also discovered its location and passed the information around certain circles—dangerous circles. A few weeks ago, some men came to our place in Washington."

Nicholas watched her from his desk. "And who were these men?"

"He said he was making a deal with the FBI but then these men came—Russian men. Steph tried to keep it all a secret from me but I knew what was going on. They wanted proof he knew where the book was. He promised them proof at Angela's gala."

"Bonnie? You brought the Russian mob to my gala?" Angela's voice was curt and she stood up and went to Bonnie at the window. "Did you?"

"I'm sorry," Bonnie said, refusing to face her. "Steph demanded someone make the deal—a go-between. They were to meet outside, before the gala began, but it was raining and—"

"Who?" Angela asked. "Petya? Being a go-between got him killed?"

"I don't know." Bonnie shook her head. "I don't. Please believe me. Steph caught me listening outside their last meeting. He was furious. He ordered me to stay out of it. He was very angry. But I think it was a façade."

Poor Nic nodded. "Of course it was. Your husband was not angry with you, but perhaps he was afraid for you."

"He was terrified—I could tell. But we needed the money. He'd gambled all we had to make this work. For months, he ran around trying to find the book. He needed this score. We were broke and he said the money he had was too hard to use—it would draw attention, whatever that meant."

Angela watched Bonnie return to her chair and slump back down. She could see the defeat in her—see her eyes begin to drain her regret of Stephanos. "Bonnie, who was Stephanos's contact? Who at the gala did he give the evidence to?"

She shook her head again and dabbed at her eyes with a tissue from her pocket. "I don't know. He wouldn't tell me, and anyway, I think they killed him before he made contact. He still had the old money after they killed him."

"Old money?" Angela looked over at Poor Nic. "Does it make sense to you?"

It did. A smile took over Poor Nic's face and he winked. "Yes, of course. The book was more than just a list of enemy businesses and spy networks. It was also Vincent's ledger of his hidden accounts—accounts from his government benefactors."

"Government payments?" Angela asked. "The FBI paid him for information?"

"Yes, of course, and other activities, too." Poor Nic stood up and went to the den's story-tall double oak doors. He opened them, called out to some unseen servant for iced tea and sandwiches, and returned to his desk where he leaned against it. "Vincent was a true entrepreneur. War was coming. The FBI had been very successful against the old families in the twenties and thirties—but Vincent's had survived by knowing what your customer wanted and providing it."

Angela's eyes lit up. "It's hard to believe our government would work with gangsters—no offense, Nicholas."

Poor Nic laughed. "None taken. Our government has been in business with those in my former profession since both were born. It's often a tenuous relationship, but a relationship no less. Especially in wartime. When the government needed something—information, covert action—it often relied upon those who had the means and the networks and above all, the right people. After all, we're all Americans, aren't we?"

Angela shrugged. "Yes, I suppose we are. But—"

"And back then," he went on, "patriotism trumped petty arrests and bad blood. No, my dear, those were unusual times. And Vincent Calaprese was an unusual man. They paid him very well for his services. And those services were very valuable indeed."

Bonnie looked at him. "You know where Steph got the money? You know all about this book? You know more than Steph or I did. Do you know who killed him and who is trying to kill me?"

"No," he said in a soft voice. "But it is over the book. Detective Braddock found ten thousand dollars on Stephanos—ten, one-thousand dollar gold certificate notes. They were in mint condition like the day they were printed." He winked at Angel. "At least, so I am told. So, Stephanos must have found the book."

Poor Nic's den doors opened and a beefy bodyguard carried in a tray of iced tea, sandwiches, and desserts. He set the tray on a server near the window, poured three glasses of tea, and served them. Then, without a word, he left.

Bonnie asked, "How do you know they're connected to the book, Nicholas?"

"Those notes were from one of Vincent's stashes." He paused and sipped his tea. "How they survived without discovery all these years I don't know. Think about it—where would those gold certificates come from if not some hidden vault of Vincent's? I don't believe in coincidences such as those, do you?"

Angela shook her head. "No, I suppose not. Bonnie, do you have any idea where he found them?"

"Does it matter? Someone's trying to kill me—staying alive is all I care about." She took a long sip of tea and looked up at him. She held his eyes and smiled a weak, forced smile. "You'll help me, won't you? And I understand if there is a fee for your services."

Poor Nic moved around to the front of the desk where he stood in front of Angela and Bonnie. He leaned down and touched Bonnie's cheek, holding it in a gentle, old-fashioned sign of warmth and comfort. "Of course, my dear. And yes, there is a cost. I wish to see this book for myself. There may be information in the book that can protect me, too. I am a retired old man, but I still must protect myself. You may keep the book, but I wish to review it for a day or so."

"Yes, of course." Bonnie took his hand. "I knew I could count on you."

"Of course, my dear." Poor Nic's grandfatherly smile returned. "Please, tell me who you fear—who you believe killed Stephanos. I know you have an idea. No?"

"I don't believe anything; I know who killed him." Bonnie's eyes were streaming. "It was Anatoly Nikolaevich Konstantinova—the biggest Russian Mob boss in the country."

Angela's eyes went wide. "Ruth-Ann Marcos was asking about Anatoly earlier, Nicholas. You said you didn't know him, right?"

"Ah, yes, Anatoly," Poor Nic said, frowning. "He and I are very dear, very old friends, Angela. Very dear friends."

FIFTY

I SEARCHED THE VINCENT House from top to bottom. I also searched all the tunnels I could find. Chevy was nowhere; and nowhere was bad. Oh, not that Chevy's absence was unexpected—he could have lied to Bear when he said he had more evidence. It's just going to be worse on Chevy when Bear catches him. I'd seen Bear bested one or two times. Once, it took three bikers and a half-dressed barmaid to take him down in a bar fight. Had it not been for the bosomy, half-naked barmaid, Bear wouldn't have lost his concentration and would have taken the bikers. Another time, a drunk driver stumbled out of his pickup, forgot to set the brake, and the truck knocked Bear over and broke his leg.

This time, Victorio Chevez rodeo-hogtied him in three seconds flat. And with his own handcuffs, too. Also, Chevy stole his car. How much humiliation can he take?

I was checking in the large dining room when I noticed the room's walls were adorned with paintings of stalwart figures—

Calapreses' no doubt—all portrayed in various rooms in the Vincent House. Their images were a timeline that began with a robust Michael Calaprese—who was the spitting image of Vincent—in a double-breasted, wide-lapeled pinstripe suit standing in the lounge. Several paintings later, there was a young man in a decorated military uniform standing in front of the den fireplace—he looked familiar in a strange, *deja vu* way. I moved from painting to painting trying to piece together the bloodline from father to son and daughter and so on until I found myself gazing at the last portrait in the room.

The painting was of a young woman standing in the library in front of Vincent's bookcases. One hand extended to the desk beside her, resting atop a stack of books, the other clutched a Bible. The image was life-like—alluring and warm. The woman had dark hair flowing around her shoulders and a classy, elegant figure. She was smiling the faintest of smiles—a guileful, taunting smile. Her black evening dress clung to her and even though it was just paint and canvas, she teased sensuality. The woman was happy—eyes wide and radiant, staring out at life beyond the canvas.

I was lost in those eyes when Coleman Hawkins began *Body and Soul*.

"Isn't she a tootie-bear?"

Sassy stood in the dining room doorway. She was wearing a cotton, above-the-knee dress that for her time was rather risqué. It fit her just right and the white cotton accentuated all her feminine parts to make me blush a little—very little. In her time or mine, she was a hottie. I can only imagine what men of her time thought—or the women.

"Hello, Sassy. Is this Frannie?"

"Yep, sure is. Francesca Calaprese-Masseria, back in her heyday. What a dish, huh?"

"Yes she was. Why didn't she stay here? Angel said she retired somewhere else?"

"She got too old to take care of the place herself, so she got rid of a lot of the good stuff and left. Then some creep broke in and messed up the place. The creep ripped up some of these paintins' good, too."

I remembered Angel telling me about the vandalism. "It looks like they fixed up the portraits like new."

"Well, not like new—no way—but they fixed them up." She giggled again. "Frannie had already taken some other paintings, books, and stuff. Stuff I wouldn't take but she wanted."

"What kind of stuff?" I made a mental note.

"Just stuff."

I changed the subject. "Sassy, you haven't seen a short, stocky Hispanic guy who looks like a bulldog, have you?"

"Maybe." She batted her eyes and lit the room with her smile. "What'll you give me if I tell you?"

"What do you want?" I was screwed the moment the words left my lips.

She wiggled across the room like a puppy coming to play. "You know ... I got a bottle of hooch hidin' upstairs in the attic. The fella you were askin' about was up there earlier. So were all the others."

"The others?"

"Yeah, the others." She batted her eyes again, this time leaning into me and letting her finger glide across my face, over my lips, and down to my chest where it lingered. "And Tuckie, it's real dark up there and we could—"

"Oh, no, Sassy, we couldn't. I'm a married man."

"To a breather. What about 'till death do us'?"

She had a point. But, "I just can't, Sassy. Special as you are."

"No kiddin'?" She put on a pout. "You know you can't do nothing with her, right?"

"I know. Believe me, I've thought long and hard about it."

"We can, Tuckie. You ever make it with a hundred-year-old doll-baby like me?"

Gulp. "No. What would Vincent think?"

"Yes," a voice boomed from the doorway, "what would Vincent think?"

It was, of course, Vincent.

"Hey, Vincent. I was admiring your portraits." I hoped he hadn't heard too much.

"I see what you've been admiring." He had. He strode in and pulled Sassy away from me. "You've been a welcome guest, Oliver. But, any man who takes advantage of another man's hospitality becomes unwelcome."

Geez, he sounded like Doc.

"It isn't like you think, Vincent. I was just—"

"Yes, *just.*" Vincent puffed on a big cigar and burned holes through me. "It's not bad enough the coppers were in here all last night and today. They turned the joint upside down again. When does it stop? When do they leave us alone?"

"I'm sorry, Vincent." I meant it, too. "But someone killed two more people and I have to find out who."

"You have to? You mean they do, right Oliver—the coppers?" He turned and glanced up at Frannie's portrait. "Over the years, my things have been stolen and destroyed. My home is becoming a museum. And I cannot even protect my family because someone has the book. You want to know who is killing all these people, Oliver?"

Dumb question. "Yes, Vincent. I do."

"Find my book."

"Ah, so if I find this book for you, you'll tell me who killed Grecco and the others?"

"No."

"No?"

Vincent tapped ash from his cigar and dismissed Sassy with a wave. He watched her march out of the room huffing and mumbling under her breath. Then he turned to me with eyes shooting daggers.

"You find the book and you find your killer. It's that simple. But you bring the book to me, you understand? No side trips. No peeking. Bring me the book and I'll tell you what you want."

"So, you know who killed Grecco? Is it the same person who killed Petya Chernyshov and Grecco's killer?"

"One and the same."

"And you're not going to tell me?"

"No."

For a dead guy, he was irritating. "Come on, Vincent. Have you considered the killer already has the book? Tell me who it is and I'll end all this and get it back."

He threw a chin up at Frannie's portrait. "Go to my daughter, Oliver. She's the last of us. She will know how to help."

"Your daughter?"

"Didn't Sassy tell you?"

"No, she left the 'your daughter' part out."

"Ah, yes, she was jealous of my Frannie. Still is. Go to her, Oliver. She can help with the book."

So Frannie was Vincent's daughter. "Why can't you, Vincent?"

"It don't work that way." He walked to the dining room doorway and turned back around. He was fading; just a silhouette and a stream of Cuban smoke. "If I did, what would motivate you to find my book?"

I started after him. "Wait, I need to know about Frannie—"

"Ask Doc. After all, he owes me—he owes me big."

"Why? What did you ever do for him?"

He laughed and faded to nothing as the rich scent of his Cuban lingered. "It's not what I did for him, it's what he did to me."

"What did he do?"

"You mean you don't know?"

Damn, he was irritating. "No."

His laughter echoed. "Why, Oliver, Doc Gilley killed me."

FIFTY-ONE

"WAIT, WHAT? DOC KILLED you?"

I started down the hall after him when Sassy slinked in behind me and wrapped her arms around me. "Tuckie, the Cuban guy is back. He's upstairs looking for something. But I hid it on him— 'cause I knew it was important. I grabbed it, see, and hid it good."

"Sassy, do you want Vincent to kill us both?"

She giggled. "That would be a trick, wouldn't it?"

"You know what I mean." It struck me what she said. "What did you hide?"

"The little lipstick-thingy. The thingy the Latin guy is looking for. He was here last week putting up these funny gadgets all over the joint. Vincent was in a tizzy I tell you."

Victorio Chevez. "You mean Chevy?"

"I don't know what he drives, Tuckie, but yeah, the Cuban fella. He's upstairs going nuts 'cause I hid his doohickey."

"Tell me what it looks like and what he was doing with it."

She did. She described a computer USB flash drive. "Show me."

We went to the northwest attic room—Chevy's secret room—where she'd shown me the ghost hunting paraphernalia yesterday. The equipment was long gone—seized first by Bear's men and then by the FBI. All that remained were an old wobbly wood table and some shelving. Outside the room, someone banged and smashed things around the attic.

"It's him, Tuckie. That's the guy who drives the Chevy."

"No, Sassy, his name is Chevy."

"Why would someone name their kid after a car?"

It was no use. Sassy was still back in 1939 with the mind of a sexy, wild party girl whose chair at Mensa would be forever vacant. But alas, she was a bubbly, good-natured gal, even for a dead one.

We followed the sounds of breaking glass and crashing furniture and found Chevy in a panic. He dumped packing boxes on the floor, kicked over old furniture, and careened around the attic like a drunken tornado. He'd worked up a sweat and stood panting and cursing beneath the attic eaves.

"Hi ya, Chevy, what are you looking for?" I asked, and when I did, I saw his EMF meter hanging on his belt flashing like a plane about to crash. "Did you lose something?"

Chevy grabbed the meter off his belt and turned in a slow circle until the row of multi-colored lights stayed on—a high-pitched whine erupted when it settled on Sassy and me. "Oh, man, not you again. Go away, *fantasma*, leave me alone."

"Tuckie, his thingy is telling on us again."

"Relax, Sassy. Where's Chevy's flash drive?"

She looked at me like I'd just asked a 1930s girl about, well, a flash drive.

I tried again. "The lipstick-thingy?"

"Oh, yeah, it's downstairs behind the bar. I hid it in the wine closet in an empty champagne bottle." She threw her hands on her hips. "Didn't I have a great idea?"

"A champagne bottle?"

"Yeah, it wouldn't fit in a wine bottle, silly."

"Of course not. Good girl."

Chevy waved the EMF meter around again, each time it flickered and chirped until he pointed it back at us. Then it shrieked a steady cry and stayed lit.

"No. No. No. Shit. You a ghost, man?"

"Yep."

"You a ghost man? Talk to me, man. Don't hurt me but talk to me." His face paled and he slid something out of his pocket. "This is a recorder, ghost ... okay? Don't get mad."

I moved closer to him, touching the thin, silver digital recorder and watched the lights light up as it turned on. "I know, Chevy. I had one just like it when I was alive."

Chevy's eyes exploded as the signal strength meter—a tiny string of red indicator lights on the top of the recorder—flashed full-power every time I spoke.

"Boo, Chevy. You looking for your flash drive?"

The signal strength meter spiked.

"Oh, man. You are here." He looked around the attic and back at the recorder. "Tell me what you want, ghost."

"Tell 'em, Tuckie." Sassy said, hooking her arm in mine. "Tell him where his thingy is. I want to see his face."

I did. "And Chevy, you better get the flash drive to Bear when you're done. He's pissed enough for handcuffing him to a radiator and stealing his car. Having the evidence you promised might keep you from getting your butt kicked."

When the signal meter weakened, Chevy clicked a couple buttons on the recorder and held it up to listen. The sounds were faint and he turned up the volume. I didn't have to listen to know when it played. His eyes erupted and his mouth dropped.

"Boo, Chevy. You looking for your flash drive?"

"¡Hijo de puta!" He jumped back and dropped the EMF meter on the ground. He spun in a circle as his face contorted and sweat broke out on his forehead. "No way, ghost. No way." He took a deep breath and listened to the remainder of the recording.

"Tell 'em, Tuckie. Tell him where his thingy is. I want to see his face ... And Chevy, you better get the flash drive back to Bear when you're done. He's pissed enough for handcuffing him to a radiator and stealing his car. Having the evidence you promised might keep you from getting your butt kicked."

I said, "Sassy, we better give him a minute. He's about to—"

Chevy's face flushed and he ran for the corner of the attic, pushed open the round window, and tried to stick his head out. When he couldn't gulp in enough air, he bent over and heaved bile and fear onto the floor. After a few moments, he stood up, turned around, and stared into the attic. Then, he flipped the recorder back on and waited.

"Easy, Chevy. We aren't here to hurt you. I'm Oliver Tucker. Bear and Angel know all about me. And this is Sassy—she's, ah, well, she's not from here. Oh, she's from the Vincent House, just not from the here and now like you and me. Long story. Trust me."

When the strength meter lowered, Chevy replayed the recording and fell back against the wall. His eyes were closed and sweat poured down his face. "*Madre de Dios, fantasmas.*" When he got his nerve, he retrieved his EMF meter and waved it around until the lights and squealing showed him where we were standing.

"You … You're … Detective Tucker?" He looked down at his recorder as I answered, waited for the meter to slow, and listened to my reply. "How?"

We found a rhythm. He asked, I spoke, he replayed the recording. For ten minutes we went through his questions and my answers. With each question, he laughed a little more, almost cried twice, and settled into a calm, disbelief-but-it's-happening mindset.

"Why are you hanging here?"

Talk—record—listen.

"Sorry, Chevy, but I don't have a lot of answers. I was murdered and I'm back. I think I'm back to help solve cases like mine. You know, I can connect with Angel and Bear and help others like me."

Talk—record—listen.

"Like you?" He didn't wait for the reply. "Oh, dead guys."

"And gals," Sassy added. "Us girls can get whacked, too, Chevrolet."

"Chevy. It's Chevy, short for—"

"Yeah, I tried to explain," I said, "but forget it. Let's go get your evidence and find Bear."

Downstairs, Sassy led us to the bar's wine closet and pointed out the dusty champagne bottle where she'd hidden the flash drive. It took a minute or two for Chevy to rattle and shake the small device free.

Sassy sat on a bar stool twirling in circles. "Come on, let's have some fun, boys. Vincent will be back soon."

Talk—record—listen.

"Who is this Vincent guy?" Chevy waved his EMF meter around the bar. "Should I worry? Will he hurt me or is he like you?"

Good questions. I didn't know the answers. "He's a gangster before gangsters were in the music business. He's from the thirties. And Chevy, he isn't like me. He doesn't have a sense of humor."

"Great. What could be worse than an angry gangster ghost?"

That was an easy one. "Bear Braddock."

"Uh-oh. I forgot about him. He's coming here, isn't he?"

Another softball. "Yeah, but relax. This flash drive will make him all happy. If it has the evidence on it you promised, anyway."

"It does. It's my get-out-of-jail-free card." Chevy stood in the open wine closet doorway. "But I need it first, Tuck. Are you stuck in this house or at home or something? Or can you guys—and gals—like, you know, go anywhere and follow people? Like on TV?"

Good question. "Well, Sassy and Vincent are pretty much here I think. I don't know why. But I can go where I want. But I can't just poof in and out and find people—not yet. And I can't do the movie stuff like know everything and do spirit tricks. So if I don't see something happen or hear it for myself, I'm no better off than you."

Talk—record—listen.

"So you just can't dial me up or something? You gotta find me like if you were alive?"

"Yes. Unless I have something personal of yours. Sometimes I can find Angel or Bear by using their personal things. Cool, huh? Why?"

Click—listen.

"'Cause I'm outta here before Braddock gets here." He stepped into the wine closet and opened the secret passage. "Sorry, man, but I got things to do." He disappeared.

"Tuckie, what is he doing? Chevy's a funny guy, ain't he?"

The front door slammed and heavy footsteps came down the hall toward us.

The stomping would be Bear Braddock—an unhappy Bear Braddock.

"Yeah, Sassy, he's a real card. He thinks he's going to hide from me. But he can't."

"No? I thought you said you can't find him with a snap? You know, like Houdini or something?" She twirled on the bar stool again and began fading as Bear walked into the room.

"Tuck? You in here?"

"Nothing like Houdini, Sassy. But I don't need to be. I know where he'll be later tonight."

FIFTY-TWO

"1930S MOBSTERS. SOVIET SPIES. Three dead guys. The Russian mob and some secret book?" Bear spat out his frustrations and downed half his bourbon. He sat in a leather recliner near the front living room window. He'd started with a tall bourbon and ice—a very tall bourbon and one tiny ice cube—it was almost gone. "Not to mention someone stalking you, Angela. And the stalker's missing. What's next?"

"Well, you forgot about Bonnie Grecco." Angel said from the couch across from him. "And—"

"And she's disappeared, too," I said and watched her look away. "Angel?"

"Nothing. I'm worried about her."

The three of us had been hashing out the entire case since Bear and I returned from the Vincent House an hour ago. He was still stinging from Chevy's second escape. Luckily for Chevy, he forgot to take Bear's cell phone when he hog-tied him to the radiator.

Bear was able to call Spence to get released—Spence rescuing him would torment him for months.

"Where does this leave us?" Angel asked, sipping a glass of red wine while she scratched Hercule's belly. He was on his back with twenty-toes up beside her on the couch. "Do you have anything on the two bodies from the tunnels?"

"All bad news," Bear said. "One was Viktor-something, a Russian mob enforcer who was supposed to be in Federal prison. Petya, the caterer, was also mobbed up with the Russians. He ran low-level scams and errands. Feds think he's laundering mob money through the catering company and get this, he's skimming payroll at the same time. Very enterprising guy."

I sat beside Hercule. "Someone pays Viktor-the-Russian-hitman to shoot Stephanos Grecco. The someone then kills Viktor—I know, because I was there. Petya got involved somehow and somebody kills him—to silence him is my guess. So we have three dead, all connected by one killer—the 'someone.' The question is, who is this someone?"

"Whoever sent Chevy to the Vincent House," Bear said. "Chevy's mysterious client. The one wanting all the video of Angel."

Angel asked. "What do I have to do with any of this?"

I remember what Sassy told me. "Angel, what can you tell me about Francesca Calaprese-Masseria?"

"Frannie?" Angel was thoughtful. "She's ninety-plus and in a retirement home. All her relatives are gone—at least the ones I knew about. She has some distant cousins and such, but they've not been in touch with her for decades."

Bear asked, "What are you thinking, Tuck?"

"The book, maybe." I told them what Sassy said about Frannie leaving and taking all 'the good stuff.' Then I added, "Maybe Frannie took the book with her, too. If so, it could be why Chevy's mysterious client had him stalking you, Angel. You met with Frannie about the foundation buying the Vincent House and all the house's antiques and such. Maybe the killer thinks you know where the book is."

"I didn't even know about the book then."

"Maybe they don't know that." I had a hunch. "What did Frannie do with all the things she took with her from the Vincent House?"

Angel sipped her wine. "I'm not sure. I had to track down three storage places to retrieve some of the original furniture. After all the years, some of it wasn't any good anymore but there was enough to put back in the house. Frannie had several personal items with her in her retirement suite—including her antique bedroom furniture."

"Sassy thought she took a lot of books from the Vincent House library," I said.

Bear jiggled his ice cubes and contemplated the empty glass. "She must have taken the book, too. Right? You said your friend, Vincent, told you she was supposed to protect it."

"Yes, he did. What about it, Angel?"

"Frannie had some books." Angel said as Hercule bounced up and went to the window to peer out. "What is it boy?"

I followed him and looked up and down the street into the dimming light but saw nothing suspicious. "Easy boy. Give a bark if you see something."

Angel went on. "Frannie had a large bookshelf in her retirement suite. And there were boxes of books in storage. Would she put something so valuable in storage?"

"You said she's over ninety," Bear said. "Maybe she wasn't thinking. Or maybe someone did it for her without knowing."

"Or it's sitting on her bookshelf." I felt a road trip coming. "We need to go see Frannie, Angel. Tomorrow morning, first thing."

Bear stood up. "Count me out. I have a date with Chevy and his client tonight—if they show. Chevy is supposed to make a pickup and drop off with this guy later this evening. I want to be there and grab both of them. If things go well, I'll be dealing with them tomorrow."

Hercule trotted over to the living room door, turned, and woofed at me. Then he disappeared into the foyer heading for my den.

"I'll be right back." I knew what Hercule wanted and followed him.

When I walked into my den Hercule was curled up in my—his—favorite leather chair. He had his favorite ball between his paws and was getting a good head scratching from Doc.

"Where have you been, Doc? I've been looking for you since yesterday."

He continued patting Hercule and didn't look up at me. Hercule moaned and was all about Doc's house calls.

Doc said, "I've been busy thinking."

"You couldn't think here? You couldn't talk to me?"

"No. It's you I've been thinking about."

"Is there something wrong?"

He looked up and bored holes through me. "Of course there's something wrong, Oliver. And we both know what it is."

We do? Oh yeah, we do. "Did you kill Vincent Calaprese?"

"Yes."

Yes? Huh? No, wait … Yes? "Ah, Doc, I need a little more than just 'yes.' I'm a detective after all."

"You're dead after all." He forced a laugh. "Come now, Oliver. Surely you've figured it out."

Surely I haven't. "Enlighten me. And give me the condensed version, okay? Angel and I are going to see Frannie—"

"To find the book. Yes, good idea. Then you'll bring it to me."

"Yeah, okay. But only if you tell me about you and Vincent—and about you and Sassy."

Doc stood and wandered to my bookcase, taking his time there and avoiding the issue. By the time he turned around, he could have memorized *War and Peace*.

"It was thirty-seven and I was a surgeon in Washington—a healer—and your grandfather was getting ready for college. I wanted things for him. Things even as a surgeon, there wasn't enough money for in those days. The country was coming out of the Depression and money was tight for everyone."

"You never told me about my grandfather, Doc. How come?"

His voice was strange—raspy, half-whisper, half-distant, and melancholy. "He was young and adventurous and I wanted him to travel and see the world. I wanted him in a good school. Those things cost money. And, no one wanted to admit it, but war was coming, too."

"No, I get it. Times were hard."

"Yes indeed things were. But it's a terrible excuse for what I did."

Boy, could Doc spin a mystery. I had no idea what he was talking about.

He looked over at me and sat on the arm of the chair beside Hercule. "One day, late in the evening, some men came to my practice in DC. They wanted me to visit an elderly patient too sick to travel. They offered me an enormous amount of money—over two-hundred dollars. It was a lot back then—so I went. They brought me here to Winchester."

Ah, a light in the darkness. "And the patient was Vincent?"

"Yes. He had pneumonia and was very ill. But, his pneumonia was not why he wouldn't come to my office—"

"He was hiding out?"

Doc nodded. "Yes, though I didn't understand it at the time. It was later—days later. So, I treated him and healed him. I stayed with them for over a week until he was back on his feet. At the end of the second week, when I returned home, some government agents were waiting."

"G-men, Doc? The FBI was waiting for you?"

"They were, yes. They wanted to know everything that happened to me. I had no idea who Vincent Calaprese was—he was using a false name while I was in Winchester. And there, I saw no one but him and his men. I had no way of knowing what I'd fallen into."

Boy, Doc was a celebrity. "What did you tell them—the feds, I mean?"

"Nothing." He shook his head. "I knew nothing so there was nothing to tell. It didn't matter. I refused to speak with them because of doctor-patient confidentiality. They threatened me—to have me audited and arrested—even to take my license and close me down. It was unbelievable what they put me through."

I watched him as he drifted away. He was lost somewhere between reminiscence and anger. "And? Did you give in? How'd you—"

"No, I did not. Not to them, anyway." He took a deep breath. "Months went by and Vincent's men came for me again. I went with them but Vincent was fine. He wanted me to be his doctor—for him and his men—in secret. When he learned the FBI had tried to coerce me and failed, he decided to trust me."

"And you agreed?"

"No. But then I met Sassy."

Of course it was Sassy. "Ah, what about my grandfather and my grandmother—"

Tears welled in Doc's eyes—something I'd never seen before. "His mother was gone, Oliver. I'd lost her five years before to flu. It was just the two of us and a housekeeper who cared for him in my absence. No, Sassy was the first woman who turned my head since my Elaina died. Sassy captivated me—she was young and fun and full of life—someone I'd never experienced. Sassy reminded me I was still a young man. She was intoxicating."

Yep, intoxicating is the right word. "And she's beautiful, too. I get it, Doc. You fell in love with her and decided to be Vincent's mob-doc."

"No, no. It wasn't so simple." He stood and went to the window, gazing out at 1938. "I agreed to help Vincent as long as he did not involve me in his affairs. I refused to tend to any, shall we say, battle-wounds. He agreed. Sassy was his companion—when his family was in New York. He was in Winchester most of the time by '38, and I imagine it was part the coming war and part Sassy."

My guess was it was more Sassy than Adolf or Tojo.

He went quiet, staring into memories I would have given anything to know. "Doc, I want to hear the good stuff, but how about skipping to the part where you killed Vincent? You know, the *really* good stuff?"

"Yes, yes, of course." His face had lost its hazy-glow of fond memories and had hardened into cold stone. "Vincent broke his promise to me. More and more I was required to handle his men's injuries—broken limbs, terrible injuries, even gunshots and unexplained deaths. I was, for all intents and purposes, part of his gang. I turned a blind eye in order to be with her—with Sassy. I sold my soul."

"You were in love with her. I understand, Doc. Don't be hard on yourself."

He nodded. "Yes, miserably in love. I'd lost all control. My sense of responsibility . . . ethics. I'd lost everything."

"Did she love you?"

He laughed—strange considering his dark mood—but he laughed just the same. "Sassy doesn't love, Oliver, she torments. I was too smitten to know the difference."

"Please say you didn't kill him for her?"

"No, Oliver, I did not. I assure you. In fact, we'd had a fight about Vincent and I broke it off with her. If Vincent had ever learned of our affair, he would have killed us both. I swore never to return to Winchester."

I raised my eyebrows and waited.

He patted Hercule as he ran after gangsters in his sleep. "No, they came for me one late evening and told me he was dying. I refused to go but they took Ollie—your grandfather—and forced me to see him. Vincent was near death. He'd been poisoned while out to dinner in DC and I had to tend to him on their return to Winchester. They told me if he died, so would Ollie."

Wow, I'm named after my grandfather. "What happened?"

"I kept him alive on the way back—how, I don't know—but I did. Because of his situation, I learned about the book."

Finally. "How do you go from Vincent being poisoned to learning about this book of gangster secrets?"

"Sassy."

Why was I not surprised? "Explain."

"Vincent was dying and there was little I could do about it. I tried everything but they got to me too late. He refused to go to the hospital—and by the time they reached me, he was too far gone. I'd never seen anything like the poison. It was vile. He was in agony. There was nothing I could do to ease his pain. He had but hours at best by the time we reached Winchester. But in getting him home, he promised no harm would come to Ollie—ever."

I thought a moment. "You never saw anything like it before? Not a medicine or anything?"

"No."

I'd read enough Fleming and Le Carré to guess. "It was the Soviet spies. They were known for their poisons." Then the image of a small restaurant in DC Northwest sparked a thought. "Doc, do you recall a restaurant in DC back then—Quixote's Windmill?"

"Yes, yes, my boy, of course I do." An odd smile cracked his face. "Quixote's was a Cuban restaurant. Vincent visited it often. He was poisoned there. How did you know?"

I told him about my trip to DC and following spies to Quixote's Windmill. "So, it was the Soviets who assassinated Vincent."

"Yes, it was." His memories were draining him.

I gave him a moment to gather himself. "The book, Doc. Tell me about the book."

"Of course." He gazed at me but I don't think he saw me. "As Vincent lay dying, he told me about the book. It was the only thing keeping the Soviets and other gangs at bay. He'd received a message at Quixote's Windmill saying he was poisoned and would be given the antidote in exchange for the book. He refused."

"Of course he did."

"Nonetheless, Vincent entrusted the book to me with instructions to safeguard it until someone came for it—with a code of sorts so I would know it was safe."

"I guess he saw a lot of spy movies, too. Who came for the book?"

"Frannie—many years later." Doc looked down and his voice grew softer. "He made me promise before I completed his last request. He could barely speak, barely breathe. He was writhing in pain and I had to make him tell me again so Sassy could hear, too."

Tears flowed down Doc's face and his voice trembled. "Dear God, I had to. There was no choice."

Had to what? "What, Doc? What did you have to do? Something from the book?"

He stood and went to the window again—not for any memory but to hide his shame.

"I'm a doctor—a healer—not a killer. He begged me—ordered me. I shot him full of enough morphine that it stopped his heart." His head dropped. "It was me. I murdered Vincent Calaprese."

FIFTY-THREE

"Come on, Doc." I stood there, watching him fade to nothing. "What about Sassy? What happened to her?"

For a second, he remained a translucent shadow—a faint outline caught between worlds. The gravel in his voice choked on the memories. "No, Oliver. I cannot talk about Sassy. I just can't. Perhaps another time. It is too painful."

"What happened to her? Tell me you two didn't—"

"No—I never saw her again." Doc was gone—nothing was left but the pain in his voice. "Don't ask me again, Oliver. Never. A man—even his ghost—has things too painful to speak of."

Hercule sprang off the leather chair, his ball still clamped in his jaws, and charged through what had been Doc. He slammed himself paws-first on the front door. The hair on his back ridged and his teeth bared. His throaty warning brought Angel and Bear from the living room.

"What is it, Hercule?" Angel asked. She flipped on the front porch light and stepped back from the window as soon as she did. "Bear, there are two people outside watching us."

Angel pulled Hercule back. "Easy, Hercule."

Bear drew his gun. "Stay here, Angela, and keep Hercule close. Lock this behind me."

"I'll go see, Bear," I said, passing him to the front porch.

Outside, Bear kept his handgun at his side but flipped on a penlight from his pocket. He went to the side of the porch and shined the beam on the two figures standing in the side yard behind some shrubs.

"Sheriff's Department. Don't move," Bear commanded. "Identify yourselves."

One of the figures raised a hand to block the light. The voice was familiar. "Detective, put the gun away. It's Ruth-Ann Marcos."

"Marcos?" Bear didn't holster his weapon. "What are you doing in the bushes? Come to the porch steps—both of you. And slow."

She led a tall, average-built man in a dark suit toward us. "This is one of my agents. It's all right. I was waiting for you to leave Professor Tucker's. I need to speak with you."

"In the bushes?" I took note of the dark-suited man and didn't like the vibes he was giving off. "ID this guy, Bear. I don't like him. He's not wearing a tie."

"Ms. Marcos, step away from him and come over here." Bear raised his gun but Marcos patted the air again. Bear said, "Now, Ms. Marcos."

"Fine. But everything is all right." She came to the bottom step of the porch just below us. "Detective, I assure you, he's with me. Put the gun away."

"I'll just hold onto it if you don't mind. There have been enough surprises in the past two days."

"I agree, and that's why I'm here." She turned to the suited man. "Jack, wait in the car. I'll be fine. And keep your eyes open. You understand."

Jack must have understood because without a word he turned, left our yard through the front gate, and walked across the street. Jack was an obedient lapdog, albeit a quiet one.

"All right, Ms. Marcos, what do you want?"

The front door opened and Angel stepped out. "Bear, is everything all right?"

"Angela, it's Ruth-Ann Marcos. She was looking for me."

"In our bushes?"

Great minds think alike. She's got a great mind. I have, well, the other kind.

Bear holstered his gun. "You were about to explain—"

"Yes, Detective, but I'd rather do it confidentially. No offense, Professor Tucker."

Angel stood beside Bear and glared down at Ruth-Ann like a hawk about to swoop onto its prey. "I do take offense, Ruth-Ann. This is the second time you arrived unannounced and dismissed me in a rude manner. Nicholas is a gentlemen but he should have thrown you out. It was his choice. This is mine. You are trespassing, hiding in my bushes. You were peeking in my windows. I should have you arrested."

"Yes, you're right. I am very sorry." Ruth-Ann climbed two steps and extended a hand to her while Bear and I waited for Angel to bitch-slap her out the gate. "I forget myself too often. Forgive me."

Angel lifted her chin and took her hand. "Anything you wish to say you are welcome to do so in my home. If you require confidentiality, I suggest you stay out of my bushes and return to your office. My front porch is not the place for any conversation."

Damn, how diplomatic. "Angel, good for you. But, she is on our side. Maybe—"

"I'd love a glass of wine." Ruth-Ann looked from Bear to Angel and back. "Detective, if you have no objections to my speaking in front of Professor Tucker."

Bear mumbled something and stepped aside for her to follow Angel into the house.

Hercule waited at the door and wouldn't move to let her through. I said, "She's okay, Hercule. Don't let her spook you. But look for the townspeople coming with torches."

Moan. He picked up his ball in the foyer, trotted into the living room, and took a defensive position on the best leather chair in the room. From there, he could guard his ball and keep his eyes on her.

Angel retrieved another glass of wine and handed it to Ruth-Ann on the couch. She left her half-full glass on the coffee table separating them. Bear ignored his bourbon and stood by the fireplace waiting for the opening salvo. He didn't have to wait long.

"Detective, please tell me what Agent Dobron is up to."

Huh? "Shouldn't she know, Bear?"

He asked the same question.

Ruth-Ann replied, "Yes, I should, but he's—let me be blunt here—playing games with information. I haven't received an update all day and he hasn't returned my calls. You have to understand, under normal conditions the Attorney General's Office has a very close relationship with the FBI. But of late, there have been some, well, issues."

"Issues?" Angel asked. "Like what?"

"I'm not at liberty to say."

Bear said, "And I'm not at liberty to discuss an investigation without my superior approving it. And for the time being, Dobron is my superior."

"Ah, yes, of course, but—"

"No buts, Ms. Marcos," Bear said. "If he wants you to know something, he'll tell you. It's not my place to—"

Ruth-Ann snapped up a hand. "His team has been under investigation by my office for months. I'm afraid he's just found out." She took a long, slow swallow of the cabernet. Then, she leaned back on the couch and crossed her legs as though she'd just joined a book club. "Tell me, what are you working on with Dobron?"

Angel looked over at me. I sat on the arm of the couch opposite Ruth-Ann and shrugged—I hadn't a clue what Ruth-Ann was up to. Angel said, "Agent Dobron is leading this investigation into Stephanos Grecco's murder. Right?"

"Regrettably, yes. I am monitoring the case from arm's length."

"Arm's length?" Bear narrowed his eyes on her. "What are they under investigation for? The Bureau runs their own professional responsibility cases."

"Ah, most often, they do. But this is unique. I've been after Anatoly Nikolaevich Konstantinova for years. Last year, I had a case ready to take him out when it began falling apart one piece of evidence at a time. At the center of it all was—"

"Dobron's men." Bear retrieved his bourbon from the table and sipped it. "And you think this Anatoly character is behind Grecco's murder? And you think it's all connected?"

She nodded. "Yes. I have a missing Federal fugitive, too. And there's an assassin in the morgue who should be in Federal custody, and a list of problems a mile long. Each one of them is connected to Dobron's team."

"Why are you telling us all this, Ms. Marcos? It seems to me you're speaking about very sensitive matters." Angel locked eyes with her. "And I'm not sure that makes sense to me."

Ruth-Ann leaned forward. "I need your help, Detective. I'm losing this case faster than I can stop it."

"My help?"

I said, "Just his help? He's lost without me."

"Quiet," Bear said, and when Ruth-Ann looked at him, he added. "Hercule was about to bark. Go on, Ms. Marcos. I don't understand what you want from me."

Her eyes watched Bear with a cutting, dark look. "I won't be defeated, Detective. So, it's simple. You are on his team. I've wanted someone inside his circle for months. There are none of his men trustworthy enough to help. It's an 'us and them' thing. A boy's club of the worst kind. Now you're there. I need eyes and ears, Detective. And Captain Sutter tells me you're the right man for it."

"She knows?"

"Yes, of course. Call her."

I said, "Bear, she wants you to snitch on the FBI. Not a good idea, pal. It's sort of like auditing the IRS. It can't end well."

Bear glanced at Angel and slipped his cell phone out of his jacket pocket. A speed dial number later, he was saying, "Cap, it's Bear. I'm here with Ruth-Ann Marcos and ... yeah, I know ... what? You gotta be kidding me. Yeah. Yeah. Okay, Cap. Okay." He hung up and emptied his bourbon. "I'm listening."

"Then we have an understanding. Good." Ruth-Ann sat back. "Bonnie Grecco was my last hope. I believe it's possible the killer meant to kill her at the gala, not Stephanos. And now, she's missing. Although I'm quite sure I know where she is."

"You do?" Angel asked. "Where?"

"Come now, Professor Tucker. We both know, don't we?"

"Do we?" Angel cocked her head. "If you know where she is, why not bring her in?"

"Because, well ... because she might be safer where she is. I'm not sure how far I can trust Dobron's men. There's someone on his team tipping off the Russian mob with every move I make. If I bring her in, I'm afraid she may not be safe."

Something tickled me. "Angel, do you know where Bonnie is?"

She nodded but said to Ruth-Ann, "Then she should stay away."

"I agree."

"Now hold on," Bear said to Angel. "What's this about Bonnie?"

I was confused, too. "Angel, what do you have to do with this? Are you aiding and abetting a fugitive?"

"Angela," Bear said, turning to her. "Do you know where Bonnie is?"

She looked at him with defiant eyes and a you-can't-make-me-tell grin.

"Oh, no." Bear shook his head. "You're an accessory. The FBI is—"

"Not to be trusted," Angel said, taking a long sip of her wine. "Ruth-Ann, how can we help?"

Bear rolled his eyes. "Sure, okay, Ms. Marcos, Captain Sutter said do it. So I'm doing it. What do you want?"

"Nothing difficult. Just watch and listen. Report what you can find out to me. I need to know what he's about to do before he does it and I need to know what he does about Bonnie Grecco and Stephanos's murder case. The moment he learns where she is, I need to know so I can get her out of the way myself."

Bear shifted his gaze from Angel to me and his bourbon glass several times. "All right, Ms. Marcos. In two and a half hours, I'm going to apprehend Victorio Chevez and his client—the one who paid him to stalk Angela. Either of them may be Grecco's killer." He went on to explain everything that had transpired, including Chevy's escape from the Vincent House and the planned rendezvous with his client later tonight.

"And tonight?" Ruth-Ann asked. "How will you handle him?"

"Dobron knows about it but told me to handle it. I have no idea what he's doing. Last I knew, he was investigating the two bodies found at the Vincent House and searching for Bonnie."

"Good." Ruth-Ann sipped her wine and looked pleased. "Keep me informed on Chevez, Detective. His role in this isn't clear. I agree his stalking Angela is no coincidence. This client of his is very interesting—if there is one. Soon as you can, contact Dobron and find out if he has anything new. Here is my private cell phone." She handed Bear a card. "It is not for anyone else's eyes."

I said, "Bear, ask her about the book."

He did.

She didn't disappoint. "It's the center of it all, isn't it? Decades ago, the Calaprese families were both targets of our government and informants for us. They were instrumental in helping flush out Nazi rings and infiltrating Soviet Intelligence cells. Yet, at the same time, we were after Calaprese's organization, too. My, what I would give to have lived then."

"I'll say," Angel said. "And it somehow got Stephanos Grecco killed."

"Yes. It's possible he found the book—or learned where it was. I believe the book has been kept up-to-date over the years by the Calaprese family. I also believe there are mob ties and enemy agents identified in the book as recently as ten to fifteen years ago. And money—let me tell you—there may be millions the book could help us locate."

I said, "Bear, do you think Dobron or his men are after the book, too? You've been around him, what do you think?"

"Dobron is clean, Ms. Marcos," he said. "I'd bet on it."

"You would?" Her eyebrows rose. "Captain Sutter told me you were her best detective and I could rely on your judgment. Perhaps she is wrong."

"No," Angel said. "What makes you so sure he's wrong about Agent Dobron?"

"Heredity." Ruth-Ann emptied her wine glass in one long, deep swallow. "Agent James Dobron's real name—before his parents changed it—was Dmitry Alexandrovich Dobronranov."

FIFTY-FOUR

IT WAS CLOSE TO midnight and Old Town Winchester still had a few pockets of sound and light. Several bars and restaurants along the walking mall remained open and their nightlife reached us from all directions. An occasional couple strolled down the brick streets beneath the nineteenth-century streetlights. Small groups of people sat at sidewalk tables enjoying the warm spring night. Music and laughter fluttered in the air everywhere.

Bear and I sat on the second floor of a Civil War era shop. The brick building was under renovation—a good many of the historic Old Town buildings were. This one was located at the center of Old Town. From the second floor windows, we could see anyone or anything moving up or down the Old Town Mall.

We were in perfect position.

The Old Town Mall was not a mall at all—not by any teenager's standards, anyway. It was a two-block area in the heart of Winchester where vehicles were prohibited and the shops and buildings were reminiscent of nineteenth-century Americana. Loudoun Street, which runs north-south through town, intersects Cork Street to the south and Piccadilly Street to the north. To the east and west are Cameron and Braddock Streets, respectively, and within these confines are restaurants, antique shops, and miscellaneous retail and businesses alike. Close to the center of the Mall is the historic courthouse—perhaps the most prominent landmark in Winchester—surrounded by dozens of historical buildings dating back to the mid-1700s. While Winchester has a long and proud Civil War heritage, its roots predate the American Revolution.

Tonight, though, Bear wasn't expecting any historic battles. He just wanted to catch one solitary killer. Just one.

He picked up a small walkie-talkie. "Spence, are you set up?"

Spence and several uniformed Winchester officers were covering the Mall at the north and south entrances. Other officers were posted at along Braddockand Cameron streets and at strategic points within the Mall.

"Yeah, Bear. We're ready," Spence radioed back. "Nothing is getting out of the mall tonight. I promise you."

"It better not."

I said, "Bear, Chevy knows you'll be looking for him. What makes you think he's stupid enough to come here anyway? He could just call his client and change the venue."

"He needs money. And he said his mysterious client wouldn't answer his calls—only one-way communication. His phone records proved it. So he can't change the meeting."

"So if he wants money he has to show."

Bear nodded and peered out into the darkness. "Besides, he thinks he's smarter than me. He'll want to show everyone he can make a fool out of me twice."

"How do you know?"

Bear leaned back from the window. "Because the stupid bastard is walking this way."

Ambling down Boscawen Street from the east, a single figure turned north up Loudoun Street heading toward the old courthouse square. He hesitated at the intersection, looked around—for us I'm sure—before increasing his pace.

"Are you sure it's him?"

"Yes. Come on." Bear headed for the stairs as he radioed Spence. "I want to be the one who grabs him."

On the Mall, Bear stayed close to the shop walls where the darkness hid his big frame. The figure stopped at the base of the Confederate War Memorial fifty yards ahead of us and faced the courthouse. As the figure looked around, the nearby street lamps cast enough hazy light to make his identification easy.

It was Victorio Chevez.

Bear waited across the square, secreted in the dark entrance to an old antique shop. "What is he doing?"

"Waiting."

"Here? Out in the open? They've been playing I-spy games and tonight they meet in the center of the square?"

Good point.

Just as Bear picked up his radio, Chevy lifted his cell phone to his ear. We couldn't make out what he said, but he tapped off the call, stood up, and walked toward the courthouse steps. He made it halfway and stopped.

A strange, whirling noise—faint at first, then louder—sounded overhead. The sound grew louder and circled us just above the treetops.

"What the hell?" Bear stepped out of the entranceway to get a better view. "Tuck, do you hear a whining noise?"

"You mean, other than yours? I do. Look."

In a descending spiral, a dark object whirled above the square spiraling moving down toward Chevy. I turned to him and stood watching a radio-controlled model helicopter finish its descent and stop to hover six feet above the ground an arm's length from us.

"I hope this isn't your ride, Chevy. What are you doing?"

No, it wasn't taking him anywhere. It wasn't intended to.

Chevy took something out of his jeans pocket and slipped it over the helicopter's landing skid. He stepped back and waved his arm in the air. Then he jumped and looked around.

Running feet approached us from both sides of the courthouse.

"FBI, freeze! Don't move!" someone yelled as two men ran out of the shadows toward Chevy. "Stay where you are. FBI."

The helicopter lifted airborne. It climbed to the rooftops with a high-pitched whine and darted south down Loudoun Street.

Chevy turned toward Bear, flipped him the bird, and took off at a dead run north up the Mall away from him and the FBI men. He was laughing.

The FBI made chase. "FBI, stop!"

"Bear," I yelled, "the flash drive's on the helicopter."

Bear was already moving. "Dobron, you bastard." He bolted after the toy helicopter shouting orders into his radio. "Spence, Chevy's northbound toward you. Cut him off. There's a model helicopter above the trees. It's heading toward Cork Street—everyone else go after it."

I followed Bear.

A hudred yards ahead of us, the helicopter rose in a sharp arc disappeared west over the rooftops. Bear turned into a parking lot entrance farther up and continued after it. At a dead run he crossed the parking lot to Braddock Street just in time to see the helicopter swoop down and crash-land into the rear of a pickup truck driving away from him. The truck make a turn west up a side street and disappeared.

He bellowed the description of the truck into the radio as he stopped, staring after it. "Unbelievable. We lost it."

"What about Chevy," I asked. "We better go help Spence."

"I'm gonna kill him."

Bear jogged back toward the square calling Spence on his radio.

"He's gone, Bear," Spence radioed. "He ducked down the alley to the parking garage. None of the units saw him come out but we can't find him. Agent Dobron is pitching a hissy-fit at me. What should I tell him?"

"Tell him to screw off," Bear yelled. "Any motorcycles around?"

Spence did a radio roll call of the other officers on the stakeout. "Negative, Bear. No one saw him drive in or out and there's no bike around here."

"Unbelievable." Bear slowed his pace. "Keep looking."

Back at the intersection of Loudoun and Boscawen, just below the window where we'd watched the square fifteen minutes earlier, Bear stopped and looked around. "What now? Where do we look for him?"

"Beats me," I said. "Ask Dobron. He's coming this way."

Agent Dobron and another FBI man jogged up. Agent Dobron's face was flush with exhaustion and anger. "Braddock, how did you let this get away from you?"

"Me? You bastard—" Bear jumped forward and drove an angry finger into Agent Dobron's chest. "You told me to handle this. You spooked him by charging out of the alley. I could have had him. What are you doing here, anyway?"

The second FBI man stepped forward and shoved Bear. He tried to grapple for Bear's arm when Agent Dobron interceded.

"Let him alone, Stevens. Take another look around. And get with Detective Spence and organize a sweep of the area. I want Chevez found—tonight." He turned to Bear. "How'd he get past your men, Detective?"

Bear cursed. "Me? You chased him. I went after the helicopter —you know, the one with the evidence on it. I would have gone for him but you two were already pursuing him. I figured the FBI could handle that much."

"You should have had more men."

"You should have told me you were here."

"I don't report to you. You report to me."

"So I guess you're still responsible then."

"You're in big trouble, Detective."

Bear jammed a gun-finger at him again. "Listen to me, Dobron. I've had it with you. You screwed up my stakeout. Because of you we lost the evidence and our suspect. Don't blame this on me. And you never answered me. Why are you here?"

Agent Dobron's mouth clamped tight and he turned away, looking around the Mall at nothing. I don't know if he was thinking of an answer or trying to decide if he could take a cheap shot at Bear's jaw and survive.

He chose right. "What did you learn from Ruth-Ann Marcos tonight?"

"Ruth-Ann?" Bear's eyes narrowed and he smiled a silly, "oh you fool" smile. "You were staking out Angela's house."

Agent Dobron didn't answer.

"You jerk. I'm off your team, Dobron. I quit. You're an asshole."

"And you're looking at a suspension. All I have to do is call Captain Sutter and—"

"And what?" Bear stepped forward again. "She'll tell you to piss-off when she hears what I got on you."

"What does that mean?" Bear ignored him. His face darkened and his voice grew tense. "I asked you a question, Detective. What are you suggesting?"

"Screw you."

Agent Dobron's face twisted. Then, after a long moment, he stepped back and held up his hands. "All right, this is out of hand. You're right, I should have informed you I joined your surveillance. But I didn't know if I could trust you after I saw Marcos leaving Tucker's house tonight."

"Trust him? Are you kidding?" I said and Bear repeated me.

"Truce, Detective." Agent Dobron patted the air again. "But I have to know—what did she tell you?"

Bear shook his head. "Sorry, it's classified. You understand."

Agent Dobron cursed. "Let me guess. She told you my team and I are under investigation. Right? Corruption? Maybe I'm a Soviet spy or something. Maybe I killed Grecco, too."

"Did you?" Bear didn't so much as raise an eyebrow. "Are you confessing?"

"No. You have to understand, Detective," Agent Dobron said. "She's running for the Senate and she needs to play hardball. Some of her cases have gone bad and she wants a scapegoat—me. But it's all politics. We're clean. I'd vouch for every one of my men. The Bureau—"

"Screw the Bureau," Bear snapped. "I don't give a damn about your politics—with either of you. I want to find a killer. Period."

Agent Dobron nodded. "Right. I get you. And I want to find two missing Federal witnesses. Okay, we'll leave you out of the politics. But I need you to trust me."

Bear didn't answer.

"I can prove my men are solid. First, tomorrow morning, we have to go see Angela Tucker. It's urgent."

"Why?" I asked.

Bear asked the same thing, adding, "She's going to see Francesca Masseria—she—"

"Masseria?" Agent Dobron's voice grew loud. "How does she know Frannie Masseria?"

"Angela met with her when Frannie sold the Vincent House to Angela's historical foundation. She also bought a lot of old family heirlooms for the museum."

"So you two think Frannie Masseria may have this mysterious book." Agent Dobron smiled a strange, thin smile. "She's wasting her time. Stephanos Grecco found it and stashed it somewhere. Bonnie Grecco is the key, not Frannie Masseria. Tell her I want to see her at your office in the morning. Forget going to Charlottesville."

"Why?" Bear asked.

"I have some questions about André Cartier I want answered."

I said, "Remember, Bear, we saw him at Vincent's last night and he went straight home. Angel hasn't heard from him since."

"Cartier?" Bear said. "What's wrong now?"

"That's what I want to find out." Agent Dobron started down the Mall, saying over his shoulder, "My boys were waiting for him at his place in DC last night. He never showed up. Cartier's missing, too."

FIFTY-FIVE

CHEVY LEANED BACK FROM the window overlooking the two men talking below him. He watched the arrogant FBI Agent walk away and leave Detective Braddock standing alone talking to himself—something he noticed Braddock do a lot. And if what he'd heard in his voice recorder wasn't his imagination, Braddock wasn't talking to himself at all. Chevy went to the other side of the room—the same room Detective Braddock used to watch for him earlier—and waited for his cell phone to buzz.

He didn't have to wait long.

"Yeah, yeah, it went as planned. You ready to pay me for this other thing?"

The voice on the other end was cryptic and out of breath.

"All right. You better not be lying to me. And the price just went up. It's gonna cost you ten-large."

The voice hesitated and grew excited.

"Easy. Everybody in town is all jacked up over this book. Somebody will pay. I just heard the lady professor is going after it tomorrow morning. Some old broad named Francesca something. Professor Tucker thinks she has it."

The voice slow—interested but cautious.

"No way, man. Ten-large if you want a copy. Twenty if you want the original with no copies made. But when you pay me, we meet face-to-face. None of this cloak and dagger crap. You know? I gotta protect myself."

Silence. An answer.

"Okay, I'll let you know if she finds it. Then, after I grab it, you gotta give me my money—face to face. If not, I sell to the highest bidder. *¿Comprende?*"

FIFTY-SIX

"A REMOTE CONTROL TOY helicopter?" Angel turned off the county road and headed deeper into the Virginia countryside. "And what about Chevy?"

"He disappeared. Dobron charged in and screwed everything up. The helicopter went one way, Chevy the other."

Angel and I had been driving to Frannie Masseria's retirement home since eight this morning. Part of the way, she'd had a blistering argument with W. Simon Hahn—"W" for pain-in-the-ass or whatever "w" word fit. He'd called at eight-thirty to grill her about André and Poor Nic again. Even threatening to send Bear to see him didn't stop him this time. Angel hung up on him in mid-threat.

"Angel," I asked, "I've been wondering about Simon. What is the 'W' for anyway?"

"Wilhelm," she said. "His family escaped from Germany in the earlier years of the war. When he got older, he dropped the name to just a 'W.'"

"Wilhelm?" Interesting. Wilhelm Simon Hahn. A very German name. Very German as in Nazi spy rings, SS troopers, and the Russian Front. I suggested as much to Angel.

"Tuck, you're getting carried away with this spy story. Not everyone is a Russian or Nazi spy."

"How do you know? Maybe they're good spies." When she rolled her eyes, I changed the subject and filled her in on the remainder of my exciting night chasing radio-controlled helicopters around Old Town. It would have been funnier if Bear had captured Chevy and retrieved the flash drive of evidence from the Vincent House.

As it stands, no one was laughing.

"And the flash drive?"

"Gone." I sat beside her in the front seat. Hercule was dozing in the back. On long trips, he only woke up when we stopped for coffee and yet another breakfast sandwich-to-go for him. "The helicopter flew over Old Town and landed in an old pickup truck heading out of town. Bear's men chased it for two miles before they got him. It turns out the guy had no idea what was going on. He was some drunk leaving the bars. They found the helicopter but the flash drive was gone."

Angel consulted her GPS "Another mile." Then she nailed it. "Whoever was at the controls was probably on the roof above the square. He flew the helicopter over the roof, grabbed the flash drive, and sent the helicopter to the first vehicle he saw. He knew Bear would be chasing the helicopter. He slipped away."

would have been out of a job. "My tutoring has paid off."

"We're here," she said, turning into a long drive past a sign that read, "Saint Vincent's Retirement Estates"

"St. Vincent? You gotta be kidding me."

She nodded. "Frannie built it with Vincent Calaprese's money when she was a younger woman. When she got older, she left the Vincent House and moved in here. No one ever knew why she didn't just stay there."

I did. "Maybe she didn't like daddy or his mistress hanging around all these years."

Ahead of us a grand estate rose up from the Charlottesville countryside. It reminded me of a Tuscan villa. Of course, I'd ever been to Tuscany, but if I had, this is how it would look. The estate was huge—a two-story stone façade with a clay-tiled roof. There was a portico entrance with tall, stalwart stone columns. On either side of the portico were twin loggias framing the entire villa—perhaps two hundred feet or more across. The entrance drive circled—you guessed it—a story-high marble fountain. The sexy, naked maiden showered water from her bucket over equally naked and sexy cherubs bathing at her feet. They frolicked in the foundation waiting for manly men to arrive and seduce them.

Well, that's what I saw.

Angel pulled around the circle to a visitor's parking space and parked. She climbed out of the Explorer, bade Hercule wait behind, and headed for the front portico.

"All right, Angel," I said, falling in behind her. "You do all the talking and I'll do all the snooping."

She rolled her eyes. "I have the same plan."

Inside, we went to a large reception desk more resembling a luxury hotel reception than an old gangster's retirement home. The young man behind the marble counter was dressed in a light colored, double-breasted linen suit from Bogart's closet in Casablanca.

"Yes, ma'am? May I help you?" His nametag read "Robert."

"Good morning." Angel flashed her best smile. "I'm here to see Francesca—"

"Masseria," Robert said turning to his computer screen below the counter top. "My, my, she is a popular girl this weekend. You're her third guest since Friday night."

"Who else has been here?" Angel asked. "I didn't think Frannie got a lot of visitors."

"She doesn't." Robert looked up from the monitor. "This weekend though, she's quite the belle of the ball."

I said, "Who else?" and Angel asked him again.

"I'm sorry, miss, miss—"

"Professor Angela Tucker. I've been to see her before, Robert. Don't you recall?"

Robert forged a fake smile and returned to his computer. "Oh, yes, Professor. I do recall after all. You're from the University something-or-other. Wonderful you could visit Frannie again. She was very pleased after your visit last month."

"And?"

"And? No, I'm sorry, I am not allowed to disclose a resident's personal information; including their visitors and family details."

Angel smiled. "Of course. Then, may we see her? It's villa G-10. Right? Around back beyond the gardens in the corner?"

I said, "Villa? She has a villa?"

"Yes ... we?" Robert looked at the front entrance. "Is there another guest with you? I'll have to sign them in."

"No, no. I left my Labrador in the car. May I bring him in?"

Robert patted the air. "No pets, I'm sorry. If Frannie is up for a walk or a visit outside, I might let you sneak him in for a visit. But only if she requests. I'll have one of the staff escort you. It will be just a few moments."

"I'll meet you there, Angel," I said. "I'll see if Frannie is in the mood for a stroll. Hercule needs to take a walk after his last egg sandwich."

She nodded and went to a nearby lounge area to wait on her escort.

I headed for Frannie's villa.

———

Frannie was not in the mood for a stroll through the gardens. In fact, Frannie was not in the mood for any more visitors this weekend either.

Frannie was dead.

I found her in the small, white stone villa—more a bungalow if you ask me—on the far side of the rear gardens. She was lying face-up on her living room couch as though she were napping. But the throw pillow beside her head was still damp from saliva and sweat. And in the center of its flowered print was an almost unnoticeable drop of blood.

"Sorry, Frannie, you didn't deserve this."

I leaned down to examine her body, looking for a tiny tear in her frenulum caused by her struggle beneath the pillow. It was there, along with a thin smear of blood on her gums. As I looked around, a door closed in the back of the house and I went to investigate. When I reached the bedroom doorway, I would have had a heart attack if I weren't already dead.

Kneeling down at Frannie's bedroom nightstand, rifling through her drawers, was André Cartier.

"André, what are you doing here?" I went inside. "Tell me you didn't kill the old lady. Please. Tell me—"

André jumped up and closed the nightstand drawer. He went around the bed with frustration drawing his face tighter. He muttered something as his eyes narrowed and darted around the room.

"Damn you, André, what have you done?"

He jerked open the other nightstand drawer and pulled out its contents—a few magazines, pens, pencils, a small flashlight, and an old, worn Bible. He tossed each of the items on the bed and took the drawer all the way out of the stand, flipped it around, and examined underneath.

Nothing.

He began stuffing the drawer's contents back inside when he picked up the Bible. The cover was loose and the book slipped out of it onto the floor. When he bent down to retrieve it, he froze.

So did I.

He held the Bible cover in his hand. The book at his feet had its own cover—a worn, tattered, black leather one. It bore no markings or titles. He picked it up and fanned it. It was three inches thick and its pages were matted and frayed. He opened it somewhere in the middle and his eyes exploded; he smiled.

"Did you find it, André?" I said, moving around to peek over his shoulder. "Vincent's book?"

His eyes ran over the hand-scribed pages; a line here, a line there. With each page, his face lightened until it was about to burst into giddy laughter.

Vincent Calaprese's mob journal.

"Dear God, you weren't lying." He placed the book on the bed and returned the journal into the Bible book cover and tucked it into his waistband under his shirt. Then, he straightened the room, erasing the telltale signs of his presence—disheveled bed linens, dresser drawers still cracked open, items on the bed.

"André, nothing is worth killing over. This is gonna break Angel's heart. And she's here."

Something called me from Frannie's dressing table across the room. There were dozens of framed photographs lined up in front of the mirror—a collage of memories spanning her life. One photograph captured my attention.

It was a five-by-seven, black-and-white print of a beautiful, young Francesca Calaprese—I recognized her from the portrait hanging in the Vincent House. She was sitting on a porch swing with a dashing young man in an Army uniform. I guessed it was during the war—World War II—and the two appeared to be in their twenties. She was lying against his shoulder with an adoring smile. His arm was around her shoulders as he kissed the top of her head.

They were in love.

There was something about the photograph. It gripped me and pulled me closer. Something strange and familiar—personal to me—caressed my thoughts and beckoned me to remember a memory I never had.

I reached out and touched the frame.

The room exploded in a shower of light and darkness.

FIFTY-SEVEN

"Can I write you?" Frannie asked the young soldier sitting on the swing beside her. "You better write me—often as you can. You will, won't you?"

He shrugged and squeezed her shoulders. "We can try writing, Frannie. But, as I tried to explain, I can't tell you what I'm doing or where I'm going. It's just the way this new outfit is. You understand, right?"

I stood at the end of a grand veranda watching the two on the porch swing. Neither knew my presence—and I was unsure if I were really there or sharing the old photograph's karma.

"No, I don't. This war is horrible. It's bad enough you can't tell me anything, but I can't write to you?"

"You can try. It'll be hit or miss if we'd get anything. But I'll write you whenever I can. The outfit has a way of getting the letters out."

Frannie sat up and pulled away, pushing his arm from around her shoulders. "I just don't understand. Soldiers are soldiers. They can't keep our letters away at a time like this—"

"It's not the same with us," he said. He stood up and moved to the porch railing. "You have to understand. I'm not even supposed to tell you this much. But I figure a girl like you would find out anyway."

She kicked him playfully behind the leg. "You mean a gangster's daughter."

"Yeah, a gangster's daughter." He laughed. "So, if you don't want me telling anyone about your dad, you can't tell anyone about me. Deal?"

What? No, this couldn't be. I was at home here—as though I'd been here many times and knew every room, every hallway. I walked up onto the porch and peeked in the window. I knew inside was a large foyer with a grand staircase rising up to the upper floors. The great hallway led to the rear of the house and the servant's kitchen. Just off the foyer was the ballroom. The lounge was on the left and then the sitting room and other visiting rooms.

The Vincent House.

When I turned and looked at the soldier, there was something unmistakable about him—something ... familiar. He was my height and perhaps twenty pounds lighter—thin, but hard and sturdy. His hair was short—a fresh-trimmed haircut. He was clean-shaven and his eyes were dark blue—friendly, inquisitive eyes—and they were soft when they looked at Frannie. His uniform had Captain's bars on the shoulders and a patch on the left arm of a gold spearhead on a black field.

I recognized the patch.

This soldier wasn't like the millions of young GIs heading off to fight the Axis. He was something special—something new. He was one of General Donovan's men. He was OSS—the Office of Strategic Services—the forerunner of the present-day CIA.

Could he be? I didn't dare think it.

Frannie stood up and fell into the soldier's arms. "How long do you have before you leave?"

"Tomorrow, Frannie. I have to go tomorrow morning."

Tears welled in her eyes. "And home? When—"

"Not 'till it's over I guess. Maybe back to DC now and then, but I'm not sure I'll be able to see you, let alone tell you I'm around." He kissed her and crushed her to him. "I'm sorry, Frannie. I can't even tell Doc."

Doc? My Doc? *Our* Doc?

She leaned back and swiped at the tears in her eyes. "How is he, Ollie? I haven't seen him since—"

"No—not since you came for the book. I know."

"How is he?"

My grandfather slipped out of her embrace and leaned back against the porch railing. "Okay, I guess. He didn't like me joining up but I had to. He demanded I go back to school to be a lawyer or doctor. I'm so tired of him trying to make me be, well, *him*."

"I know, I do. We're both trying to escape our fathers, aren't we?" She looked down and half-smiled. "What about us? Have you told him about me—about us?"

Ollie Tucker threw his head back and laughed. "Are you kidding me, Frannie? He would have kittens. I wouldn't have to worry about Adolph, honey. He'd kill me himself."

"Why, Ollie? He can't blame me." Frannie's eyes rained and she didn't try to stop them. "Can he?"

"No." Ollie tried to smile. "It's the other way around. He blames himself for your dad's murder. He says he should have been able to save him. And the book terrifies him."

"It shouldn't. The book is the only thing keeping my family safe. Maybe Doc, too. And it's not his fault, Ollie. Those people—they murdered him. They wanted the book."

Ollie looked away. "I don't understand any of it, Frannie. Vincent's gone and the book is still so dangerous. It's been five years. What could be so important this long?"

Frannie gazed over the front yard. "Because it proves who killed him. And it proves why. There are things in the book that could destroy some very powerful families in Washington, Ollie. And they know it."

Ollie wrapped his arm around her and kissed her forehead again. "Then keep it safe, honey. And when I get back, I'll use it to get every last one of them Commies. And I'll start with Vasily Kishkin."

The name sent a harpoon of fire into me and I felt myself leaving the veranda. The light danced around me as Frannie and my grandfather embraced. With all my strength, I tried to stay just a moment longer. I willed it but it wasn't to be—the light danced and faded, pulling me away.

"Vasily Kishkin? Granddad, who is he?" I tried to reach out for them but I was already being swept away. "Frannie, tell me more. I don't understand."

Frannie kissed Ollie on the cheek. She took his hand and guided it down between them, resting it on her belly where she moved his hand in gentle, loving circles. "You have to come home safe, Ollie. For all of us."

FIFTY-EIGHT

WHEN THE TORNADO OF light dissipated, I was back in Frannie's bedroom staring at the photograph of Frannie Masseria and OSS Captain Ollie Tucker. My head spun with a million memories of my childhood; a life growing up without family or heritage—wondering about who and where I came from. The answers poured over me like a cold shower—shocking but invigorating. My family roots began with a brilliant old curmudgeon surgeon and a rough and tumble gangster. And then there was Frannie and Ollie. Two young people trying to escape their roots and make their own way during the madness of 1944. A gangster's daughter and an OSS agent—Grandma and Grandpa.

Unbelievable.

The loud banging on the front villa door shook me out of my daydream. I ran to the door. Angel and an orderly were outside. The orderly pummeled the door, calling out for Frannie to answer. Angel prodded him to hurry and get inside.

Frannie wasn't entertaining this morning.

I slipped outside just as the orderly keyed their way in.

"Angel, it's too late. Frannie's been murdered. We have to go."

Angel stood in the doorway as the orderly rushed in and knelt down beside Frannie's body lying on the couch. She said, "She's dead."

"Yes, I'm afraid so," the orderly answered, standing. "Looks like she died in her sleep. Maybe a heart attack."

I grabbed Angel's arm and the intensity of the moment gave me the energy to connect with her. "Angel, someone smothered her—murdered her. We have to get back to Winchester. André found the book. He was—"

"André?"

The orderly turned around. "No, Charlie, ma'am. You better go. I have to get the facility doctor to check Mrs. Masseria. I'm sorry for your loss."

Angel nodded and followed me out as I tugged her through the door. "The book, Angel. André has the book. I don't know what's going on, but we have to find him."

Outside, Angel shook off the shock and walked to the Explorer. Hercule was behind the steering wheel howling out the half-open window—either nature or Frannie's death woke him from his snooze. As we walked him around the parking lot, I explained everything I'd witnessed inside Frannie's villa suite.

Fifteen minutes later, we were headed home. On the way, she called Bear and filled him in too—less my visit with my dead grandparents, of course. As she hung up with Bear, I had an idea and next had her call Poor Nic. She put it on speaker.

"Yes, I'm fine, Nicholas," she said after explaining what had just happened. "But that's not why I'm calling. Have you ever heard the name Vasily Kishkin?"

A pause. "Yes, my dear, of course. Why do you ask?"

"Vasily killed Vincent Calaprese back in—"

"1939, yes. I am well aware of the family lore, Angela. What of it?"

Angel looked over at me and I gave her my thoughts. She said, "Nicholas, Vasily Kishkin was a Russian spy—and he had a network in Washington, right?"

"Yes, he did. He was a very dangerous man."

"Is it possible his family continued his business all these years? Perhaps the book proves as much?"

"Yes, my dear, it will—and more. Angela, what you know is very dangerous. Please, come to my home before you do anything rash."

"Nicholas, I think you should keep Bonnie with you—"

"I'm afraid that is not possible." Poor Nic sighed. "She left here this morning without explanation. I don't know where she went. But I fear the worst."

Angel frowned. "Nicholas, you're not telling me everything."

"There is no time." He paused and spoke to someone in the background but we couldn't hear. To Angel, he said, "I will explain when you arrive. It's far more complicated than you can imagine. Know this, Angela. No one is who they pretend to be. No one."

Boy, the last time I heard that line, Ernie Stuart had just killed me.

FIFTY-NINE

THE TRIP HOME WAS torturous as Angel shaved time off our drive. Along the way, I tried to dial into André and ghost-express to him. It didn't work. I couldn't connect to him and learn where he was and what he was doing. Whatever connection we had in the past was gone.

Angel's cell phone rang and she looked at the display. "Tuck, it's André." She put it on speaker. "André, what the—"

"Angela, listen to me, please." His voice was rushed and strained. "Something terrible has happened. Where are you? I must see you at once—without Braddock."

"What's happened?" Angel glanced over at me and said, "I went to see Frannie Masseria."

Silence. "Then you know. There's no time to explain. We're heading for the Vincent House. Meet me there. Hurry."

The line went dead.

Angel slammed her foot on the accelerator and the needle closed on ninety. "I cannot believe it, Tuck. Not André. What has he gotten into? What has he done? And who is 'we'?"

Something tickled me. "He's with Bonnie Grecco."

The Explorer groaned under her foot. Hercule laid down in the backseat and moaned.

She said, "Then he's in bigger trouble than he knows."

———

Fifteen minutes later, Angel wheeled into the Vincent House drive and skidded to a stop. Hercule howled his relief as Angel got out and opened his door.

In front of us were two vehicles—André's convertible and another luxury sedan neither of us recognized.

"Angel, you better let me go in first. I'll find Sassy and—"

A gunshot cracked inside the house.

"Angel, get down!"

The Vincent House's front door flew open and a man stumbled out. He ran toward us, looking back at the house at the same time. He tripped down the veranda stairs and stumbled forward.

W. Simon Hahn.

"Simon?" Angel called.

At a fast clip, he careened against André's Mercedes and crashed into Angel's Explorer before he landed on the ground out of breath. He lay stunned and confused.

"Simon, stop. What's wrong?" Angel took his arm and helped him to his feet. "What are you doing here?"

His golf shirt was covered in blood. So were his hands—and in one of them was a stainless steel revolver.

"I didn't see this coming. Angel, call Bear. Simon just shot somebody."

Angel's eyes swept from the gun to his bloody clothes. "Simon? What have you done?"

"I, I ... nothing. No." He lifted the .38 and his face paled when he saw it in his hand—he tossed it onto the ground like it burnt his fingers. "No, Angela. It's not ... I didn't ... I, I shot ... there's a man inside. He's dead."

I said, "I'll check it out, Angel. Just in case, get your gun."

She retrieved the .380 Walther I'd insisted she lock in the glove box this morning.

Simon stared at the Vincent House. His face was drained of color and lucidity. His mouth was agape and hands hung motionless at his sides. He looked lost, frightened, and unfamiliar. Twice he glanced at Angel and twice he tried but couldn't speak.

I pointed at Simon and said to Hercule, "Watch him, boy. He's a cat person."

Grrrrrrrr.

Inside the Vincent House, I found Simon's demon.

Chevy lay face down in the middle of the lounge. His arms were outstretched and his legs bent—he'd fallen where he stood. His right shoulder was bloody—he'd been shot—and he was not moving. I knelt down beside his body and touched his arm.

He was alive.

I ran back outside. "Angel, Chevy's been shot, but he's alive. Call for an ambulance."

"André?"

"I don't see him."

Simon was bent over beside André's Mercedes retching. When Angel connected with 9-1-1 and told them the situation, he looked up, listened, and retched again. Then he stood, leaned on the car, and wiped his mouth. "I didn't kill Chevez. You have to believe me, Angela. I was meeting him inside when Cartier showed up. He fought with Chevez and shot him. Then he ran off."

I checked the gun lying on the ground. "It's been fired, Angel. Just now."

Angel covered the phone. "We heard a shot, Simon. Your gun has been fired."

"No, yes ... I shot someone—you wouldn't believe me. Yes, I shot at someone, but not Chevez."

"Are you sure you didn't shoot him?" Angel asked. "Who did you shoot?"

"I don't know ... someone ... appeared behind the bar watching me. I was trying to help Chevez and this ... this ... mobster ... He told me to get out of his house. He had a gun and I panicked. There was a gun beside Chevez so I grabbed it and shot the man. He ... was ... disappeared."

"Who, Simon?"

I already knew the answer—and more. "Simon is Chevy's client, Angel. He came here to get the book. I don't know how Chevy got it from André, but he did, and he was selling it to Simon. The question is, why?"

Angel gestured for him to sit against André's convertible. "Chevy was working for you? To get the book?"

Simon's face fell. He looked at his blood-covered hands and began shaking. "I'm so sorry, Angela. I am. I just wanted Ernie's position at the University. The Regents think you're so perfect—brilliant—amazing. I had no choice. The job should be mine!"

Oh crap, I got it. "Simon had Chevy following you, Angel. He was gathering everything he could to discredit you with the Regents. Chevy recorded anything to make you look bad—talking to me and visiting Poor Nic. Then, when Grecco was murdered, he saw an opportunity to sink you. He was trying to connect you to it all."

"Connect me? He was trying to ruin me," Angel said. She walked over and slapped Simon across the face. "You were stalking me for a job? My job?"

Simon stared—wide-eyed—as a red mark blossomed on his cheek. He cried. "I'm sorry, Angela. It got out of hand. I wanted the job. It was mine, after all. I've been waiting years for Ernie to retire. Now they wanted you. You talk to yourself—to him—and you act like he's right there with you. The Department needs someone grounded—"

"Grounded?" She slapped him again. "Like someone stalking and lying and trying to destroy me over a job? The Regents need someone like that?"

"No. No. You don't understand."

"I understand everything."

He pushed off André's car hood but Hercule suggested he sit back down. He did. "No, Angela. I did not shoot Chevez. He met me to give me my recordings and get paid. Cartier shot him. I tried to help him but I heard someone in the house and got scared. Then I—"

I said, "What about the book?" And Angel repeated me.

"Book?" Simon's face twisted. "Chevez had videos showing you on this insane investigation. He gave me half last night and was to give me the rest this morning. The videos had you and Braddock, together, talking to your dead husband. That would keep Braddock off my back, too. What book are you talking about?"

There was something about Simon's delivery that was believable. Maybe it was the confused look on his face when Angel mentioned the book. Maybe it was the stupidity of his confession. Or maybe it was the vomit caking his shoes and slacks.

"Angel, stay here. I'm going to look for André."

"Okay, Tuck. Bear should be here soon."

Simon's eyes went wild and he looked around. "Tuck? You're talking to him again?"

"Yes." Angel didn't hesitate. "He never left me, Simon. He's been here the whole time."

His face was ashen. "Yes, I believe he has."

W. Simon Hahn—"W" for wrong place, wrong time, bent over and retched again.

SIXTY

ANDRÉ CARTIER WAS NOWHERE in the Vincent House.

I'd searched it top to bottom and returned to the lounge, hoping to find Vincent and get his help. "Vincent? Ollie-ollie-oxen-free."

Frankie Carle—*Oh, What It Seemed to Be* played…

"You're making a mess in my home, Oliver." Vincent appeared behind the bar with a long Cuban and a hefty glass of bourbon. "I hope this will be over soon." He poured me a drink. "You have my book?"

"Not yet." I swooped up the glass and downed it before he changed his mind. "It's here somewhere. But then, you know that already, don't you?"

He grinned and refilled my glass. "Of course I know. And I know my Frannie is gone, too. You never got to meet her."

"No, and I'm sorry I didn't." I sipped my drink. "Do you know who killed her?"

"No, if I did, they would be dead already. Do you?"

I considered the possibilities. "The jury's out on that one."

"Ah, interesting phrase. Be careful, Oliver. Juries are often wrong, and they can be bought. I should know. I've owned a few in my time."

I took a long pull on my drink and wiped the warmth from my lips. "Okay, Vincent—or should I say, Great Granddad?"

He laughed—a big, raucous belly laugh. "Yes, yes. There is so much more to tell you, too. But I'll let Doc fill you in. Hurry, you must find my book and get Frannie's killer. Avenge our family, Oliver."

"Avenge? We'll see, Vincent. My friend André is here some-where."

"Did he kill my Frannie?"

"I don't know. But he found your book. Someone else has it now."

Vincent puffed on his Cuban and watched me through the smoke. "The Cuban fella—Chevez—they're all as bad as the Reds—he had it but now he doesn't."

"Who took it from him?"

"Your friend—and I'm displeased."

Sassy appeared beside me. She smacked my cheek with a big kiss. "Your friend is in the carriage house, Tuckie. You better hurry. I'm not sure how long he's gonna be breathin'. He's in big trouble."

"You mean André?" I emptied my drink. "What's happening?"

"The bimbo's with him. And he's in big trouble—"

André Cartier was in big trouble. He was in the carriage house, standing outside the old horse stall. The false wall was open to the stairs behind him. His hands were bloodied and his face was ashen. Blood stained his pants and shirt, but he seemed unaware of it all. His eyes were fixed on the gun pointed at his face.

And Bonnie Grecco held it.

I walked in and stood beside her.

"André, what have you got yourself into?"

Bonnie was shaking and waving the gun around. "You stay back, André. You stay away from me."

"Bonnie, put the gun down. I had to do it—I had no choice."

"Had to do what?" I asked.

"Why, André, why?" Bonnie wailed.

He didn't answer me of course but he did speak to Bonnie. "To get the book back, Bonnie. We need the book. It's the key to Stephanos's murder. It'll prove everything."

"But you shot him, André," Bonnie cried. "I can't believe it. Did you kill Steph, too? Tell me you didn't, André, please."

I went to André. "Yeah, André, tell her. Tell us both. I'm not sure anymore."

He raised his hands and took a step toward Bonnie. "Put the gun down, Bonnie. Let me explain."

"Explain? You shot a man over this book? Did you kill Stephanos for it, too?"

"No." André's face twisted and he stepped closer. "I didn't kill Stephanos. Agent Dobron did."

Bonnie thrust the gun out. "Dobron? He said you—"

"Yes, of course he said it was me." André patted the air. "I've been working with Ruth-Ann Marcos, Bonnie. She's been after Dobron for months—he works for the Russian mob."

Bonnie's face flushed. She lowered her gun a few inches and looked over it at him. "No, no. Steph made a deal with Agent Dobron—to get us a new life—we were going into witness protection. And then we found all the money in those paintings at the Vincent House. We were—"

"No, Bonnie." André took another step. "Dobron wanted the book for the Russian mob. He was using Stephanos to get it."

"The mob? It was all a lie?" Bonnie shook her head and lowered the gun more. Her eyes welled up and she had trouble forming words. "What about you and me, André? It was all a lie, too? To get the book?"

"No, it wasn't a lie. I didn't know anything about the book when we met. I didn't know about you and Stephanos either. But when we got together, Ruth-Ann Marcos approached me to find the book first before the Russians got it."

"She came to you because of me?"

He nodded.

Right. I get it. The question was, when did he know what he was doing and how deeply was he involved?

Bonnie wiped black mascara from her cheeks and choked back tears. "Everyone thought I was using you. And it was the other way around."

"No, Bonnie. I wasn't using you. I can't explain—not here. But I'm on your side, Bonnie. You and I are real."

"You didn't kill Stephanos? You promise?"

"Yes, I promise. I told you, Dobron killed him." André started to move closer but Bonnie lifted the gun and he stopped. He went on. "Stephanos made a deal with Dobron for the book, but he double-crossed him and tried to sell it to someone else. Dobron found out and killed him before he could."

"He wasn't going to get a new name and new place to live? It was for the money?"

André nodded.

"What about me?"

"Yeah, André? What about her?" I already knew the answer.

André walked forward and wrapped his arms around her. "I'm still here, Bonnie. We can try again if you want—you and me."

Bonnie erupted in violent quakes of tears and sobs. "The book."

Footsteps approached us from outside and Angel walked through the side door.

"André? Bonnie? What—"

"Angel, you're not gonna believe all this," I said, "André's been working for Marcos—and Dobron killed Stephanos."

Angel's eyes flared and she looked from Bonnie to André and then fixed on the gun in Bonnie's hand. "André, what's going on? Agent Dobron killed Stephanos?"

"Yes, Angela. I'm afraid it's true." André took the last step and slipped his hand over Bonnie's gun and held tight. "And there's more—terrible things. I shot that man, Chevez. I found the book and went to your house looking for you."

"Did you kill Frannie Masseria?"

André's face tightened and his eyes went wide. "No. I found her dead. I found the book and went straight to your house. I wanted to explain everything to you. But Chevez was waiting there and jumped me. He took the book and ran straight here. Bonnie was with me, she saw it all."

Bonnie's face went blank. "This is insane. It's all insane. You're all lying. It can't be happening. I've got to get out of here."

"No, Bonnie," André said. "I'm telling you the truth."

"No. No. No. You're lying. It's the book."

Angel watched her for a second and then turned back to André. "Did you know Chevy worked for Simon Hahn?"

André shook his head. "No. What's it all about? I followed Chevy here to get the book back before it got into Dobron's hands."

"If you're working for Ruth-Ann, why didn't you just let her handle this?"

He looked at the ground. His face fell. "I should have. Things got out of control. When I lost the book, I called her but she was in Washington. I had to get it back fast. I went too far. When I confronted Chevez inside the house, he pulled a gun and we struggled. I shot him. It was an accident, I swear."

"All right, André, all right." Angel turned to Bonnie. "We'll wait for Bear and he'll figure all this out."

"No." Bonnie pulled the gun free from André's grip and jabbed it at him. "Both of you get back. I don't trust any of you. It's the book. It's always been the book."

"Angel, she's losing it," I said, watching the anger rising in Bonnie's face. "She's really gone—"

"Give me the book, André." Bonnie cocked the revolver and leveled it at André's face. "I want it. You all killed Steph over the book. We wanted a new life. It's my turn. I'm gonna get what I want. Give it to me."

"Do it, André," Angel said. "Give her the book. Bear is on his way."

"So is Agent Dobron," Bonnie said in a strange, eerie whisper. "Then we'll see who's lying."

André took the book out of his jacket pocket and handed it to Bonnie. "Bonnie, please. Don't do anything rash. We need this book for evidence. We need—"

"I don't care." Bonnie backed toward the stall entrance to the tunnels. "Leave me alone. Both of you. If everyone wants this book so bad, then they can deal with me." She turned and ran through the entrance.

"Wait, Angel." I went to the passage door and watched her disappear into the tunnel. "We gotta find Bear. I don't know what's going on, but we have to get the book back before Bonnie does something stupid."

Angel turned to André. "You've been working with Marcos? Why didn't you say anything when you were arrested for Grecco's murder? Why didn't you tell us?"

"I couldn't," he said, staring after Bonnie. "Dobron was involved and I couldn't let on I was. Ruth-Ann has been trying to trap Dobron for months. This was the last chance. The book will prove who he really is."

A car pulled up outside in the drive. I went to the door and looked out the window. "It's Dobron, Angel. If André's telling the truth, then we have to get the book before Dobron does."

"And if he's lying?" She said, ignoring André's stare. "What then?"

"Then he's up to his neck in four murders."

SIXTY-ONE

At the bottom of the Carriage House passage stairs and the tunnel entrance, Angel flipped on a flashlight application on her cell phone.

"Stay close, André, remember she has a gun."

"Then keep your flashlight low, too. It's a target down here."

"Good point. But it's too dark to see without it."

"Angel, I'll go up ahead. Move slow and be ready to get back if I yell."

I ran down the tunnel but found no one ahead of us. I reached the hub where the tunnels converged and called for Angel and André. When they caught up, I said, "I don't know where she went so let's go to the antechamber at the end and see if she went through into the basement."

"All right. We'll need Bear's help searching the rest of the tunnels. She could be anywhere."

André leaned back against the wall. His voice was shallow and sad. "I'm sorry, Angela. I tried to help but made a mess of this. I killed Chevez. Dear God what have I done?"

"Chevy's alive, André," Angel said. "Let's find Bonnie and get the book. Bear will sort the rest out after. Focus on Bonnie and the book."

His face fell. "Yes, of course. The book will prove everything I've said is true."

"It better," I said. "Or there are a lot of dead bodies for nothing."

Angel nodded, patted André on the shoulder, then led him to the antechamber.

We made it without finding any sign of Bonnie. But when we reached the chamber, André pulled Angel behind him and stopped.

The door through the basement storage racks was open.

"Wait, Angela. Bonnie could be waiting inside. Stay here—"

A shot cracked and the bullet slammed into the stone wall beside André.

Bonnie stepped out of the darkness behind us. Her gun was level with Angel's chest. "Don't either of you move. I mean it. I'll shoot."

"Bonnie, no! Calm down." Angel held up a hand. "Let's get Bear and sort this out."

"No. I'm gonna get my money and run." Bonnie sidestepped us and moved to block our escape into the basement. "Move away. I don't know who to trust—but I know it's not you. Just stay away." She jutted her gun toward Angel and cocked the hammer. "Get back."

André shoved Angel onto the floor and lunged for Bonnie.

"No, André, don't!" I yelled.

A shot erupted.

Bonnie stood there, gun wavering between Angel and André. Her eyes were as big as the red blossom in her shoulder. Her mouth quivered—unspoken words—and she dropped to the stone floor.

We all looked back.

Special Agent Jim Dobron—aka Dmitry Alexandrovich Dobronranov—stepped into the antechamber from the tunnel behind us. His gun was still aimed at Bonnie lying at my feet.

SIXTY-TWO

"Are you two all right?" Dobron asked. "I was afraid—"

"We're fine." Angel dropped down beside Bonnie and checked her pulse. "She's alive. We have to get a doctor."

"Angela, come over here," André said. "Get behind me."

Angel looked over at Dobron. Her voice was icy. "Call an ambulance, Dobron."

"There's one upstairs for Chevez. I'll get someone down here." Dobron lifted his cell phone. "No signal. I'll have to go back—"

"Jim, put your gun down. It's over." Ruth-Ann Marcos said from the cellar entranceway. "Put it down, Jim." She stepped into the chamber with Bear behind her.

Bear had his gun trained on Dobron.

"What are you doing?" Dobron looked from Ruth-Ann to Bear. "Detective, get your gun off me. I'm not asking."

Bear shook his head. "Drop your weapon."

Spence appeared beside Bear. His gun was aimed at Dobron, too. "One of us will get you. So put it down."

I said, "Thank God, Bear. Where have you been?"

Bear glanced at Angel. "Angela, you and André step back. Dobron, I told you to drop your gun."

Dobron's face tightened and his eyes went black. "All right, Detective, we'll do this your way—for now." He slid his handgun into the holster on his hip. "Bonnie was about to shoot Professor Tucker and Cartier. I shot her. She needs an ambulance."

"Bear," Angel said. "André shot Chevy—it was self-defense, I'm sure. Chevy stole the book from him and Agent Dobron—"

"André, you have the book? Good." Ruth-Ann turned to Bear. "Get an ambulance team down here. The rest can wait."

Bear issued orders into a radio but never took his gun off Dobron.

"Ruth-Ann, please," André said, "tell them about me. They don't believe me."

All eyes fell to Ruth-Ann. I said, "Yes, Ruth-Ann, tell us."

"Of course," she said with a strange, cocky smile. "André has been working with me at Justice—to make a case against Dobron. I learned Stephanos was searching for the book for Dobron. Dobron wanted to turn it over to the Russian Mob. Bonnie's relationship with André gave me my chance to trap him once and for all."

"Agent Dobron?" Angel asked. "You're sure?"

"Yes, Angela, very. And the book may very well prove it." Ruth-Ann walked over to Bonnie's still form, stooped, and pulled the book from her pocket. "And we have it after all this time." She nodded to Bear. "Detective, André has been working under my authority.

We'll sort out what he may or may not have done later. I'm sure we can reach a mutual accommodation."

Dobron tried to step forward but Bear's gun stopped him. "What are you accusing me of, Ruth-Ann?"

"Oh, please, Jim. You've been working for Anatoly Konstantinova. Once Grecco found the book—you'd give it to Anatoly. When Grecco decided on a different deal, you had him killed."

"Bullshit!" Dobron's face flashed rage and he jumped forward. "You lying—"

Bear and Spence grabbed him and pushed him against the antechamber wall. Spence pulled Dobron's gun from its holster and Bear held his on target. "Don't move again, Dobron. Let's all get upstairs and talk this out."

An ambulance crew called out from the cellar and Spence left and brought them into the antechamber where they went to work on Bonnie Grecco.

"Yes, let's go chat, Jim." Ruth-Ann looked at Dobron and smiled. "Isn't it odd, Detective Braddock, how Agent Dobron is alone here today?"

"I was thinking the same thing." Bear pointed into the cellar. "Spence, take him up and make sure he doesn't get lost."

"Sure, Bear." Spence shoved Dobron into the cellar room and followed.

We all went upstairs to the lounge. Dobron slumped into one of the chairs around a playing table. Spence sat behind him. Angel and André settled on two bar stools and Ruth-Ann stood in the doorway talking on her phone.

Me, I stood by the bar watching the show. "Bear, how's Chevy?"

"Chevy's gonna make it. He's on the way to the hospital—still unconscious but he'll pull through."

"Good, another witness." Ruth-Ann closed her phone. "I've got one of my men waiting at the hospital. I don't want any of Dobron's men there, Detective. Understand?"

Bear shrugged. "Sure, I'll have my—"

"Just my men. Chevez is a federal witness. I'm not losing another one."

"Another one?" Angel asked.

Ruth-Ann walked over to Dobron. "Do you want to explain Katalina Kishkin or shall I, Jim?"

Dobron didn't blink.

"Have it your way." Ruth-Ann went to the bar and leaned back against it. "Katalina Kishkin was an insider in Anatoly Nikolaevich Konstantinova's organization. She was family—related by marriage to Petya Chernyshov. Petya was a low-level thug for Anatoly's gang."

"Kishkin?" The pieces started to fall into place. "Angel, Kishkin—"

"I remember," Angel said. "Vasily Kishkin killed Vincent Calaprese decades ago. He's where all this started."

"Vasily Kishkin killed the old mobster?" Ruth-Ann forced a laugh. "Vasily wasn't so bad after all."

"Ruth-Ann," Bear said, "tell us the rest."

She did. "Katalina worked for Anatoly but she got cold feet and went to Dobron's people. She wanted out of the Russian mob and wanted into WITSEC. She didn't know Dobron was working for Anatoly."

I whispered to Angel, "She means witness protection."

She rolled her eyes and nodded.

"Anatoly was onto her. I can only imagine who reported her, right Jim? Katalina disappeared. I believe she's under Nicholas Bartalotta's protection as we speak."

"Nicholas?" Angel asked. "Ruth-Ann, is this what your problem with me has been? You thought I knew?"

"Yes, Angela. I'm sorry, but I felt you were complicit in this from the beginning. Knowingly or not."

André gestured to Dobron. "Dobron was trying to find her and kill her, Angela. Ruth-Ann was trying to save her."

"Yes," Ruth-Ann glared at Dobron. "As I said before, every case I've had against Anatoly has gone bad. Dobron made sure. Katalina doesn't even know who betrayed her. But it was Dobron."

"Screw you, Ruth-Ann," Dobron growled. "My team is solid. Is yours?"

"We'll soon find out, won't we?" She waved toward the door and a dark-suited man—one I recognized from Ruth-Ann's entourage at Poor Nic's place—walked in with Jack, the man in our bushes last night. "I have a warrant for you, Jim. My men will escort you to the WFO. I've spoken with the Director personally. They're looking forward to seeing you."

"Ruth-Ann, wait." Angel raised a hand. "He did save our lives. It must count for—"

"Nothing, Angela. He silenced another witness against him. That's all he did."

André said, "Angela, he'd already killed Stephanos and the others. Bonnie was the last link to him."

"I didn't murder anyone." Dobron snapped. "Stephanos was going to turn the book over for a deal—for he and Bonnie. We do it all the time; information for a deal."

"And you say Grecco was making a deal?" Ruth-Ann folded her arms. "My office would have to know about such a deal—and there's no record of one. The only deal you were making was with Anatoly."

"Screw you." Dobron stood up and poked holes in the air between them with his gun-finger. "This is all lies, lady."

Ruth-Ann handed the book to one of her men. "Agent Michaels, Agent Cary, please take him into custody."

The two headed for Dobron. Michaels said, "You're under arrest."

"Screw you, too." Dobron lunged forward, landing a hard right-cross into Michael's jaw and sending him to the floor. He swung a wild left at Cary but it never collided. Cary stepped in, blocked the punch, and delivered a crushing jab to Dobron's chin. Cary followed it with a second, powerful punch to his stomach—collapsing Dobron in half. Then, the struggle ended when Cary's knee drove into Dobron's face and he collapsed onto the floor.

Both men descended on Dobron, grappled his arms behind him, and used his own handcuffs to restrain him. They had him back on his feet clutched between them in seconds.

"Dammit, let me go." Dobron tried to twist free but couldn't. "Ruth-Ann, I'll—"

"Save it, Jim. Don't add threatening a federal officer to the charges."

Ruth-Ann's men escorted him from the room.

I said, "Holy crap, Angel. I never saw this coming."

She shook her head. "Neither did I."

Ruth-Ann shot her a sideways look and walked over to Bear. She extended her hand. "Detective, I had my doubts about you, but you've been an invaluable asset. I'll pass along my congratulations to Captain Sutter."

Bear nodded. "Thanks. What about—"

"I'm sealing this case, Detective. You'll be called as a witness— all of you. But all facts and evidence relative to Stephanos Grecco, Anatoly Konstantinova, and Frannie Masseria will be under a gag order. It's all classified as of this moment." She walked to the lounge door and turned around. "André, you'll need to come with me. I'll need to debrief you."

André looked at Angel and shrugged. "I don't know what to say. I, well, I'll explain the rest when this is over. I'll call as soon as I can. I'm so sorry I've lied to you."

And without another word he strode out the door behind Ruth-Ann Marcos.

SIXTY-THREE

As Bear called Captain Sutter and a crime scene team, Angel sat at the bar. Her head was shaking as she tried to make sense out of all the events unfolding. I wasn't much help so I went looking for Vincent again.

I followed Benny Goodman's *And the Angels Sing* to the dining room and found Vincent gazing at the portrait of Frannie Masseria.

"My Frannie was a good girl, Oliver. You would have liked her."

"I'm sure, Vincent. I have some questions."

Woof. Hercule bounded into the room following Doc as he walked over to me and put a hand on my shoulder. "Questions later, Oliver. For now, just listen." He turned, stone-faced, and looked at Vincent.

"Hello, Vincent."

Vincent walked up to him and without a word, threw his arms around him in a long, emotional bear hug. The two stood there, embracing in a silent, long-ago moment. After a few more moments, Vincent released him and stood face-to-face holding his shoulders.

"Benjamin, it has been too long. Why haven't you come to see me?"

Doc's eyes were filled with tears. "It was my fault, Vincent. Mine. Our kids were crazy in love and I almost kept them apart. All because of your book. It took your life and I couldn't save you. I was terrified it would take theirs, too—I am so very sorry."

Vincent patted his shoulders. "It took your life, too, my friend. And many others."

Huh? "Hold on there, Vincent. Rewind a little. Doc was killed over the book? And who else—"

"Me." Sassy sashayed into the room and threw an arm around me. "Hi ya, Tuckie. Good to see the old boys together again, ain't it?"

Was it? "Someone tell me what's going on."

She did. "Them Commies came for the book a few months after Vincent died. They busted in and tore this place apart. I was hiding upstairs in our secret place—you know—in the attic. I came down too soon and they nabbed me. They tried to make me talk but I wouldn't. Like I told you, I ain't no snitch."

Doc went to her, kissed her cheek, and wrapped old, tired arms around her. "I'm so sorry, Sassy. You didn't deserve what happened. You weren't involved in any of this."

"Nope, I wasn't. Lousy commies." She kissed him hard on the mouth. "But it's okay. It's a long time ago and it saved Frannie and Ollie—for a while. So what the heck, right?"

"I too am sorry, Doc." Vincent patted Doc on the back. "The book was to protect us all—but it couldn't save you."

"Doc?" I asked. "Don't leave me hanging."

He looked at me and his eyes were lost in bad memories and hard times. "Your grandfather—Ollie—was a war hero. He came back and married Frannie. By then, using the book, she had built up enough of an empire to keep the hounds—and Vasily—away. She and Ollie were safe."

"But not you." Sassy kissed him on the cheek again. "Commies wanted revenge. They figured out who Doc was after a while. Frannie tried to keep them away but she couldn't. The book protected her and Ollie and your father, Tuckie. But not everyone."

Doc lowered his head.

"It took them years but they got their revenge," Vincent said. "The battles went on year after year and they lost most of them. Then, after some shenanigans in the fifties, they made a move on Frannie. But their plan failed and they got beaten even harder. In retaliation, they hit Doc instead."

Hercule came over and woofed at the three of them. He stood there, wagging and moaning up a storm until Sassy knelt down and rubbed his ears. Herc had a way with beautiful women—dead or alive.

I just stood there, trying to grasp it all. Each of them had died—horrible deaths—because of the damn book. But as much as it took away, it had saved my grandparents—at least for a while— and my father.

I asked, "Tell me about my dad. Tell me about Frannie and Ollie, too."

"Another time, Oliver." Doc knelt down beside Sassy and gave Hercule a good head-rub. "You're not done, Oliver. Vasily Kishkin's heirs are about to exploit the book—they finally have it after all these years. And it is more dangerous than ever."

What? "No, Doc. Bonnie's in custody—maybe dead. Dobron is in custody, too, and the Justice Department has the book. Who's left?"

"Who's left?" Vincent's voice boomed. "The killer, Oliver."

Oh, no. "You can't mean—"

Doc nodded to me. "How could you miss it, Oliver? It's right there in front of you. A Cuban family owned Quixote's—they were the first of the socialists who came here in the thirties."

"Cubans? So what do the Cubans have to do with—"

Vincent raised a hand. "Vasily Kishkin was a Soviet agent who used Quixote's as a hideout. His sister worked at the restaurant, too, and had a crush on the owner's son. They married. They created a very dangerous and ruthless alliance when the Soviets befriended the dictator, Fidel, years later."

I knew where this was going. "Come on, how was I supposed to know all the history? You could have told me that days ago."

"Ah, yes, perhaps we're being hard on you, Oliver," Doc said. "All right then. Vasily's sister and the Cuban boy had a child. Their child started a long family line of spies and gangsters who still exist today."

Sassy stood and linked her arm with mine.old, "Tuckie, you'll never guess whose family owned Quixote's."

Yes, I can. "Ruth-Ann Marcos."

SIXTY-FOUR

I RAN TO THE lounge where Bear and Angel were talking.

"We've got this all wrong, Angel. Dobron wasn't the killer," I said. "It was—"

"Ruth-Ann?" Angel said, looking past me.

Poor Nic stood in the doorway behind me. He shoved Ruth-Ann Marcos into the room at gunpoint. Behind them, a pretty, dark-haired woman followed along with André Cartier. Poor Nic waved the girl to a chair and kept the gun trained on Ruth-Ann. "Detective Braddock, please place Miss Marcos under arrest. I don't enjoy holding this gun."

Bear's mouth dropped. "What are you talking about?"

"Oh, lord, I screwed up, Angela. I really screwed up," André said, walking over to her and giving her a big, long embrace. "I was so wrong. I trusted her, Angela."

"Detective," Poor Nic said, "if you will call your office, you will find one of her men just tried to kill young Victorio Chevez at the hospital. My men were waiting and interceded. We have also detained the others, too, and they are with Agent Dobron. He is well."

Angel stood up. "But, they were escorting him to the Washington FBI office, Nicholas. What are you doing?"

"Stopping the madness." Poor Nic kept his gun on Ruth-Ann who stood silent beside Bear. "I may be an old man, but I still know Washington is east. They were heading west into the mountains. No, Angela, they were taking Agent Dobron elsewhere and not for interrogation."

Bear took Ruth-Ann by the arm. "Sit down, Ruth-Ann."

"You're going to listen to this thug?" she yelled. "André, don't listen to him. I'm a—"

"Spy." Poor Nic's words were ice and steel. "From a long line of spies. No, Ruth-Ann, you will not be continuing your treason as a Senator."

I said, "Bear, Angel, you have to hear this." I told them everything I'd learned from Doc and Vincent—the condensed version. And each time Poor Nic or Ruth-Ann started to speak, Angel held up her hand to silence them—awkward as it was. When I was through, I dropped into a bar stool.

Angel looked at Ruth-Ann. "You killed them all didn't you— Grecco, Viktor, Petya, even Frannie Masseria? And you used André. You set him up with Bonnie to get the book. And when you killed Stephanos, you framed him for the murder to confuse things."

André's voice was dry and hollow. "She and I drove together to the gala from DC. She must have planted the driving glove and left the .22 bullet in my car. I was so naive. She told me Dobron set me up, so I continued to lie for her—to find the book."

"You see," Poor Nic said, "Murder is like a magic trick. If you manipulate the audience, you can make anyone believe whatever you wish. She used you, André, to find the book and frame Dobron. And you were her unwitting theatrical assistant."

Bear shook his head. "What's your proof, Nic?"

Poor Nic raised a finger. "Well first, you should call your office. Then, we'll see."

Bear made the call on his cell phone and he took his time. When he was through, he looked at Ruth-Ann and took out his handcuffs. "Nicholas' boys just dropped off your two men along with Agent Dobron at our office. They checked Ruth-Ann's men out—one of them is on work-release from Federal prison—he shared a cell with Petya Chernyshov two years ago."

"Ah, then you have your proof," Poor Nic said. "You see, Bonnie and Stephanos *were* searching for the book. And they did make a deal with Agent Dobron. Stephanos was in trouble with the wrong people. Agent Dobron, of course, told Ruth-Ann about them and it all began."

"Thank God he's all right." Angel turned and smiled a fake, plastic smile at Ruth-Ann. "Are her men talking yet, Bear?"

"How foolish." Ruth-Ann laughed. "Russians don't talk. Ever."

Bear gritted his teeth. "There's always a first time, Ruth-Ann."

"What about Chevy?" Angel asked. "Why did he steal the book from André? Was he involved with her, too?"

All eyes fell to Ruth-Ann again but she remained defiant.

"We'll have to wait and see—if he pulls through," Bear said. "Without his statement, we won't know."

"Now, as for more proof, Detective Braddock," Poor Nic said, nodding to the dark-haired girl sitting across the room. "May I introduce Katalina Kishkin. Granddaughter to Vasily Kishkin—of whom you are familiar."

"You're Vasily's granddaughter?" Angel asked. "Ruth-Ann has been looking for you."

"Yes, this is true—she wishes to kill me." Katalina stood up and walked over to Ruth-Ann. She leaned in and kissed her on both cheeks, saying in a thick, Russian accent, "Hello cousin, how good it is to see you."

Ruth-Ann's glare was ice.

"Cousin, please." Katalina patted her cheek. "Viktor—he like me very much. He tell me he will kill this Stephanos Grecco. He tell me he kill Grecco for you—my cousin—for much money. Tell them how you send Anatoly to kill me, too. Please. I am asking nice. Tell them or I make you tell."

Ruth-Ann threw her head back and laughed. "You betrayed us. You sold our blood out for them. For what?"

"To end madness." Katalina leaned into Ruth-Ann again. "When would it end? Our family has hunted for book for generations—killed so much. Who can count? We thought it was over when the old woman went away. But no. You had to find it. You had to kill much more."

Bear said, "What about André and Stephanos?"

Katalina patted Ruth-Ann's cheek again and smiled. "*Da*, yes. She try make deal with Stephanos. Book has her family inside. Book tells whole story; story she not want in news I think. Story about her family before the big war and about restaurant—Quixote's Windmill— and how they are spies all this time. They always spies. Even today, my cousin, she is spy."

"Since the '30s?" Angel asked. "All this time? And Ruth-Ann is one of them?"

"*Da*, of course. Our family—her family—come to this country before war. My family come from Russia. Ruth-Ann's from Cuba. They become one family. All spies. This book, it tells; it has her secrets. And to keep secrets, she kill Stephanos, maybe later Bonnie, too, and frame Dmitry."

"Ah, so Dobron is innocent?" Bear rubbed his jaw. "Dammit, I owe him an apology." He winked at Angel. "Naw, he'll get over it."

Katalina gave a dismissive wave. "Perhaps, if you think he kill these people. Dmitry is good man—he try help me but my cousin made it impossible. I don't know more, by then, I was hiding. But Viktor and Petya—they are dead. Who else would kill them? Must be my cousin—the she-bitch-killer."

Ruth-Ann jumped from her chair but Katalina was too quick. She lashed out and struck Ruth-Ann with a vicious punch to her face, knocking her back into her chair. "You cow. This country good to me. To all of us. You don't know—you were not sent home to live so long as me. If you had been, you too would see truth and would help end this madness."

"I could have been a United States Senator. Think what I could accomplish."

"No, my cousin, no. When I learn you with Anatoly, I knew what you would do with power." Katalina turned away. "No. If I not stop you now, I would kill you later."

"No." Ruth-Ann's chin rose and her eyes turned hard and black. "You would have failed."

Katalina nodded to Poor Nic. "Nicholai, I wish to go. Please. I cannot stand to be by her."

"Nicholas," Bear said. "You've been hiding her all this time? She's a federal witness."

"Katalina is the key to ending Ruth-Ann's power. She had to be protected and the feds who wanted her were not to be trusted." Poor Nic's eyes softened. "And Detective, an old man has a right to be chivalrous, does he not?"

Bear looked over at Ruth-Ann and shook his head. "Yeah, sure Nicholas." He turned back to Poor Nic. "I have men outside. She'll be safe with them until Agent Dobron can move her."

Katalina shrugged and nodded. "Yes, Nicholai. I am safe with them. The queen bitch—she is no more."

Bear went into the hall and returned with Spence and a uniformed deputy. They introduced themselves to Katalina and gestured toward the door. Before she followed them out, Katalina went to Poor Nic and gave him a big Russian hug, kissing him on his cheeks.

"Nicholai, you are good man. I am in your debt. When this through, I wish to visit."

"Then I will look forward to that day, my dear."

Spence led Katalina Kishkin out the door as a deputy fell in behind them.

I said to Bear, "Ask Poor Nic where the book is."

Bear did. "Nic, Captain Sutter said your men brought in Marcos' men and Agent Dobron. Funny, though, no one had the book."

"How odd." Poor Nic walked over to Angel and kissed her on both cheeks as Katalina had done him. "My dear, it has been a pleasure once again."

"Nicholas?" Angel eyed him. "What about the book? The FBI will need it to go after Ruth-Ann's connections."

Poor Nic touched Angel's face and smiled. Then, he turned to Bear and extended his hand. "Detective Braddock, do not trouble yourself. I'm sure the book will surface soon—perhaps two, maybe three days. The necessary contents will be provided to Agent Dobron. You have my word."

"The necessary contents?" Bear shook his hand. "What about the rest?"

"Do not concern yourself." Poor Nic walked to the lounge door and turned around. "I would like to have known Oliver's family, Angela. I believe they, like me, were good people. Complicated, perhaps, but good people."

I said, "He knew all along who my family were. Angel, ask him—"

"Nicholas, wait." She was way ahead of me. "I'd like to know about his family, too. So—"

"Another time, my dear. I have some reading to do. Call on me soon, perhaps next week. I have some photographs and letters I think will interest you. A few things Frannie left with me."

Bear held up a hand. "Wait, Nic, I can't let you keep the book."

"No? But, Detective, who says I have it?" He smiled and winked. "The book has protected the Calapreses for decades. It must continue to do so for a short time longer. Do not attempt to intercede, Detective. I am still a complicated person, remember?" And with a sly, thin smile, Poor Nicholas Bartalotta—retired gangster and good-fairy extraordinaire—walked out.

"Angel, let's go home," I said as Bing Crosby crooned *I'll Be Seeing You*. Vincent, Doc, and Sassy appeared around a table in the rear of the lounge. "Hey, Vincent, isn't that tune a little after your time—in the forties?"

"It is," he said. "But it's not after your grandfather's time."

I watched Hercule sitting beside Sassy and basking in 1939. "Traitor. Nice legs and a pretty smile, eh, boy?" I winked at Angel. "Just saying."

Sassy giggled. "Hey, Tuckie. The Cuban fella left you something behind the bar—one of his doohickies."

I went behind the bar and looked around. Tucked beside several old, empty whiskey bottles, hidden among some bric-a-brac, was a small, digital video camera.

"Angel, a little help?"

She came over and pulled the camera from its hiding place and turned it on, flipping up the view screen for all of us to see.

Chevy's face appeared on the screen. "Hey, ghost-man, I know you'll find this. I didn't mean to hurt your wife, man. Things got out of hand. But I'm making it up to you. See, I found some good video—stuff I didn't know I had. I shot it before your big party, man. But first, I'm gonna get the book everyone wants so much so

I can catch the Grecco-dude's killer. She thinks I'm selling the video and the book for twenty-five g's. Fat chance, man. I'll get her, Braddock, and when I do—this makes us even, man. Deal's a deal. And when you see who it is, man, are you gonna owe me forever."

The video went dark and started again, this time, it was secreted somewhere looking down into the lounge. The screen was an eerie green and gray—night-vision video—of a man and woman standing behind the bar. I recognized the man right away. It was Viktor, the hit man. He spoke to the woman and then disappeared into the wine closet where the secret door led to the upstairs rooms. The woman waited a second and looked around the lounge—when she did, she turned and gave the camera a picture-perfect profile.

Ruth-Ann Marcos.

Angel switched it off. "There's more on there. Seen enough, Bear?"

"For now." Bear was nodding and smiling. "You got it, Chevy. Deal's a deal."

I said, "Chevy's a good guy, Bear. Give him a break."

"I will."

Sassy giggled again. "You stayin' for a drink, Tuckie? Or you going home with the missus?"

"I have to go, Sassy. But I'll be back later to have a few with you, Doc, and Vincent. If it's okay with him."

"Anytime," Vincent said, raising a glass with Doc. "We're family, after all."

Angel looked around the room but didn't see anything. "You done flirting, Tuck?"

"Yeah, let's go home."

I looked at Sassy, Doc, and Vincent. They were my family. My past—a gutsy, hard-living gangster and a feisty surgeon during a time when the world came apart. Frannie and Ollie—my grandparents—broke molds forged by family before them. But nothing could stop the past from catching up to them—to all of us. I don't know what became of my dad. Perhaps Vincent and Doc will tell me. But the others—Doc, Vincent, Sassy, even Frannie Masseria—they died for their past.

In the end, I guess we all answer for what we've done and where we came from.

My family did.

Now though, being dead isn't all bad. I've got family around—the living and the dead. In time, perhaps, I'll have to choose between them. When the time comes—if it does—I don't know which I'll choose. But for now, Angel and Bear still need me here.

Woof.

Hercule, too.

Artie Shaw played *Stardust* and I called for Hercule. He planted a big, sloppy wet-one on Sassy that made her giggle again, and then he bounded over to me. Doc nodded. Vincent raised a glass. Sassy blew me a kiss—oh, maybe it was for Hercule.

As I followed Angel and Bear out the door, images of Frannie and Ollie came to me and Vincent's words touched my thoughts—the book took so many lives. Did it take my father's? My mother's?

It didn't matter. What did matter was whatever held me here—among the living but not one of them—wasn't through with me.

Family needed me—and there might be others, too, who needed my help to find their killers and end their madness.

It's what detectives do.

THE END

© TJ O'Connor

ABOUT THE AUTHOR

Tj O'Connor is an international security consultant specializing in anti-terrorism, investigations, and security programs—life experiences that drive his novels. With his former life as a government agent and years as a consultant, he's lived and worked around the world in places like Greece, Turkey, Italy, Germany, the United Kingdom, and throughout the Americas—among others. He was raised in New York's Hudson Valley and lives with his wife and three Lab companions in Virginia, where they raised five children. *Dying for the Past* is the second of his novels to be published. Learn more about his world at www.tjoconnor.com